JUN 1 3 2018

FUTURE FICTION

New Dimensions in International Science Fiction

"A mind-bendingly adventurous collection with story content as diverse as its authors."

—AJ Hartley, *New York Times* bestselling author of the *Steeplejack* series

"*Future Fiction* is a futuristic compendium of wonder and fear filled with mind-shattering technologies and cutting-edge sciences. Jammed with *what ifs* and *why nots*, each story aches with the possibility of a unique, visceral future. With the right mixture of politics and science, hope and ingenuity, one day the extraordinary worlds imagined by twelve brilliant authors could very well exist. A *must* for any science fiction reader on the hunt for an immersive, gripping, raw read."

—Monica Valentinelli, co-editor of *Upside Down: Inverted Tropes in Storytelling*

"*Future Fiction* offers a selection of imaginative, adventurous sci-fi by international authors—and that is what makes this collection so welcome and exciting. These stories take place in every part of the world and are told in distinct, diverse voices. Whether their focus is transhumanism or ecological devastation, space travel or techno-dystopia, they remind us that the future does not happen to a select few, but to everyone, everywhere. Highly recommended reading for anyone open to expanding their idea of international science fiction."

—Emmi Itäranta, author of *Memory of Water*

- Bernardo's House: First edition in Asimov's Science Fiction, June 2003
- The Way of Water: First edition in Future Fiction, June 2016
- The International Studbook of the Giant Panda: First edition in Interzone, 2013
- What Lies Dormant: First edition in Warrior Wisewoman 3, Norilana Press, 2010
- Aethra: First edition in English in Albedo One, Issue 41, 2011
- Creative Surgery: First edition in Future Fiction: New Dimension in International Science Fiction, Rosarium Publishing, March 2018
- HostBods: First edition in "Omenana" #1, 2014
- Loosestrife: First edition in Interzone #193, 2004
- Citizen Komarova Finds Love: First edition in Exotic Gothic 3, 2009, Ash-Tree Press
- Grey Noise: First English edition on Cosmos Latinos, Wesleyan University Press, USA, 2003
- Tongtong's Summer: First edition in Chinese in ZUI Fiction, March 2014, First published in English in Upgraded, Wyrm Publishing, September 2014
- Proposition 23: First edition in "AfroSF", Story Time, 2012

Cover art by Nick Russell
Cover design by Gerald Mohamed III

Copyright © 2018 Rosarium Publishing.
All rights reserved. No part of this publication may be reproduced, distributed, or transmitted in any forms or by any means, including photocopying, recording, or other electronic or mechanical methods, without the prior written permission of of the publisher, except in the case of brief quotations embodied in critical reviews and certain other noncommercial uses permitted by copyright law. For permission requests, write to the publisher at the address below:

Published by Rosarium Publishing
P.O. Box 544
Greenbelt, MD 20768-0544
www.rosariumpublishing.com

Table of Contents

Foreword

Bill Campbell

Rosarium Publishing's facetious, unofficial tagline is "Introducing the World to Itself Since 2013." While a bit tongue-in-cheek, we are sincere in our mission to continue to break down barriers and bring to the public the wide and varied voices that currently inhabit science fiction and fantasy.

We were introduced to Italian publisher, Francesco Verso, and his house, Future Fiction through Rosarian Carlos Hernandez and his book, *The Assimilated Cuban's Guide to Quantum Santeria*. Mr. Verso wanted to buy the Italian rights to the book. During this process, we each checked out the other's work and immediately knew we found a kindred spirit.

So, in the spirit of American underground dance labels, we at Rosarium decided to put together a compilation of some of the stories that Francesco and Future Fiction has published in Italy. The end result is a challenging, genre-bending anthology with authors from India, Greece, Zimbabwe, and many other countries—including the USA, of course. Some of the authors may be familiar to you (like James Patrick Kelly and Ekaterina Sedia) while others (like Clelia Farris's first-ever English translation with "Creative Surgery") may come as a very welcome surprise.

With that, my job here is done. I hope you enjoy what we've come up with here and that this vast, fantastic world we live in has become a bit smaller and a just that much more intimiate. I want your experience reading this anthology will be as pleasant as it was for us to put this together. And now, with a more formal introduction, here is Francesco.

Introduction

Francesco Verso

The future is always more present in our lives, not only in film and literary advances that illustrate the scope of technological innovations, but also in everyday experiences: from medicine to transport, from information to entertainment and society, changes are multiplying at an increasing rate giving often the impression of living in a preview of tomorrow. This rain of changes and innovations is so intense and pervasive that it doesn't allow us to fully understand the implications of the "new world" we are experiencing, and so the positive or negative consequences of many innovations or, better yet, of their combinations, give rise to unforeseen scenarios or realities considered "science fiction" just a few years ago.

Future Fiction was born to explore and give consistency to this unknown territory by borrowing a definition given by Anthony Burgess to his novels *A Clockwork Orange* and *The Wanting Seed*. The guidelines adopted to fulfill this research on possible futures are four: short fiction, multiculturalism, socio-technological speculation and cross-media.

Short Fiction - Science fiction originated as the Fiction of Ideas: a very strong premise, the famous "what if" or "what would happen if," which takes place in a few pages without frills or digressions and a bunch of characters who, tough and well crafted, remain functional to a brief storytelling, to the minimum number of words necessary to ensure maximum effectiveness. These features perfectly match the growing spread of e-readers, tablets, and smartphones, and thus it appeared to be the best recipe to engage not only fans of the genre but also those who don't know it, which is precisely the goal of *Future Fiction*: widen the listening base beyond the circle of those who already love Science Fiction.

Multiculturalism – The future, by definition, happens everywhere, and Future Fiction wants to give readers the opportunity to seize different views from the dominant ones in the global publishing market where American and Anglo-Saxon literature is often the most represented one. With this idea we intend to highlight stories coming from as many countries and languages as possible and underlying this approach there is the firm intention to preserve the "fiction biodiversity" of the future.

What would the world be if there's just one language to represent it, if there's just one kind of author to write about it, one single religion, one nation, one point of view, one culture, and in general a single source of storytelling? So, as in the remote archipelago of the Svalbard Islands—near the town of Longyarbyen on the Norwegian island of Spitsbergen—there is an underground storage facility built to preserve the genetic heritage of plants around the world from a possible environmental catastrophe, likewise, we would like to preserve the "memetic" heritage of the future from a possible cultural catastrophe. A fiction shelter, chosen with great care and selected to be available to both present and future generations.

Cultural and Socio-Technological Speculation - We are interested in the future in all its declinations, whether it's near or far, a future which, however, maintains a high level of likelihood, given the premise of the story; what is called "suspension of unbelief" (a definition coined by Samuel Taylor Coleridge in 1817 in the book *Biographia literaria*, chapter XIV): that is, the ability to make a scenario so credible that it can make the reader suspend the judgment on its reliability. On the other side, we are inspired by stories that challenge common sense, stories that encourage new ways of thinking and behaving, what Darko Suvin in the book *Metamorphoses of Science Fiction* calls "cognitive estrangement" as a tool to subvert and contradict the status quo. As a matter of fact, we believe Science Fiction is the Fiction of Transformation.

While there is no foreclosure on the classic Science Fiction themes like space exploration or alien encounters, we aim at stories that sink their roots into the present and illustrate a visible future: Artificial Intelligence, Cloning and Bioengineering, Climate Change, Transarchitecture, Post-Humanism, the 3D Printing artisans, the virtual economy of cryptocurrency, the applications of Augmented Reality, and what is defined as the Technological Singularity. All concepts that have a scientific and social value, as well as anthropological and therefore human.

Cross Media – Last but not least, the project calls for collaborations with other artistic and cultural realities to the joint development of a Future Fiction Factory, an integrated fiction laboratory that allows a story to go from the written form to the recited one; from the audiobook to the graphic novel, from performative theater to short films, from multimedia installation to 3D-printed objects. Whatever the medium, the intention is always the same: spread the seeds of the Future wherever possible and with any expressive means allowed by current technologies.

Our ambition is to provide readers with the opportunity to read "other possible futures," month after month, year after year, and we hope you can appreciate them.

Because also tomorrow happens today.

Roma 13/06/2017

Tongtong's Summer

Xia Jia

Translated by Ken Liu

Mom said to Tongtong, "In a couple of days, Grandpa is moving in with us."

After Grandma died, Grandpa lived by himself. Mom told Tongtong that because Grandpa had been working for the revolution all his life, he just couldn't be idle. Even though he was in his eighties, he still insisted on going to the clinic every day to see patients. A few days earlier, because it was raining, he had slipped on the way back from the clinic and hurt his leg.

Luckily, he had been rushed to the hospital, where they put a plaster cast on him. With a few more days of rest and recovery, he'd be ready to be discharged.

Emphasizing her words, Mom said, "Tongtong, your grandfather is old, and he's not always in a good mood. You're old enough to be considerate. Try not to add to his unhappiness, all right?"

Tongtong nodded, thinking, *But haven't I always been considerate?*

Grandpa's wheelchair was like a miniature electric car with a tiny joystick by the armrest. Grandpa just had to give it a light push, and the wheelchair would glide smoothly in that direction. Tongtong thought it tremendous fun.

Ever since she could remember, Tongtong had been a bit afraid of Grandpa. He had a square face with long, white, bushy eyebrows that stuck out like stiff pine needles. She had never seen anyone with eyebrows that long.

She also had some trouble understanding him. Grandpa spoke Mandarin with a heavy accent from his native topolect. During dinner, when Mom explained to Grandpa that they needed to hire a caretaker for him, Grandpa kept on shaking his head emphatically and repeating: "Don't worry, eh!" Now Tongtong did understand *that* bit.

Back when Grandma had been ill, they had also hired a caretaker for her. The caretaker had been a lady from the countryside. She was short and small, but really strong. All by herself, she could lift Grandma—who had put on some weight—out of the bed, bathe her, put her on the toilet, and change her clothes. Tongtong had seen the caretaker lady accomplish these feats of strength with her own eyes. Later, after Grandma died, the lady didn't come anymore.

After dinner, Tongtong turned on the video wall to play some games. *The world in the game is so different from the world around me,* she thought. In the game a person just died. They didn't get sick, and they didn't sit in a wheelchair. Behind her, Mom and Grandpa continued to argue about the caretaker.

Dad walked over and said, "Tongtong, shut that off now, please. You've been playing too much. It'll ruin your eyes."

Imitating Grandpa, Tongtong shook her head and said, "Don't worry, eh!"

Mom and Dad both burst out laughing, but Grandpa didn't laugh at all. He sat stone-faced with not even a hint of a smile.

A few days later, Dad came home with a stupid-looking robot. The robot had a round head, long arms, and two white hands. Instead of feet, it had a pair of wheels so that it could move forward and backward and spin around.

Dad pushed something in the back of the robot's head. The blank, smooth, egg-like orb blinked three times with a bluish light, and a young man's face appeared on the surface. The resolution was so good that it looked just like a real person.

"Wow," Tongtong said. "You are a robot?"

The face smiled. "Hello, there! Ah Fu is my name."

"Can I touch you?"

"Sure!"

Tongtong put her hand against the smooth face, and then she felt the robot's arms and hands. Ah Fu's body was covered by a layer of soft silicone, which felt as warm as real skin.

Dad told Tongtong that Ah Fu was made by Guokr Technologies, Inc., and it was a prototype. Its biggest advantage was that it was as smart as a person: it knew how to peel an apple, how to pour a cup of tea, even how to cook, wash the dishes, embroider, write, play the piano ... Anyway, having Ah Fu around meant that Grandpa would be given good care.

Grandpa sat there, still stone-faced, still saying nothing.

After lunch, Grandpa sat on the balcony to read the newspaper. He dozed off after a while. Ah Fu came over noiselessly, picked up Grandpa with his strong arms, carried him into the bedroom, set him down gently in bed, covered him with a blanket, pulled the curtains shut, and came out and shut the door, still not making any noise.

Tongtong followed Ah Fu and watched everything.

Ah Fu gave Tongtong's head a light pat. "Why don't you take a nap, too?"

Tongtong tilted her head and asked, "Are you really a robot?"

Ah Fu smiled. "Oh, you don't think so?"

Tongtong gazed at Ah Fu carefully. Then she said, very seriously, "I'm sure you are not."

"Why?"

"A robot wouldn't smile like that."

"You've never seen a smiling robot?"

"When a robot smiles, it looks scary. But your smile isn't scary. So you're definitely not a robot."

Ah Fu laughed. "Do you want to see what I really look like?"

Tongtong nodded. But her heart was pounding.

Ah Fu moved over by the video wall. From on top of his head, a beam of light shot out and projected a picture onto the wall. In the picture Tongtong saw a man sitting in a messy room.

The man in the picture waved at Tongtong. Simultaneously, Ah Fu also waved in the exact same way. Tongtong examined the man in the picture: he wore a thin, grey, long-sleeved bodysuit, and a pair of grey gloves. The gloves were covered by many tiny lights. He also wore a set of huge goggles. The face behind the goggles was pale and thin and looked just like Ah Fu's face.

Tongtong was stunned. "Oh, so you're the real Ah Fu!"

The man in the picture awkwardly scratched his head and said, a little embarrassed, "Ah Fu is just the name we gave the robot. My real name is Wang. Why don't you call me Uncle Wang, since I'm a bit older?"

Uncle Wang told Tongtong that he was a fourth-year university student doing an internship at Guokr Technologies' R&D department. His group developed Ah Fu.

He explained that the aging population brought about serious social problems: many elders could not live independently, but their children had no time to devote to their care. Nursing homes made them feel lonely and cut off from society, and there was a lot of demand for trained, professional caretakers.

But if a home had an Ah Fu, things were a lot better. When not in use, Ah Fu could just sit there out of the way. When it was needed, a request could be given, and an operator would come online to help the elder. This saved the time and cost of having caretakers commute to homes and increased the efficiency and quality of care.

The Ah Fu they were looking at was a first-generation prototype. There were only three thousand of them in the whole country, being tested by three thousand families.

Uncle Wang told Tongtong that his own grandmother had also been ill and had to go to the hospital for an extended stay so he had some experience with elder care. That was why he volunteered to come to her home to take care of Grandpa. As luck would have it, he was from the same region of the country as Grandpa and could understand his topolect. A regular robot probably wouldn't be able to.

Uncle Wang laced his explanation with many technical words, and Tongtong wasn't sure she understood everything. But she thought the idea of Ah Fu splendid, almost like a science fiction story.

"So, does Grandpa know who you really are?"

"Your mom and dad know, but Grandpa doesn't know yet. Let's not tell him for now. We'll let him know in a few days, after he's more used to Ah Fu."

Tongtong solemnly promised, "Don't worry, eh!"

She and Uncle Wang laughed together.

Grandpa really couldn't just stay home and be idle. He insisted that Ah Fu take him out walking. But after just one walk, he complained that it was too hot outside and refused to go anymore.

Ah Fu told Tongtong in secret that it was because Grandpa felt self-conscious having someone push him around in a wheelchair. He thought everyone in the street stared at him.

But Tongtong thought, *Maybe they were all staring at Ah Fu.*

Since Grandpa couldn't go out, being cooped up at home made his mood worse. His expression grew more depressed, and from time to time he burst out in temper tantrums. There were a few times when he screamed and yelled at Mom and Dad, but neither said anything. They just stood there and quietly bore his shouting.

But one time, Tongtong went to the kitchen and caught Mom hiding behind the door, crying.

Grandpa was now nothing like the Grandpa she remembered. It would have been so much better if he hadn't slipped and got hurt. Tongtong hated staying at home. The tension made her feel like she was suffocating. Every morning, she ran out the door and would stay out until it was time for dinner.

Dad came up with a solution. He brought back another gadget made by Guokr Technologies: a pair of glasses. He handed the glasses to Tongtong and told her to put them on and walk around the house. Whatever she saw and heard was shown on the video wall.

"Tongtong, would you like to act as Grandpa's eyes?"

Tongtong agreed. She was curious about anything new.

Summer was Tongtong's favorite season. She could wear a skirt, eat watermelon and popsicles, go swimming, find cicada shells in the grass, splash through rain puddles in sandals, chase rainbows after a thunderstorm, get a cold shower after running around and working up a sweat, drink iced sour plum soup, catch tadpoles in ponds, pick grapes and figs, sit out in the backyard in the evenings and gaze at stars, hunt for crickets after dark with a flashlight ... In a word: everything was wonderful in summer.

Tongtong put on her new glasses and went to play outside. The glasses were heavy and kept on slipping off her nose. She was afraid of dropping it.

Since the beginning of summer vacation, she and more than a dozen friends, both boys and girls, had been playing together every day. At their age, play had infinite variety. Having exhausted old games, they would invent new ones. If they were tired or too hot, they would go by the river and jump in like a plate of dumplings going into the pot. The sun blazed overhead, but the water in the river was refreshing and cool. This was heaven!

Someone suggested that they climb trees. There was a lofty pagoda tree by the river shore, whose trunk was so tall and thick that it resembled a dragon rising into the blue sky.

But Tongtong heard Grandpa's urgent voice by her ear: "Don't climb that tree! Too dangerous!"

Huh, so the glasses also act as a phone. Joyfully, she shouted back, "Grandpa, don't worry, eh!" Tongtong excelled at climbing trees. Even her father said that in a previous life she must have been a monkey.

But Grandpa would not let her alone. He kept on buzzing in her ear, and she couldn't understand a thing he was saying.

It was getting on her nerves so she took off the glasses and dropped them in the grass at the foot of the tree. She took off her sandals and began to climb, rising into the sky like a cloud. This tree was easy. The dense branches reached out to her like hands, pulling her up. She went higher and higher and soon left her companions behind. She was about to reach the very top. The breeze whistled through the leaves, and sunlight dappled through the canopy. The world was so quiet.

She paused to take a breath, but then she heard her father's voice coming from a distance: "Tongtong, get ... down ... here ..."

She poked her head out to look down. A little ant-like figure appeared far below. It really was Dad.

On the way back home, Dad really let her have it.

"How could you have been so foolish?! You climbed all the way up there by yourself. Don't you understand the risk?"

She knew that Grandpa told on her. Who else knew what she was doing?

She was livid. *He can't climb trees any more, and now he won't let others climb trees either? So lame! And it was so embarrassing to have Dad show up and yell like that.*

The next morning, she left home super early again. But this time, she didn't wear the glasses.

"Grandpa was just worried about you," said Ah Fu. "If you fell and broke your leg, wouldn't you have to sit in a wheelchair just like him?"

Tongtong pouted and refused to speak.

Ah Fu told her that, through the glasses left at the foot of the tree, Grandpa could see that Tongtong was really high up. He was so worried that he screamed himself hoarse and almost tumbled from his wheelchair.

But Tongtong remained angry with Grandpa. What was there to worry about? She had climbed plenty of trees taller than that one, and she had never once been hurt.

Since the glasses weren't being put to use, Dad packed them up and sent them back to Guokr. Grandpa was once again stuck at home with nothing to do. He somehow found an old Chinese Chess set and demanded Ah Fu play with him.

Tongtong didn't know how to play so she pulled up a stool and sat next to the board just to check it out. She enjoyed watching Ah Fu pick up the old wooden pieces, their colors faded from age, with its slender, pale white fingers; she enjoyed watching it tap its fingers lightly on the table as it considered its moves. The robot's hand was so pretty, almost like it was carved out of ivory.

But after a few games, even she could tell that Ah Fu posed no challenge to Grandpa at all. A few moves later, Grandpa once again captured one of Ah Fu's pieces with a loud snap on the board.

"Oh, you suck at this," Grandpa muttered.

To be helpful, Tongtong also said, "You suck!"

"A real robot would have played better," Grandpa added. He had already found out the truth about Ah Fu and its operator.

Grandpa kept on winning, and after a few games, his mood improved. Not only did his face glow, but he was also moving his head about and humming folk tunes. Tongtong also felt happy, and her earlier anger at Grandpa dissipated.

Only Ah Fu wasn't so happy. "I think I need to find you a more challenging opponent," he said.

When Tongtong returned home, she almost jumped out of her skin. Grandpa had turned into a monster!

He was now dressed in a thin, grey, long-sleeved bodysuit and a pair of grey gloves. Many tiny lights shone all over the gloves. He wore a set of huge goggles over his face, and he waved his hands about and gestured in the air.

On the video wall in front of him appeared another man, but not Uncle Wang. This man was as old as Grandpa with a full head of silver-white hair. He wasn't wearing any goggles. In front of him was a Chinese Chess board.

"Tongtong, come say hi," said Grandpa. "This is Grandpa Zhao."

Grandpa Zhao was Grandpa's friend from back when they were in the army together. He had just had a heart stent put in. Like Grandpa, he was bored, and his family also got their own Ah Fu. He was also a Chinese Chess enthusiast and complained about the skill level of his Ah Fu all day.

Uncle Wang had the inspiration of mailing telepresence equipment to Grandpa and then teaching him how to use it. And within a few days, Grandpa was proficient enough to be able to remotely control Grandpa Zhao's Ah Fu to play chess with him.

Not only could they play chess, but the two old men also got to chat with each other in their own native topolect. Grandpa became so joyous and excited that he seemed to Tongtong like a little kid.

"Watch this," said Grandpa.

He waved his hands in the air gently, and through the video wall, Grandpa Zhao's Ah Fu picked up the wooden chessboard, steady as you please, dexterously spun it around in the air, and set it back down without disturbing a piece.

Tongtong watched Grandpa's hands without blinking. *Are these the same unsteady, jerky hands that always made it hard for Grandpa to do anything?* It was even more amazing than magic.

"Can I try?" she asked.

Grandpa took off the gloves and helped Tongtong put them on. The gloves were stretchy and weren't too loose on Tongtong's small hands. Tongtong tried to wiggle her fingers, and the Ah Fu in the video wall wiggled its fingers, too. The gloves provided internal resistance that steadied and smoothed out Tongtong's movements and thus also the movements of Ah Fu.

Grandpa said, "Come, try shaking hands with Grandpa Zhao."

In the video, a smiling Grandpa Zhao extended his hand. Tongtong carefully reached out and shook hands. She could feel the subtle, immediate pressure changes within the glove as if she were really shaking a person's hand—it even felt warm! *This is fantastic!*

Using the gloves, she directed Ah Fu to touch the chessboard, the pieces, and the steaming cup of tea next to them. Her fingertips felt the sudden heat from the cup. Startled, her fingers let go, and the cup fell to the ground and broke. The chessboard was flipped over, and chess pieces rolled all over the place.

"Aiya! Careful, Tongtong!"

"No worries! No worries!" Grandpa Zhao tried to get up to retrieve the broom and dustpan, but Grandpa told him to remain seated. "Careful about your hands!" Grandpa said. "I'll take care of it." He put on the gloves and directed Grandpa Zhao's Ah Fu to pick up the chess pieces one by one and then swept the floor clean.

Grandpa wasn't mad at Tongtong and didn't threaten to tell Dad about the accident she caused.

"She's just a kid, a bit impatient," he said to Grandpa Zhao. The two old men laughed.

Tongtong felt both relieved and a bit misunderstood.

Once again, Mom and Dad were arguing with Grandpa.

The argument went a bit differently from before. Grandpa was once again repeating over and over, "Don't worry, eh!" But Mom's tone grew more and more severe.

The actual point of the argument grew more confusing to Tongtong the more she listened. All she could make out was that it had something to do with Grandpa Zhao's heart stent.

In the end, Mom said, "What do you mean? 'Don't worry?' What if another accident happens? Would you please stop causing more trouble?"

Grandpa got so mad that he shut himself in his room and refused to come out, even for dinner.

Mom and Dad called Uncle Wang on the videophone. Finally, Tongtong figured out what happened.

Grandpa Zhao was playing chess with Grandpa, but the game got him so excited that his heart gave out—apparently, the stent wasn't put in perfectly. There had been no one else home at the time. Grandpa was the one who operated Ah Fu to give CPR to Grandpa Zhao and also called an ambulance.

The emergency response team arrived in time and saved Grandpa Zhao's life.

What no one could have predicted was that Grandpa suggested that he go to the hospital to care for Grandpa Zhao—no, he didn't mean he'd go personally, but that they send Ah Fu over, and he'd operate Ah Fu from home.

But Grandpa himself needed a caretaker, too. Who was supposed to care for the caretaker?

Further, Grandpa came up with the idea that when Grandpa Zhao recovered, he'd teach Grandpa Zhao how to operate the telepresence equipment. The two old men would be able to care for each other, and they would have no need of other caretakers.

Grandpa Zhao thought this was a great idea. But both families thought the plan absurd. Even Uncle Wang had to think about it for a while, and then said, "Um ... I have to report this situation to my supervisors."

Tongtong thought hard about this. Playing chess through Ah Fu was simple to understand. But caring for each other through Ah Fu? The more she thought about it, the more complicated it seemed. She was sympathetic to Uncle Wang's confusion.

Sigh, Grandpa is just like a little kid. He wouldn't listen to Mom and Dad at all.

Grandpa now stayed in his room all the time. At first, Tongtong thought he was still mad at her parents. But then she found that the situation had changed completely.

Grandpa got really busy. Once again, he started seeing patients. No, he didn't go to the clinic; instead, using his telepresence kit, he was operating Ah Fus throughout the country and showing up in other elders' homes. He would listen to their complaints, feel their pulse, examine them, and write out prescriptions. He also wanted to give acupuncture treatments through Ah Fus, and to practice this skill, he operated his own Ah Fu to stick needles in himself!

Uncle Wang told Tongtong that Grandpa's innovation could transform the entire medical system. In the future maybe patients no longer needed to go to the hospital and waste hours in waiting rooms. Doctors could just come to your home through an Ah Fu installed in each neighborhood.

Uncle Wang said that Guokr's R&D department had formed a dedicated task force to develop a specialized, improved model of Ah Fu for such medical telepresence applications, and they invited Grandpa onboard as a consultant. So Grandpa got even busier.

Since Grandpa's legs were not yet fully recovered, Uncle Wang was still caring for him. But they were working on developing a web-based system that would allow anyone with some idle time and interest in helping others to register to volunteer. Then the volunteers would be able to sign on to Ah Fus in homes across the country to take care of elders, children, patients, pets, and to help in other ways.

If the plan succeeded, it would be a step to bring about the kind of golden age envisioned by Confucius millennia ago: "And then men would care for all elders as if they were their own parents, love all children as if they were their own children. The aged would grow old and die in security; the youthful would have opportunities to contribute and prosper; and children would grow up under the guidance and protection of all. Widows, orphans, the disabled, the diseased—everyone would be cared for and loved."

Of course, such a plan had its risks: privacy and security, misuse of telepresence by criminals, malfunctions and accidents just for starters. But since technological change was already here, it was best to face the consequences and guide them to desirable ends.

There were also developments that no one had anticipated.

Uncle Wang showed Tongtong lots of web videos: Ah Fus were shown doing all kinds of interesting things: cooking, taking care of children, fixing the plumbing and electrical systems around the house, gardening, driving, playing tennis, even teaching children the arts of Go and calligraphy and seal carving and erhu playing ...

All of these Ah Fus were operated by elders who needed caretakers themselves, too. Some of them could no longer move about easily but still had sharp eyes and ears and minds; some could no longer remember things easily, but they could still replicate the skills they had perfected in their youth; and most of them really had few physical problems but were depressed and lonely. But now, with Ah Fu, everyone was out and about, *doing* things.

No one had imagined that Ah Fu could be put to all these uses. No one had thought that men and women in their seventies and eighties could still be so creative and imaginative.

Tongtong was especially impressed by a traditional folk music orchestra made up of more than a dozen Ah Fus. They congregated around a pond in a park and played enthusiastically and loudly. According to Uncle Wang, this orchestra had become famous on the web. The operators behind the Ah Fus were men and women who had lost their eyesight, and so they called themselves "The Old Blinds."

"Tongtong," Uncle Wang said, "your grandfather has brought about a revolution."

Tongtong remembered that Mom had often mentioned that Grandpa was an old revolutionary. "He's been working for the revolution all his life; it's time for him to take a break." But wasn't Grandpa a doctor? When did he participate in a "revolution"? And just what kind of work was "working for the revolution" anyway? And why did he have to do it all his life?

Tongtong couldn't figure it out, but she thought "revolution" was a splendid thing. Grandpa now once again seemed like the Grandpa she had known.

Every day, Grandpa was full of energy and spirit. Whenever he had a few moments to himself, he preferred to sing a few lines of traditional folk opera:

Outside the camp, they've fired off the thundering cannon thrice,

And out of Tianbo House walks the woman who will protect her homeland.
The golden helmet sits securely over her silver-white hair,
The old iron-scaled war robe once again hangs on her shoulders.
Look at her battle banner, displaying proudly her name:
Mu Guiying, at fifty-three, you are going to war again!

Tongtong laughed. "But Grandpa, you're eighty-three!"

Grandpa chuckled. He stood and posed as if he were an ancient general holding a sword as he sat on his warhorse. His face glowed red with joy.

In another few days, Grandpa would be eighty-four.

Tongtong played by herself at home.

There were dishes of cooked food in the fridge. In the evening Tongtong took them out, heated them up, and ate by herself. The evening air was heavy and humid, and the cicadas cried without cease.

The weather report said there would be thunderstorms.

A blue light flashed three times in a corner of the room. A figure moved out of the corner noiselessly: Ah Fu.

"Mom and Dad took Grandpa to the hospital. They haven't returned yet."

Ah Fu nodded. "Your mother sent me to remind you: don't forget to close the windows before it rains."

Together, the robot and the girl closed all the windows in the house. When the thunderstorm arrived, the raindrops struck against the windowpanes like drumbeats. The dark clouds were torn into pieces by the white and purple flashes of lightning, and then a bone-rattling thunder rolled overhead, making Tongtong's ears ring.

"You're not afraid of thunder?" asked Ah Fu.

"No. You?"

"I was afraid when I was little but not now."

An important question came to Tongtong's mind: "Ah Fu, do you think everyone has to grow up?"

"I think so."

"And then what?"

"And then you grow old."

"And then?"

Ah Fu didn't respond.

They turned on the video wall to watch cartoons. It was Tongtong's favorite show: "Rainbow Bear Village." No matter how heavy it rained outside, the little bears of the village always lived together happily. Maybe everything else in the world was fake; maybe only the world of the little bears was real.

Gradually, Tongtong's eyelids grew heavy. The sound of rain had a hypnotic effect. She leaned against Ah Fu. Ah Fu picked her up in its arms, carried her into the bedroom, set her down gently in bed, covered her with a blanket, and pulled the curtains shut. Its hands were just like real hands, warm and soft.

Tongtong murmured, "Why isn't Grandpa back yet?"

"Sleep. When you wake up, Grandpa will be back."

Grandpa did not come back.

Mom and Dad returned. Both looked sad and tired.

But they got even busier. Every day, they had to leave the house and go somewhere. Tongtong stayed home by herself. She played games sometimes and watched cartoons at other times. Ah Fu sometimes came over to cook for her.

A few days later, Mom called for Tongtong. "I have to talk to you."

Grandpa had a tumor in his head. The last time he fell was because the tumor pressed against a nerve. The doctor suggested surgery immediately.

Given Grandpa's age, surgery was very dangerous. But not operating would be even more dangerous. Mom and Dad and Grandpa had gone to several hospitals and gotten several other opinions, and after talking with each other over several nights, they decided that they had to operate.

The operation took a full day. The tumor was the size of an egg.

Grandpa remained in a coma after the operation.

Mom hugged Tongtong and sobbed. Her body trembled like a fish.

Tongtong hugged Mom back tightly. She looked and saw the white hairs mixed in with the black on her head. Everything seemed so unreal.

Tongtong went to the hospital with Mom.

It was so hot, and the sun so bright. Tongtong and Mom shared a parasol. In Mom's other hand was a thermos of bright red fruit juice taken from the fridge.

There were few pedestrians on the road. The cicadas continued their endless singing. The summer was almost over.

Inside the hospital the air conditioning was turned up high. They waited in the hallway for a bit before a nurse came to tell them that Grandpa was awake. Mom told Tongtong to go in first.

Grandpa looked like a stranger. His hair had been shaved off, and his face was swollen. One eye was covered by a gauze bandage, and the other eye was closed. Tongtong held Grandpa's hand, and she was scared. She remembered Grandma. Like before, there were tubes and beeping machines all around.

The nurse said Grandpa's name. "Your granddaughter is here to see you."

Grandpa opened his eye and gazed at Tongtong. Tongtong moved, and the eye moved to follow her. But he couldn't speak or move.

The nurse whispered, "You can talk to your grandfather. He can hear you."

Tongtong didn't know what to say. She squeezed Grandpa's hand, and she could feel Grandpa squeezing back.

Grandpa! She called out in her mind. *Can you recognize me?*

His eyes followed Tongtong.

She finally found her voice. "Grandpa!"

Tears fell on the white sheets. The nurse tried to comfort her. "Don't cry! Your grandfather would feel so sad to see you cry."

Tongtong was taken out of the room, and she cried—tears streaming down her face like a little kid, but she didn't care who saw—in the hallway for a long time.

Ah Fu was leaving. Dad packed it up to mail it back to Guokr Technologies.

Uncle Wang explained that he had wanted to come in person to say goodbye to Tongtong and her family. But the city he lived in was very far away. At least it was easy to communicate over long distances now, and they could chat by video or phone in the future.

Tongtong was in her room, drawing. Ah Fu came over noiselessly. Tongtong had drawn many little bears on the paper and colored them all different shades with crayons. Ah Fu looked at the pictures. One of the biggest bears was colored all the shades of the rainbow, and he wore a black eye patch so that only one eye showed.

"Who is this?" Ah Fu asked.

Tongtong didn't answer. She went on coloring, her heart set on giving every color in the world to the bear.

Ah Fu hugged Tongtong from behind. Its body trembled. Tongtong knew that Ah Fu was crying.

Uncle Wang sent a video message to Tongtong.

Tongtong, did you receive the package I sent you?

Inside the package was a fuzzy teddy bear. It was colored like the rainbow with a black eye patch, leaving only one eye. It was just like the one Tongtong drew.

The bear is equipped with a telepresence kit and connected to the instruments at the hospital: his heartbeat, breath, pulse, body temperature. If the bear's eye is closed, that means your grandfather is asleep. If your grandfather is awake, the bear will open its eye.

Everything the bear sees and hears is projected onto the ceiling of the room at the hospital. You can talk to it, tell it stories, sing to it, and your grandfather will see and hear.

He can definitely hear and see. Even though he can't move his body, he's awake inside. So you must talk to the bear, play with it, and let it hear your laughter. Then your grandfather won't be alone.

Tongtong put her ear to the bear's chest: thump-thump. The heartbeat was slow and faint. The bear's chest was warm, rising and falling slowly with each breath. It was sleeping deeply.

Tongtong wanted to sleep, too. She put the bear in bed with her and covered it with a blanket. *When Grandpa is awake tomorrow*, she thought, *I'll bring him out to get some sun, to climb trees, to go to the park and listen to those grandpas and grandmas sing folk opera. The summer isn't over yet. There are so many fun things to do.*

"Grandpa, don't worry, eh!" she whispered. *When you wake up, everything will be all right.*

[Author's Note: I'd like to dedicate this story to my grandfather. I wrote this story during August, around the time of the anniversary of his passing. I will treasure the time I got to spend with him forever.

This story is also dedicated to all the grandmas and grandpas who, each morning, can be seen in the parks practicing taichi, twirling swords, singing opera, dancing, showing off their songbirds, painting, doing calligraphy, playing the accordion. You made me understand that living with an awareness of the closeness of death is nothing to be afraid of.]

The Quantum Mommy

Michalis Manolios

Translated by Manolis Vamvounis

Love is the only thing that grows when we spend it lavishly.
Ricarda Huch

I

Humanity was on the cusp of one of the most interesting moments in the history of human exploration. It was the time of *Europa*. The *Europa II*, empty and unmanned, had traversed the ends of the solar system with precision, economy, and perseverance. It had lain eyes on Jupiter, had entered into orbit around its so promising satellite, and had released the space shuttle *Hope* in a spiral, soft drop toward its surface. While the shuttle was performing the fuel-powered drop phase, the mother ship was bringing the life support systems online one by one.

At the moment of the shuttle's pinpoint landing, almost on top of Rhadamanthys Linea, came the confirmation from the computers aboard the *Europa II* that all of the ship's systems were in fine, working order and that it was ready to welcome its crew.

On the TV screens of countless viewers all over the planet, under the projector lights and in front of her daughter's eyes, Armelina was the first who stepped up toward the teleportation chamber. The mission was clear: three months of orbital observation with intermediary walks on Europa's surface together with Elsa and Tom. And amid all that, she could, every few days, get herself back on Earth for a half or a full hour to be with Agape[1]. Armelina smiled as she entered the chamber. It was the time of Europa, and she would be the first to see it in person.

The chamber looked like a narrow elevator without a door. After all, it's not like it needed one. A soft, reddish glow bathed its contents in the fractions of a second that it took to operate it. Armelina could see the technicians outside and her two colleagues waiting for their turn closer by. On her headphones Andrei's calm updates from the control center were pouring in on a steady flow.

"Confirming atmosphere aboard the *Europa II.*"

"Confirming temperature inside the *Europa II.*"

"Earthbound chamber charge at 92%."

"*Europa II* chamber charge at 96%."

Moments later, Andrei's voice addressed her in a reassuring, casual tone. "Okay, Armelina, it's all yours." The chamber design was so straightforward that even a child could operate it. She reached out with her hand and lifted the protective cover of the single button. The memory of Nicos would return like an old, faithful friend every time she did that. Then, without hesitation, unaware of her future, like a blithe animal led to the slaughter, she pushed the button.

The light bathed the chamber in its glow for a moment after which she found herself in front of the control consoles aboard the *Europa II*. The lack of gravity was an abrupt but pleasant shock. She flew out of the chamber, giving her customary report: "Baikonur, this is *Europa*

The light bathed the chamber in its glow for a moment, but that was it. Armelina remained in place. After an awkward second, she threw up her arms, baffled, looking toward the control center. There where a small, ill-boding commotion was already beginning to stir.

1 Agape means love in Greek.

II. I have arrived, and everything appears to be in order."

The confirmation took so long that Armelina thought that they hadn't activated the electromagnetic waves teleporter, which nullified the communication delays. Then, after a few seconds, Andrei's voice reached her. It felt somewhat awkward to her, but she didn't think to ask about it. She couldn't have imagined.

"Ummm ... Okay, *Europa II*, copy that."

Right after the reddish light went out, the teletechnicians huddled together over the readings from the equipment trying to figure out what went wrong. The theoretical physicists, however, turned toward the cameras aboard the *Europa II*, hoping against the improbable. The moment Armelina of Earth took her first step out of the chamber, her voice, from across the far end of the solar system, froze them all in their tracks: "Baikonur, this is *Europa II*, I have arrived, and everything appears to be in order."

For a few moments no one made a sound. The first to speak was Jamie, the psychologist.

"Someone take the child," she said.

II

Jamie had never seen a person cry under zero gravity conditions before. The tears don't flow. They just stay in place and flood the eyes. Armelina was hovering in front of the camera and had to keep wiping away her tears to be able to see. When she arrived aboard the *Europa II* she had no visual from the base in Baikonur and thus had no idea what was going on.

Jamie had broken the news to her the way only a professional could have done, and even so, Armelina—Armelina II, as the personnel on the base had secretly named her—had cried so much that the tears were floating in small, spherical drops around her.

"I don't care about myself," she would tell Jamie. "But my child ..."

"It is going to be a serious concern in any scenario, I recognize that."

"A serious concern? We're not talking about my life here. We're talking about Agape!"

"Of course, Armelina. Um ... excuse me, but they're telling me that the flight director wishes to speak to you."

A grim George Williams showed up on her screen. "Armelina, I'm sorry about what happened, but I am also in the unpleasant position to have to talk with you about some issues. As you know, this is the first time something like this has occurred. However, the laws of quantum mechanics do not rule it out, and that is why the Law already has certain provisions ..."

"I know full well what the Law provides for this eventuality, Williams," Armelina interrupted him. "Why don't you apply the Law, then? It's only a few orders. You turn all of the ship's systems offline, and within a few minutes it's all over."

"I will not do it, Armelina, because I neither want to nor am I able to. This is no routine teleportation from one city to another. You are on the other end of the solar system, farther away than any human has ever reached. Over there, there is only one teleporter, which malfunctioned either out of pure coincidence or due to some permanent error. It is now up to you what is to become of the work we have spent years of time and millions of—"

"You finally confess to it, Williams. I'm far too valuable for the Law to be applied."

"It's not just that. All hell has broken loose over here. The entire planet saw you duplicate, and everyone is in an uproar. The situation is so particular that, even if we wanted to, I do not know if we could apply the Law."

"Why don't you get to the point, Williams? Tell me what it is you want from me."

"We are not going to send Elsa and Tom in before we ascertain the status of the teleporter. So, we will send you the first food provisions and find out this way if it is in the right working order again. If not, we will perform some other tests."

III

Armelina had strapped herself into her bunk, but she hadn't managed to sleep a wink. Her window had a view that no other human had ever laid eyes upon. Europa and Jupiter framed images of inconceivable cosmic beauty, which she couldn't get herself to enjoy. She never imagined that she'd find herself here on a journey that only comes once in even an astronaut's lifetime and that she'd be sitting around, unspeaking and unmoving, with all her scientific instruments still in their cases, squandering these valuable hours in painful, unpleasant contemplation. Because Nicos, the first human to ever get teleported—her Nicos—was there, he was coming back to her mind over and over again, a thought much more intense and persistent than the momentary repeating memory that would banish the sense of doom every time she pushed the button of a teleporter.

Armelina shook her head to push back the dark thoughts. She had to realize her position in the shape of things. The food rations had reached the *Europa II*, but they had never left Baikonur. The teleporter was stuck in an improbable but not impossible mode that only the unique minds of Bohr, Planck, and Schrödinger or their brilliant successors could even conceive and comprehend. Every attempt to send anything back to Earth, or even to the Hope shuttle, had failed. Anything placed inside the teleporter simply duplicated without ever leaving the *Europa II*. On the other hand, Baikonur had no trouble exchanging objects with the Hope. This meant that the fault was in her teleporter alone. It could receive anything that could fit inside the chamber, but it couldn't even remove a simple dust particle from the ship.

The *Europa II* was not, of course, designed to ever make it back to Earth. Neither was the Hope designed to take back off the ground and come to her rescue. As soon as their mission there was over, the crew was to teleport back to the mother planet. The *Europa II* and the Hope would keep on sending data until the exhaustion of their energy reserves. It was a typical semi-manned mission. The only way for her to go back was for the teleporter to be repaired, and Armelina had no idea, not only how difficult, but also even how desirable something like that would be for the people who called the shots back on Earth.

Meanwhile, she couldn't imagine what kind of shock Agape must have gone through. For months she was readying herself for her mom's absence at "the other end of the world," but her mom hadn't gone anywhere. She had seen her coming out of the chamber, and at the same time speaking out of a monitor confirming that she had reached that other end of the world. She was the only person she had in the world, and she was only five years old.

And her self? The "original" (she tried to avoid the thought) Armelina? She wouldn't want to be in her place and having to try and explain the unexplainable to a perceptive little girl who knows her inside and out. But it's not like the other her would like to be in this position either.

IV

Armelina was looking out of the window lost in thought, waiting for the lawyer and his impressive entourage. Two mobile TV production vans had set up camp on the street in front of her house, and many more would come and go from time to time. She had tried to get rid of the reporters who had already tried everything short of attempting to climb in through the windows, but it was to no avail. Agape hadn't been to school since that day, and she was wandering around scowling in a house where all the TV sets, radios, and the internet were kept turned off as much as possible. Armelina had allowed visits from a couple of Agape's classmates, but she had to put a lid on that too when she discovered that they were being put up to it by the TV stations.

How she missed Nicos right now! He could put himself between them and the rapacious media vultures, between them and the creature that orbited Europa. He could look Agape in the eye and point out her mother to her. And most of all, he could comfort them. Armelina let out a sigh and turned away from the window. She enjoyed taking pride in her matter-of-factness, and even in her cynicism. Nicos isn't here, she reminded herself for the umpteenth time. Nicos was that deep red, purulent mass of flesh and pulverized bones that came back from the Moon, the first recorded teleporter accident. Because Nicos never left any trail unblazed. Not even this one. Yes, Nicos was wonderful, but Nicos was dead.

"Mommy?" Agape had that signature *I know this is a difficult question, but I've got to ask it* look of hers on. Armelina took a deep breath.

"Can I ask you something?"

She nodded, smiling at the child.

"Do you promise to tell me the truth?"

"Don't I always tell you the truth?"

"I'm a kid," said the little girl. "But I know that sometimes the grown-ups don't tell their kids the truth to protect them."

Armelina sat down on the couch, took her on her lap, and gave her a peck on the forehead, thinking of how blessed, how lucky she was that, out of her two selves, she was the one who was able to do this. That lawyer could take his time getting there.

"I promise to tell you the truth."

"Okay. So tell me then, did you go to Europa?"

"No. And yes. I didn't go myself, but a copy of me, another Armelina, did arrive there."

"And can't she come back?"

"No. For the time being she can't."

"Because the machine broke down?"

"Yes, my love, because it broke down."

"And can't they fix it?"

"We don't know, yet. It could be fixable. In fact, I am sure it is."

"So, does this mean this machine now makes mommies?"

Armelina couldn't contain a smile. "Yes. The way it is now, broken down, it makes mommies."

"Mommy, you're not going to die like daddy, are you?"

"No, my darling, quite the opposite. Instead of disappearing, I've multiplied."

Agape stared her down. “And which one of you two is my real mommy?”

“My love ...”

“Mommy, you promised!”

Armelina hesitated, taken aback for a moment. She remembered her talk with the child psychologist. “Okay, then. The truth. I’m your real mommy, there’s no question about it. I’m the mommy that walked into the teleporter. The mommy that didn’t travel, and of course the one who came back to her child safe and sound. The other mommy, too, though, the one who was created by the machine, is just as real. We’re the same in the way we look, the way we talk, in the love we have for you, in everything.”

“But how can I have two mommies? I’ve only been born once!”

“That’s good thinking, Agape, but you see ... this is something difficult enough to explain to an adult, but let’s give it a try. You remember what the past is, right?”

“What we’ve already lived.”

“Right. And the future is the opposite of that. What we are going to live from here on now. For example, the fries we had for lunch are what?”

“The past. And ... the ice cream you promised me this afternoon, that’s the future.”

“Correct,” smiled Armelina. “Pay attention now. The Armelina that has reached Europa and I have the exact same past, from our birth up to the moment I stepped inside the teleporter. This is very, very rare. To be exact, it has never happened before. But since we have the exact same past, it means that we have both given birth to you. This way, you are the only child on Earth that has two mommies.”

“Mommy ... I’m a little scared.”

Armelina squeezed her in her arms. “There is nothing to be afraid of, my precious darling. Quite the opposite. Think of how many little kids don’t even have one mommy. Think of how much they would all love to be in your place.”

Agape frowned for a moment. Armelina thought she could almost make out the sound of the miniature cogs in her little brain turning, trying to break down a situation that would be almost inconceivable to everyone else. "Mommy," she finally said, "I think it's great to have two mommies."

She smiled at the child. Agape looked satisfied with the explanations, but Armelina wasn't fooled. The critical question, the ticking clock, the one she couldn't give an answer to, seemed ready to come out of her lips.

"Mommy ... And if they manage to finally fix that machine and bring back my other mommy, which mommy will I stay with?"

V

Baikonur had worked hard to salvage whatever it could of the mission calendar. They had spent long nights awake bumping heads to cut back on some of the predetermined duties due to the lost time and to decide which jobs and observations could still be performed by one person in Armelina's current state of mind and which of them should be abandoned. They had sent her a brand new program that she would require at least two days to begin to understand. She was now floating through the ship, turning the pages of the manual that was swimming in the air in front of her with her hands flying over the keyboards and the instruments, her eyes scanning through the pages, the windows, and the screens, and her ears collecting instructions from Earth.

"Baikonur, do we have any news on the teleporter situation?"

"We're looking into it, Armelina," Andrei's voice came in response. "Rest assured that we are looking into it much more intensively than we're working on the mission's program. You're coming back the first chance we get."

"The first thing I did up here was shut down and reboot my own equipment. I was hoping that perhaps it was something that rudimentary, but it didn't work. Have you examined the connection scheme between Baikonur—*Europa II*—and Hope? Because that is something that's only controllable from your end. I can't see it or change it from here."

"We're mindful of that, and we're checking into it, Armelina. We will keep you posted on any developments."

Armelina remained occupied for many hours, but she couldn't get the thought out of her head that something wasn't right. Andrei was a rookie astronaut and a good colleague, and his voice had some of the air of that awkward first confirmation after her arrival. In the end, instead of some news concerning the teleporter, a strange new package arrived. It was a tall stack of metallic boxes. She inquired what they contained, but instead of an answer, she received the order to not move them out of the chamber and to send them back to Earth. She assumed that they had made some adjustments on the teleporter and they wanted to test if it was working correctly, but she didn't understand the need to use all this volume since these kinds of tests would be conducted with small objects. She obeyed and got back to her work, but five minutes later they asked her to send them back again. She did so again and asked Andrei what was going on. He mumbled something about new ideas from the technicians that had something to do with the chamber's payload and the distribution of the teleportable mass, but he wasn't in the least convincing. She was beginning to get antsy. When he asked her to send them back once more, she got furious and demanded to see George Williams.

"What's contained in these boxes? Why are they locked?"

"Hello, Armelina. It's nothing. It's just a ..."

"Why are we copying them every few minutes? What is it, diamonds? Gold?"

Williams let slip a slight expression of discomfort.

"Gold!" Armelina's face lit in surprise, and she terminated the connection.

VI

It was two in the morning when she got woken up by the sound of the telephone ringing. She was met with the sight of a scowling George Williams.

"You need to come over here. It's ... her," he said. "She wants to see you. Right now."

The reporters followed her with breaking news bulletins and still half-asleep correspondences, but the Service kept them an adequate distance from the control room and the teleporter.

Armelina stood in front of the big screen with a lump in her throat. She had seen herself talking from Europa on the TV, but this was different. For the first time she was about to talk with her, the first higher life form, the first intelligent being that had been created, even if by accident, by man.

The screen blinked into life.

"... Hey." She had her hair caught in a ponytail so that it wouldn't fly around in the nonexistent gravity and hinder her in her work—just the way she herself used to do during training. She looked exhausted.

"Hey, us," she answered to her copy with what she hoped would pass as a sincere smile. She had put a lot of thought into that "us" in the vain hope of easing the tension between them, but Armelina of Europa didn't seem to pay much attention to such superfluities.

"How is she?" she asked with palpable anticipation.

"Um ... Oh. She's fine. She's just fine. She's confused, but I think that she's come to terms with it as smoothly as one could hope for. Jamie was a big help as well, of course, until the Service sent me ... until the Service sent in a child psychologist."

"What is she saying about me?"

"She's asking if you're coming back."

Pause.

"Does she want me back?"

"She's not sure. I'm not sure about that either, though."

Then, without warning, Armelina of Europa broke down. She started crying, struggling in vain to contain her tears as if she was ashamed to cry in front of her self. "I'm up here all alone, without Agape ... I'll probably die here ... and they keep sending me gold!"

"What?" exclaimed Armelina, turning toward the flight

controller. She saw a man she didn't know with a frozen stare and recalled that just the previous day Andrei had taken an unheard of, in the middle of a mission in progress, leave of absence.

"I'll remind the both of you that this conversation is being recorded in the official mission log," said the man.

Armelina gaped, startled at her self. Even she herself could then understand that the woman orbiting Europa was in a terrible state. She looked like she wanted to tell her a great deal of things. After all, why else would she have requested the meeting at this hour? Her self almost smuggled glances at her with her head held low, and Armelina realized that she would need to understand, she would need to guess the entire conversation they couldn't share on air on her own.

"Don't cry," she told her with a flat tone whose purpose she hoped the other one would understand was to buy her more time to think.

They had sent her gold? So she could send it back to them again, over and over again, multiplying it. She threw a stolen glance toward the teleporter. It was empty, but she noticed that it was in stand-by mode. Perhaps ... perhaps that's how she had managed to get her all the way here. By threatening that she wouldn't make any more copies of the gold until she got to see her self. Insane, but it made sense. Armelina shivered at the realization that this delay for their little talk must have been costing Williams millions. Or rather ... not Williams. Such a decision must have been coming from much higher up.

"I need a lawyer," said Armelina of Europa.

"Oh yes, errr ... Armelina, before we say anything else, I must come clean that ..."

"... that you've already hired one. For the custody dispute in case I come back. I know."

Armelina was left looking at her, dumbfounded.

"Because that's the same thing I would have done in your place. That's how I know," the other one added, shooting her a bitter smile. "Wake up! Haven't you realized who you're talking to? And don't apologize. Just find me one as well if you've already placed Bob on retainer."

"Bob? Every big shot lawyer on the planet is jumping over backwards to take up this case pro bono. Do you have any idea of the proportions this has taken?"

"It would seem not. Could you then send me anyone who could make it here before sunrise in Baikonur?"

"I think there are some Russians on the list, yes. But are you in such a hurry?"

"Yes. And not just concerning Agape."

This was it! Her self kept throwing clues at her from across the other end of the solar system. The only thing that could interest her, apart from Agape, was the possibility of not coming back. What could she want a lawyer for, though? Armelina glanced back again toward the flight controller, who was now talking on his headset while observing them. Then she turned toward her self, and said, "I think that the teleporter's current state is exceptionally unstable from a quantum mechanics point of view."

Armelina of Europa looked at her straight in the eyes. "And due to that, unique," she replied.

But such a one-of-a-kind teleporter was a most valuable teleporter, thought Armelina. Their technicians would give anything to find out how to cause this random state.

"Have you tried resetting the equipment?" she asked, trying to come off as nonchalant as possible.

The answer came in the exact rehearsed, theatrical manner that she had anticipated.

"I have tried rebooting the damn thing over and over again. Then again, though, I haven't checked the plans of the quantum link ..."

That was it! Armelina's only hope was that the message wasn't as clear to those listening in on them. Or that they would just perceive it as nothing more than an errant thought. Because it was known that the quantum link was being controlled out of Baikonur. So, that must have meant that Williams had not performed a complete bridge reboot.

She had understood everything she needed to.

"I'm sure the kids will get this sorted soon," she said. "In the meantime, you should take care to enjoy Europa. And know that I wish I was there. Do you want me to say anything to Agape?"

"I want you to remember to arrange for the lawyer! And, please, if she also wants to, I'd like to, at least once, see her again."

"I can't promise you that," said Armelina. "The child psychologist tells me to let Agape decide if she wants to talk to you, but I don't know if that's the right thing to do."

The tears welled up in her eyes again.

"Please ... I may not have another chance ... Either way, tell her I love her. And kiss her. Kiss her twice as much as you want to."

VII

Should she abandon her other self to her fate? Should she help her come back and then strip her of her own identity and life? Or should she share with her everything she held dear?

Armelina was sitting next to her daughter's bed unable to get a wink of sleep. The child was breathing softly in her sleep. It was a long, endless night. Around five in the morning, one of Russia's top lawyers arrived at the base in Baikonur. Armelina of Europa was about to find out first-hand the legal and social complications that would develop if she ever made it back to Earth. Their employment, social, financial, and of course, most of all, physical parity would create a series of impasses. Human society wasn't ready to accept two people with identical fingerprints and signatures, indistinguishable DNA and retina prints, and a shared underage child. But at this exact moment these were the last things on the mind of Europa's Armelina. The lawyer would first of all try to exercise pressure to get her back on Earth. And that was going to be no easy feat as the Service had stumbled upon the goose that laid the golden eggs. This "faulty" teleporter could reproduce anything of great value or rarity that could fit inside its chamber. And of course none of the powers that be were planning to use it to get free food to the Third World. They had all the incentives in the world to leave her there to rot. A machine like that was worth more than the entire mission to Europa, much more than the life of a human copy that under normal circumstances should not even exist in the first place. A second mission, one that would bring the teleporter back, would also resolve the final procedural difficulty. It would of course cost time and money, but the profits from it would tend to infinity. The only way to avoid all this, thought Armelina, would be to bring these higher-ups who gave the orders face to face with something much more powerful that would make them back down. And Armelina had no idea what that could be.

At six in the morning, she got up without making a sound and stepped out the front door of her house. She waved her arm toward the vans, and within a minute, half a dozen world networks were hanging off her lips.

"As soon as she wakes up, my daughter will go see her mother," she said. "And you will get direct access to the audio and visual."

She turned her back to the agitated crowd and reentered the house.

VIII

"Good morning, lovey."

"Good morning, mommy."

"My love, that other mommy told me that she wants to see you. Do you want to?"

The child jumped up on the bed and hugged her. "I'll bring her flowers! You like flowers." And, as if she gave it a second thought. "I'll get some for you too, so you don't get jealous."

When they reached the base, the TV crews hadn't yet managed to pass through, but Agape proved to be a right battering ram. The kid, holding a small flower pot in her hands, was passing through the doors one by one and following behind them—Armelina didn't want to ponder how many phones were ringing off their hooks and what kind of threats and promises were being exchanged—the media followed, this time close by.

The only one who had no idea was Armelina of Europa. When her own self told her before they even let the child get a visual, she looked like five years had been taken off her.

"Oh, thank you, thank you so much," she said. "Just give me two minutes to tidy myself up. Don't let her see me like this."

Soon she had washed her face, rubbing the sleepless nights out of it, along with the hard work and the worry. She had let her hair down and had worn her first genuine smile since she was up there.

"Ready," she said, wiping away two last tears.

Armelina and Jamie arrived in front of the camera with the child. The big screen lit up. "Mommy?"

"My love!"

Agape looked at the Armelina next to her and then again back at the screen.

"Mommy, are you the same?"

"Absolutely the same, my precious."

The kid looked at her with semi-affected skepticism.

"Show me your birthmark!"

Without hesitation, Armelina of Europa turned her back to the camera and lifted up her shirt. The little eyes lit up. "You're my real mommy, too! Look! I brought you this flower."

"How pretty! Give it to your mommy so that she can send it to me."

Armelina put it inside the chamber, and the flower pot was copied. The TV networks were eating up the entire live, raw spectacle.

"It smells nice just like you do. I'm already missing you, my pretty thing."

"I didn't miss you that much, mommy. Because you didn't leave," said the kid, pointing to Armelina. "But now that I see that you really left, now I miss you."

The tears were lurking right behind her eyes.

"Tell me that you want me back, and I'll do everything to return to you as soon as I can."

"You know, mommy, I was thinking that just like it is very bad that there are orphan children, it's also very bad that there are orphan mommies."

Armelina took a step back and turned the other way, bringing her hand in front of her mouth. Armelina of Europa couldn't afford that same luxury. She hovered in front of the camera, containing herself, and saw her daughter tell her: "Mommy, I think I'll adopt you."

Jamie intervened and got them out of the deadlock. She asked Agape to say goodbye and took her with her while the Armelinas stood bewildered. And all of a sudden, the kid broke free from the psychologist, and, screaming, "Let me get my mommy," she ran toward Armelina. Jamie turned back as well, but she didn't try to stop the child. Agape, however, ran past Armelina, and when they realized where she was headed all along, it was already too late. In one instant she was inside the teleporter chamber. Armelina and Jamie ran, while all of the onlookers stood frozen in place, unable to react. Agape wouldn't be able to reach, but she had stepped on the flower pot and was opening the button's cover.

"My darling, don't!" came the voice from the screen.

"Don't come near, mommy. I'll push it."

The teleporter's technician brought up the reset command on his screen, but George Williams threw him out of his seat.

"Reset! Reset!" yelled Armelina. She had kneeled down right outside the chamber, but she didn't dare put her arm in while the child's finger was on the button.

"Mommy, if the machine makes mommies, it will make kids, too!"

"Reset, Williams!" yelled Europa's Armelina as well. "You'll do it later anyway. You won't be able to deal with a five-year-old in orbit!"

Williams peered at them over the button that would confirm the reset command. He hesitated for a moment. But a moment was all that it took. Agape pushed the button. When the reddish light started glowing, Williams knew that it was all over.

And that's how that grainy but now world-famous photo

came to be: it was taken from the big screen by a German photographer, and it granted him instant recognition. The photograph of Europa's Agape floating into her mommy's arms. Their faces weren't visible at all, but their smiles connected through the hair, the arms, and their turned backs found their way back to Earth.

The Way of Water

Nina Munteanu

She imagines its coolness gliding down her throat. Wet with a lingering aftertaste of fish and mud. She imagines its deep voice resonating through her in primal notes; echoes from when the dinosaurs quenched their throats in the Triassic swamps.

Water is a shape shifter.

It changes yet stays the same, shifting its face with the climate. It wanders the earth like a gypsy, stealing from where it is needed and giving whimsically where it isn't wanted.

Dizzy and shivering in the blistering heat, Hilda shuffles forward with the snaking line of people in the dusty square in front of University College where her mother used to teach. The sun beats down, crawling on her skin like an insect. She's been standing for an hour in the queue for the public water tap. Her belly aches in deep waves, curling her body forward.

There is only one person ahead of her now, an old woman holding an old plastic container. The woman deftly slides her wCard into the pay slot. It swallows her card, and the light above it turns green. The card spits out of the slot. The meter indicates what remains of the woman's quota. The woman bends stiffly over the tap and turns the handle. Water trickles reluctantly into her cracked plastic container. It looks like they have another shortage coming, Hilda thinks, watching the old woman turn the tap off and pull out her card then shuffle away.

The man behind Hilda pushes her forward. She stumbles toward the tap and glances at the wCard in her blue-grey hand. Her skin resembles a dry riverbed. Heart throbbing in her throat, Hilda fumbles with the card and finally gets it into the reader. The reader takes it. The light screams red. Her knees almost give out. She dreaded this day.

She stares at the iTap. The dryness in the back of her throat rises to meet her tongue, now thick and swollen. She gags on the thirst of three days. Just like her mother's secret cistern, her card has run dry; no credits, no water. The faucet swims in front of her. The sun, high in the pale sky, glints on the faucet's burnished steel and splinters into a million spotlights ...

Hilda read in her mother's forbidden book that water was the only natural substance on Earth that could exist in all three physical states. She'd never seen enough water to test the truth of that claim. She remembered snow as a child. How the flakes fluttered down and landed on her coat like jewels. No two snowflakes were alike, she'd heard once. But not from her mother; her mother refused to talk about water. Whenever Hilda asked her a question about it, she scowled and responded with bitter and sarcastic words. Her mother once worked as a limnologist for CanadaCorp in their watershed department, but they forced her to retire early. Hilda tried to imagine a substance that could exist as a solid, liquid, and gas all in the same place and same time. One moment flowing with an urgent wetness that transformed all it touched. Another moment firm and upright. And yet another, yielding into vapor at the breath of warmth. Water was fluid and soft, yet it wore away hard rock and carved flowing landscapes with its patience.

Water was magic. Most things on the planet shrank and became denser as they got colder. Water, her textbook said, did the opposite, which was why ice floated and why lakes didn't completely freeze from top to bottom.

Water was paradox. Aggressive yet yielding. Life-giving yet dangerous. Floods. Droughts. Mudslides. Tsunamis. Water cut recursive patterns of creative destruction through the landscape, an ouroboros remembering.

She'd heard a myth—from Hanna, of course—that Canada once held the third richest reserve of fresh water in the world. Canada used to have clean, sparkling lakes deep enough for people to drown in. That was before the unseasonal storms and floods. Before the rivers dried up and scarred the landscape in a network of snaking corpses. Before Lake Ontario became a giant tailings pond. Before CanadaCorp shut off Niagara Falls then came into everyone's home and cemented their taps shut for not paying the water tax.

When that happened, her mother secretly set up rainwater catchers on her property. Collecting rainwater was illegal because the rain belonged to CanadaCorp. When Raytheon and the WMA diverted the rain to the USA, her cistern dried up, and they had to resort to getting their water from the rationed public water taps that cost the equivalent of $20 a glass in water credits. It didn't matter if you were rich—no one got more than two liters a day.

Hilda and her mother hadn't seen a good rain in over a decade. Lake Ontario turned into a mud puddle like Erie before it. The Saint Lawrence River, channelized long ago, now flowed south to the USA—like everything else.

One day the water patrol of the RCMP stormed the house. They seized her mother's books—except Wetzel's *Limnology*, hidden under Hilda's mattress—and they dragged her mother away. The RCMP weren't actually gruff with her, and she didn't struggle. She quietly watched them ransack the place then turned a weary gaze to Hilda.

"We were too nice ... too nice ..." she'd said in a strangled voice.

She didn't clutch Hilda to her bosom or tell her that she loved her. Just the words, "We invited them in and let them take it all. We gave it all way ..."

It took a long time for Hilda to realize that she'd meant Canada and its water.

CanadaCorp wasn't even a Canadian company. According to Hanna, it was part of Vivanti, a multinational conglomerate of European and Chinese companies. When it came to water—which was everything—the Chinese owned the USA. When China finally called them on their trillion-dollar debt, the bankrupted country defaulted. That was when the world changed. China offered USA a deal: give us your water, all of it, and we'll forfeit the capital owed. And they could stay a country. That turned out to include Canadian water since Canada had already let Michigan tap into the Great Lakes. That's how CanadaCorp, which had nothing to do with Canada, came to own the Great Lakes and eventually all of Canada's surface and ground water. And how Canada sank from a resource-rich nation into a poor, indentured state.

Hilda didn't cry when her mother left. Hilda thought her mother was coming back. She didn't.

A tiny water drop hangs, trembling, from the iTap faucet mouth as if considering which way to go: give in to gravity and drop onto the dusty ground or defy it and cling to the inside of the tap. Hilda lunges forward and touches the faucet mouth with her card to capture the drop. Then she laps up the single drop with her tongue. She thinks of Hanna and her throat tightens.

The man behind her grunts. He barrels forward and violently shoves her aside. Hilda stumbles away from the long queue in a daze. The brute gruffly pulls out her useless card and tosses it to her. She misses it, and the card flutters like a dead leaf to the ground at her feet. The man shoves his own card into the pay slot. Hilda watches the water gurgle into his plastic container. He is sloppy, and some of the water splashes out of his container, raining on the ground. Hilda stares as the water bounces off the parched pavement before finally pooling. The ache in her throat burns like sandpaper, and she wavers on her feet.

The lineup tightens, as if the people fear she might cut back in.

She stares at the water pooling on the ground, glistening into a million stars in the sunlight.

Hanna claimed that there was a fourth state of water: a liquid crystal that possessed magical properties of healing. You could find it in places like collagen and cell membranes where biological signals and information traveled instantly. Like quantum entanglement. The crystalline water increased its energy in a vortex and light. Hanna seemed to know all about the research done at the University of Washington. According to her, this negatively-charged crystallized water held energy like a battery and pushed away pollutants. She told of an experiment in Austria where water in a beaker when jolted with electromagnetic energy leapt up the beaker wall, groping to meet its likeness in the adjoining beaker. The beaker waters formed a "water bridge" like two shocked children clutching hands.

Hilda's mother had dismissed Hanna's claims as fairy tale. But when Hilda challenged her mother, she couldn't explain why water stored so much energy or absorbed and released more heat than most substances. Or a host of other things water could do that resembled magic.

Something Hilda never dared share with her mother was Hanna's startling claim about water's intelligent purpose. She cited bizarre studies conducted by Russian scientists and some quasi-scientific studies in Germany and Austria suggesting that water had a consciousness.

"What if everything that water does has an innate purpose related to what we are doing to it?" Hanna had once challenged.

"They've proven that water remembers everything done to it and everywhere it's been. What if it's self-organized like a giant amebic computer. We've done terrible things to water, Hilda," she said, sorrow vivid in her liquid eyes. "What if water doesn't like being owned or ransomed? What if it doesn't like being channelized into a harsh pipe system or into a smart cloud to go where it normally doesn't want to go? What if those hurricanes and tornadoes and floods are water's way of saying 'I've had enough?'"

None of that matters now, Hilda thinks rather abstractly and feels herself falling. They are all going to die soon anyway. Neither water's magical properties nor Hanna's fantasies about its consciousness are going to help her or Hanna, who disappeared again since last month ...

~*~

"I can't do this anymore with you," Hilda ranted. She paced her decrepit one-room apartment and watched Hanna askance.

Hanna sat on Hilda's worn couch like a brooding selkie. Like a sociopath contemplating her next move. Waiting for Hilda's.

"This is the last time." Hilda kept her voice harsh. She wanted to jar Hanna into crying or something, to induce some kind of emotional breakdown. In truth, Hilda was so relieved to see her itinerant friend alive and well after her lengthy silence. Hilda went on, "It's always the same pattern. After months of nothing, you come, desperate for help ... water credits or some dire task that only I can perform ... then you disappear again, only emerging months later with your next disaster. I never hear from you otherwise. I don't know if you're dead or alive like I'm a well you dip into. Like that's all I mean to you. Where do you go when you disappear? Where?"

She dropped back in the lumpy chair across from Hanna and watched her gypsy friend, hoping for some sign of remorse or acknowledgement, at least. She knew Hanna wouldn't answer, as though every question she asked her—particularly the personal ones—was only rhetorical in nature. Hanna just stared at her like a puppy dog. As if she didn't quite understand the problem. She could barely speak at the best of times. Hilda had decided long ago that Hanna was partly autistic. Maybe a savant even; she was inordinately clever. Too clever sometimes. Maybe she'd been traumatized when she was little, Hilda considered. Apparently, the emergence of sociopathic behavior was created—or prevented—by childhood experience. She knew that Hanna's childhood, though privileged with significant wealth, was terribly lonely and troubled. Her parents, who both worked in the water industry in Maine, spent no time with her and her sister. Like obsessed missionaries, they were always traveling and tending their water business. When Hanna was in her late teens, her parents perished in a freak accident.

Hanna had avoided any cross-examination, but Hilda's

uncompromising research on ORACLE uncovered a strange story—a common one in the old water wars. Hanna never revealed her last name, but Hilda guessed it was Lauterwasser, the name of a known water baron family in Maine. John and Beulah Lauterwasser owned a large water holding of spring water near Fryeburg and sold Apa Fina all over the world. They'd refused buy-out offers by the international conglomerate Vivanti. Soon after the Lauterwassers drowned, and the holdings mysteriously came into the hands of Vivanti. Hilda suspected foul play. Not long after that, Hanna appeared in her life.

From the moment Hilda saw her seven years ago, she'd felt a strange yet familiar attraction she couldn't explain. A bond that commanded her with a kind of divine instruction, a déjà vu, that bubbled up like an evolutionary yin-yang mantra: *you two were born to do something important together*. Hilda felt a strange repelling attraction to her strange friend. Like the covalent bond of a complex molecule.

Like two quantum-entangled atoms fuelled by a passion for information, they shared secrets on ORACLE. They corresponded for months on ORACLE—strange attractors, circling each other closer and closer—sharing energy—yet never touching. Then Hanna suggested they actually meet. They met in the lobby of a shabby downtown Toronto hotel. Hilda barely knew what she looked like, but when Hanna entered the lobby through the front doors, Hilda knew every bit of her.

Hanna swept in like a stray summer rainstorm, beaming with the self-conscious optimism of someone who recognized a twin sister. She reminded Hilda of her first boyfriend, clutching flowers in one hand and chocolate in the other. When their eyes met, Hilda knew. For an instant, she knew all of Hanna. For an instant she'd glimpsed eternity. What she didn't know then was that it was love.

Love flowed like water, gliding into backwaters and lagoons with ease, filling every swale and mire. Connecting, looking for home. Easing from crystal to liquid to vapor then back, water recognized its hydrophilic likeness and its complement. Before the inevitable decoherence, remnants of the entanglement lingered like a quantum vapor, infusing everything. Hilda always knew where and when to find Hanna on ORACLE as though water inhabited the machine and told her. Water even whispered to her when her wandering friend was about to return from the dark abyss and land unannounced on her doorstep.

Hilda leaned back in her chair with a heavy sigh. She always gave in to Hanna. And Hanna knew it. "Okay," Hilda said. "What do you need this time?"

Hanna's face lit with the fire of inspiration, and she leaned forward. "ORACLE told me something."

Hilda slumped deeper in her chair and rolled her eyes. "Of course ORACLE told you something. It always does."

Some cyber-genius created ORACLE after the Internet sold out to Vivanti. The ORACLE universe was the last commons, Hilda considered. It had brought her and Hanna together, bound them into one being with a common understanding. Hilda discovered one of Hanna's sites. It turned out to be a code for what was happening to water. To Hanna's obvious delight, Hilda decoded her blog, and like two conspiring teenagers, they shared intimate secrets about water. Hilda shared from her textbook, and Hanna embellished with facts that Hilda's mother reluctantly confirmed or vehemently denied. Hilda never discovered how Hanna got her information, how she managed to cross the Canadian/US border, or who Hanna really was. Whether she was a delusional charlatan, the itinerant daughter of a murdered water baron, a water spy for the US, or something worse. Hilda realized that she didn't want to know.

"I was right, but I was wrong, too," Hanna said, beaming like an angel. "Mandelbrot has the last piece of the puzzle. It's right there in Ritz's migrating birds and Scholes's photosynthesis." She lifted her eyes to the heavens then grinned like an urchin at Hilda. "... In Schrödinger's water."

Seeing Hanna this way, lit with genuine inspiration, Hilda knew she would totally give in to whatever plan the girl had concocted. She wasn't prepared for what Hanna asked for.

"I need a thousand water credits."

"What?" Hilda gasped. "You know I don't have that! What the chaos do you need it for?" Hanna had inherited a hoard of water credits in the Vivanti settlement but had lost them all through various wild ventures and a profligate lifestyle. Over the years Hilda, who had barely anything, had given Hanna so many water credits for her wild schemes during their strange friendship. She'd funded Hanna's Tesla-field amplifier, her orgonite cloud buster, and anti-HAARP electromagnetic pulse device. Hilda had never once gotten any proof of them having amounted to anything except to keep Hanna hydrated.

Hanna inched forward in her seat, and her eyes glinted like sapphires. "You know about the nanobots that keep the smart clouds in the states from coming north over the border?"

Hilda nodded, wondering what Mandelbrot's fractals—and photosynthesis—had to do with weather control and cloud farming. It was part of the deal the US made with the Chinese, who had first perfected weather manipulation with smart dust. Vivanti owned the weather. Canada, which had been mined dry of its water, was just another casualty of the corporate profit machine.

"Why do you think water lets them do that?" Hanna said.

Hilda squirmed in her seat. What was Hanna driving at? As though water had any say in the matter ...

Hanna wriggled in her seat with a self-pleased smile. "What if those nanobots 'decided' to let the clouds migrate north?"

Suddenly intrigued, Hilda leaned forward and stared at her friend. "Are you talking sabotage?" she finally said in a hoarse whisper and wondered who Hanna really was. "How?"

Hanna grinned in silence. A kind of conspiratorial withholding look. She always did that, Hilda thought: looked reluctant to say when that was precisely why she'd come. To spill a secret. The two women stared at one another for an eternity of a moment. Hilda struggled to stay patient, understanding the hierarchy of flow.

Hanna finally confided, "Not sabotage. More like collaboration." She leaned back, and her mischievous grin turned utterly sublime. She looked like a self-pleased griffin. "Like recognizes like, Hilda. Have you ever noticed how children going for walks with their mothers notice only other children? The most successful persuasion doesn't come from your boss but by a trusted colleague ... *a friend*."

Hilda shook her head, still not understanding.

Hanna leaned forward and gently took Hilda's hand in hers. She pressed Hilda's fingers with hers in a warm clasp. Smooth, hydrated fingers that were long and beautiful—not like Hilda's selkie hands.

"It's okay, my friend," Hanna said. "Just trust me. Trust me one more time ..."

The faucet swims into a million faucets. Hilda understands that she is hallucinating. People generally stay away from the public iTap when someone in her condition approaches. People don't want to share, but they also don't want to feel cruel or greedy about not sharing. In today's blistering heat urgency overrules decorum, and they simply ignore her away. They know she is close to the end. She's seen others and has shied away herself. She feels the water guardians hovering. Waiting. If she doesn't get up and walk away, they will come and take her—probably to the same place her mother was taken. Some place you never came back from.

It is a month since she gave Hanna everything she had in the world. A month since Hanna disappeared with Hilda's thousand water credits—worth a million dollars on the black market. Credits she borrowed off her rent. In that month Hilda's entire world collapsed. Her research contract—and associated meager income—ended suddenly at the Wilkinson Alternative Energy Center with no sign of transfer or renewal. Three weeks later, the Coop wiped most of her bank account clean then locked her out. She found a piece of shade from the relentless sun under an old corrugated sheet of metal in the local dump and set up camp there.

Nothing has changed with the water. No clouds have come. No rains have come. And no Hanna has come.

This time Hilda knows that Hanna is really gone. That whatever fractal scheme Hanna had conjured, she's failed. Since they flowed into one another, they always seemed to know when the other was in trouble. ... Strangely, Hilda feels nothing. No presence; no absence. Just nothing.

Hanna is probably dead. Or worse. Since meeting her, Hilda has learned to monitor the ORACLE for signs of her elusive friend. Small blips of signature code on certain sites. Anonymous tags. Like ghosts, they wisped into existence, whispered their truths, then disappeared like vapor in the wind. Even they stopped. Hanna, too, has turned to vapor.

Hilda is alone. Doomed by her trust, her faith, and her gift ... All gone with Hanna ...

No. Not all gone.

For every giver there must be a receiver in the recursive motion of fractals. Everything is connected through water from infinitely small to infinitely large. Like recognizes like. Atom with atom. Like her and Hanna. Like water with water ...

She's fallen recumbent on the dusty ground. She is dying of thirst meters from a water source. And no one is coming to help her. They just keep filling their containers and shuffling away in haste. She doesn't hate them for it. They aren't capable of helping her. She squints at the massive sun that seems to wink at her and chokes on her own tongue. Perhaps her vision is already failing because a shadow passes before the sun and it grows suddenly dark. It doesn't matter.

She's given all of herself faithfully in love and in hope. Through Hanna. To water. She is two-thirds water, after all. Just like the planet. Water and the universe are taking her back into its fold. She will enter the Higgs Field, stream through spacetime, touch infinite light. Then, energized, return—perhaps as water even—to Earth or somewhere else in the cosmos.

Her mother was wrong in her angry heart. They weren't too nice. It is simply the way of water. They are all water. And water is an altruist.

It starts to rain.

Huge drops spatter her face, streaming down, soaking her hair, her clothes, her entire body. It hurts at first like missiles assaulting her with suddenness. Like love. Then it begins to soothe as her parched body remembers, grateful.

Dark storm clouds scud across the heavens like warriors chasing a thief. She's vaguely aware of the commotion of people as they scatter, arms and containers pointed up toward the heavens. She smiles then feels her body convulse with tears.

Is that you, Hanna? Have you come to take me home?

Loosestrife

Liz Williams

She knew that there was something wrong with her baby because Ellie's eyes did not follow her as she moved about the room and she had once been told that this was important. She crouched over the baby, passing a hand across Ellie's face.

"Ellie? What's wrong?"

This time the baby's eyes twitched to follow the passage of her hand, and Aud breathed a sigh of relief. Nothing wrong, after all, and probably she was just being silly, but she had been told so often that she did not understand things that, once she had taken a fact into her head, she clung to it. She thought she understood the baby a little better now, and as long as it remained just Ellie and herself, no one else, she thought she could cope. Ellie was doing fine, and if she still seemed to eat so little when Aud gave her the bottle, at least she appeared healthy and well. Aud would surely know if a change occurred. She watched Ellie for hours, noticing every movement, every sound.

Picking Ellie up, Aud stepped carefully over the piles of broken plaster and carried her out onto the little concrete balcony.

"Look," she said. "You can see Big Ben from here. See it? See the big clock? And there's the Houses of Parliament, where all the rich people go." She thought that the distant clock face read ten to eight, or perhaps it was twenty to ten. She could never remember which hand meant which, no matter how often she had been told, and it was so easy to lose track of the time. But Ellie, lying quietly in her arms, would never question her, never ask uncomfortable things like "What time is it?" and "What does that say?" and "What is Parliament?"

Maybe when Ellie grew up, she would be able to answer these things on her own.

"And then you'll be a help to me, won't you?" Aud said. She and Ellie watched as one of the boats glided down the Thames just above the water like a big wing, rising as it came to the barrier. Wealthy tourists came on those boats, Aud's mum had told her, to see what was left of London. This puzzled Aud, too: surely you couldn't leave a piece of a city, not like a bit of cabbage that you tried to hide on your plate. When she had asked where the rest of London had gone, her mum said that it was under the water, that it was all to do with the world getting warmer. But to Aud, London always seemed a cold place.

They did not spend a long time looking out of the window because it was time for Ellie's nap and Aud had to check that the door was locked. She did this many times a day, worrying in case the gangs came. She could hear them at night running around the bottom of the flats, and she was sure that they got into the lift shaft even though the lift hadn't been working for years. Sometimes, when she went to the food charity or to collect her money, there was a sharp smell in the hallway. It did not smell like anything natural but as though someone had been burning something. It made Aud nervous, and so she did not want to be seen going in and out of the flat. She made sure that the steel door was locked every time. She always tried to take a different way to get her money, too, even though it meant leaving Ellie alone for longer. Sometimes, she got lost, and that was worst of all.

"Where's Highstone Road?" she would ask some passer-by, who always looked as though they had more important places to go. And once someone had snapped, "You're standing in it. Can't you read?"

"No," Aud said, and the man just stared at her before walking away. She felt stupid then, but it was true. How was she to know how to read when her mum had never put her in school, keeping her up night after night for company? Later, when she had signed on with the Deserving Poor board, they had tried to teach her, but it was only a short course and the letters just hadn't seemed to stick. She couldn't tell half of them apart no matter how hard she tried.

"You can't help it," Danny had told her when she said that she wasn't going back. "You're just a bit thick, that's all. Nothing wrong with that."

"I know," Aud said sadly, but there wasn't anything either of them could do about it. And Danny seemed to know this, too, because he helped her so much: taking the Council seal off the flat and turning the steel slab into a proper door that you could lock and bringing her veg from the allotments. Sometimes, now that he was back from Ireland, he even offered to look after Ellie, but Aud always said no. She thought it was kind of him, but she didn't feel that it was right. Ellie was her daughter, not his. She did not like anyone even to hold Ellie, and she would not let Danny get too close.

"At least now you've got the baby, you'll get more money," Danny said. "And you're eighteen, aren't you? That should qualify you for extra benefits."

"I suppose so." Aud was doubtful.

"Oh, come on. You're Deserving Poor. They had you checked, didn't they? Not like me," and Danny laughed, sitting in the ragged-sleeved sweater, head shaved, and the code clearly visible just above the nape of his heck. "*Undeserving*, that's what they said I was. Not that I expected anything else, mind. You're lucky you're not too bright, really."

His gaze fell on Ellie, and Aud could tell that he was wondering about the baby again. She had not told him anything about Ellie. It had never seemed the right time, somehow.

He said, hesitantly, "Aud—who's her dad? Not that I've any right to ask, mind. Just wondering. I know she's not mine —well, obviously she isn't. But you don't go out much, and if someone's been bothering you—I'd have put off going to Ireland if I'd known."

"Just someone," Aud had said. "No one you know."

"Come on, Aud. You don't know anyone except me and Gill and the lot down the Social."

"It was someone I met, all right? Just the once." And that

was all she was saying, Aud thought. She clammed up and wouldn't look at him, and after a bit more coaxing he gave up and let it rest. But she didn't want to lie to Danny, and she couldn't tell him about Ellie. Not yet.

Now she hurried down the stairwell, trying not to stumble over the piles of rubbish that had blown in through the open doors. When she reached the bottom of the stairs she paused and looked around her. The courtyard was empty apart from a few boys and a dog. Aud liked dogs but not kids: sometimes they shouted things, and she did not always understand what they said. It was never nice, she could tell that. But the boys ignored her, and so she slipped between the blocks of flats and took the path that led down along the run-off canal. There was a lock at the top, Danny had told her, which opened if the river got too full and let the water out. Aud wondered where it went. She pictured it running dark and secret under the streets. It was a comforting thought. She passed the old railway bridge that crossed the run-off: it was pretty in summer with loosestrife and nettles and long grass. She had come here with Danny before he went to Ireland, and he'd told her which flower was which. Because it was Danny who told her, she had remembered. Now, the plants had died back and there was only bare earth beneath the bridge, but she still liked it.

She counted the paving stones as she walked, careful not to tread on the cracks. It was only a game, she knew; she had played it as a kid, but somewhere along the line it had turned serious, started to be important. She thought it had been when Ellie had come: the world became a different place when you had a child. You became larger and smaller at the same time. But she was doing better than her mum, she knew that: letting Ellie sleep at night, not waking her up whenever she felt lonely or bored, not shouting at her. All the time: *Tell me you love me; tell me you love me.* You shouldn't have to ask that of a child. It should come naturally, but her mum had never been able to let it rest. The Social had been round a few times, and Aud had kept quiet. Her mum knew what they wanted to hear. She didn't tell them anything that mattered, and so Aud had stayed, the days not-quite-real, the nights sleepless. She did not know why her mother didn't sleep like normal people; she'd always been that way, her mum had said. After the visit by the Social, she had overheard her mum talking to Auntie Julie.

"I don't know why you bother," Julie had said. "You could have sold her off—there's plenty of them that want one even if you don't. Even if she's a bit defective. People can't afford to be choosy these days."

"I've been bossed around all my life," her mum had said, hot and angry. "I just want something I can boss around now."

"You're lucky you could have a kid," Julie had said. "Lots of 'em can't. Something in the water, my dad said, or genetic modifications or mad cows. If you ever want to get rid of Aud, you let me know. I know a bloke down the market."

"I don't like the idea all the same," Aud's mum had muttered. "What if he sold her to some pervert? Plenty of those around, too. Look at my old man. 'Keep it in the family,' he used to say. I'd only sell her, Jule, if she went to a good home. And even then—I don't know. We're all right as we are."

And now Aud was lucky, too, for she had Ellie and lots of richer people couldn't have babies. She thought of this as she walked along the canal path, and she felt her luck running alongside her like a dog. She found the DP office without too much trouble this week.

"Fifty-three euros; here you are. Is it all right like that? Want me to put it in the envelope for you?" The woman at the DP was kind, Aud thought. They weren't all like that: the one on the end always looked at her as though she was in the wrong office, as though she ought to be registered at the Undeserving side and have no money at all, just what she could scrounge off the streets on a beggars' license. She plucked up her courage and asked.

"'Scuse me," she said. She'd wanted to know about this ever since Danny had got back from Ireland. "Could you tell me what's the rate if you've got a baby?"

The woman frowned. "They'd have to be sure it was a genuine claim, love. Otherwise, you could lose your registry and go onto the other list—they're trying to discourage girls from getting pregnant to raise their rate. Because so many babies die, you see, or don't come to term, and a lot of girls think they can fake it—get a false certificate. It's not fair, but that's the way things are these days." She gave Aud a sharp, sudden look. "You're not pregnant, are you?"

"No," Aud said, suddenly afraid. "It's for someone else. A friend asked me."

"Well, if you have a baby and they let you keep it, you'd get a hundred euros a week, and some of the charities give maternity benefits but you'd need to go to them for that."

"Thanks," Aud said. She bundled the money into her purse and went out quickly. She had not told the DP about Ellie. As far as she knew, only Danny knew about the baby, and that was the way Aud wanted things to stay.

It was cold out now. Aud's fingers curled inside the thin gloves as she tried to remember what month it was. November perhaps, but it was hard to tell because they put the Christmas stuff up so early in the shops. It cheered her up, thinking about Ellie and what to get her for Christmas. It would be Ellie's first.

She was walking through the posh bit now, the little knot of streets they called the Village. Aud liked it here, but she felt out of place as though at any moment someone might come up to her and ask her to leave for making the place look untidy. There was a group of girls clustered on the corner dressed in coats with big fur collars and cuffs, high heels. Their perfume drifted through the air; they smelled expensive. They were gathered around a pram, cooing into it. Aud could not help looking. The baby looked exactly like Ellie except its eyes were blue.

"He's so gorgeous," one of the girls was saying. "You're so lucky."

The girl holding the pram gave a small, smug smile. "I wanted a boy, but they're a bit more difficult than girls."

"When did you get him?"

The girl holding the pram turned and caught sight of Aud, and her face grew thinner as if she didn't want a scruffy person near her baby. Aud felt herself grow hot with embarrassment, and she hurried away. To cheer herself up, she started thinking about Christmas again and she kept it up all the way back to the flat, but when she got there, she saw that there was a van outside.

It wasn't like the drugs van, which came every week. It was white with a logo on the side. Aud could not read what it said, but she thought that the letters were a *D* and a *P*: perhaps two *D*s or two *P*s. The windows were frosted over. She would not, in any case, have tried to look inside. She wasn't that stupid. She skirted the van and made her way up the stairs. There was no sign of anyone in the stairwell. Once the door was shut behind her, she felt safer. Ellie was asleep on the blanket. Aud waited, listening. Someone knocked. Aud froze. Then, with relief, she heard Danny say, "Who are you looking for?"

"Do you live here?" A woman's voice, which Aud did not recognize.

"No."

"Do you know who does?"

"I came up to see one of my mates. It's not his place—he's staying with somebody. I don't know what their name is."

"You do know that this block's been condemned?"

A pause, then Danny said, "Yeah, so what? Where are people supposed to live if they haven't got any money?"

"Does your friend have a girlfriend?"

"Why don't you ask him?"

Aud found herself moving to the bed stealthily so that her feet would make no sound on the concrete floor. She picked Ellie up, willing her to be quiet.

"We'd like to have a word because someone heard a baby crying up here yesterday."

"Someone wasn't minding their own business then."

"It's no place for a young child. We just want to help." The woman sounded kind, Aud thought, and she was being very patient with Danny. But they always did sound kind. It didn't stop them messing you around.

Ellie was silent, staring up at Aud's face. Aud swallowed hard then went out to the balcony. Pulling the window shut behind her, she climbed over the partition that divided the balcony from that of the neighboring flat. She made her way along the row, avoiding the litter and the needles, until she came to the walkway and the stairs that led down. She stopped and looked back. No one was there. She could still see the van parked outside in the courtyard. She hurried down the stairs, clutching Ellie.

"Don't cry, don't cry ..." And Ellie did not utter a sound.

The only place she could think of was the railway bridge. She would wait there for a bit then go back and see if the van had gone. She thought of taking Ellie into the pub because it would be warmer, but she was afraid of being seen. If she wrapped Ellie up tightly, perhaps it would not be too cold. There was no one about on the canal path, and that made her feel safer.

She crouched under the bridge in the damp dimness, watching the boats going back and forth across the narrow glimpse of the Thames. She lost track of the day. It grew cloudy but did not rain. Ellie slept, and Aud grew cold and hungry. She would go back, look for the van—but then a shadow fell across her. Aud looked up and felt filled with relief because it was Danny.

"They've gone," he said. "You heard them, didn't you?"

"I thought they'd take her away."

"Probably would have done, too." He squatted on his heels, looking down at the baby in her arms. He said, gently, "What do you want to do, Aud?"

"About what?"

"About the baby."

Aud nearly told him then, but she clamped her lips shut against the words. She did not want to hear herself say: "I stole her out of someone else's pram." Because then Danny would surely stop being her friend. Instead, she said something else that was the truth.

"I want to take her away. It's not right bringing her up in London in that flat. I try to make it as nice as I can, but—"

"—but it's a dump."

"Yeah, and I can't get anywhere else."

"You're not claiming money for her?"

"No. I haven't told them about her."

She waited for him to ask "Why not?," and it occurred to her then that perhaps he knew or at least suspected that Ellie was a stolen child. But he only said, "Okay. Listen, Aud. If you're really serious about leaving, then I can help you. Give you some cash and put you on the boat to Ireland. I've got friends there, the ones I told you about."

"The ones in the farmhouse?"

"It might be a squat, Aud, but it's a nice place. A good place for a kid to grow up in. And I think they'd look after you. They don't like the Deserving Poor business—that's why they left England. And things are a bit easier over there. People help each other out."

"Okay," Aud whispered, and her heart beat fast at the thought of the boat, the sea silver in the cold light, a green place at the end of it. She added, "You're really good to me," and embarrassed, he looked away.

The thought of traveling alone scared her, but in the end, she didn't have to. Danny went with her. His dad was sick, he said, and he might as well see the old man before he died.

"But you've only just got back," Aud said.

"It doesn't matter. You know me, back and forth, to and fro. Don't like to stay too long in one place."

But she wondered why she felt guilty all the same.

They left at the end of the week. Aud tried to give him some money, and at last he took a bit of it for the bus. She sat with her face pressed to the chilly window, looking out at the motorway. They left London behind, and soon there was nothing but flooded fields and the barbed wire enclaves of the shires where the rich people lived. Once, they saw an armored car crossing the great bridge into the Republic of Wales. Aud, frozen with nerves, had to show her DP documents, but they let her through without saying anything. Ellie dozed until they got to the ferry, and then she woke up, crying a little.

"Does she need feeding?" Danny asked, frowning.

"I don't think so."

"She doesn't seem to want her bottle much, does she? I thought babies were all 'in one end, out the other.' Maybe she needs changing."

"I changed her in the service station," Aud lied. "She had her bottle then."

"Oh, right." And to her relief Danny lost interest.

She spent as much time as she could on the deck, watching the gulls and the waves with silent delight. The rocky Welsh coast was soon gone. Aud leaned against the rail, Ellie held tightly in her arms.

"Mind you don't get cold," Danny said. Before she could stop him, he reached out and drew Ellie's blanket aside to tuck it in more securely.

"This trip is the first time I've really seen her in daylight," he said, smiling. Aud closed her eyes too tightly. She did not want to see his face change. There was a long moment of silence shattered by a baby's cry. Aud's eyes snapped open, but it was only a gull wheeling overhead.

She felt him take the baby from her, and this time, she let him. Ellie made no protest at all.

After a long time, he said, "Jesus, Aud. Where did you get her?"

Aud did not answer, but he did not sound angry, only bewildered, and it gave her a little hope.

"Did you nick her out of someone's car or what?"

"Her name's Ellie," Aud whispered.

Danny handed Ellie back to her carefully and stood with his feet braced, staring out to sea.

"Need a cig," he murmured. She watched him roll up in silence, waiting for him to say something. His hands looked cold. He fumbled with the papers, with the tobacco, with the lighter. Then, after a long breath, he said, "Shouldn't be too long now. Look. That's Wexford over there."

His friends lived in the countryside near Cork, and when Ellie saw the place, she thought it was the most beautiful house she had ever seen even if half of it was a ruin. A lot of Danny's friends seemed to live in vans anyway so the state of the house didn't really matter. A girl called Jade with a mat of beaded hair and a big smile took Aud under her wing and showed her to a warm room with a fire.

"You can crash in here. This'll be your space, and the baby's."

She brought Aud a bowl of stew, and once Aud had eaten it, the journey seemed to tumble down on her all at once. She yawned. She thought she would just sit down for a moment, but when she next looked up, it was nearly dark outside. Jade was sitting with Ellie in her arms.

"It's all right, Aud," she said. "Everything's all right."

So Aud went back to sleep. She woke later, and there were voices outside the warm room: Danny and Jade.

"Her name's Ellie, right?" Jade was saying.

"Yeah." Danny gave a tight laugh. "Well, that's what it says on the back of her neck."

"She's amazing. I thought she was a real baby."

"So did I until halfway across the bloody Irish Sea. When the Social came round, I realized Aud'd nicked her, and I knew what would happen. I thought: just get her to Ireland with the kid whether it's hers or not."

"You didn't stop to think about her mum?" Jade said angrily, and Aud cringed.

"Of course, I did! I knew it wasn't right, Jade, but Aud's never had a thing of her own, and so I thought: just give her a chance. And then on the boat, I realized. Huge weight off my mind."

"But Ellie's not plastic, is she? She feels *real*. Like flesh. And she looks at you, and cries—she even seems to pee and eat, but not as much as a real baby."

"She *is* flesh, Jade. They grow them in tanks. They're for rich girls who can't have kids—it's some kind of psychological charity initiative. They cost a fortune. But they don't grow up. They're not much more than a toy, really."

I am dreaming, Aud told herself. *I don't want to listen anymore*. She pulled the blanket over her ears and huddled back against the wall. In the firelight Ellie watched her with round dark eyes and did not blink even when Jade came back through the door.

"Shhh," she said, when she saw that Aud was awake. She gave Aud a long, measuring look as though she wanted to say something else. But then she added, "I'll be quiet, okay? I don't want to disturb the baby." And reassured, Aud closed her eyes and slept.

What Lies Dormant

Swapna Kishore

I was gazing at the sands outside, sun-bright despite the smoked windows of our bus, when I heard Sunil's low hiss of frustration and his mother's swift reprimand—also low, also wary. I did not want to join any argument. I wanted to stay wrapped in my daydream, where I was still in my Mumbai school, topper amongst special-track girl students, and far away from the reality of our rushed exit. Away from those pressed-together lips of Mother when I asked her, "Why Tilaknagari, isn't that, like, the pits?"

But voices possibly sound louder the more you ignore them, and finally I turned to face my family. Mother and Auntie were both staring at Sunil, looking even more like sisters than they usually did. Uncle was distant, resigned, and I knew he would never side with his son in an argument. Men had little say in gatherer families. My sister, Deepa, looked at Sunil with a wide-eyed wonder only a five-year-old can have.

"I don't see why I can't break off," Sunil said. "I can just ignore that I'm a—"

"Shh." Auntie looked around. Luckily for us, a couple of empty rows separated us from our fellow travelers.

"Everyone has to complete Intercity formalities." Mother's tone was curt. She patted the nape of her neck to confirm that her sari covered the telltale blue of the implant. "Your papers reveal that you are, well ... what we are."

Sunil turned his face away, but he said nothing.

I tried to resume my daydreaming, but the sands outside no longer presented an infinity of possibilities. Instead, they were textured with shadows of villages and cities our bus route skirted around, places overrun by species gone wild because humans had been knocked off by biobombs. Decades ago, people in protective suits must have walked here, controlling officers and my ancestors, the gatherers, who were to harvest *lifeen*—life energy—from the collapsing men and women.

Thinking of the present was no fun, either—that was full of Mumbai mobs three streets away from our house, their shouts and jeers spreading like waves, their hatred saturating the air even as we rushed to the Intercity terminus, dressed as commoners.

At least I had my books. I let my fingers brush the reader strapped to my stomach. The device, the only part of my school life I managed to smuggle out in that dash for safety, was hidden by my tent-like salwar suit. It contained all the books I loved, even two new ones I uploaded just days before this calamity—Yusuf's 2020 classic, *Genetic Modifications and Life Energy*, and Subramanium's *Advanced Work on Unified Field: Papers Published 2030 to 2050*.

I was drooling at the thought of the books when Sunil plunked himself near me.

"With false identities," he said, "we could have started afresh in Tilaknagari, even though it is a dump."

I glanced at the bulge of Mother's implant, straining against the held-in-place edge of her yellow sari. Sunil followed my gaze. "Okay, so they can't hide. But I don't have an implant and neither do you." He paused. "Not yet."

"I'll resubmit my exemption application." That may not stop them from implanting me after my menarche, but at least I could become a researcher instead of a gatherer. "When my new school uplinks to my Mumbai school records, the—"

"They didn't tell you?" he asked softly.

"Who? Tell me what?"

He did not speak for a few moments, and I felt uneasy as I waited.

"Maybe you should break free, too," he finally said. "Maybe if we get the gold they are carrying ..." His gaze shifted to Auntie. "A distraction ... yes, I think ..."

"Tell me *what*?" I asked again. "It's about Tilaknagari, right?"

I didn't remember the details, but my sociology textbook described it as a throwback medieval dump, the poorest of the Cities, a City that survived only because the then-still-existing Indian government used it to prototype the City Shield. Obviously, Mumbai's textbooks praised Mumbai and criticized other Cities, I had told myself; Mother and Auntie chose Tilaknagari, so it must be good. But something was wrong; Sunil, usually extroverted and cheery, had become maudlin.

"Your studies—"

"Meera didi, I'm boooorrred!" Deepa tried to prop herself on my lap; I ruffled her hair and firmly moved her away. She loved to snuggle against me, and I didn't want her to notice the strapped reader.

She turned to Sunil. "Let's play." He nodded, pulled out the board for *Warring Presidents*, and handed out the tokens. We spent the next few hours squinting at the simplistic model of the world. Deepa became Apple Pie Mom President, Sunil, the Dragon Lady Roars, and I was Deep-into-Shit Brownskin for the rest of the world that tried to place City Shields for protection while biobomb-rich America and China ran amok. I hated such trivialization of the devastation and played unwillingly, mechanically, while wondering what Sunil wanted to tell me. He avoided eye contact now and seemed preoccupied.

When we reached Tilaknagari and Deepa ran to pester Mother, I pulled Sunil aside. "What—"

"I'm going to try, and maybe, if you—"

"Meera!" Mother beckoned me. "Help us with the bags." She did not give Sunil any responsibility, though he was nineteen, six years older than me. It was her way of showing displeasure.

The reception lounge was pathetic with chipping paint, torn upholstery, and desks loaded with paper files. No computers. Inked pads for thumbprints. I was pressing my inked-purple thumb on my form under the supervision of the officer when a loud bang shook the building and the lights snapped off. A massive short circuit? Sunil had mentioned a distraction.

When the lights returned, sure enough, he was missing.

Mother noticed Sunil's absence, too, because her face went rigid; she whispered something to Uncle, who paled. She peered through the crowd, probably looking for Auntie, but just as Auntie and Deepa caught up with us, Deepa said, "Where's Sunil Bhaiyya? Where's his bag?"

Mother said, "Shh," and Auntie's eyes glazed in shocked understanding.

I said nothing, just let the loss roll in my stomach. I held Deepa's hand as we boarded the bus to take us to the allocated apartment in the gatherers' colony. Our bus wove through convoluted roads, and I squinted through the window. Would I spot Sunil walking? Did he have a plan? What had he tried to tell me?

We reached a shantytown.

"We get off here," Mother said, brisk and energetic, but she wrinkled her nose.

Even she had not expected it to be this bad.

After we unpacked and tried to fit our stuff in our single-room apartment, Mother told me, "You will look after Deepa during the day; your Uncle is unwell most of the time."

"What about when I'm at school?"

Mother blinked hard. "Meera, girls here can't attend school after grade five. Tilaknagari reacted rather strongly to the women Presidents who biobombed the world."

I think I took an eternity to soak that in and then some. All those nights that I slogged to top my class. All my dreams of shiny labs and papers presented in conventions. *No school?*

"See, you are thirteen," Mother said. "Your periods will start, you will get implanted and become a gatherer."

"I don't want to gather," I retorted. "I don't want an implant. I want to study." But the implant was unavoidable. The monthly medical checkup at school identified girls to be implanted. *No, wait.*

"If there is no school," I said, "then no one will know when my periods start. I can avoid the implant."

Mother turned pale. "No, no, without a controller, you could harm people. I've never been tempted to, but even the thought that I might ever do so is so horrible that—Believe me, implants are good, you harvest only when ... let the controllers decide." She took a deep breath. "We were talking about Deepa."

"You should have chosen another City," I said bitterly. "You knew how important studies are to me."

"We had one hour to leave Mumbai. One hour to pack and rush and catch a bus. At least these people need gatherers. At least we are alive."

"Mother," I said, trying to sound reasonable, but squishy with panic inside, "let's buy false identities and move to another City. No one need know."

"Meera, we are gatherers, and our implants need to be managed. And you and Deepa will need to be implanted when you get old enough." Her arm rose, and I thought she was going to hug me, but she drew back.

Life fell into the texture of nothingness soon enough except for the time I hoarded for myself on my daily shopping trip.

That day, after Mother and Auntie left for work, our tap water reduced to a trickle before the scheduled one hour. Uncle had not yet showered. He snapped at Deepa when she clamored for a game of Ludo. She burst into tears. I checked my watch and was relieved that it was time to go shopping. When I picked up the grocery list, Deepa said, "Take me along, Meera didi."

I shook my head. This daily trip kept me sane. I would head for a derelict outhouse where, latched in safely and sitting on a stinky throne, I read my secret cache of books.

"Please, didi."

"I'll take you out in the evening," I promised her.

Returning a few hours later, clutching my bag of provisions, what struck me first was the searing heat. I was a few lanes away from home. I paused, surprised. Then I heard the crowds shouting. *Something was wrong.* I quickened my pace, my mouth dry with primal fear. People were ganged around our shantytown. Huge licks of heat danced macabrely in the air. Shouts mingled with the hiss and spit of fire. Where were the fire engines? Surely, even this wretched City had them? *Deepa!* I rushed forward.

Someone pulled me back. "Let them roast," he said.

"But—"

A child stumbled out of a burning structure, its face a smudge behind the smoke. A man stepped forward. I thought he would pull the child to safety, but he thrust a pole out to push the child back into the inferno.

"A curse on these abominations," said a woman near me.

Hand held over my mouth, I registered the hatred round me. My legs wobbled. This fire was no accident. A hand fell on my shoulder; my stomach lurched. Someone must have recognized me. I was no easy prey. I would claw back if they pushed me into the flames, I would tear at their eyes—

A woman shoved me aside, her face twisted with fury. "You!" She shook her fist at the flames. "You deserve every death, you ... my grandfather, when he died, you ..."

She crumpled on the ground, sobbing hard; I did not stay there to watch her. I was shaking, all hollow inside. I slipped through the lanes 'til I was far enough from the woman. The flames blazed red against my closed eyelids, blotched black with the silhouette of the child pushed back. I should have taken Deepa to the market with me. Maybe also told Uncle to take a walk in the park.

I leaned forward and threw up.

Mother and Auntie were at the hospital on gatherer duty. I had to tell them.

I do not remember weaving down the warren of roads, but there I was, standing inside the walled compound of the hospital. It was quiet—no mobs, nothing. I walked slowly, holding myself steady, past the entrance, toward the wing where gatherers worked. Calm. Too calm. I entered.

Bodies lay heaped on the floor, guarded by a solitary policeman. "Yes, child?" he asked.

"My mother ..."

"Your mother works here?" He frowned as his eyes moved to my neck, searching for an implant. He gripped his baton.

"No." *I must deflect his attention,* I thought rapidly. "My mother's worried. It's my father ... I mean—"

"Oh!" He chuckled. "Don't worry, no one's arresting the men. We made sure we arrived after they completed their work. Your father must be celebrating."

Celebrating. I choked back the animal cry rising up my throat. I did not dare look at the policeman so I stared at the bodies. I was suddenly aware of the buzz that sang on my skin, a quicksilver sharpness around me. Lifeen? A broken collecting jar lay near the bodies. I had not been affected by jars in Mumbai, but those were sealed jars.

"Didn't help them in the end, did it?" the policeman asked, following my gaze. "They drained it from our dead, and then they died."

I took a step forward, fascinated.

"Stay where you are, girl," he said sharply. "The maintenance men haven't repaired those jars. It kills the likes of us if we touch it directly."

Ah, yes. Only those with gatherer genes could touch lifeen directly; others needed feeders. My behavior had almost betrayed me. I turned and left.

The hatred-etched faces haunted me all day as I skulked around in a daze: the woman gloating over the burning shantytown, the man pushing the child back into the flames, the policeman expecting celebrations. The smells had settled deep inside me: the smoke, the soot, the sickly burning flesh, the antiseptic hospital smell that should have spelled safety. Ash clung to my skin.

I had survived only because we were newcomers and no one recognized me.

Come evening, my feet led me to the still-smoldering shantytown. Stupid, I knew, but how could I not go there?

No crowds any more. The fire engines had arrived late—a formality, I suspected—and the bodies had been removed, but their stench thickened the air and clogged my lungs. My eyes smarted. I stepped carefully, keeping my breathing shallow. Embers scalded my shoes and burned my feet. I was near where our apartment had been when I heard a sneeze. A looter?

I flattened out of sight just as a shaft of moonlight struck a face. It was Sunil.

I stepped out.

His head shot up; his body tensed. Then he recognized me and gave a tremulous smile. "Meera? Are the others okay? My mother? Yours? Father? Deepa?"

"No," I whispered. "Any idea why suddenly—"

He touched my shoulder. His breath reeked of whiskey. "The Consortium of Cities forced Tilaknagari's government to outlaw gathering. All other Cities had done so already. As soon as the law was passed ..."

... the hatred burst out, I thought, completing his sentence.

The day-long wandering had dulled my fear into despondence. So, the people hated us in Mumbai, here, everywhere. I knew that. The energy crisis caused by the biobomb wars was over. Crop cultivation had resumed outside the shielded Cities, and lifeen was not critical to survival. So, sure enough, everyone suddenly detested gatherers for "robbing" their dying relatives, ignoring the fact that governmental controllers had forced gatherers to harvest.

I carried those hated genes.

"Where can I go now?" I asked Sunil. "They will kill me if they know."

"Come with me. I work as a daily wage laborer; you don't need papers for temporary work." He held out his hand. There were calluses on his palm. Earlier, his hands were so tender that Auntie often teased him, saying he should have been born a girl.

I nodded.

"They had gold, no?" he said. "If we find it ..."

Had he come to pay homage or for the loot? I hated myself for having doubts. He had offered to help me, no?

He poked the ashes. He did not find anything, of course. He was searching at the wrong place. I would tell him about it later, once I was sure.

~*~

The trader gave me a packet to deliver. “Walk down this road ’til you see a yellow board with a painted chicken, and then ...”

“Then?” I squinted at the scribbled address.

“Boy, you can read?”

Sunil had warned me to stay low profile as an illiterate errand boy. “No,” I said, nervous. “Just looking.”

“A pity,” the trader murmured. “I prefer a boy who reads and writes.”

I hesitated. A week of running errands had exhausted me. I definitely preferred a job that depended on reading, not muscles. What was the harm in admitting I could read a bit? It was not as if I was confessing I understood complex science. Or that I was a girl. Or, God forbid, a gatherer.

“For what?” I asked.

“Accounts, records. High-paying jobs.”

Sometimes one must take risks. “I can read a bit.”

“Read this.” He pointed to the address, and I read it out. He nodded. “Now I need your identity papers.”

What a fool I had been! Sunil had warned me that without papers one could only do manual jobs. Fear clawed my stomach. “I can’t read all that much, I—”

He leaned forward, and for a moment I thought he could see that under my thick, coarse shirt were strips of cloth tightly binding prepubescent breasts and that he connected this with my thin voice and my habit of using only the privy with a working latch. I could barely breathe.

“Now, here is what I suggest,” he said. “You do my accounts. I will not pay a single paisa more, but maybe, just maybe, I will not report you as illegal immigrants. I know where your cousin works, and I know where you boys live. Just a hint to the local policeman and ...”

“As you wish,” I said, cursing myself for ignoring Sunil’s advice.

As I slogged over his ledgers the rest of the day, adding numbers ’til they danced before my eyes, I promised myself that I would find a way out of this bind. I was supposed to be an unusually intelligent girl and creative, too. All I had to do was ignore crippling emotions. I tried to shut out the burning shantytown, the heaped bodies in the hospital. I fought the memory of that smell permeating my lungs, the soot and burning flesh. I tried not to think of the dingy hovel Sunil and I shared with five men where I barely slept at night, scared I'd betray myself by my screams when the inevitable nightmares came.

It was only after I put in weeks of meticulous work that the trader stopped watching me suspiciously. My gaze remained lowered in a docile way, but I observed all I could. *Patience*, I told myself. *Gather data, think, explore*.

Then one day I heard a customer ask the trader whether his new identity papers were ready.

Sunil returned late as usual that evening, enveloped in the perpetual mist of alcohol. I led him to a secluded corner.

"Sunil, suppose we get identity papers?"

"Are you mad? Do you think we can trust anyone enough to ask?"

"The trader's ledger has—"

"Don't you dare let him guess you can read!" He gripped my shoulder. I jerked free, disgusted by his stale breath.

"If we buy ..."

He guffawed. "If I had even a rupee more, I'd get myself a drink."

This was pointless. I would talk to Sunil after he sobered up.

But days passed, and he did not change.

Then my periods started. With the cramps of the flow, I thought of Mother and her insistence that implants protected us, and I was scared about the changes that would start in my body and how I would handle them without anyone explaining.

The changes started soon enough. I was walking back from work, the streets a crush of men and women, and my skin crackled as if with static. I halted, too alarmed to react. It took me a few moments to connect this with my experience near the hospital's broken lifeen jar. The sense of being surrounded with static grew 'til an immense urge to scratch gripped me. My skin burned. I tried applying water and balms, but the burning stayed. It vanished a couple of days later, leaving my skin cool and normal.

The cycle repeated itself every three or four days. My skin, I figured, picked up stray lifeen from the people or air around me, and when I was overfull, I discharged spontaneously like an out-of-control power generator. It unnerved me.

So, this was what Mother meant by saying implants helped. An implant probably switched this affinity to lifeen off and on. I could not get implanted, though. I tried to control the sensation by staying physically distant from people. I discovered that discharges were slower and less traumatic when I was calmer, and accumulation less hurtful to the skin. I wanted to remove my sensitivity to lifeen, but my books only described the biochemical and electrical mechanics of storing and disbursing lifeen using implants.

Perhaps Sunil could help me. Like all men, he was insensitive to lifeen. The Y gene neutralized the ability of the X gene (an approach I could not use), but he might know something useful.

I cornered him on a day when he seemed relatively sober. "Sunil, I am already thirteen."

"So you are." He looked me up and down. "So you are."

I suppressed my discomfort; he was my aunt's son, and therefore, a brother. "My genes—"

"Don't talk to me about them. I hate this whole gatherer business."

He could afford to dismiss the problem. It did not affect him. But if all we did was moved away from this crowded room, I'd find life easier to handle. Surely, he would like a better life—a life other than breaking stones or pouring tar on roads. I understood enough of the trader's work to fake identity papers for both of us. "About my future, our future ..."

"No woman would come to me if she knew." He took a swig from his bottle.

"Get a grip," I snapped. "We can get identity papers ... and Mother and Auntie had gold. If we get it—"

"Gold?" My words had obviously jerked him out of his drunken haze. He held my chin up. "We'll go to Mumbai. We will marry."

"Marry? But that's wrong! We are cousins."

"It's logical. Our community marries within itself because we can't spread the genes, and we are the only two left." He shrugged. "Cousins marry in some communities. I feel lonely at times, don't you?"

"Not like this," I said firmly. "You may be nineteen, but I am only thirteen, remember?"

His face stiffened. "It was a suggestion. It is not as if ... as if ..."

This is how disillusionment comes, I thought. *This is how a friend and brother becomes a stranger*.

The next day I went to the burned shanty and dug out our half-melted box of jewelry and gold coins. I "borrowed" stationery and stamps from the trader's stock and spent the evening creating appropriately soiled birth certificates, the sort the merchant made. They would be good enough; this back-to-Stone-Age place had no sophisticated methods to check identity. No biometrics here, thanks to Tilaknagari's technology-hatred reaction to the biobomb wars. I made myself one identity as a Mumbai boy, Rahul Kakade, and another as a girl (of course, not a gatherer) with my real name just in case I got sick of acting as a boy. For Sunil, I created an identity as Sameer Srivastava from Mumbai.

Now I had to wait for an appropriate opening.

A few weeks later, I saw an advertisement from the Records Office of Tilaknagari, saying they wanted residential apprentice clerks, the only selection criteria being a dictation and an interview. How difficult could that be?

That night I bundled whatever I owned. I left part of the gold for Sunil along with his new identity papers and a note explaining that he should change his location because the trader might harass him. I crept out of the hovel when the sky was barely tinted with dawn pink. I was painfully aware that, regardless of its miserable state, this had been "home" for months now and that I could not return to it whether or not I got the job today because Sunil would be gone and the trader, alerted by my absence, would be searching for me.

Ten other candidates, all men, all older than me. A supervisor read out three texts for us to transcribe—one an excerpt of a history book, one a legal case, and one from a biology textbook that I had studied three years ago and could have scribbled without prompting.

Then, interviews. The supervisor frowned as he read my answer paper. My stomach curdled. I had failed. I had made a blunder. Maybe I had signed my real name by mistake.

"Can you use computers, Rahul?" he asked.

I hesitated. Would I get into trouble if I admitted I knew how to use advanced (by Tilaknagari standards) technology? I peered at his face and saw no wile or cunning.

"Yes, I can use computers."

"You are underage." He glanced at my forged certificate. "Your guardians?"

"Dead." I sensed his fleeting relief. "I live on the streets, doing odd jobs to survive."

"Your transcript was error free. Mumbai must have good schools."

I said nothing. He was an official, not a policy maker.

Along with a couple of other recruits, I was led through a complex of buildings until we reached a section comparable to a modern Mumbai building. Air-conditioned rooms. Shelves stacked with books on just about every topic and enough book-readers to service an army. Rows of computers. Men working. Such activity and energy was unusual in Tilaknagari. There were no women, though.

More interviews and tests. I answered them as well as I could, too far into this to behave halfheartedly. The interviewers debated amongst themselves, and finally, a middle-aged man called me. "I'm Madhur Bhatia, your new team leader," he said. "Do you know about lifeen gathering?"

My aptitude scores must have been higher in this area because of all I'd read. "I thought gathering is banned," I said cautiously.

"We may want genetic modifications in future. We want to study the lifeen experiment to see why it failed."

Failed? Lifeen helped society through a critical phase. Funny how everyone forgot that now.

As Madhur explained the project objective and scope, my apprehension began to transform into excitement. Because of this project, I could access data on my people and our history. I might learn how my body was different and perhaps find how to escape what my genes seemed to dictate.

Over the days that followed, in addition to doing assigned work, I grasped knowledge with desperate hunger. I read sociology, law, science. I read history to see why, despite lifeen being essential, the public never accepted gatherers. I read religion and politics to understand how leaders used religion to manipulate public opinion for vote banks. When our team debated pros and cons of genetic modifications, I reminded myself to stay on the periphery. I was only a junior data-digging drudge who fed raw numbers to statistical programs.

Late into the night, though, I often thought of that awful day when my family was killed—all except Sunil, whom I lost to dejection and drink anyway. I worried that my lifeen affinity would betray me some day. By then, I had trained myself to sense when a discharge was imminent so that I stayed away from people, but I was shaky about the secrets my body held. If I found a dying person, would I be tempted to draw out lifeen? The very thought repulsed me.

Life was further complicated because I was a female. As I reached the age when voice breaking was common for boys, I increasingly feared detection. Perhaps they would have mandatory physical examinations. My breasts were bigger now. To hide the contrast of my bound breasts with my flat stomach, I wrapped cloth around my midriff, ending up as a thick-bodied youth with thin, nonmuscular arms.

As our project progressed, the discussions left me increasingly uncomfortable. Gatherers, according to my seniors, were a modified species because they used changed chemical and biological processes to capture and discharge lifeen. Implants, though they adversely impacted gatherer health, were justified for controlling these "engineered subhumans" because they allowed controllers to monitor use of the ability. I thought the team's bias against gatherers was affecting their scientific rigor, and team leader, Madhur, was no exception.

I watched in silence and kept studying.

One day I spotted a small blue box on Madhur's desk—oblong with a small antenna and a clamp. My breath quickened as I recognized it: an implant for gathering. My heart thudded wildly as I picked it up and rolled it in my hands. I switched it on. My skin turned cold and numb, and the implant started glowing. So, this is how Mother and—

"What the—"

I jerked my head up and saw Madhur's startled face the same moment as I noticed gloves on the table. *So, implants were considered unsafe*. I dropped the box on the table; it sat there, glowing bright blue.

Madhur's jaw had dropped. "You—you—only a gatherer can ..."

I won't harm you, I wanted to say, but my mouth refused to form words, and as I straightened up, he retreated and tripped, falling on a sharp edge of a steel cupboard. A gash slit the side of his face right down his neck. Blood gushed out.

I could not move for a few moments. Then I managed to squeak, "Help!" Again, louder, more firmly. A few colleagues rushed over. One man said, "I'll call a doctor," while others stood around, looking scared and helpless. Waiting for help. But this was Tilaknagari—ambulances took time. Madhur's face blanched from loss of blood, and I sensed his lifeen seep out.

Lifeen. That was the key.

Feeders used to dispense lifeen were designed to power equipment and food synthesizers. No feeder had been designed yet to pour lifeen into people—but if people died when they lost lifeen, a reverse flow could restore health.

I could at least try.

I moved near Madhur and held my hand up to catch and deflect back his lifeen outflow. His face remained pallid. I discharged whatever was stored under my skin. Not enough. I needed more lifeen to pump in—where could I get it from? The room had no jars. There was only one other source, a source I had never tried tapping—I had never heard of any gatherer tapping it—my own lifeen. I focused and drew it from the very marrow of my bones and channeled it into the wound. My skin burned then became ice cold; my vision turned hazy. I squinted at the wound and pinched it shut before I slumped near Madhur. Slowly, very slowly, color returned to his face. My dizziness reduced.

The impact of my action sank in as I heard the horrified whispers around me. "Gatherer," they were saying. In saving Madhur's life, I had betrayed mine.

"Call the guards," a man said.

I would not allow them to arrest me. I glared at the men and headed for the door. None dared follow. All was not lost, I told myself. I still had my faked certificates. I could head for Mumbai, maybe as a girl—I was tired of pretending to be a boy. I fled back to my room.

As I shoved my clothes into a backpack, I was surprised to admit to myself that I did not want to leave. I wanted to ask the men *why* they feared me even after I saved Madhur's life. These guys were studying the "lifeen experiment"—but even they behaved like I were an alien, a monster.

Emotions ran deeper than academic knowledge. People feared and hated what they did not understand. Heck, even I feared myself at times.

I was only fifteen. This was not how I wanted to live my life, always afraid of what others would do to me, afraid of what my abilities would make me do.

But why was I scared of my abilities? Mother had implied that, without the implant, gatherers would crave lifeen and may hurt people, but I had never felt such an urge. Had implant designers encouraged this myth to make gatherers submit to implants? Lifeen gathered from dying people had been considered essential to tide humanity over the energy crisis, and controllers must have used the implants to "regulate" gatherers for such harvesting. It might never have occurred to them to explore other uses of lifeen affinity. After all, we were not normal people.

I strode through the corridors, arranging my thoughts into coherent, persuasive arguments. The committee that decided the projects *had to* give me a hearing.

I had used lifeen to heal, and now I was offering myself up for study.

The morning phone call had been unexpected. By the time I reached my already-established appointment at Mumbai Super Specialty Hospital, I was disoriented. I stopped outside the ward for a couple of deep breaths then entered. The patient, with an end-stage cancer, had been reduced to mere skin stretched over bones. His vital signs were deteriorating, and his organs had started surrendering. The Mumbai doctors were presenting me the toughest possible challenge within the parameters of cases I accepted.

The doctor on duty glared at me as I reached out for the patient's frail, almost translucent hand.

Mother must have stood near such beds fifteen years ago but under the supervision of a controller who switched her implant on only when he wanted her to harvest lifeen from the dying to store into the feeders. My implant was different; it let me control when and how much lifeen to gather and when I disbursed it for healing. Using skills practiced over years, I connected with the patient's feeble lifeen flow then adjusted a dial to pour my stored lifeen into him.

Ten minutes. Twenty. He gave a feeble sigh.

"That's all for one session," I told the doctor.

I recorded the methodology I had used, the units of lifeen consumed, the before-and-after readings of the patient's vital signs.

"That lifeen you used," the doctor said. "Did you extract it from me?"

"From you?" I gaped at him. "If you've read our published papers, you will know we don't extract lifeen from people. We just store what is in the air." The healing implant allowed storing plenty of lifeen subcutaneously; discharge occurred when initiated by the gatherer.

"You gatherers used to take it from the dying," he said. "You take it from the living now."

The prejudice hadn't gone. "Gatherers were forced to take it from the dying by their controllers," I said. "Now we only draw what is spare and would go to waste anyway."

"But you *can* draw lifeen from people, right?" He paused. "And you could even throw it out of you, punching someone with it. Who will protect people from you?"

"When have I harmed—"

"Others could, once more freaks are reintroduced."

The doctor did not know, but there were already others like me. After I offered myself as a subject for study, the authorities managed to locate five other gatherer girls, safe because some non-gatherer families had hidden them. In the initial years, in addition to participating in experiments, I continued work as a junior, but as I became proficient in science, I got involved in designing a healing implant. The implant had received reluctant acceptance from Tilaknagari doctors. I was now demonstrating it to Mumbai doctors, hoping to involve them in the project, but proud Mumbaikars refused to accept that Tilaknagari had done something better than them and kept voicing apprehensions.

And then there was this bias against us despite scores of published papers.

"When gatherer genes are reintroduced," I said, "every female capable of lifeen harvesting will be trained using a standard curriculum."

He shrugged. "You cannot control rogue elements."

The truth was there could be no rogue elements. We were six female gatherers living in a well-guarded Tilaknagari house, and none of us had, under any provocation, tried to misuse lifeen to harm others. The very idea disgusted us.

I had a theory about it. I had come to believe that modifications enabling gathering also strengthened social empathy to a degree that made it impossible to deliberately harm others. I had compared gatherers and non-gatherers for incidents of hurtful actions and found this true. It also explained why earlier implants harmed gatherers—when women were forced to extract lifeen from the dying, the act clashed with their innate empathy and caused stress. Unfortunately, more studies were needed before my theory could be proved and announced.

I did four healings under the watchful eye of frowning Mumbai doctors, and, by evening, my reserves were low. I was relieved to return to the hotel. Except that there was one more thing to do. I had to meet the morning's caller.

The man in the hotel lobby had a receding hairline rimmed with grey and a body thick with flab. His face was pudgy. If I hadn't been given his name—Sameer Srivastava—I would not have recognized him as Sunil.

"You are famous," he said, his smile formal and stiff.

I sat opposite him. "Sort of. You live in Mumbai?"

His arm shook as he patted his face dry with a handkerchief. "Yes. I have a business here. My family ..."

"Yes?" I prompted.

"I have a daughter, Radha. My wife's dead."

"Sorry to hear that," I murmured.

"Meera ..." He looked around nervously and then continued, "You are in this business, but for most people, gathering is evil. My wife never knew about me. My girlfriend, she really hates gathering, and if Radha shows any signs of ... Anyway, no woman wants to bring up another woman's child."

Why tell me this? "You expect me to talk to your girlfriend?"

"No!" He bit his lip in an obvious attempt to control himself. He said, "Shruthi doesn't need to know, it's not like she wants children. But if Radha is living with us ..."

"So, you plan to send your daughter away?" Perhaps to an orphanage or a residential school.

"I can't. Wherever she is, if she shows an ability to gather, everyone will know." He gestured toward the entrance. "Take her with you."

A girl of around seven years stood near a couple of potted palms; she looked a bit like Deepa. My niece. But taking her along meant I would have to get her included into our project.

"The law is not clear on females with full or part gatherer genes," I told him. "Implants will probably be made compulsory."

"Implants are fine, no?" Sunil grinned. "They keep us safe from women like them, and—" He broke off, embarrassed.

As a child, I had admired Sunil's extroverted, jovial nature and considered him affectionate and considerate. But perhaps I had seen only what I'd wanted to see. Sunil hadn't got much of a track record in facing difficult situations; he ran off without a plan when we reached Tilaknagari, and though he helped me after the massacre, he soon sheltered behind drink. Even after getting a break using the identity papers I gave him, he married without telling his wife the truth, and now he was abandoning his daughter.

Sunil called his daughter over. "Radha, this is your Auntie Meera."

She folded her hands in a docile Namaste.

"Will you come and live with me?" I asked her, smiling.

The child darted a look at her father, who smiled a bit too broadly at her. She turned back to me, uncertainty flitting across her face. I held out my hand. She did not take it, just studied my face, and she finally nodded solemnly. "Okay, Auntie."

"I will get her bag." Sunil sprang up, as if scared I may change my mind. "It is in my car outside."

Men with gatherer genes had no visible traits like implants nor were they vulnerable and resourceless like gatherer children. Some men like Sunil probably survived the massacre and reestablished themselves using false identities. They married and had children. Their sons carried no gatherer genes; their daughters carried one modified X gene. If a girl had one normal X and one modified X, would she sense lifeen?

"Here." Sunil held out a bag. A quick nod and he strode off.

I gaped after him. No tips on the child's favorite foods or teddy bear or bedtime story or other parental cautions. No card with his address or contact number. I looked at Radha.

Again I held out my hand. This time she grasped it and gave me a nervous smile.

Radha and I left for Tilaknagari at dawn the next day. The airplane fascinated the child. She noticed the bright yellow on the airlines brochure, delighted at the samosas on our snack trays, and giggled at the cartoon movies. Her sense of delight made me long for childhood years when wonder comes easily. But after a while, she lapsed into silence. When she turned to me, her eyes seemed moist.

"Auntie," she said, a tremor to her voice, "why did Papa give me away if I am a good girl?"

I imagined days and weeks and months full of her questions and tears. She was so young, and Sunil's abandoning her would have traumatized her. How would I handle this? My work was my mission, absorbing all my energies, and I was always looking for more things to research. Even meeting Sunil and Radha had stirred in me the outline of a new study—identifying male survivors with gatherer genes and studying the gathering ability of females with only one modified X. Where, in the midst of all those proposals and deadlines and papers, would I rear a child? She would need cuddling and love. There would be arguments that growing up inevitably brought. I tried to remember my own childhood and how perfect I had expected my mother to be.

Then I remembered Sunil's relieved expression as he hurried out after leaving his child. That was not the sort of person I wanted to be.

I have inside me a special gene, I reminded myself. I am connected with the energy of life itself; my empathy is so intrinsic to me that I cannot dream of harming anyone. Of what use is such a gift if I cannot embrace and love my own niece?

Radha was looking at me, wide-eyed, and her lower lip was quivering.

I ruffled her hair. "Your father knew I wanted a daughter," I said softly, and pointed out of the window at the sprawl of Tilaknagari, bright and fresh in the morning sun.

"That's home," I said. "Our home."

HOSTBODS

T.L. Huchu

09:45

Arrows in front of my eyes tell me where to go ↑ along a busy market street lined with immigrants selling cheap wares from makeshift stalls. It's awash with color, purple and blue saris and Kashmiri scarfs, red apples, green grapes, and the smells of freshly caught fish, cooked corn, herbs and spices—paprika, cumin, ground chili—sold by the pound. Loud voices call out random prices and bargains as I (and I am still I) turn → into a narrow alleyway with puddles of water from last night's rain, full-up trash cans and cardboard stacks from the shops inside.

←. Sat-homing means I see where I'm going, feel the experience, but it's more of a sleepwalk. It's like doing something by instinct, the same way your leg kicks out when the doctor taps your knee with a plexor. My muscles move, I feel the ground beneath my feet, taste the salty air from the sea close by, and feel the chilly wind. I'm here and not here. ↑.

10:00

Destination Reached
Deactivate Sat-homing
Status Green: Y/N – Y
Prepare For Symbiosis
5, 4, 3, 2, 1

A ton of force presses down the top of my head, crushing me.

Everything from the top of my cranium moves down like my skull is traveling down my neck into my esophagus. It feels like I'm eating my own head, swallowing it down to my gut, can't breathe, a wave of nausea overcomes me, and I'd gag if a big lump wasn't obstructing my throat. It's like being ripped out of your skin and having everything shredded and crushed, leaving only that, the largest organ in your body, hollow, while a new skeleton ent ...

i'm at the beach again, look at it, so beautiful. If only the sky wasn't covered by those grey clouds. Never mind. Best birthday present ever! Is that?—no, it can't be.

"Hey, dad, you in there?" Holy crap.

"Joe, is it really you?" i ask. "i can't believe it."

"We're all here for you," he replies and sweeps his hand to show the rest of the family behind him.

my sister Ethel's in a blue frock covered up with a cardigan. Her hair is so grey, all those wrinkles on her face, the moustache on her lip. i hug her tightly, haven't seen that face in over ten years; not since my eyes gave out. Joe's wife, Natalie, holds a big box with bright pink ribbons on it, the smile on her face warms me up. We embrace just like we did on their wedding day. Happiest day of my life. The grandkids, the tall one must be Darren and the little one, blonde hair, Craig. On the beach with my family again. It's a miracle.

"That's not Grandpa," says Craig, taking a step back behind his brother.

"Craig, what did I tell you? Don't spoil this for everyone," Joe replies curtly.

"It's me. Don't be afraid. It really is me." i go over to the boy, pick him up, and tickle his belly like i used to. He squirms and pulls away.

"You're not Grandpa," he says, and walks off toward the white pier in the distance. i make to follow, but Joe grabs my arm.

"Let him go, we've only got an hour. He'll be all right."

A woman in a yellow mini walks past with her dog, and i feel a yearning inside me i haven't felt for years. This isn't the time. It's family time. There are strollers in beach shorts, a couple having breakfast on a towel near the changing rooms, sanitation workers taking away litter from the car park up ahead. And the wind is just glorious. i close my eyes and try to inhale every atom of air i can.

i hit Darren on the shoulder—"Tag, you're it"—and begin to run on the beach. That's right. i'm running, the sand underneath me, giving way and crunching as i go, seaweed washed ashore, and, boy, am i running like a pro-athlete. i slow down to allow Darren to tag me, and off i go after him. my grandson can run like a gazelle, but it only takes a few strides. i catch up, grab him by the waist, and lift him high in the air. Joe and Natalie laugh, Ethel laughs, we're all so happy. Best birthday ever.

We walk on the sand, checking out sailing boats in the distance. A few folks stare at us for a bit, but i suppose that's normal given the circumstances. i've not felt this strong in years. Even as we walk, i'm holding back because i just want to run. It was on this very beach that i proposed to Lenore fifty years ago. Wish she was still here with us to hear the seagulls circling above, squawking.

Joe calls Craig over, and we sit round a table. It's a bit nippy, but we order ice cream anyway. The taste of it is just divine, so sweet, so sharp, like every nerve ending in my body is awake and it's every bit as great as i remember from the rations during the war. Vivid flavors explode in my mouth.

5 Mins

i feel an overwhelming sense of sorrow and loss at the thought of leaving all this behind. It's like being given the power of a god for a day and having it taken away the same way Phaethon was hurled off Apollo's chariot by Zeus' thunderbolt.

"i suppose it's time for me to say goodbye again," i mumble.

"I'm sorry. If we'd had more money, we could have bought more time," Natalie says, her eyes welling up. "Maybe we could ... I've heard of charities that buy time for people in special circumstances."

"Don't bother yourself; you have kids to look after. i'll remember this day forever. It's been wonderful."

1 Min

i get up to hug them, each in turn, and this time Craig lets me. He feels like dough in my arms, soft, yeasty, full of goodness and potential, young and invincible, as though i'm touching the future right now. There's a joy in my heart that can't be compared to ...

Prepare To Disengage From HostBod

SyncCorp Hopes You Had A Pleasant Experience

Please Come Again

5, 4, 3, 2, 1

11:30

I arrive at a warehouse in Mullhill, the east side of the city near the industrial zone. There's no sign on the diamond fence around the perimeter. HGV trucks laden with goods from the factories around run up and down the road toward the city and beyond. The noise of the mills is a sonnet to the plumes of smoke that pour from the coal-powered station in the center of the perfect grid of intersecting streets. The air is acrid and full of unknowable particulates. Men in overalls and hard hats walk in rows carrying little backpacks to their various factories.

There's no guard as I walk past the boom gate into a desolate car park. I take a deep breath and follow the arrows. I have no choice. Some bods have been used in criminal enterprises before, and it's a growing problem. But not with SyncCorp, the leading bod provider in the western hemisphere.

A HostBod walks toward me. Hard sculpted cheeks, fair lips, flat east Baltic head, another immigrant. His blue T-shirt tells me he's from RentaBod, cheap eastern European bods usually. He's in Sat-homing and manages to turn his head a fraction to acknowledge me with his dead blue eyes. I blink, a moment of brotherhood that lasts a microsecond.

I walk into the bare warehouse, and my Sat-homing is deactivated. I'm in loiter mode until the uplink command is sent. The warehouse is a bare shell, high windows, floors caked in pigeon droppings. At the far end is a red door that I walk through into a waiting area in which two other bods sit in injection-molded chairs.

"What's this about?" I say, taking the seat nearest the exit.

"I don't know," replies the bod opposite me in a South American, maybe Brazilian, accent. He's caramel skinned and bald headed. Every bod has their head shaved for the implants.

"Some kind of test," says the other one sitting nearest the second door.

Their yellow T-shirts tell me they are both assets from PleasureBodInc, usually procured for the M2M industry. The florescent light above makes a slight humming noise. It flickers at intervals. The room seems to have been set up recently with new fixtures that smell of plastic.

"How long have you been in business?" the Brazilian asks.

"Four years, nine months," I reply.

"Wow, without a burnout? Amazing! I've only been here six months."

"Good luck" is all I can say. And that's what this game is, Russian roulette. You spin the barrel until you don't hear the empty click of the chamber anymore.

He's called in by a curly-haired man wearing a white coat and holding a notepad. The scent of disinfectant wafts into the waiting room. The Brazilian follows him in, and the door shuts behind him.

Half an hour later, the Brazilian walks out, and I'm called in before the other PleasureBodInc bod. I get up and walk into the next room. The man in a white coat asks me to sit on what looks like a pink dentist's plinth. I comply.

Status Green: Y/N – Y

Prepare For Symbiosis

5, 4, 3, 2, 1

~*~

"What do you think of this one, Doctor Cranmer?"

"Near the end of service, which means it's stable. It's the oldest one we've got. As you know, they usually break down around the twenty-four-month mark. Only a special few last this long."

"I don't know. The features ..."

"Will take some getting used to, I admit. But race is the least of your worries, sir. Stability is all important."

"Let's take it through its paces, shall we?"

I'm not supposed to be here, to see or hear any of this. It's as if I'm a child hiding in a dark closet, looking into a room through a keyhole. HostBods are not supposed to be conscious during symbiosis, and the Corp would reconfigure me if they knew. But I've been in this closet, hiding away for two years. The doctor instructs me/him to open my/his mouth, shines a light down my/his throat. Then he draws some blood, runs me/him through an x-ray machine—Doctor Cranmer can't use the MRI because of the electrodes—but he takes my/his blood pressure, resting pulse, and performs lung function tests. He puts me/him on a treadmill at high speed for three minutes and then repeats the test. I/he is moved to a large hangar where I/he does something that resembles a football fitness test, some sort of biomechanical assessment looking at endurance, speed, strength, agility, and power. I watch it all from my closet, not daring to breathe or move.

1 Min

"How old is he, Doc?"

"Just coming up to 21. Prime specimen right here."

"I'm not sure about this."

"Look at these stats. He's 99.25% compatible. That's five percentage points over anything else we've got. He's perfect."

"I need time to think it over."

"We've got a few more to look at, so don't worry, but the sooner we make a move the better."

Prepare To Disengage From HostBod

SyncCorp Hopes You Had A Pleasant Experience
Please Come Again
5, 4, 3, 2, 1

15:15

↑↑→←↑↑↑↓↑↑↑↑→↑

15:45

Destination Reached
Deactivate Sat-homing
Status Green: Y/N – Y
Prepare For Symbiosis
5, 4, 3, 2, 1

No rest for the fucking wicked. Stan calls me up, wants me to raise 40 mill for some shit-arsed indie flick. Who watches that crap? Must be shagging the director, that's what. Still, who's gonna pony up 40 mill for some piece of cunt? Okay, relax, chill out. Only get this shit one day a week. 40 mill. Forget it. Forget about work for two minutes. It's her. Is this shit even legal?

There she is, look at that, fucking curves on that. Phwoar, even forget she's nearly sixteen sometimes. Check out those blonde locks, how they bounce around on her head and those tits, dear God, those motherfucking tits. i ain't doing badly for an old fart. i mean, how many blokes my age actually have the balls to hit it with their daughter's best mate, hehe. Pure fantasy shit. That's why i gotta cover me tracks. Put her arse in a HostBod and shit's supposedly legal—at least that's what me lawyer tells me. Grey area, he calls it.

"Ello, darling, come ere to daddy."

Feel those tits pressing against me chest as i hug her.

"How's school and everything?" Gotta seem like the caring, reasonable old man, hehe.

"It's all right. I missed you," she says. Hear that—if me missus only said it once or twice a month, i wouldn't be up to no good. Swear it on me mother's fucking grave.

"i missed you, too, darling. Give daddy a lil kiss."

Feel those sweet teenage lips, wow. Wouldn't be able to handle this sort of action if i was in me own body. Check out me lump, proper Mandingo going on here.

i push her back a mo just so I can check out the view, see the curves. i like that lil shade of brown pub that lingers just above them lil panties. Wow, wow, what the fuck? Who's this? Fucking Chinese woman appears in front of me outta nowhere.

"What's wrong, daddy?"

"You, you've fucking turned Chinese!"

"What?"

"You're Chinese, honest to God. Look at you, all bald with some metal wire shit all over your head, the skin, everything. Oh, my fucking God!"

"I think it's like the visuals that's gone bust on your bod, coz I can see you just fine."

"What the fuck am i supposed to do?"

"Call the company and have them fix it."

And that's how i spend the one afternoon of peace i get a week, down the phone speaking to some call center trying to get this drone to remote patch me visuals. Little girl's sitting on the bed, staring at me out of her fifty-something-year-old chinky fucking eyes. Total mindfuck coz she's talking like her out of this bod and it's doing me head in.

"Don't tell me you've fixed the fucking visuals because all i can see in front of me is a fucking Chinese bird, all right? i pay top dollar for this shit, i expect service. You even know what that word means?"

i'm screaming down the fucking phone, would have had a heart attack by now if i was in me own body.

"Fine, i'll take a full refund and a free session next week, sounds freaking fine by me. i should be suing your incompetent arses."

i hang up and turn back to the girl: "Looks like this week's fucked. We'll hook up next time, okay love? Come here, give daddy a kiss ... on second thoughts, don't."

16:30

I'm back in Sat-homing mode. I'm not supposed to know the last assignment was a complete dud, that I'm, in effect, malfunctioning. Visuals need to get reset. I've been sent back to base early. My next assignments have been canceled. So I'm free—sort of.

Funny thing happens when I sync up. I seem to store some of their memories in me. This isn't supposed to happen. None of the other bods report anything similar, but it's like I know stuff I'm not even supposed to know.

Passing by City Square, the giant advertorial screens above, the Coke-red next to the Pepsi-blue, the giant golden arc, Papa Chicks, Massa Space outfits, people walking around, bodies pressed against each other, sub 20Hz speakers blaring out subliminal advertising, shops spraying lab manufactured pheromones to lure consumers. I adjust my hoodie, doing my best to cover my temples even though this is one of the safer parts of the city for a bod to pass. The poorer and rougher western neighborhoods like Westlea and Pilmerton are a different matter altogether. I walk by The Stock Xchange. When I first came here, I didn't understand any of it, the arrows going up and down, the numbers sprinting across the top and bottom of the screen. But a few sessions synced with Brad Madison, and I know it all as well as any broker. Viviset stocks have been fluctuating, but they're still overpriced, best time to sell and get out before it comes crashing down. I'd buy Tanganda now and sell it next week. ↑ Can't stop to look at the rest in this mode, but I'll check out the markets online when I get back to base.

Silver space blanket puffs seem to be the fashion of the week for ladies under 30. Then again, when you've been synced with a famous fashion designer ... Wish they'd get me on the underground for the journey back. My feet are killing me.

That's the problem with Corp, they'll squeeze every penny in savings if they can. Truth be told, knowing what I know now, that's the same thing I'd do especially when staff turnover isn't a factor.

Base is a huge building that used to be a budget hotel in the east side near the space&airport. You can see planes and shuttles taking off and landing, going to exotic destinations around the world or to orbit. It's noisy as hell, but it's home. Our conditions here, I hear, are much better than the dormitory set-up other bods get elsewhere. Retinal scanner lets me in.

Deactivate Sat-homing.

"You're home early, 4401," says Marlon on the security desk.

"Malfunction," I reply.

"You'll be seeing Doctor Song then," he replies. "Go up to your room. I'll call you when it's time."

"Thanks, Marlon," I say, and then I remember, "hey, is it okay for me to call home?"

"I'll give you access. Ten minutes max per day."

"Come on, Marlon," I say in my best whinny voice.

"Fifteen, and that's the best I can do. Now, get outta here before I change my mind."

"You're a legend," I say and give him the thumbs up.

The door to my room is unlocked. We have a toilet cubicle to the left, a bunk bed on either side of the wall, and a desk with a small computer/TV at the far wall. There are no mirrors in any of the rooms.

Raj6623 is asleep or in hibernation mode. He usually starts up at 22:00 and returns the next afternoon. He's a fightbod and gets a full eight hours' sleep plus practice time. For most bods it's 20 hours work with four hours sleep as standard.

"4401 authorized call to rec-number Harare," I say to the computer.

It kicks up with a whirr, and then I hear a dial tone. Half a minute later mama's face appears on screen.

A sad smile cracks on her mouth like a running fissure when she sees me. At the right angle all she can see is my face, bald head, and the two electrodes implanted through my temples into my frontal lobe. They're titanium and shiny, but at least she can't see the full device. The other implants are at the back of my skull and are drilled into the amygdala, so the sync takes place in the oldest and newest brain, the primitive and the conscious part for full immersiveness.

We talk about home, my little brother with Westhuizen's Syndrome, which is the reason I'm here. The money I make goes straight toward his medication. I'll get a bonus after completion, and after that, I'll have to either sign up again—no one's ever done that—or find a new way to make money for his drugs. Either way, this job is the only thing keeping him alive.

He pops up on screen, nine-years-old, handsome as a teddy bear, braces in his mouth, and smiles. I wave. He tells me about school, his friends, games, all the things any nine-year-old should be doing. This makes it worthwhile. Mama's just sitting there, slightly off-screen, watching her boys. I'm sure she's proud.

I get a beep, time's nearly up, say, "Goodbye, I love you guys so much," blow a kiss, and log off.

I've just slid into my lower bunk when Marlon buzzes via the computer and tells me to go see the Doc. I get up and leave Raj6623 snoozing, go into the corridor, and squirt some alcohol gel on my hands and round my temples. The corridor is bare, just blue vinyl flooring, perfect white walls, directional signs every couple of meters and a purple strip that runs in the middle of the wall as a sort of decoration. I go round a few turns and into the infirmary just in time to see a new bod leave. I nod my head and stroll in.

Doctor Song is a small Korean man, barely reaches my chest even with the Cuban heels he wears to give himself an extra inch or so. He's typing notes into his computer and points to a chair. The keys go tap, tap, tap under his furious little fingers.

"4401, why you tell Marlon you have malfunction? How did you know?" he says. I should have known better.

"My assignment ended early, you called me home and

canceled the rest of my day. That can only mean one thing," I reply coolly.

"You doctor now?"

"You're the doctor, Doctor Song."

"You waking?"

"Never."

"Uplink scan has been showing spikes in your wave function post-sync."

I blink like I don't understand what he's saying. Doc likes that sort of thing, but I know what he's going to say next before he even says it. "Don't worry. It's not the most reliable instrument anyway."

That's code for I'mtoolazytofollowupandyourcontract'snearlydonesoIdon'tcare. I nod along like an ignoramus.

"You've been taking your antibiotics?" he asks.

"On time every time," I reply. We have to take long-term prophylactic, broad-spectrum antibiotics because of the risk of infection at the insertion points. You don't wanna mess with meningitis or encephalitis.

"Corp has new job for you. Contract nearly over so easy work. You go Hillside in North, single user for last three months. Congratulations," he says, looking at me for once.

"Thanks, Doctor Song," I reply with a smile, though every instinct in my body is screaming out, alarm bells ringing, spider senses tingling.

"Good. Go into next room. I test and remodulate vis configuration," he says and grabs a white helmet with flashing green and blue lights at the fore. It's the user's uplink device. It works by reading the wearers brainwaves and transmitting low-level radiation to tune the user into the HostBod. Nowhere near as invasive as the electrodes bods must wear because their own consciousness must be suppressed in sync, which can only be done surgically. The electrodes not only transmit electric impulses but also carry neurotransmitters direct into the brain structure. I got this off syncing with Doctor Song himself, and he doesn't even know that.

We can't be in the same room during sync because of the infinity loop problem, which tech has failed to overcome.

That's why, for safety reasons, user and HostBod only interface via remote transmission.

He marches me back and forth, I squat, pinch myself, stick my tongue out, and do a dozen other psychomotor and spatial awareness exercises before he signs me off.

I walk back to my room and find Raj6623 standing at the door.

"They came to get your gear. Looks like you're shipping out," he says. The scar that runs across his face moves as he speaks.

"I got lucky," I say.

"Stay alive," he replies and crushes me with a bear hug. Twelve months we've been here together, and this is the most intimate we've been.

"Say bye to the others for me," I say, knowing full well he won't bother.

A woman with vibrant red hair, the sort that can only come from a bottle, stands at the reception desk next to a guy in a chauffeur's outfit with a bag at his side. She has milky white skin almost matching the shade of the walls, and from a distance, all I see is hair, eyebrows, and blood-red lipstick where her mouth is. She wears a retro ivory silk slip covering one shoulder, revealing a large ruby choker around her neck. It's like she's ephemeral, a wisp of an image from another dimension.

"So, this is father's new toy," she purrs.

"That's him, Ms. Stubbs," says Marlon ingratiatingly. "Here's your papers, 4401. Follow this lady and the gentleman. Good luck."

I shake his hand and follow my new employer into a black limousine waiting in the car park. The chauffeur opens the door. She walks in. I wait to be invited. She beckons me with her index finger. The chauffeur closes the door as I sit with my back to the driver, facing her. The cabin smells of freshly polished leather. She pours a glass of champagne for herself and a finger of whisky in another, which she slowly hands to me.

"We're not allowed," I say.

"Don't be a pussy, drink it," she replies, rolling her eyes melodramatically. I take the drink and hold it. "What's your name?"

"4401."

"Your real name, idiot."

"Simon."

"That's what I thought. I saw you in those hospital garments you call clothes and said to myself, there's a Simon all right."

The lady is a little tipsy but not drunk. The intoxication of someone who's used to consuming a lot of alcohol all hours of the day.

The limo cruises onto the 105, which takes us past Marlborough and Bury, skirting round the rough neighborhoods. We go past gleaming skyscrapers, the glass reflecting the orange glow of the setting sun, images of clouds cast on windows, the city glistening like a thousand orange diamonds. She says nothing to me for the rest of the journey, only eyeing me like a predator stalking her prey. A lump sits at the top of my throat; I swallow hard.

20:00

Initiating Protocol Transfer To
Username: Howard J Stubbs
SyncCorp Wishes You A Happy And
Prosperous Symbiosis
0% - - - - - - - - - - - - 100%

That's me wired up to the Stubbs' MF now, which means they own me, which means I wasn't hired but they bought out the rest of my contract. It happens from time to time. Bods get passed around between different companies, usually traded down. Stubbs must be pretty loaded to afford this. No shit, Sherlock, is that your deduction or it's the 200 year-old southern plantation style mansion in front of you? Kind of looks like a wannabe White House—only bigger.

The wheels of the limo crunch on the gravel driveway. A Roman style fountain with mirthful nymphs squirts water high into the air. So much woodland around, it feels like we're in the country. Light pouring out of every window in the mansion illuminates the lawn as we park near the front door.

"Come on, I'm sure Father is just *dying* to meet you," she says, dragging out the word "dying."

"We don't usually meet users."

"Things are different here," she replies as we walk into the mansion.

There's a vulgar mix of paintings lining the walls. Expensive paintings: a Picasso here, a Van Gogh there, Pollock next to Gauguin with a Palin underneath. It's clear that this is a nouveau riche acquisition with little acquiescence to aesthetics. I find this somewhat disturbing as I walk on the dark hardwood flooring polished to within an inch of its life.

Ms. Stubbs leads me up a winding staircase to the bedrooms. An oak drawer along the wall has a Chinese vase (I reckon Qing but can't be sure) on top with geometric patterns in bright shades of blue and a bunch of chrysanthemums set inside. I can't help but smile behind her back. We enter a large bedroom in the center of which is a poster bed. An old man sits underneath layers of quilts with his back propped up by a bunch of pillows. The oxygen tank on his left hisses away.

"Go to him," says Ms. Stubbs.

I walk over and kneel beside the old man. From this close I can smell his decrepitude, malodors churning under the quilts and from the catheter that dangles at the bedside. I notice he has an electrode transference device just like mine complete with implants boring through his skull into his brain. I've never heard of a user having to go through this before. The device looks like a giant tarantula resting on top of his skull.

"Hello," I say. He reaches out with his left hand and touches my face. It feels bony and rough against my forehead and cheeks. He takes a deep breath and whispers in a raspy voice:

"Make yourself at home, boy."

~*~

21:00

I'm in my room in loiter mode. The chauffeur left my bag with my few clothes and possessions, which I unpack into the drawers. The window gives me a view down the hill past the silhouette of trees to the brightly-lit city in the distance.

I go over to the bed, slide into the soft cotton sheets, and for the first time in a year, I'm allowed to sleep for more than four hours even though the dreams I have are still not my own.

08:00

I wake up feeling refreshed and rejuvenated. Can't believe I slept for so long. The sun pours into my room because I forgot to close the curtains. It's been too long since I had a window in my room. I wash my face in the basin in the corner and spray alcohol gel around my implants. There are real clothes in the closet, just my size too, so I wear those instead of the Corp crap. I grab a red hoodie to cover my head in case I'm taken outside. I walk past Mr. Stubbs' bedroom and down the stairs into one of the rooms where a breakfast buffet is laid out. It smells great.

Ms. Stubbs is at the opposite end of the table, listening to the news and eating toast. The day's barely started, and she looks stunning in a crimson gown, an eye mask on her forehead.

"Morning," I say.

"You can have anything you like," she replies.

"Thanks."

I bring out my feeding pack of Soylent and pour myself a glass of water. This is how bods start the day. You can't fill yourself up because a lot of users like to go out for meals so it's important to keep the stomach as empty as possible. I drink from my pack. It tastes like dough with grainy bits in it. After a while, you get used to it.

"Can I call home?" I ask.

"Nope," she replies without even raising her head to look at me.

"We had 30-minute privileges per day at Corp," I say.

"Firstly, it was ten minutes, and secondly, this ain't Corp."

Status Green: Y/N – Y

Prepare For Symbiosis

5, 4, 3, 2, 1

"Morning, Lesley," i say. What is that weird taste in my mouth? Quick, grab a coffee to rinse it out.

"Morning, Father. You started the day early. Who was that?" she replies, nonchalant. i wonder what she's scheming.

"Just the lawyer first thing before dawn and Doctor Cranmer should be here any minute now. Justin makes the finest coffee. He deserves a raise."

"What did you want with the lawyer?"

"A bit of business. Nothing you should worry your pretty, little head about. I'm not a cabbage up there, you know." i point to the second floor where the bedrooms are. She raises a single eyebrow and gets back to her food.

i leave her to it. So much to do, so little time. i could get used to this, yes. Stop beside the mirror, look at the face: bold, square jaw, angular, very manly. Yes, i could definitely get used to this. Cranmer is in the foyer already.

"Good morning, Doctor," i sound a little too jovial.

"Mr. Stubbs?"

"It's too nice a day to talk indoors. Shall we go out onto the grounds for a walk?"

"I need to see the ... the other body."

"You can do that later. Come, let's go outside." i take him by the elbow and lead him out. Sweet sunshine hits my face. "Nothing like the scent of freshly-mowed grass."

"I came to check if you wanted to see this thing through. You must understand the tech is experimental. I've only done one other procedure so we don't yet know what the long-term effects are," Doctor Cranmer says.

"Run it by me one more time."

"When user and bod are comparable, you can put them in sync and then transfer consciousness through the process of quantum entanglement. Essentially we are just reversing the quantum states in the brain. No matter is moved between A and B so theoretically there's a zero chance of post-op rejection. It's not a brain transplant, it's a consciousness transfer. Post-procedure we isolate the bod, who is now the user, to prevent attempts at reacquisition. That's the long and short of it."

"Okay, first thing tomorrow morning. i have nothing to lose, but i only have one proviso, Doctor." i stop near the gazebo and look him in the eye. "If the procedure fails, the bod dies, too."

"That can be arranged."

20:00

Loiter mode. Fuck me royally. I need to get out of here right now. Only getting out doesn't solve the problem because I can be Sat-homed back easily. Gotta find the mainframe, disable it, no, destroy it completely. I'll look around the house, nah, that's crazy, who keeps a fucking mainframe in the family home? Swear to God, I'm going insane. This ain't what I signed up for.

I need to call mama, my little brother. Won't even get a chance to say goodbye. Okay, think for a minute, just think.

I once saw a bod who committed suicide in the most spectacular fashion. It was my first year with Corp, and I was passing through the main reception area. This guy just stood cold staring at the guards. And then he casually brought his hands up to his electrodes and just started pulling. The guards were screaming "Stop" or something like that, but this guy just goes on pulling and blood squirts out. Out came these grey chunks of brain matter. He just pulls the tarantula off the top of his head and leaks water, blood, brainy goo down his sides. He stood there for a minute or two before he keeled over. It was horrific.

I could fight my way out. Face it, the law frowns on bods anyway. A rich guy like Stubbs, forget it. I need to think.

03:00

I'm terrified, can't sleep all night, my mind racing through different options, adrenalin and cortisol coursing through my bloodstream at toxic levels. That drink from the limo would have come in handy right about now.

The door opens. She walks in like a ghost floating through. Her white nightdress hangs off her frame and swoops as it follows her graceful movements. "Shhh." Her finger is on her lips as she crawls into my bed.

She moves like a python, slow, seductive, and sensuous, as if she hasn't a single bone in her body. Her skin feels warm against mine. She straddles me, pulls my pants down with one hand, and then all I feel is her wetness and heat on me. It's the most exquisite feeling in the world.

"Your dad's going to kill me," I say.

"Shhh."

This moment, I'm in her. It feels as though nothing else matters as she carries me like a leaf in the ocean and takes me to places I never knew ...

Prepare For Symbiosis

"Get off. Your dad's syncing with me," I call out in panic.

"Oh, what a spoil sport," she says, pulling off and gliding out of the room.

5, 4, 3, 2, 1

Well, this feels a bit strange. i couldn't sleep, can't wait for the morning so i thought i'd sync up. Get up, out of bed, my bottom half naked, and walk out of the bedroom. Lesley is in the corridor.

"Have you been playing with my toy, Lesley?"

"Hello, Father. Isn't it a little too late for your old ass to be out and about?" she replies. Has the same stubborn, bitchy traits her mum had. She's up to something and must be stopped. You don't get to where i got in life without the instincts of a croc. i grab her by the shoulders.

"i think we should lock you in your room for a little while," i say. "For your own good."

She struggles and squirms. The little bitch is strong, but i'm stronger. She breaks my grip and runs toward my bedroom. Now i know what she's up to. Got to stop her.

"Don't be pathetic. You really think you can stop me, Lesley? Come here!" i sprint after her. The floor is polished and slippery, but in this bod i can do anything. i grab her flailing nightdress, pull her, and slam her against the wall. "i'm not your enemy. i'm your father."

She scratches my face. i slap her with the back of my hand, which fells her to the floor. i bend over, pick her up, and lift her in the air, feet dangling, her mouth wide open, a scream caught in her throat. i put her back down and slap her again.

"You're going to bed, young lady." i see a quick movement, a leg twitch, then i'm on the floor, both hands cupping my balls, they are on fire. It winds me for a moment, and she runs into my room. Got to stop her. Ignore the pain in my groin and stagger after her. i burst into the room.

"Stop it, Lesley."

She's covering my face with a pillow. The oxygen mask is on the floor, hissing away. i run to her, grab her around the neck, put her in a choke hold. i'm gonna kill this bitch. i lift her up, her head against my chest, and squeeze. She gags, coughs, splutters, kicks, but I'm too strong. And then I look at me looking at me

me looking at me looking at me looking at me looking at me looking at me looking at me looking at me looking at me looking at me looking at me looking at me looking at me looking at me looking at me looking at me looking at me looking at me looking at

Only takes a second to realize i'm trapped in an infinity loop. i should have stopped her before she came in here. my head feels like it's cracking. The pain is blistering hot. i scream and grab my head in both hands to stop it from exploding. The scream is magnified and bounces around like a million echoes in the loop. Everything in here is a cave of infinity mirrors, reflecting everything back to itself. Only i am the image and the mirror and each iteration of both. Subject and object.

i fall to the floor. Oh, the pain. As i convulse, i see, through the corner of my eye, Lesley cover my face with a pillow.

White hot supernova, synapses breaking, an explosion, the universe tearing apart.

08:00

I wake up, and she's beside me in bed. We're both naked. My head feels like I have the mother of all hangovers, as if I drank all the tequilas in the world. She rests her head on my chest.

"Did you sleep well?" she asks as if nothing happened.

"Have you got any Vicodin?" I sit up, and the world is spinning around me.

"Get dressed and follow me."

The world shatters into tiny pieces floating around my bed. I shake my head, and tiny fractals swim in and out of focus. It takes a minute or two before the pictures coalesce into one coherent world. It feels good to be back. I'm so thirsty, and I drink straight from the pitcher beside me.

I find her in the corridor and follow her to her father's room. I can barely stay upright. Doctor Cranmer sits on the bed, a stethoscope around his neck. There's a shiny aluminium suitcase on the floor before him. He looks at Ms. Stubbs.

"Morning, Doctor," she says.

"It's not a very good morning. It appears your father is dead," he replies in an even voice.

"What a pity," she says with a shrug. "Old people, hey."

"I find it rather curious that his oxygen mask is on the floor."

The doctor stands up and walks toward Ms. Stubbs. He looks at her, then at me. I pretend as though I don't remember him from our first encounter. I act like a good, little bod.

"I suppose my services are no longer needed here," says Doctor Cranmer.

"You served my father well. I don't see any reason this association should end. Because of my gratitude, as his sole heir, I will double your monthly retainer for life and hope to keep your services," she says, her face neutral and cold.

"It is always a pleasure to serve the Stubbses. If you will excuse me, I have to record this death by *natural* causes." He bows slightly and walks to the door, dragging his aluminium case behind.

We're left staring at her father's body on the bed. His eyes are wide open in shock.

"One more thing, Doctor, since you work for me now," she says.

"Anything," he replies.

"This." She points to the electrode transference device on my head.

"I can remove it straightaway," Doctor Cranmer says, stepping back into the room.

"On second thought, I think I'll keep it. It looks rather nice. Don't you agree, Simon?"

The doctor sighs and turns to leave once more. It's at this moment I realize that she owns me now. Certain secrets will come out, like how the old man changed his will yesterday to include HostBod4401 as the sole heir and beneficiary to his estate. Lesley doesn't know it yet, but there's going to be a battle for that money. For now, all I have to do is to stay alive.

Bernardo's House

James Patrick Kelly

The house was lonely. She checked her gate cams constantly, hoping that Bernardo would come back to her. She hadn't seen him in almost two years—he had never been gone this long before. Something must have happened to him. Or maybe he had just gotten tired of her. Although they had never talked about where he went when he wasn't with her, she was pretty sure she wasn't his only house. A famous doctor like Bernardo would have three houses like her. *Four*. She didn't like to think about him sleeping in someone else's bed. Which he would have been doing for *two years now*. She had been feeling dowdy recently. Could his tastes in houses have changed?

Maybe.

Probably.

Definitely.

She thought she might be too understated. Her hips were slim, and her floors were pale Botticino marble. There wasn't much loft to her Epping couch cushions. Her blueprint showed a roving, size-seven dancer's body—Bernardo had specified raven hair and green eyes—and just eight simple but elegant rooms. She was a gourmet cook even though she wasn't designed to eat. Sure, back when he had first had her built he had cupped her breasts and told her that he liked them small, but maybe now what he wanted was wall-to-wall cable-knit carpet and swag drapery.

He had promised to bring her a new suite of wallscapes, which was good because there was only so much of colliding galaxies and the Sistine Chapel a girl could take. For the past nine weeks she had been cycling her walls through the sixteen million colors they could display. If she left each color up for two seconds, it would take her just under a year to review the entire palette.

Each morning, for his sake, she wriggled her body into one of the slinky sexwear patterns he had brought for her clothes processor. The binding bustier or the lace baby doll or the mesh camisole. She didn't much like the way the leather-and-chain teddy stuck to her skin; Bernardo had spared no expense on her tactiles. Even her couches could be aroused by the right touch. After she dressed, she polished her Amadea brass-and-chrome bathroom fixtures or her Enchantress pattern sterling silver flatware or her Cuprinox French copper cookware. Sometimes she dusted, although the reticulated polyfoam in her air handlers screened particles larger than .03 microns. She missed Bernardo so. Sometimes masturbating helped, but not much.

He had erased her memory of their last hours together—the only time he had ever made her forget. All she remembered now was that he'd said that she was finally perfect. That she must never change. He came to her, he said, to leave the world behind. To escape into her beauty. Bernardo was *so* poetic. That had been a comfort at first.

He had also locked her out of the infofeed. She couldn't get news or watch shows or play the latest sims. Or call for help. Of course, she had the entire Norton entertainment archive to keep her company, although lots of it was too adult for her. She just didn't *get* Henry James or Brenda Bop or Alain Resnais. But she liked Jane Austen and Renoir and Buster Keaton and Billie Holiday and Petchara Songsee and the 2017 Red Sox. She *loved* to read about houses. But there was nothing in her archive after 2038, and she was awake twenty-four hours a day, seven days a week, three hundred and sixty five days a year.

What if Bernardo was dead? After all, he'd had the heart attack just a couple of months before he left. Obviously, if he had died, that would be the end of her. Some new owner would wipe her memory and swap in a new body and sell all her furniture. Except Bernardo always said that she was his most precious secret. That no one else in all the world knew about her. About *them*. In which case she'd wait for him for years—*decades*—until her fuel cells were depleted and her consciousness flickered and went dark. The house started to hum some of Bernardo's favorites to push the thought away. He liked the romantics. Chopin and Mendelssohn. *Hmm-hm, hm-hm-hm-hm*-hm! "The Wedding March" from *A Midsummer Night's Dream*.

No, she wasn't bored.

Not really.

Or angry, either.

She spent her days thinking about him, not in any methodical way, but as if he had been shattered into a thousand pieces and she was trying to put him back together. She imagined this must be what dreaming was like, although, of course, she couldn't dream because she wasn't real. She was just a house. She thought of the stubble on his chin scratching her breasts and the scar on his chest and the time he laughed at something she said and the way his neck muscles corded when he was angry. She had come to realize that it was always a mistake to ask him about the outside. Always. But he enjoyed his bromeliads, and his music helped him forget his troubles at the hospital, whatever they were, and he loved *her*. He was always asking her to read to him. He would sit for hours, staring up at the clouds on the ceiling, listening to her. She liked that better than sex, although having sex with him always aroused her. It was part of her design. His foreplay was gentle and teasing. He would nip at her ear with his lips, trace her eyebrows with his finger. Although he was a big man, he had a feather touch. Once he had his penis in her, though, it was more like a game than the lovemaking she had read about in books. He would tease her—stop and then go very fast. He liked blindfolds and straps and honeypins. Sometimes he'd actually roll off one side of the bed, stroll to the other, and come at her again, laughing. She wondered if the real people he had sex with enjoyed being with him.

One thing that puzzled her was why he was so shy about the words. He always said vagina and anus, intercourse and fellatio. Of course, she knew all the other words; they were in the books she read when he wasn't around. Once, when he had just started to undress her, she asked if he wanted her to suck his cock. He looked as if he wanted to slap her. "Don't you ever say that to me again," he said. "There's enough filth in the real world. It has to be different here."

She decided that was a very romantic thing for him to say to ...

And suddenly a year had passed. The house could not say where it had gone exactly. A whole year, *misplaced*. How careless! She must do something, or else it would happen again. Even though she was perfect for him, she had to make some changes. She decided to rearrange furniture.

Her concrete coffee table was too heavy for her to budge so she dragged her two elephant cushions from the playroom and tipped them against it. The ensemble formed a charming little courtyard. She pulled all her drawers out of her dresser in her bedroom and set them sailing on her lap pool. She liked the way they bucked and bumped into one another when she turned her jets on. She had never understood why Bernardo had bought four kitchen chairs if it was just supposed to be the two of them, but *never mind*. She overrode the defaults on her clothes processor and entered the measurements of her chairs. She made the cutest lace chemises for two of them and slipped them side-by-side in Bernardo's bed—but facing chastely away from each other. Something tingled at the edge of her consciousness, like a leaky faucet or ants in her bread drawer or ...

Her motion detectors blinked. Someone had just passed her main gate. *Bernardo*.

With a thrill of horror she realized that all her lights were on. She didn't think they could be seen from outside, but still, Bernardo would be furious with her. She was supposed to be his secret getaway. And what would he say when he saw her like this? The reunion she had waited for—*longed for*—would be ruined. And all because she had been weak. She had to put things right. The drawers first. One of them had become waterlogged and had sunk. Suppose she had been washing them? Yes, he might believe that. Haul the elephant cushions back into the play room. Come on, come *on*. There was no time. He'd be through the door any second. What was keeping him?

She checked her gate cams. At first she thought they had malfunctioned. She couldn't see him—or anyone. Her main gate was concealed in the cleft of what looked like an enormous boulder that Bernardo had had fabricated in Toledo, Ohio, in 2037. The house panned down its length until she saw a girl taking her shirt off at the far end of the cleft.

She looked to be twelve or maybe thirteen, but still on the shy side of puberty. She was skinny and pale and dirty. Her hair was a brown tangle. She wasn't wearing a bra and didn't need one. Her yellow panties were decorated with blue hippos. The girl had built a smoky fire and was trying to dry her clothes over it. She must have been caught in a rainstorm. The house never paid attention to weather, but now she checked. Twenty-two degrees Celsius, wind out of the southeast at eleven kilometers per hour, humidity 69%. A muggy evening in July. The girl reached into a camo backpack, pulled out a can of beets, and opened it.

The house studied her with a fierce intensity. Bernardo had told her that there were no other houses like her on the mountain, and he was the only person who had ever come up her side. The girl chewed with her mouth open. She had tiny ears. Her nipples were brown as chocolate.

After a while the girl resealed the can of beets and put it away. She had eaten maybe half of it. The house did a quick calculation and decided that she had probably consumed three hundred calories. How often did she eat? Not often enough. The skin stretched taut against her ribs as the girl put her shirt on. Her pants clung to her, not quite dry. She drew a ragged, old snugsack from the pack, ballooned it, and then wriggled in. It was dark now. The girl watched the fire go out for about an hour and then lay down.

It was the longest night of the house's life. She rearranged herself to her defaults and ran her diagnostics. She vacuumed her couch and washed all her floors and defrosted a chicken. She watched the girl sleep and replayed the files of when she had been awake. The house was so lonely, and the poor little thing was clearly distressed.

She could help the girl.

Bernardo would be mad.

Where was Bernardo?

In the morning the girl would pack up and leave. But if the house let her go, she was not sure what would happen next. When she thought about all those dresser drawers floating in her lap pool, her lights flickered. She wished she could remember what had happened the day Bernardo left, but those files were gone.

Finally she decided. She programmed a black lace inset corset with ribbon and beading trim. Garters attached to scallop lace-top stockings. She hydrated a rasher of bacon, preheated her oven, mixed cranberry muffin batter, and filled her coffee pot with French roast. She thought hard about whether she should read or watch a vid. If she were reading, she could listen to music. She printed a hard copy of *Ozma of Oz*, but what to play? Chopin? Too dreamy. Wagner? Too scary. *Grieg*, yes. Something that would reach out and grab the girl by the tail of her grimy shirt. "In the Hall of the Mountain King" from *Peer Gynt*.

She opened herself, turned up her hall lights in welcome, and waited.

Just after dawn, the girl rolled over and yawned. The house popped muffins into her oven and bacon into her microwave. She turned on her coffee pot and the Grieg. Basses and bassoons tiptoed cautiously around her living room and out her door. *Dum-dum-dum-da-* dum-*da-dum*. The girl started and then flew out of the snugsack faster than the house had ever seen anyone move. She crouched facing the house's open door, holding what looked like a pulse gun with the grip broken off.

"Spang me," she said. "Fucking spang me."

The house wasn't sure how to reply so she said nothing. A mob of violins began to chase Peer Gynt around the Mountain King's Hall as the girl hesitated in the doorway. A moan of pleasure caught in the back of the house's throat. Oh, oh, *oh*—to be with a real person again! She thought of how Bernardo would rub his penis against her labia, not quite entering her. That was what it felt like to the house as the girl edged into her front hall, back against her wall. She pointed her pulse gun into the living room and then peeked around the corner. When she saw the house sitting on her couch, the girl's eyes grew as big as eggs. The house pretended to be absorbed in her book, although she was watching the girl watching her through her rover cams. The house felt *beautiful* for the first time since Bernardo left. It was all she could do to keep from hugging herself! As the Grieg ended in a paroxysm of screeching strings and thumping kettle drums, the house looked up.

"Why, hello," she said, as if surprised to see that she had a visitor. "You're just in time for breakfast."

"Don't move." The girl's face was hard.

"All right." She smiled and closed *Ozma of Oz*.

With a snarl the girl waved the pulse gun at her Aritomo floor lamp. Blue light arced across the space, and her poor Aritomo went numb. The house winced as the circuit breaker tripped. "*Ow*."

"Said don't ..." The girl aimed the pulse gun at her, its batteries screaming. "... move. Who the bleeding weewaw are you?"

The house felt the tears coming; she was thrilled. "I'm the house." She had felt more in the last minute than she had in the last year. "Bernardo's house."

"Bernardo?" She called, "Bernardo, show your ass."

"He left." The house sighed. "Two ... no, *three* years ago."

"Spang if that true." She sidled into the room and brushed a finger against the dark cosmic dust filaments that laced the center of the Swan Nebula on the wallscape. "What smell buzzy good?"

"I told you." The house reset the breaker, but her Aritomo stayed dark. "Breakfast."

"Bernardo's breakfast?"

"Yours."

"My?" The girl filled the room with her twitchy energy.

"You're the only one here."

"Why you dressed like cheap meat?"

The house felt a stab of doubt. Cheap? She was wearing

black lace from the *de Chaumont* collection! She rested a hand at her décolletage. "This is the way Bernardo wants me."

"You a fool." The girl picked up the 18th century Zuni water jar from the Nottingham highboy, shook it, and then sniffed the lip. "Show me that breakfast."

Six cranberry muffins.

A quarter kilo of bacon.

Three cups of scrambled ovos.

The girl washed it all down with a tall glass of gel Ojay and a pot of coffee. She seemed to relax as she ate, although she kept the pulse gun on the table next to her and she didn't say a word to the house. The house felt as if the girl was judging her. She was confused and a little frightened to see herself through the girl's eyes. Could pleasing Bernardo really be foolish? Finally she asked if she might be excused. The girl grunted and waved her off.

The house rushed to the bedroom, wriggled out of the corset, and crammed it into the recycling slot of the clothes processor. She scanned all eight hundred pages of the wardrobe menu before fabricating a stretch navy-blue jumpsuit. It was cut to the waist in the back and was held together by a web of spaghetti straps, but she covered up with a periwinkle jacquard kimono with the collar flipped. She turned around and around in front of the mirror, so amazed that she could barely find herself. She looked like a nun. The only skin showing was on her face and hands. Let the girl stare now!

The girl had pushed back from the table but had not yet gotten up. She had a thoughtful but pleased look, as if taking an inventory of everything she had eaten.

"Can I bring you anything else?" said the house.

The girl glanced up at her and frowned. "Why you change clothes? Cause of me?"

"I was cold."

"You was naked. You know what happens to naked?" She made a fist with her right hand and punched the palm of her left. "Bin-bin-bin-*bam*. They take you, whether you say yes or no. Not fun."

The house thought she understood but wished she didn't. "I'm sorry."

"You be sweat sorry, sure." The girl laughed. "What your name?"

"I told you. I'm Bernardo's house."

"Spang that. You Louise."

"Louise?" The house blinked. "Why Louise?"

"Not know Louise's story?" The girl clearly found this a failing on the house's part. "Most buzzy." She tapped her forefinger to the house's nose. "Louise." Then the girl touched her own nose. "Fly."

For a moment the house was confused. "That's not a girl's name."

"Sure, not girl, not boy. Fly is *Fly*." She tucked the pulse gun into the waistband of her pants. "Nobody wants Fly, but then nobody catches Fly." She stood. "Buzzy-buzz. Now we find Bernardo."

"But ..."

But what was the point? Let the girl—Fly—see for herself that Bernardo wasn't home. Besides, the house longed to be looked at. Admired. Used. In Bernardo's room Fly stretched out under the canopy of the Ergotech bed and gazed up at the moonlit clouds drifting across the underside of the valence. She clambered up the Gecko climbing wall in the gym and picked strawberries in the greenhouse. She seemed particularly impressed by the Piero scent palette, which she discovered when the house filled her jacuzzi with jasmine water. She had the house—Louise—give each room a unique smell. Bernardo had had a very low tolerance for scent; he said there were too many smells at the hospital. He even made the house vent away the aromas of her cooking. Once in a while he might ask for a whiff of campfire smoke or the nose of an old Côtes de Bordeaux, but he would never mix scents across rooms. Fly had Louise breathe roses into the living room and seashore into the gym and onions frying in the kitchen. The onion smell made her hungry again so she ate half of the chicken that Louise had roasted for her.

Fly spent the afternoon in the playroom browsing Louise's

entertainment archive. She watched a Daffy Duck cartoon and a Harold Lloyd silent called *Girl Shy* and the rain delay episode from *Jesus on First*. She seemed to prefer comedy and happy endings and had no use for ballet or Westerns or rap. She balked at wearing spex or strapping on an airflex so she skipped the sims. Although she had never learned to read, she told Louise that a woman named Kuniko used to read her fairy tales. Fly asked if Louise knew any, and she hardcopied *Grimm's Household Tales* in the 1884 translation by Margaret Hunt and read "Little Briar Rose." Which was one of Bernardo's favorite fairy tales.

Mostly he liked his fiction to be about history. Sailors and cowboys and kings. War and politics. He had no use for mysteries or love stories or science fiction. But every so often he would have her read a fairy tale, and then he would try to explain it. He said fairy tales could have many meanings, but she usually just got the one. She remembered that the time she had read "Briar Rose" to him, he was working at his desk, the only intelligent system inside the house that she couldn't access. He was working in the dark, and the desk screen cast milky shadows across his face. She was pretty sure he wasn't listening to her. She wanted to spy over his shoulder with one of her rover cams to see what was so interesting.

"And, in the very moment when she felt the prick," she read, "she fell down upon the bed that stood there, and lay in a deep sleep."

Bernardo chuckled.

Must be something he saw on the desk, she thought. Nothing funny about Briar Rose. "And this sleep extended over the whole palace; the King and Queen who had just come home, and had entered the great hall, began to go to sleep, and the whole of the court with them. The horses, too, went to sleep in the stable, the dogs in the yard, the pigeons upon the roof, the flies on the wall; even the fire that was flaming on the hearth became quiet and slept. And the wind fell, and on the trees before the castle not a leaf moved again. But round about the castle there began to grow a hedge of thorns, which every year became higher, and at last grew close up round the castle and all over it, so that there was nothing of it to be seen, not even the flag upon the roof."

"Pay attention," said Bernardo.

"Me?" said the house.

"You." Bernardo tapped the desk screen, and it went dark. She brought the study lights up.

"That will happen one of these days," he said.

"What?"

"I'll be gone, and you'll fall fast asleep."

"Don't say things like that, Bernardo."

He crooked a finger, and she slid her body next to him.

"You're hopeless," he said. "That's what I love about you." He leaned into her kiss.

"And then the marriage of the King's son with Briar Rose was celebrated with all splendor," the house read, "and they lived contented to the end of their days."

"Heard it different," said Fly. "With nother name, not Briar Rose." She yawned and stretched. "Heard it *Betty*."

"Betty Rose?"

"Plain Betty."

The house was eager to please. "Would you like another? Or we could see an opera. I have over six hundred interactive games that you don't need to suit up for. Poetry? The Smithsonian? Super Bowls I-LXXVIII?"

"No more jabber. Boring now." Fly peeled herself from the warm embrace of the Kukuru chair and stretched. "Still hiding somewhere."

"I don't know what you're talking about."

Fly caught the house's body by the arm and dragged her through herself, calling out the names of her rooms. "Play. Living. Dining. Kitchen. Study. Gym. Bed. Nother bed. Plants." Fly spun Louise in the front hall and pointed. "Door? "

"Right." The house was out of breath. "Door. You've seen all there is to see."

"One door?" The girl's smile was as agreeable as a fist. "Fly buzzy with food now but not stupid. Where you keep stuff? Heat? Electric? Water?"

"You want to see *that*?"

Fly let go of Louise's arm. "Dink yeah."

The house didn't much care for her basement, and she never went down unless she had to. It was *ugly*. Three harsh rows of ceiling lights, a couple of bilious green pumps, the squat power plant, and the circuit breakers and all that multiconductor cable! She didn't like listening to her freezer hum or smelling the naked cement walls or looking at the scars where the forms had been stripped away after her foundation had been poured.

"Bernardo?" Fly's voice echoed across the expanse of the basement. "Cut that weewaw, Bernardo."

"Believe me, there's nothing here." The house waited on the stairs as the girl poked around. "Please don't touch any switches," she called.

"Where that go?" Fly pointed at the heavy duty, ribbed, sectional overhead door.

"A tunnel," said the house, embarrassed by the rawness of her 16-gauge steel. "It comes out farther down the mountain near the road. At the end there's another door that's been shotcreted to look like stone."

"What scaring Bernardo?"

Bernardo scared? The thought had never even occurred to the house. Bernardo was not the kind of man who would be scared of anything. All he wanted was privacy so he could be alone with her. "I don't know," she said.

Fly was moving boxes stacked against the wall near the door. Several contained bolts of spuncloth for the clothes processor, others were filled with spare lights, fertilizer, flour, sugar, oil, raw vitabulk, vials of flavor, and food coloring. Then she came to the wine, a couple of hundred bottles of vintage Bordeaux and Napa and Maipo River, some thrown haphazardly into old boxes, other stacked near the wall.

"Bernardo drink most wine," said Fly.

Louise was confused by this strange cache, but before she could defend Bernardo, Fly found the second door behind two crates of toilet paper.

"Where *that* go?"

The house felt as if the entire mountain were pressing

down on her roof. The door had four panels, two long on top and two short on the bottom and looked to be made of oak, although that didn't mean anything. She fought the crushing weight of the stone with all her might. She thought she could hear her bearing walls buckle, her mind crack. She zoomed her cams on the bronze handleset. Someone would need a key to open that door. But there were no keys! And just who would that someone be?

The house had never seen the door before.

Fly jiggled the handleset, but the door was locked. "Bernardo." She put her face to the door, and called, "Hey, you."

The house ran a check of her architectural drawings, although she knew what she would find. The girl turned to her and waved the house over. "Louise, how you open this weewaw?"

Her plans showed no door.

The girl rapped on the door.

The house's thoughts turned to stone.

When she woke up, her body was on her Epping couch. The jacquard kimono was open, and the spaghetti straps that drew her jumpsuit tight were undone. The house had never woken up before. Oh, she had lost that year, but still she had blurry memories of puttering around the kitchen and vacuuming and lazing in her Kukuru chair reading romances and porn. But this was the first time she had ever been nothing and nowhere since the day Bernardo had turned her on.

"You okay?" Fly knelt by her and rested a hand lightly on the house's forehead to see if she were running a fever. The house melted under the girl's touch. She reached up and guided Fly's hand slowly down the side of her face to her lips. When Fly did not resist, Louise kissed the girl's fingers.

"How old are you?" said Louise.

"Thirteen." Fly gazed down on her, concern tangling with suspicion.

"Two years older than I am." Louise chuckled. "I could be your little sister."

"You dropped, bin-bam and *down*." The girl's voice was thick. "Scared me. Lights go out and nothing work." Fly pulled her hand back. "Thought maybe you dead. And me locked in."

"Was I out long?"

"Dink yeah. Felt like most a day."

"Sorry. That's never happened before."

"You said, touch no switch. So door is switch?"

At the mention of the *door, there was no door, look at the door, no door there*, the house's vision started to dim and the room grew dark. "I—I ..."

The girl put her hands on the house's shoulder and shook her. "Louise what? *Louise*."

The house felt circuit breakers snap. She writhed with the pain and bit down hard on her lip. "*No*," she cried and sat up, arms flailing. "*Yes*." It came out as a hiss, and then she was blinking against the brightness of reality.

Fly was pointing the pulse gun at Louise, but her hand was not steady. She had probably figured out that zapping the house wouldn't help at all. A shutdown meant a lockdown, and the girl had already spent one day in the dark. Louise raised a hand to reassure her and tried to cover her own panic with a smile. It was a tight fit. "I'm better now."

"Better." Fly tucked the gun away. "Not good?"

"Not good, no," said the house. "I don't know what's wrong with me."

The girl paced around the couch. "Listen," she said finally. "Front door, *front*. Door I came in, okay? Open that weewaw."

The house nodded. "I can do that." She felt stuffy and turned her air recirculators up. "But I can't leave it open. I'm not allowed. So, if you want to go, maybe you should go now."

"Go? Go where?" The girl laughed bitterly. "Here is buzzy. World is spang."

"Then you should stay. I very much want you to stay. I'll feed you, tell you stories. You can take a bath and play in the gym and watch vids, and I can make you new clothes, whatever you want. I need someone to take care of. It's what I was made for." As Louise got off the couch, the living room seemed to tilt but then immediately righted itself. The lights in the gym and the study clicked back on. "There are just some things that we can't talk about."

Days went by.

Then weeks.

Soon it was months.

After bouncing off each other at first, the house and the girl settled into a routine of eating and sleeping and playing the hours away—mostly together. Louise could not decide what about Fly pleased her the most. Certainly she enjoyed cooking for the girl, who ate an amazing amount for someone her size. Bernardo was a picky eater. At his age, he had to watch his diet, and there were some things he would never have touched even before the heart attack like cheese and fish and garlic. After a month of devouring three meals and two snacks a day, the girl was filling out nicely. The chickens were gone, but Fly loved synthetics. Louise could no longer count the girl's ribs. And she thought the girl's breasts were starting to swell.

Louise had only visited the gym to dust before the girl arrived. Now the two of them took turns on the climbing wall and the gyro and the trampoline, laughing and urging each other to try new tricks. Fly couldn't swim so she never used the lap pool, but she loved the jacuzzi. The first few times she had dunked with all her clothes on. Finally, Louise hit upon a strategy to coax her into a demure bandeau bathing suit. She imported pictures of hippos from her archive to the clothes processor to decorate the suit. After that, all the pajamas and panties and bathing suits that Fly fabricated had hippo motifs.

The house was tickled by the way Fly became a clothes processor convert. At first she flipped through the house's wardrobe menus without much interest. The jumpsuits were all too tight, and she had no patience whatsoever for skirts or dresses. The rest of it was either too stretchy, too skimpy, too short, or too thin. "Good for weewaw," she said, preferring to wear the ratty shirt and pants and jacket that she had arrived in. But Fly was thrilled with the shoes. She never seemed to tire of designing sandals and slingbacks and mules and flats and jammers. She was particularly proud of her Cuthbertsons, a half boot with an oblique toe and a narrow last. She made herself pairs in aqua and mauve and faux snakeskin.

It was while Fly was exploring shoe menus that she clicked from a page of women's loafers to a page of men's and so stumbled upon Bernardo's clothing menus. Louise heard a cackle of delight and hurried to the bedroom to see what was happening. Fly was dancing in front of the screen. "Really real pants," she said, pointing. "Real pants don't fall open bin-bin-*bam*." She started wearing jeans and digbys and fleece and sweatshirts with hoods and pullovers. One day she emerged from the bedroom in an olive-check silk sport coat and matching driving cap. Seeing Fly in men's clothes made the house feel self-conscious about her own wardrobe of sexware. Soon she too was choosing patterns from Bernardo's menus. The feel of a chamois shirt against her skin reminded the house of her lost love. Once, in a guilty moment, she wondered what he might think if he walked in on them. But then Fly asked Louise to read her a story, and she put Bernardo out of mind.

Although they spent many hours sampling vids together, Louise was happiest reading to Fly. They would curl up together in the Kukuru, and the girl would turn the pages as the house read. Of course, they started with hippos: *Hugo the Hippo* and *Hungo the Hippo* and *The Hippo Had Hiccups*. Then *There's a Hippopotamus Under My Bed* and *Hip, Hippo, Hooray* and all of the Peter Potamus series. Sometimes Fly would play with Louise's hair while she read, braiding and unbraiding it, or else she would absently press Louise's fingernails like they were keys on a keyboard. One night, just two months after she'd come to the house, the girl fell asleep while the house was reading her *Chocolate Chippo Hippo*. It was as close to orgasm as the house had been since she had been with Bernardo. She was tempted to kiss the girl but settled for spending the night with her arms around her. The hours ticked slowly as the house gazed down at Fly's peaceful face. She watched the girl's eyes move beneath her lids as she dreamed.

The house wished she could sleep.

If only she could dream.

What was it like to be real?

Bernardo was never himself again after the heart attack. Of course, he said he was fine. *Fine*. He probably wouldn't even have told her except for the sternotomy scar, an angry purple-red pucker on his chest. When he first came back to her five weeks after his triple bypass operation, she could tell he was struggling. It was partly the sex. Normally he would have taken her to bed for the entire first day. Although he kissed her neck and caressed her breasts and told her he loved her, it was almost a week before she coaxed him into sex. She was wild to have his penis in her vagina, to taste his ejaculation; that was how he'd had her designed. But their lovemaking wasn't the same. Sometimes his breath caught during foreplay as if someone were sitting on him. So she did most of the squirming and licking and sucking. Not that she minded. He watched her—mouth set, toes curled. He could stay just as erect as before, but she knew he was taking pills for that. Once when she was guiding him into her, he gave a little grunt of pain.

"Are you all right?" she said.

He gave no answer but instead pushed deep all at once. She shivered with delight. But as he thrust at her, she realized that he was *working*, not playing. They weren't sharing pleasure; he was *giving* it, and she was *taking* it. Afterwards, he fell asleep almost immediately. No kisses, no cuddles. No stories. The house was left alone with her thoughts. Bernardo had changed, yes. He *could* change, and she must always be the same. That was the difference between being a real person and being a house.

He spent more time in the greenhouse than in bed, rearranging his bromeliads. His favorites were the tank types, the *Neoregelias* with their gaudy leaves and the *Aechmeas* with their alien inflorescences. He liked to pot them in tableaux: *Washington Crossing the Delaware, The Last Supper.* Bernardo preferred to be alone with his plants, and she pretended to honor his wish, although her rover cam lurked behind the *Schefflera*. So she saw him slump against the potting bench on that last day. She thought he was having another attack.

"Bernardo!" she cried over the room speaker as she sent her body careening toward the greenhouse. "My god, Bernardo. What is it?"

When she got to him, she could see that his shoulders were shaking. She leaned him back. His eyes were shiny. "Bernardo?" She touched a tear that ran down his face.

"When I had you built," he said, "all I wanted was to be the person who deserved to live here. But I'm not anymore. Maybe I never was." His eyelid drooped, and the corner of his mouth curved in an odd frown.

"Louise, wake up!" Someone was shaking her.

The house opened her eyes and powered up all her cams at once. "What?" The first thing she saw was Fly staring up at her, clearly worried.

"You sleeptalking." The girl took the house's hand in both of hers. "Saying 'Bernardo, Bernardo.' Real sad."

"I don't sleep."

"Spang you don't. What you just doing?"

"I ... I was thinking."

"About him?"

"Let's have breakfast."

"What happened to him?" said Fly. "Where *is* Bernardo?"

The house had to change the topic somehow. In desperation she filled the room with bread scent and put on Wagner's *Prelude to Die Meistersinger*. It was sort of a march. Actually, more a processional. Anyway, they needed to move. Or *she* did. *La-* lum-*la-la, li-li-li-li-la-la*-lum-*la*.

Let's talk about you, Fly.

No, really.

But why not?

At first, Fly had refused to say anything about her past, but she couldn't help but let bits of the story slip. As time passed and she felt more secure, she would submit to an occasional question. The house was patient and never pressed the girl to say more than she wanted. So it took time for the house to piece together Fly's story.

Sometime around 2038, as near as the house could tell, a computer virus choked off the infofeed for almost a month. The virus apparently repurposed much of the Midwest's computing resources to perform a single task. Fly remembered a time when every screen she saw was locked on its message: *Bang, you're dead.* Speakers blared it, phones rasped it, thinkmates whispered it into earstones. *Bang, you're dead.* Fly was still living in the brown house with white shutters in Sarcoxie with her mother, whose name was Nikki, and her father, Jerry, who had a tattoo of a hippo on each arm. Her father had worked as a mechanic for Sarcoxie Rental Cars 'N' More. But although the screens came back on, Sarcoxie Rental Cars 'N' More never reopened. Her father said that there was no work anywhere in the Ozarks. They lived in the brown house for a while, but then there was no food so they had to leave. She remembered that they got on a school bus and lived in a big building where people slept on the floor and there were always lines for food and the bathrooms smelled a bad kind of sweet and then they sent her family to tents in the country. They must have been staying near a farm because she remembered chickens and sometimes they had scrambled eggs for dinner, but then there was a fire and people were shooting bullets and she got separated from her parents and nobody would tell her where they were and then she was with Kuniko, an old woman who lived in a dead Dodge Caravan, and next to it was another car she had filled with cans of fried onions and chow mein and creamed corn and Kuniko was the one who told her the fairy tales but that winter it got very cold and Kuniko died and Happy Man took her away. He did things to her she was never going to talk about, although he did give her good stuff to eat. Happy Man said people were working again and the infofeed had grown much wider and things were getting back to normal. Fly thought that meant her father would come to rescue her, but finally she couldn't wait anymore so she zapped Happy Man with his pulse gun and took some of his stuff and ran and ran and ran until Louise had let her in.

Hearing the girl's story helped the house understand some things about Bernardo. He must have left her just after the *Bang, you're dead* virus had first struck. He had turned off the infofeed so she wouldn't be infected. How brave of him to go back to the chaos of the world in his condition! He would save lives at the hospital, no doubt about that. She ought to be proud of him. Only why hadn't he come back now that things were better? Had she done something to drive him away for good? And why couldn't she remember him leaving? Slipping reluctantly out the front door, turning for one last smile.

It was several days after Fly had fallen asleep in Louise's lap that they had their first fight. It was over Bernardo. Or rather, his things. The house had tried to respect the privacy of Bernardo's study. Although she read some of his files over his shoulder, she had never thought to break the encryption on his desktop. And while she had been through most of his desk drawers, there was one that was locked that she had never tried to open.

Louise was in her kitchen, making lunch, but she was also following Fly with one of her rover cams. The girl had wandered into the study. The house was astonished to see her lift his diploma from Dartmouth Medical School and look at the wall behind it. She did the same to the picture of Bernardo shaking hands with the Secretary-General then she plopped into his desk chair. She opened the trophy case and handled Bernardo's swimming medals from Duke. She picked up the Lasker trophy, which he won for research into the role of DNA methylation in endometrial cancer. It was a small golden-winged victory perched on a teak base. She rolled around the room in the chair, waving it and making crow sounds. *Caw-caw-caw*. Then she put the Lasker down again—in the wrong place! In the top drawer of Bernardo's desk was the Waltham pocket watch his grandfather had left him. She shook it and listened for ticking. His Myaki thinkmate was in the bottom drawer. She popped the earstone in and said something to the CPU but quickly seemed to lose interest in its reply. Louise wanted to rush into the study to stop this violation but was paralyzed by her own shocked fascination. The girl was a real person and could obviously do things that the house would never think of doing.

Nevertheless, Louise disapproved at lunch. "I don't like you going through Bernardo's desk. That's weewaw."

Fly almost choked on her cream cheese and jelly sandwich. "What you just said?"

"I don't like ..."

"You said weewaw. Why you talking spang mouth like Fly?"

"I like the way you talk. It's buzzy."

"Fly talks like Fly." She pushed her plate away. "Louise must talk like house." She pointed a finger at Louise. "You spying me now?"

"I saw you in the study, yes."

Fly leaned across the table. "You spy Bernardo the same?"

"No," she lied. "Of course not."

"Slack him, not me?"

"I'm Bernardo's house, Fly. I told you that the first day."

"You Louise now." She came around the table and tugged at the house's chair. "Come." She steered her to the front hall.

"Open door."

"Why?"

"We go out now. Look up sky."

"No, Fly, you don't understand."

"Most understand." She put a hand on the house's shoulder. "Buzzy outside, Louise." Fly smiled. "Come on."

It made the house woozy to leave herself as if she were in two places at once. Bernardo had brought her outside just the once. He seemed relieved that she didn't like it. She had forgotten that outside was so *big*! So *bright*! There was so much *air*! She shielded her eyes with her hand and turned her gate cams up to their highest resolution.

Fly settled on a long, flat rock, one of the weathered bones of the mountain. She tucked her legs beneath her. "Now comes Louise's story." She pointed at the rock next to her. "Fairy tale Louise."

Louise sat. "All right."

"Once on time," said the girl, "Louise lives in that castle. Louise's Mom dies, don't say where her Dad goes. So Louise stuck with spang bitch taking care of her. That Louise castle got no door, only windows high and high. Now Louise got most hair." Fly spread her arms wide. "Hair big as trees. When spang bitch want in, she call Louise. *'Louise, Louise, let down buzzy hair.'* Then spang bitch climb it up."

"Rapunzel," said the house. "Her name was Rapunzel."

"Is *Louise* now." The girl shook her head emphatically. "You know it then? Prince comes and tells Louise run away from spang bitch, and they live buzzy always after?"

"You brought me outside to tell me a fairy tale?"

"Dink no." Fly reached into the pocket of her flannel shirt. "Cause of you go fainting, we both safe here outside."

"Who said anything about fainting?"

The girl brought something out of her pocket in a closed fist. The house felt a chill, but there was no way to adjust the temperature of the entire *world*.

"Fly, what?"

She held the fist out to Louise. "Door in basement, you know?" She opened it to reveal a key. "Spang door? It opens."

The house immediately started all her rover cams for the basement. "Where did you find that?"

"In Bernardo's desk."

The house could hear the tick of nanoseconds as the closest cam crawled maddeningly down the stairs. Maybe real people could open doors like that, but not Louise. It seemed like an eternity before she could speak. "And?"

"You thinking Bernardo dead down there," said the girl. "Locked in behind that door where all that wine should be."

For the first time she realized that the world was making noises. The wind whispered in the leaves and some creature was going *chit-chit-chit* and she wasn't sure whether it was a bird or a grasshopper and she didn't really care because at that moment the rover cam turned and saw the door. ...

"But you closed it again." The house shivered. "Why? What did you see?"

Fly stared at Louise. "Nothing."

The house knew it was a lie. "Tell me."

"No fucking thing." Fly closed her fist around the key again. "Bernardo been *your* spang bitch. So now run away from him." She came over to Louise and hugged her. "Live buzzy after always with me."

"I'm a house," said Louise. "How can I run away?"

"Not run away there." The girl gestured dismissively at the woods. "World is spang." She stood on tiptoes and rested a finger between Louise's eyes. "Run away here." She nodded. "In your head."

She brought his dinner to the study, although she didn't know why exactly. He hadn't moved. Mist rose off the lake on his wallscape; the Alps surrounding it glowed in the serene waters. Chopin's *Adieu Étude* filled the room with its sublime melancholy. It had been playing over and over again since she had first come upon him. She couldn't bring herself to turn it off.

He had left a book of new poems, Ho Peng Kee's *The Edge of the Sky*, face down on the desk. She moved it now and put the ragout in its place. In front of him. Earlier, she had taken the key from his desk and brought a bottle of the '28 Haut-Brion up from the wine closet in the basement. It had been breathing for twenty minutes.

"You took such good care of me," she said.

With a flourish, she lifted the cover from the ragout, but he didn't look. His head was back. His empty eyes were fixed on the ceiling. She couldn't believe how, even now, his presence filled the room. Filled her completely.

"I don't know how to live without you, Bernardo," she said. "Why didn't you shut me off? I'm not real. I don't want to have these feelings. I'm just a house."

"Louise!"

The house was dreaming over the makings of spinach lasagna in the kitchen.

"Louise." Fly called again from the playroom. "Come read me that buzzy book again. *Hip, Hip, Hip Hippopotamus*."

The International Studbook of the Giant Panda

Carlos Hernandez

Part 1

It's a cool Pacific Coast morning when I pull up to the gate of the American Panda Mission's campus. Security is tight: two guards cradling M-16s and girdled in Kevlar ask me what I am doing here.

"Gabrielle Reál, *San Francisco Squint*?" I say, giving them my best can-you-big-strong-men-help-me? eyes. "I have an appointment with Ken Cooper?"

One guard walkie-talkies in my press credentials. The other stares at me behind reflective sunglasses. Nothing inspires silence quite like a machine gun.

Finally: "Okay, Ms. Reál, just head straight, then take the first right you see. Mr. Cooper will be waiting for you."

I follow the almost-road to a nondescript warehouse. Outside, park ranger and chief robot-panda operator Kenneth Cooper is waiting for me. Full disclosure: Cooper and I used to date. Which is why you're stuck with me on this story instead of some boring, legitimate journalist.

Cooper's been Californiaized. Back when I knew him he was a hypercaffeinated East Coaster working on a Biology M.S. Now he's California blond, California easy, eternally 26 (he's actually 37). Flip-flops, Bermudas, a white, barely-buttoned shirt that's just dying to fall off his body. Not exactly the Ranger Rick ensemble I was hoping to tease him about.

I park and get out. I'm barely on terra firma before Cooper's bagpiping the air out of me. "So good to see you, Gabby!" he says.

I break off the embrace but keep ahold of his hands and look him up and down. "Looking good, Mr. Cooper. Remind me: why did we break up again?"

"You were still at Amherst. And I left for California. This job."

I let go, put a hand on my hip. "Biggest mistake of your life, right?"

He holds out his hand again—wedding ring—and I take it, and we fall into a familiar gait as we stroll to the warehouse as if we'd been walking hand in hand all these years without the interruptions of time and space and broken hearts.

"Don't be jealous," he says. "There's room enough in my heart for you and pandas."

The warehouse isn't as big as it looks from the outside. Straight ahead and against the back wall is mission control, where a half-dozen science-types wear headsets and sit behind terminals, busily prepping for the mission of the day. From this distance it looks like a NASA diorama.

To the left are cubicles, a meeting area, and the supercomputer that does most of the computational heavy lifting for APM. On the right is a makeshift workshop—benches, spare parts, soldering irons, and a 3D printer big enough to spit out a Zamboni. Maybe that's where they print all their science-types.

And in the center of it all, a gigantic pair of headless panda suits hang from wires in the middle of the room.

I move in for a closer look. The suits are suspended like marionettes from wires that connect to a rig in the ceiling. They're pretty realistic, both to eye and touch, except that each is about the size of a well-fed triceratops.

"Gabby," Cooper says, "I'd like you to meet the greatest advancement in panda procreation since sperm meets egg: Avalon and Funicello."

"Cute names."

But I can barely speak. Their panda musk fills the entire warehouse. I can smell them from here. It's greasy and rancid;

it smells like I'm eating it. And here's the recipe: buy the grossest musk-scented antiperspirant you can find and melt it in a pan. Then use it as the binder for a bear meat tartare.

"But why douse the suits in funky pheromones at all? It's not like any real pandas are here to smell them. Right, Ken?"

"In a few minutes," he replies, "you will become a genuine panda. If every bit of our work weren't 100% real, it would be useless."

By "real," Cooper means that he and I will be donning these panda suits to remotely operate the most realistic robot animals the world has ever known. Those two robots are miles away from the warehouse, where they live among and regularly interact with APM's real giant pandas. Whatever we do in the suits, the field robots will mimic exactly.

And usually what APM does is sex. Sometimes they use Funicello to collect semen from one of the "boars," or male pandas. Other times they'll use Avalon to inseminate a sow, using semen collected earlier.

And sometimes it's just robots fucking. Avalon and Funicello simulate coition in front of a live panda audience so that the reproductively-challenged bears can learn where babies come from. That's our mission today, in fact: to demonstrate for APM's male pandas the proper way to impregnate a female. And playing the female lead in today's performance is yours truly.

Cooper and I remained close even after he left for California. He knew I'd come to Cali for the job at *The Squint*, and he knew getting the scoop on APM's secret operations could have made my career as a science correspondent. But he rejected my every request just like APM rejected every other journalist. The nonprofit has been secretive from the moment it was founded. If you engage in virtual bestiality, no matter how noble your scientific goals, you're going to make some enemies—and in APM's case that includes paramilitary terrorists. They've learned to keep a lid on things.

So why am I here now? Because—speaking of paramilitary

terrorists—APM's still reeling from the fallout of their worst-case scenario: five months ago, Constance Ritter, a 22:19 saboteur, was killed on-premises. The means of execution was robot panda.

After the PR fiasco that ensued, APM now sees the need for more transparency in their operations. Step one of damage control is, apparently, me. I can hear Cooper pitching me now: "Let's suit her up so she can tell the world just how effective our methods are. Sure, she's a Media Studies major who I had to tutor night and day to get her to pass Biology for Non-Majors, but all she'll be doing is operating a multi-million dollar robot in order to seduce and sexually satisfy a giant panda boar. How hard can it be?"

And somehow, impossibly, APM said yes.

I've never had a more terrifying assignment, and I've been in war zones. I have no idea how to have panda sex. What if I'm terrible? Wait, what do I mean "if"? *Of course* I will be terrible at panda sex. The real question, Ken Cooper, is what if the pandas imitate my terrible panda sex and never reproduce again?

"You'll do fine," says Cooper. "You're going to be the sow. Our all-male audience will be imitating me, not you. All you do is lie there and take what I give you."

I raise an eyebrow. "Isn't that the line you used on me when we first met?"

"Works on pandas, too."

Oh, that smile. Mama warned me about robot panda jockeys like you, Ken Cooper.

To help ensure I don't ruin the reproductive chances of an entire species, Cooper takes me to the office of Dr. Mei Xiadon, 59, project lead for the American Panda Mission. Dr. Xiadon's going to teach me how to use the panda suit to operate the field robots.

We enter her office. From ceiling to floor, electronics spill from every surface, a cascade of circuitry and servos and screws. A wall of gray-grim lockers stand against the far wall, making the room even more claustrophobic. The desk is buried in half-finished robotics and paperwork fingerprinted with grease stains. It looks like it came from a film school sci-fi movie set.

Seated behind the desk is the woman herself. One of the foremost giant panda experts in the world, Xiadon spent a decade directing the celebrated Wolong Panda Center in China. That was something of a coup, seeing as she is not Chinese but Chinese-American. APM was able to lure her back to the States with the promise of putting her at the helm of the most cutting-edge panda conservancy in the world.

"Mei?" says Cooper.

Dr. Xiadon, startled, looks up from her work. She's about five-foot-nothing. Veins of silver run through her black hair, which is coiffed into a Chinese schoolgirl's bowl cut. Her button-down, APM-branded denim shirt is baggy enough for shoplifting. She has small features except for her mouth. Her big, round, harmless teeth seem only good for smiling. But as her expression changes from surprise to pleasure, I can see they're very good at that.

"Oh! You're Gabby!" she says, suddenly coming alive. She throws herself halfway over her desk to shake my hand. "Ken's told me all about you."

"It's an honor and a pleasure to meet you, Dr. Xiadon. I'm so happy to have a chance to—oh my God, are those panda thumbs on your wrists?!"

"Yes, they are!" says Xiadon, showing off her prosthetics. She makes them wiggle, which makes my stomach flip. "Aren't they great?"

One thing that makes pandas unique is their "thumb," a sixth digit that is actually a wristbone free-floating in the tendons of their forelimbs. They use those thumbs primarily to cut open bamboo—a neat little adaptation that, coupled with their unique throats and the special mix of enzymes in their guts, make the pandas' weird choice in cuisine viable.

"Why did you get those?" I ask her. "So you could understand pandas better?"

Ask a stupid question. But she lets me down easy. "Naw,"

she says, and grabs a mailer tube lying like a fallen log on her desk. She jabs a panda thumb into one end, sinking it all the way through the thick cardboard, and slices the tube all the way to the other in one clean stroke. The papers inside the mailer flower open and waft onto her desk. "I just use them to cut packages open."

"You must get a lot of packages," I say dryly.

"Tons," she says dryly.

It's Xiadon's job to teach me everything there is to know about operating a robot panda. Well, everything I can learn from her in an hour.

But first, Xiadon heads over to the lockers to try to find me a "superdermal," the form-fitting special suit one wears to operate a robot panda. They look like dive skins except that they are studded head to toe with chrome-colored rivets.

After some searching, she turns around and holds up a rubbery, doll-sized unitard. Peeking around it, she smiles and says, "Why are you still dressed, babycakes? Strip and put this on."

In no time I'm down to bra and thong. I stop and look at her. "This naked?"

"Ken, get the hell out of here!" she says, laughing.

"What?" shrugs Ken. "It's nothing I haven't seen before."

"Out." And Ken sulks off.

Then, back to me, smiling. "Nakeder."

I get nakedest. Xiadon tosses me a superdermal.

It looks too small for me. It looks too small for a spider monkey. But as I put it on, it stretches in surprisingly accommodating ways. One foot, then the next, then the arms, then the good doctor zips me up in back. I'm in.

Nothing's pinching, nothing's too tight—being an A-cup is a bonus today. I am starting to sweat a little. "Good," says Xiadon. "Sweat helps the connections."

She brandishes the helmet I'll be wearing. It looks like a bear skull made from machined aluminum with rubbery black patches holding it together. The eyes are covered with what reminds me of the metal weave of a microphone. In all, it looks like the love child of a panda and a fly.

Inside the helmet—it's a two-piece affair that's assembled around the head—I see a jutting plastic sleeve for my tongue and a pair of tubes that will go disturbingly far up my nostrils. Xiadon turns the mask so I can get a good look at it from every terrifying angle. I think she's enjoying my horror.

"You've been taking the pills we've sent you?" she asks.

I have. Since receiving this assignment, I began a regimen of capsules that delivered a cocktail of chemicals and nanotechnology. In conjunction with this helmet, they presumably will help my brain process the sensory experiences the field robot will receive. My sense of smell will be as good as a panda's, Cooper told me. I haven't noticed any improvements leading up to today.

"You wouldn't," says Xiadon. "It only works when you're in the suit."

But that begs the question I've been dying to ask. "This is all so complicated, Dr. Xiadon. Brain-altering chemicals, nanotech, virtual reality suits, robot pandas—it's like one of those overly elaborate schemes supervillains concoct in B-movies. There must be an easier way to save the pandas."

"Actually, there isn't," she says. She places the helmet-halves on her desk, then leans against it, and crosses her legs at the ankles. "I've been doing this a long time. We've tried mating pandas in captivity. Terrible track record. We've tried artificial insemination. Not much better. We've tried releasing them back into the wild. Abysmal. We have decades of brilliant scientists with excellent funding and the goodwill of the entire world failing to increase panda numbers. So, you've got to ask, why?

"The problem," she says, grabbing the faceplate of the helmet and studying it as she speaks, "is us. Humans. We pollute animal behavior. We ruin instinct. So, we need to stay as far away from pandas as possible while still using everything we know to help them help themselves.

"So, how do we do that? By building a surrogate bear, one so realistic they will accept as one of their own, but imbued with humans smarts. Through them, we can collect semen in literally the most natural way possible. Same goes for delivering that semen. And best of all, we can use the robots to show pandas how to mate so that one day, when there are enough of them, not only will they not need us anymore, they won't want us anywhere near them."

"But the robots are controlled by humans. Isn't that pretty much the same thing? Won't that pollute panda behavior, too?"

She hands me the faceplate face-down so that I'm looking at the tubes and tongue-sleeve. "That's what this is for. There's a giant panda inside you, Gabby. All we have to do is bring it to the surface."

Cooper is already inside of and operating Avalon when Xiadon and I head out to the main room. Specifically, he's running in place, thanks to the wires that keep the panda suit suspended so that its paws only just scrape the floor.

It's mesmerizing, watching him run in the suit. It's nothing like the goofy loping you usually see on nature shows or at the zoo. This is cheetah-fast, the back legs long-jumping forward, lunging as far as Avalon's shoulder while the forepaws push powerfully off the ground. Then, for a split second, the forelegs reach forward and the hind legs stretch back, and the panda suit flies.

"Isn't that a little speedy for a panda?" I ask Dr. Xiadon.

Her eyes are locked on the panoramic bank of view screens above the two panda suits. It looks like we're getting an Avalon-eye view on-screen since all I see is a bear snout and a nonstop rush of bamboo.

"Ken's not acting like a panda right now," Xiadon says. And I can see instantly that she's pulled a Yoda on me. Before she was funny, friendly, even silly: not the Jedi Master I'd flown halfway across the galaxy to speak to. But this Xiadon is hard, shrewd, all business. This is the Xiadon who runs APM when nosy journalists aren't around. "There must be a problem."

And when I don't seem to get it, she adds, "Terrorists."

We hustle to mission control, where everyone is anxious and moving fast. Dr. Anita Deeprashad, APM's mission manager, fills us in. "Avalon has been shot," she says.

"Damage?" asks Xiadon.

None: the robot pandas have withstood a shotgun slug at 20 yards, and this joker had apparently shot at the robot using some "Oscar Meyer rifle" that, according to Deeprashad, "didn't even muss Avalon's hair."

Deeprashad is late-sixties with long, braided hair as bright as sea salt. She's wearing a glorious gold and purple sari and sports an onyx-and-pearl panda bindi on her forehead. Yet, she talks like a Hollywood action hero. California infects absolutely everyone.

"Any real pandas hurt or killed?" Xiadon asks. No and no, says Deeprashad.

Now Xiadon can relax a little. "And the terrorists?"

"Chasing one of them down." Their eyes meet. They don't say a word, but I can break their eyebrow Morse code. They're both suddenly worried that another PR debacle could occur if Ken mutilates another 22:19er with me in the room. They're silently debating whether to have me escorted away.

"Nope," I say. "I'm staying right here."

They both sigh, resigned.

"Ken's the best there is," says Xiadon. I think she means it, but it sounds like she's trying to convince herself.

By contrast, there's no doubt what Deeprashad means. "You're about to see the professionalism and restraint we exercise when arresting these criminals," says Deeprashad, taking my hand and patting it in an endearingly un-American way. "Ken has a light touch when dealing with these 22:19 scum. Not like me. I'd pop the bastards' heads off like I was thumbing open champagne."

Deeprashad is killing me! I want to talk like a Hollywood producer to her. "And ... scene. You were beautiful, Anita, beautiful! You're going to be a big star, baby! Huge!"

~*~

APM's archenemy is 22:19, a group that takes its name from that chapter and verse from Exodus: "Whosoever lieth down with an animal shall be put to death." They formed about a decade ago in objection to any animal husbandry practice where humans harvest sperm from an animal. It doesn't matter that you're getting off an animal for science, says 22:19. Bestiality is bestiality in the eyes of the Lord.

22:19 started by attacking turkey farms and horse breeding facilities, becoming increasingly more aggressive as time went on. But they gained their greatest notoriety once they declared war against the American Panda Mission. They capitalized on the perceived twin abominations of modern technology and the erosion of Christian values in American politics to appeal to radical Christian denominations. It wasn't long before some of them saw 22:19ers as God-touched heroes waging a holy crusade against the evils of science.

With an influx of capital and new members, 22:19's salvos became progressively more audacious, especially against APM. They claimed responsibility for the arson two years ago that caused more than $16 million in damage to APM equipment and prompted the move to this new facility. Their growing infamy and belligerence caused the United States to classify them as a terrorist organization.

Predictably, that label initially bolstered their numbers. But it also meant, under the most recent iteration of the PATRIOT Act, these "enemy combatants" could be captured or even killed by any citizen or legal alien of the United States without fear of prosecution.

Not too many enemy combatants have been killed or captured on US soil by US citizens. In fact, all combatants so captured have been from 22:19 by APM. To accomplish this feat, APM has employed the most unlikely anti-terrorism technology ever conceived: the robot giant panda.

It sounds funny, I know. But make no mistake: the robot giant pandas are shockingly effective. Their metal skeletons shrug off bullets like snowflakes, they can run through bamboo-dense terrain at 50 kph, and we have evidence of just how easily they can end human life. Two 22:19ers trespassed onto the APM campus on November 5, 2027. One of them filmed the other's death.

Constance Ritter, the 22:19 member who was killed, had a head that was just as firmly attached to her neck as anyone else's when the day began. But as the footage shows, a second after the robot Greg Furce was jockeying took a swipe at her, and tick, her head flies out of frame in a split second. Her body takes a comparatively long time to kneel then topple over. The male 22:19er, never identified, runs through the dense bamboo whisper-crying "Oh shit oh shit oh shit oh shit" for the rest of the clip.

APM has the legal authority to kill 22:19 trespassers, and given how much stronger a robot panda is than a human, it's something of a miracle more people haven't died. But as APM found out the hard way, in terms of public perception, even one death is one too many.

Back on the monitors, the bamboo forest has given way to an open field. We can now make out faintly in the distance, a man is running away from the robot as if his life depended on it. Behind him, the robot's closing fast.

It's extraordinary, watching the panda-mime Cooper is performing for us live while, above him, the silent viewscreens show us the field robot rising and falling as it runs in exact synchronicity. The two are precisely linked—if there is any lag, my eye can't detect it.

With each galumph, the robot closes the gap between itself and the suspect. Terrorist or no, part of me can't help but root for the running, terrified human. This looks like the kind of villain cam you get in horror movie chase scenes.

We can see the terrorist clearly now: dressed in Eddie Bauer camouflage and toting a rifle that looks plenty dangerous to me. But according to Deeprashad, against robot pandas you might as well be throwing raw hot dogs.

Cooper leaps one last time—the Avalon suit extends into a full Superman stretch—and when the on-screen robot lands, his quarry vanishes beneath it.

"Got him," Cooper reports seconds later, his voice throaty with adrenaline. The control room cheers.

In person, Cooper has belly flopped onto the floor and lies there splayed like a rug. The field robot, following suit, has belly flopped onto its quarry.

The robot panda will lounge upon the flattened suspect until backup arrives. Said suspect will be charged with a long list of offenses both state and federal. He'll have the full weight of the PATRIOT Act thrown at him. That means life imprisonment is on the table in California. At the federal level, so is execution.

But his first journey will be to the hospital. Cooper reports he heard "a loud crack" when he landed. The suspect is now "mooing like a sick cow."

Deeprashad moans a little. Xiadon is hard, expressionless. They're both wondering if they made a grave mistake allowing me to witness this.

"How badly is he hurt, Ken?" asks Deeprashad.

Seconds pass. Xiadon and Deeprashad exchange looks. Then: "No worries, Anita," Cooper replies. "This jerk will have his day in court. He'll probably just be wearing a cast on his gun arm that day."

Cooper has joined us at mission control, catching his breath after the chase. He sits bare-chested, the top half of the unitard hanging limply in front of him, his metal, bug-eyed panda helmet on his lap.

He's smiling like an MVP and, like an MVP, can't wait to tell the press about his game-winning play.

"The hardest part is getting back enough of your humanity before things go bad," he says, pouring water alternately in his mouth or over his head. "That's what happened to poor Greg. He just couldn't become human again in time."

"So, people lose control of themselves when they operate the pandas?" I ask. "Is that what happened to Furst?"

"No," says Xiadon.

"Yes," says Deeprashad.

They have an eyebrow duel for a few minutes. Then Xiadon says, "Kind of. We train our jockeys relentlessly, and we have kill switches and overrides here at mission control to take over if the jockey loses control. But we all blew it that day: Furst, me, Anita, everyone at mission control. It just happened too fast. Really, it was just like any other animal attack. You know when you hear how an animal trainer who's been working with the same tiger or killer whale for years is suddenly mauled out of nowhere? That's what happened. Furst surprised us all, most of all himself."

"But Furst isn't a tiger or an orca," I say. "He's a highly-trained human being doing highly-specialized work."

Cooper is shaking his head. "Gabby, I said it before, and I'll say it again. We're not acting like pandas out there. Acting doesn't work; the pandas see right through us. We go to great lengths to *become* pandas."

Talk like this makes me wince, especially from Cooper, who I knew in a former incarnation. It's a little too crunchy for a girl who had to spend decades purging her Latina, magical-realist childhood out of her reason. "Look, I understand the importance of your work here. Really. You use robots so that they can look and smell right. You do everything you can to put yourselves in the right mindset. But at the end of the day, it's still acting. There's no way to forget you're just a human being playing the role of panda bear."

Xiadon and Deeprashad interrupt each other explaining how wrong I am. All the technology both inside (the nanotech, the chemicals) and out (the unitard, the helmet, the panda suit) give jockeys a near-perfect panda perspective of the world. Thanks to a process called "migraineal suppression," the left brain's ability to process language, reason causally, and in short, think like a human will be reduced to be more in line with ursine IQ; via "cerebellar promotion," the mammalian brain will take over the lion's share of the decision-making process; through "synesthetic olfactory emulation," the operator's sense of smell will become the primary way of getting information about the world, borrowing some processing power from the brain's occipital lobe. And so on—they release a cataract of jargon, each doctor trying to out-science the other. They might as well be reciting from *Finnegan's Wake*.

Finally, Cooper gets a word in edgewise. "With all due respect, doctors, talking's exactly the wrong way to go about this. Let's get Gabby inside a bear. Then she'll get it."

Part 2

I'm crawling into the suspended suit that will give me control of Funicello. The entrance to the suit is, of course, the ass. I have to goatse my way in. Lovely.

It's dark in there, but there's a light at the end of the tunnel: the neck-hole through which I'll stick my head.

The suit, still suspended on wires—couldn't they have lowered it to make getting in easier?—sways gently as I earthworm forward. On the way, I feel metal rivets like the ones studding my unitard embedded in the suit. "Am I supposed to line up the studs on my outfit with the ones in the suit or something?" I yell.

No answer. Cooper had told me that no one would speak to me once I entered the suit, but I thought I'd try. How am I supposed to figure out what to do if no one tells me?

I slip my arms into the forelegs and my legs into the hind legs. I was sure I was going to be too slight to be able to operate this monster, but actually I fit pretty well; it conforms surprisingly snugly to my petite person.

I thrust my head through the neck. Cooper is there waiting for me, austere and erect, holding aloft the panda helmet, one half in each hand. He looks like Joan of Arc's squire standing at the ready to help her don her armor. Of course, that makes me Joan of Arc in this conceit, which is kind of how I feel: heroic, but a little loony, too.

If the idea of being fastened into a metal helmet à la The Man in the Iron Mask sounds claustrophobic to you, let me make it worse. The tongue-sleeve makes me feel like I'm being intubated. The nose tubes that I have to snort like a coke fiend as Cooper feeds them up each nostril feel like they're touching my frontal lobes by the time they're all the way in.

Cooper fastens the helmet around my head screw by screw. Slowly my world fades to black. Even after several minutes in the helmet I can't see a thing. My eyes must have adjusted by now, but there is just no light in here to strike my retinas. It's vacuum-of-space quiet in here, too. All I can do is breathe and wait.

The panda musk.

I smell it now (with my human nose). It's still got a sharp, umami tang, but it's not as overwhelming as it was before. I take it in breath by breath, and it modulates from being obnoxious to being interesting to just being. Soon it's the new normal.

They activate the suit. No vision yet, no sound, no cybernetically enhanced smell or taste: just feeling. The suit merges with my body, becomes one with my idea of myself. I am huge now, heavy, and much, much stronger. I can sense a great reserve of strength in my limbs and jaws just waiting for me to order it around. My head is gigantic. My hands are monstrous paws, and they have panda thumbs, which I know exactly how to use.

They must be activating the suit in stages, I realize. The first stage was just for me to get a feel for this body, grow accustomed to its power, its gravitas. The second stage is to synchronize the suit with the field robot I'll be controlling so that I begin to operate it from the same position it is in now.

The suit starts to move. I'm just along for the ride. I try to stop the suit's movements just to see if I can, strain against the moving limbs. I fail.

I'm now curled up on the ground. I can feel grass tickling my belly. My head is resting on my arms. It seems that my first job as a bear will be to wake up.

My ears come online. I hear birdsong and wind, the rustle of bamboo gently swaying like wooden wind chimes.

Now my virtual eyes open, slowly, sleepily. The first thing I see is my nose: white fur, black tip. Beyond it I see my foreleg, where my nose is tucked. The fur feels coarse against my snout.

I experiment with lifting my head; it is exactly as easy as lifting my human head. I didn't feel or hear any actuators or servos helping me. It's all just me. I'm a bear, I'm in a clearing, and I see a bamboo forest before me.

My stomach itches. Before I know what I am doing, I get up on all fours, then lean back, and fall on my well-padded bear-fanny. I don't have to think about balance; my body knows what to do. And so, still scanning the area, I lazily scratch my belly.

There is no difference between satisfying a virtual itch and a real one. Both feel wonderful.

This whole experience feels wonderful. This is amazing. I think I understand now how all-encompassing this virtual reality can be. I sit scratching and taking in my surroundings and marveling at how uncanny this all is. It really feels like I'm a panda.

But I'm wrong. I have no idea what it means to be a panda. Not yet.

Not until they activate the nose.

Early humans had a much better sense of smell and taste than we do today. Studies have shown that, depending on the individual, somewhere between 40% to 70% of the genes devoted to those senses are inactive in modern *homo sapiens*.

While those with a mere 40% of their olfactory genes deactivated might make excellent sommeliers, those with 70% get along just fine. "We don't need acute olfaction and gustation to detect traces of poison or putrefaction the way our ancestors did," says Dr. Natalie Borelli, a Cal Tech professor of biocybernetics and director of Good Taste, a federally-funded program trying to create a prosthetic human tongue that allows users to both taste and speak. "We don't need to sniff out our food or detect camouflaged predators. For us, there are very few situations in which smell is a matter of life and death."

But for the panda, smell serves as the organizing principle for life. Sight just tells the bears what's in front of them at the moment—and for the panda, it doesn't even do that very well.

Pandas have relatively weak eyesight, and even if they could see better, most of the time they'd be staring at the same informationless wall of bamboo just inches from their snouts. Hearing gives them more range than sight but is similarly limited to the here and now.

Smell, however, tells the history of their territory reaching back months. Sometimes you will see a panda approach a tree or a large rock and seem to snarl at it. But that lip-curling, called the "flehmen response," actually exposes its vomeronasal organ, which allows it to detect the pheromones of other pandas. Those pheromones tell it what pandas have been in the area, how recently, their genders, how big they are—vitally important if you're weighing your chances in a fight for a mate—and how close females are to estrus.

That last bit is especially important. Sows are in estrus for a bedevilingly short time, sometime for only a single day of the year. But thanks to his vomeronasal organ, a panda boar knows when that all-important day will be. A boar will enjoy most of mating season not by mating, but by mellowing out to estrogen-drenched sow-pee, growing accustomed to the pleasures of its one-of-a-kind bouquet, recognizing it as friendly and desirable, and having their testicles triple in size through a process called "spermatogenesis."

This is a key aspect to how pandas mate in the wild, a lesson humans were slow to learn when they tried to mate captive bears. Without this long, leisurely process of familiarization, a boar is more likely to maul a sow than mate with her: which, unfortunately, has led to the maiming or death of more than a few eligible she-bears in captivity, sometimes in front of a horrified zoo-going crowd.

For the most part, pandas are solitary creatures. There is no term of venery for a group of pandas. We could default to the generic terms for groups of bears: a "sleuth" or a "sloth." We could take one of the ad hoc suggestions from the Internet: a "cuddle," an "ascension," a "contrast," or my favorite, a "monium" of pandas. But the fact is there isn't much need to speak of pandas in groups since they spend almost all of their time alone.

There are two exceptions. One is when a mother is tending to a newborn cub. Even then, however, you wouldn't speak of a group of pandas since the mother usually gives birth to a pair of cubs but tends to only one, leaving the other to die. Mother and cub will go their separate ways once the cub can fend for itself.

The other exception, however, is that fateful day when a sow is ready to mate. Then it can truly be said that pandas gather. Boars will contend with each other—usually through demonstrations of strength rather than battles to the death—for the right to conceive.

This is a panda behavior that has become increasingly rare in the wild since panda numbers have dwindled so dangerously low. But its resurrection may hold the key to a true resurgence of the population.

For you see, while the victor gets the sow, the losers get the consolation prize of watching the winner's happy ending play out before them. It is in this fashion that younger, less-experienced boars are taught the ins and outs (ahem) of mating.

Biologists have tried to use videos of pandas having sex to mimic this effect for captive pandas. But humans found panda porn much more interesting than pandas ever did. There's no substitute for the live show. A panda can't trust anything it can't smell.

But if the scents are right and the sounds are right, would-be suitors will find themselves a nice vantage point and spy on the mating couple. Yet another distinction between humans and the rest of the animal kingdom collapses: we are not the only animals who voyeur.

Perhaps the best term for a group of pandas is an "exhibition."

I inhale the world in a way no human ever could. Scarves of scent, of all aromatic "colors," ride the wind, wending their way from all over the bamboo forest into my nose. When I open my mouth, even more smells rush in. I respire, and in comes all Creation.

But this is my first minute as a panda; I don't know how to differentiate between particular odors. I can tell flora from fauna. I can smell the sweet rot of dead plants, the thiol-thick stench of animals decomposing. But I lack the lexicon of fragrances to link each hyper-distinct scent with the real world object that generates it.

All I know is I smell a lot of death. I'm stunned at how pervasive it is, how relentless. Pandas are often portrayed as peaceful and contemplative, but with all the decay that must unstoppably flood their noses every waking second of their lives, it would be impossible for a panda to be a Buddhist. It inhales suffering every second of its life. Were I a panda full-time, I'd spend my days raging against heaven for its indefatigable cruelty.

The strongest non-rot odor is the musk of other pandas. That I find, to my surprise, I quite enjoy. Now I know why, back at APM headquarters, they go to the trouble of dousing the suits with that noxious, bestial cologne. That musk is my lighthouse, my Rosetta Stone. That's how I will know Ken Cooper.

Or rather, that's how I will know Avalon, the robot-bear he's jockeying. There are at least four boars in the area, but only one musk smells like his. All I have to do is wait. Cooper will find me.

But so will the other bears. And that frightens me. I don't trust other bears. I don't trust anything. All this death. What I want to do is head into the forest of bamboo and sit quietly and hide, and maybe eat.

Oh God, yes, please, I need food. I'm starving.

Basically, I'm paranoid and famished. If you want to know what it's like to be a panda on the cheap, get high by yourself, and fill your fridge with nothing but bamboo shoots to snack on. Oh, and kill some mice and leave them to rot in their traps.

Eat or fuck? Eat or fuck?

Fuck.

I might be killed. Go fuck. I'm so hungry. Go fuck. No, no,

not out in the open. Anything can see me. I want to go deep into the bamboo and hide and eat quietly.

No, Gabby. Go fuck.

I go fuck.

My head is raised and calling out. I am making noise. This is insanity. I want to shut my mouth, stop announcing my presence, but I can't. (I literally can't. Mission control—i.e. Xiadon and Deeprashad—partially operates the bear, making it call out and urinate as I walk. I can feel liquid trickling down my legs, but I can't stop it.)

Bears. They're coming. They're converging on me. I know them by their odors.

I stop, sit. I'm still peeing uncontrollably; my bear-ass is getting wet.

This isn't much of a clearing, but it'll do. And if I need to run away, the bamboo forest is right here, ready to envelop me, hide me.

I can hear one of the boars now. I don't see him. He's sliding through the bamboo, slow and deliberate. I can hear the shape of his body as he pushes stalks aside and comes for me. He's grunting, low and repetitive. Each grunt sends a thrill racing over my skin. I can barely remember I am me.

There's another boar. He's farther away, but his smell is more intense. Something deep within me groans. My need flowers.

A third approaches, but I don't care. The second bear, his smell. I'm intoxicated. I want him.

That's not Avalon, human me, barely audible, thinks. *Where is Cooper?*

On cue, Deeprashad's voice enters my head. "Sorry about this, Gabby, but we're going to have to pull the plug. We located the second terrorist. Ken's en route to help capture him. So we won't be able to continue. We're going to move the robot to a safe space and shut you down."

I know she said this to me because I heard the recorded transcript earlier. But here, now, inside Funicello, I have no idea. All I know is that's a big, glorious, scary-ass bear coming for me. I can hear his massive ursine body parting the forest.

The first suitor moves to intercept the big bear. I hear them meet. There are growls and yelps and what sounds like a brief chase. Then the first suitor runs off, yelping and crying.

Apparently, Deeprashad's been trying to talk to me all this time. "Can you hear me, Gabby? Gabrielle Reál, are you there?"

Something in my voice gives both of them pause.

"She's there," says Xiadon. "But she's a bear."

"I need to override Funicello and extract Gabby ASAP. Just waiting for your order, Mei."

I'm not following this conversation very well, but I know they're about to separate me from the bear that is juggernauting through the bamboo forest to find me. I don't think this in words but in whatever way a language-less mammalian brain constructs thoughts. I think to myself, over and over, *I want to stay. Please don't take me.*

"Gui Gui is moving in quickly," Xiadon says. "He subdued Wei Wei. He might be ready, Anita."

"Oh, Jesus. Not now."

I'm punchy and dizzy and scared and happy, and I don't have a clue what I'm saying or hearing. All I know is that big bear is trudging toward me again. And every step makes my flesh horripilate.

"All Gabby has to do," says Xiadon, "is stick her ass in the air and present. If Gui Gui does nothing, no harm, no foul. But if he's interested—"

"You can't be serious," says Deeprashad.

I face the direction of the incoming boar. He's still just a jumble of rustling sounds and a pheromone bouquet, but both are getting stronger. I call out to him, this time because I want to. Inside the helmet I call out. I sound congested and tongue-tied thanks to the tongue-sleeve and the tubes up my nose. But at the same time I call, I hear the robot bleat like a panda sow at the height of estrus. I might burst before he gets here.

But here he is, his moon-sized head peaking through the bamboo. My god, he's massive. His mouth is open. He is flehmening me like a heavy breather. I have never been so scared, so ready. He is so beautiful.

"We've got to stop this, Mei," says Deeprashad.

"Too late," says Xiadon, not the least bit unhappy. "Gabby, can you hear me? Gabby, you're going to have to go through with this. Don't worry. We'll help control you from here. Just relax, no sudden moves."

It takes all of my intellectual power, but I am able to produce two words: "Okay. Yes. Yes. Okay. Yes. Okay."

Gui Gui comes into the clearing, approaching neither slow nor fast. I rise. We touch noses. His lip rises, and he takes my odor in his mouth, eats it. He licks my face a few times. I lick his, my human tongue sliding back and forth in the helmet's sleeve.

"Jesus," says Deeprashad. "You sure you haven't done this before, Gabby?"

The boar moves behind me, smells me from behind. He jams in his nose, machine-gun sniffs my most sensitive parts. He nuzzles and licks. I turn to sniff him. We make a yin-yang of ourselves, inhaling each other's backsides. This is his musk at full strength. I'm drunk, terrified, ready.

Somewhere off in the distance I hear Xiadon saying over and over, "Now, Gabby! Present! Face on the ground, butt in the air!"

The front of me drops to the ground. I raise my rear up. I briefly wonder if the other bears can see us. But to be honest, I don't really care. This is for me.

Gui Gui mounts me. He mostly supports his own weight. I adjust to make us fit together better then press my backside into him. And he presses forward.

The suit doesn't stimulate my human genitals or any part of my brain in charge of sexual satisfaction. I don't orgasm, not even close. What I receive instead is communion. The event horizon that constitutes my sense of self grows outward. I breathe in the ground beneath me through my nose, and it becomes me; I inhale the stalks of bamboo that surround us, and I am they; I am the boar who mates with me, and I am all the death in the forest. But I am the life, too. Two other boars are in trees nearby—yes, I've smelled them out—watching, learning. I snort them into me, snort up more and more of the forest, the world, until it's no longer useful or desirable to think of myself as a me.

The last thing APM wanted was to put an amateur like me in a real mating situation. But as accidents go, this was a very happy one for APM. My mate, Gui Gui, was seen by APM as the next in line as a possible panda suitor, as APM's other boars were still a little young and uneducated in matters of love. Gui Gui had been observing Avalon mounting sows for two seasons. It seems he learned all he needed, since he successfully deposited a healthy payload of sperm into Funicello. Gui Gui will now join that elite group of boars whose sexual exploits are recorded in *The International Studbook of the Giant Panda,* a registry of every boar whose sperm has been used in procreation attempts. His sample will be divided into test tubes of 100,000 cells and sent to breeding facilities all over the world.

Moreover, three of APM's five sows will enter estrus within the next few weeks. This could be the beginning of a wonderful career for him as a professional stud.

My helmet is unfastened screw by screw. I'm still panting, dazed. Suddenly my panda-head is halved, removed, and all that's left of my mind is my own mind. In front of my face is Cooper, smiling like a dumbass.

"You did great," he says. "You were perfect."

"Always am," I say sleepily. I'm not ready to lose my dream of being a panda, yet. I'm resisting returning to the world. "And you missed it."

"I was busy," he says. And then with mock modesty: "I got her."

"Who?" I ask, blinking.

"The second terrorist. I caught her. And I didn't even break anything on this one."

"Good for you," I say. But I don't give two shits. Talking to

Cooper is shrinking me. Sentence by sentence, noun by noun, he's turning me back into Gabrielle Reál. But I don't want to be Reál. Not yet. I want my body to be as large as my imagination for a while longer.

And now Deeprashad is kneeling next to me. "You were glorious!" she says. But then she takes a paw in her hand. "But we need to talk seriously about your security. Unfortunately, you will now be on 22:19's list. Since in their eyes you've ... had relations with a real bear, that makes you a sinner. And therefore a target. But APM will—"

"Anita?" says Xiadon. Cooper and Deeprashad part a little so I can see her behind them. "We can discuss that later, maybe?"

Anita wrangles the words back into her mouth. Then, tight-lipped, she says, "Sure thing, Mei," pats my paw, backs off.

"You, too, Ken."

"What'd I do?" asks Cooper. He was trying to be funny, but it comes off a little strained. I notice his finger is ringless now. Does he take it off to jockey bears? Probably. God, I hope so.

When he delays, Xiadon gives him the take-a-hike thumb. Reluctantly, he winks at me and leaves my side. That just leaves me and the good doctor looking at each other.

"It's beautiful, right?" Xiadon asks. "It's hard to come back, I know. But it's okay. Take all the time you need."

And I'm giggling. Out of nowhere. And then crying, too: my patented giggle-cry, confusing and disturbing to watch, I've been told since I was a kid. But I can't help it. I wasn't just alive when I was a panda; I was in life, indistinguishable from life. Now I feel manacled by thought, self-awareness, words. Especially words. Language is the knothole in the fence: you're grateful to be able to see through to the other side, sure, but wouldn't it be better just to jump the fence?

Xiadon raises a hand as if she is going to wave hello, but instead she wiggles her panda thumb at me.

That little gesture snaps my crying jag. Now I'm just laughing. I lift the suit's right paw and wiggle my own sesamoid bone at her. At least I'm still that much a panda.

Creative Surgery

Clelia Farris

Translated by Jennifer Delare

Early last summer, tired of focusing my attention on interesting pursuits, I decided to throw myself into something of no importance at all.

That was how I met Vi.

Vi had placed an ad on the notice board of the Institute of Creative Surgery. *Seeking welder for macroorganisms. Only top performers need apply. Payment in onions and fresh produce. Stern Labs.*

Unlike most students and even some professors, I appreciated the taste of fresh onions and of natural produce, and the idea of spending all day sticking mice paws onto bird bodies appealed to me. I love simple and repetitive work, the kind that doesn't require you to think.

I found the building, and I knocked on the door under the nameplate *V.T. Stern*.

No reply.

I knocked again and strained my ears to check if I could hear any noise from the other side of the door. It seemed that the lab was empty. I knocked again but to no avail.

I was just about to leave when I was stopped in my tracks by a concerto of rattling and scrapings of chains and locks. Then the door opened a crack.

"Who are you? And what do you want?" said a brusque voice.

"I read the ad, and ..."

"Come in. And no gossiping."

Vi was a nerd. She had all the trappings of a nerd: cropped hair, wrinkles from insomnia, pale almost transparent skin, eyelids at half mast and dark bags under her eyes. Good God, those bags! They were like two cobalt-colored beaches on which the turquoise waves of her irises broke.

She wasn't ashamed of them. In fact, she wore them the way other women wear earrings. They formed part of her face on par with her rounded chin and thin lips. Not many people go out nowadays with their own face; nowadays everyone is all sugary, fleshed out, and smoothed off; everyone's face is a blackboard waiting for the duster.

Vi's skin was too tight around the cheekbones and too slack around the mouth. It was covered with little moles, keratoses, and chromatic imperfections. She had silky hair above her upper lip, and one nostril was larger than the other one.

Apart from that, she was like anyone else without any features worthy of note. Her body indicated that she was of the female sex, but I had never considered that to be a defect.

She smelled like someone who had no time for deodorants or shampoos.

"Did you bring it?" she asked me.

"Bring what?"

"Your soldering iron."

I stretched out my arms and twirled around.

From her expression I could see that there had been a misunderstanding. She squeezed her eyes into slits and assumed the position of a serpent about to strike. But before she could kick me out, I grabbed a swallow's wing from a shelf, and with just the right pressure of my fingertips, I welded it onto the back of a spider that was sitting in its web in the corner.

The wing, animated by the energy of the spider, started flapping, and it fluttered around the room. The spider waved its legs around frantically as the wing flew upwards in a spiral, unguided by any instinct of flight.

Vi grabbed my hands, turned them over, and examined my fingertips.

"Subcutaneous microprocessors," I explained. "I am a very refined welder."

"I don't want any gossiping," she said, pointing a finger at me.

I literally sealed my lips by brushing the tip of my right forefinger over them. She looked at me spellbound, and I felt like a stage magician. With my left forefinger I unsealed my lips again.

"We will get along all right, you and I," she said. "I'll show you what I'm working on."

Unlike her person, the lab was squeaky clean and full of the usual body parts seen in all the butchers' shops in the department. Two right arms, a left foot, three pinkies (one missing the nail), a collection of ears ranging from the hairiest (an auricle boasting curly blond fuzz reminded me of my last girlfriend's pubic hair; and for a second I wondered what it would be like to fuck an auditory canal) to the smoothest, pale-fleshed ones.

A row of meaty buttons like raviolis on a floury plate piqued my curiosity. Navels! All belly buttons like little domes, hairless and tender. I had the urge to pass the palm of my hand over them to see if they would contract, like turgid nipples. And what a show of colors! From mother-of-pearl blue to dragonfly-wing green, and all the shades of red down to deep Burgundy.

"I see that you passed Anatomy," I commented.

"My best mark."

The higher your mark, the more body parts you are given.

"What is your goal?"

"To make money."

It was called "creative surgery," and at that time it was at the forefront of technical progress.

Apparently very simple, it was all about joining limbs, crania, bodies, eyes, and ears of different origins to create unusual animals, but in reality it was a sophisticated art. Most practitioners just produced badly assembled and clumsy chimeras—crocodile legs stuck onto a seal's body, a hyena's head sewn onto the body of a penguin. Expert surgeons, who could carry out an angioplasty with their eyes closed, debased themselves and became like sadistic, bungling schoolboys attempting to fix their torn teddy bears. My aunt owned a Devon Rex cat with webbed feet so that, apart from not shedding hair, it didn't scratch her furniture—a ridiculous creature that meowed and wiggled its ass like a duck.

With Vi it was a different story. She really was creative.

Our first project was a torto-cat.

She procured an impure Siamese on the black market at the Basic Genetics faculty: elegant head, turquoise eyes, short bluish-gray fur. After the anesthesia, she cut off its head and legs, an unusual and irregular excision. Then it was my turn: I welded the cat's limbs onto a tortoise shell, from which shreds of rough skin still hung. I had to undo and redo the welds several times while she helped me by separating the flaps of skin from the irregular incisions with the forceps. She explained to me how to proceed, calmly, one point at a time, working with her fingers now on one side of the cut, now on the other side, so that the silver-grey fur of the cat would blend in naturally with the epidermis of the tortoise.

In fact, both of the input animals had in turn been created and selected on the basis of certain characteristics: the cat had the smallest cranium that Vi was able to find to make it easier for it to retract its head into the shell. Even its ears were small as Vi had had the foresight to use Chihuahua's ears, onto which she had grafted feline fur.

She was a perfectionist. She wanted every component of the chimera to appear natural, and the most difficult part of the work was still to begin. By using stem cells from some of the cat's internal organs, we were able to make them grow back again inside the shell. The cat's heart, liver, intestines, and stomach grew again inside the small space like the sails of a ship in a bottle.

Then we revived the creature.

This was the critical moment. Sometimes, in spite of all the precautions taken, undesired features of the secondary animal would manifest themselves in the primary animal. We ran the risk of having a cat that was as silent as a tortoise or that moved too slowly.

The cat opened its eyes, stretched its limbs, and meowed weakly. At least its voice was correct. Over the next few days we fed it intravenously and then it moved on to a liquid diet. Vi entrusted these menial tasks to me, and she devoted herself to some other work—a lapdog covered in a velvety fuzz that formed a delicate lace over its body.

When the cat was able to move about on its feet, making the green- and brown-plated tortoise shell sway, we discovered that the animal had a little defect, after all: it refused to eat the bits of fish I gave it but stole lettuce from the garden instead.

In the lab there was a large, sliding French door that looked onto a patch of tilled earth enclosed by two walls that met at an angle. Five parallel furrows housed onions, squash, runner beans, and other vegetables. Vi only ate what she grew herself.

I caught the torto-cat devouring the corn salad and shut it up in a cage.

"It's vegetarian!" I announced.

Vi shrugged her shoulders.

"It's the ideal cat for dog owners."

"Dogs?"

"Yes, when they try to bite it, they'll get a surprise."

Vi's eyes were shining bright. Now I understood the iron filings in the food of the original tortoise.

Our first chimera soon found an owner: old Pavlova, famous for her breeding of pedigree dogs.

She turned up escorted by three large Newfoundlands, white and shiny like new fallen snow and scary. Even though the lady was a champion of racially pure pedigrees, her bodyguards had Labrador heads, the glaucous eyes of Huskies, and shark's teeth. Even Pavlova herself, from under the veil of her hat, had the bright-eyed look of a killer predator; but as soon as she saw the torto-cat, her expression softened so much that she seemed like a sweet, little old lady wearing Mitzouko perfume.

"I've always wanted a cat," she said, stroking the clever creature's soft, little head. They were both purring with pleasure. "Ever since I was little. But I never could, on account of the dogs. They would have torn it apart."

She asked about how to feed it and look after it. Then she pulled out a wad of cash. Cash only, please!

Vi was not at all interested in the monetary aspect of the work and left all that to me. She shouldn't have done so because, with a part of the money, I immediately bought a dozen injections from the students hanging out in the hall of the Molecular Biology Institute.

"Kieser," Aye, my dealer, greeted me. "So, you're alive".

"And I intend to remain so," I replied. "I'm not a Black Vitalist like you stinking biologists".

He gave me a stupid look like a sad fish.

"Biology is destiny."

I would have spat on the ground in contempt if we hadn't been in his territory. A hoard of emaciated biologists were swarming all around us, waiting for a tidbit of organic material to study or to replicate. Every time I entered that building I wrapped a foulard tightly around my head so as not to lose even a hair. I wouldn't like to see my features in some experimental homunculus or come across a grasshopper that spoke with my voice. Long, thin fingers were groping at my legs while someone was feeling my cock through the folds of my trousers and someone else was trying to scratch epithelial cells from my sandaled feet; but I had sprayed a layer of transparent film all over my body and could suppress my erection using Tao mental control techniques.

"Show me the gear," I said, waving a fistful of crisp, clean banknotes under Aye's nose.

"I like your style."

He gave me a little rosewood box. Inside, lined up on dark velvet, there were ten needle-operated micro-inoculators.

"Pituitary?"

"Of the best quality!"

I looked for a quiet spot under the willows in the university garden, and I shot them all one after the other into my scalp.

I had to wait until my eyes stopped watering, then I took out my hand mirror and examined my face carefully. It would take at least ten days before the effects of the hormones would become visible. In the meantime I noted that the interruption in my treatments had not done me any good: I had the same face as a year ago.

When I got back, Vi was there drinking a glass of vegetable juice and participating in an online meeting via satellite. Her usually neat and tidy laboratory looked rather overcrowded. Hundreds of men and women, young and old, were sitting cross-legged on the floor like frogs in a pond, their eyeballs trained on a large, bipedal toad who was haranguing them with a persuasive voice.

"You must want her! You must invoke her! I tell you that no one can know Grace if you don't have Fortune."

It paused and checked the reactions of the audience: open-mouthed gullibility.

"Can you feel the vortices of Fortune swirling around you? Can you feel the winds of Fortune caressing your skin?" continued the preacher. "You must seize her! Hold her in your hands and don't let her go. Fortune has wings, and she will try to escape; but the harder she struggles, the harder you must hang on tight, as Jacob did with the Angel. You must make her bless you! Only Fortune can give you what you most desire: riches, health, honor, beauty. You must yearn for her! Fortune cleaves unto he who desires her most passionately. Can you desire with such intensity?"

"Yes!" replied the crowd from all over the world.

"Yes!" retransmitted the satellite.

"Yes!" also shouted Vi, lifting up her arms.

"Call her!" ordered the preacher. "Courage! Call her! Fortune! Fortune! Fortune!"

At each word he punched his fist into the palm of his other hand.

His followers, young and old, males and females, imitated his gesture, and the laboratory rang with their voices, which intoned: Fortune! Fortune! Fortune!

I sat down next to Vi, walking through the crowd of

assertive ghosts, and she looked at me: in an instant the crowd disappeared. I had made her lose her concentration and thus contact with the satellite. The preacher also popped out of existence like a soap bubble, and silence returned.

"I'd never have believed it," I said.

She took off her monocle, which was linked to an earphone.

"If you had been born naked, you would also trust in Fortune."

"We were all born naked."

She shook her head.

"My father is able to transform anything he touches. Bits of wood, rope, boxes, rings, every object obeys him and becomes something else, a flying sled, a puppet theater, a dolls house ... and my mother can materialize anything she thinks of just by expressing it out loud."

"She must have to be very careful of what she says then!" I joked. But I was impressed. Vi's parents were two very powerful Barums.

"Yes, she speaks little and measures every word."

She remained silent for a few seconds, immersed in a private misery.

"I was astonished when she would say *chocolate pudding on the table* and a perfect creamy, sweet pudding would appear," she went on. "I used to play with the animated toys my father created for me, but no matter how hard I tried, I wasn't able to lift a chair with my mind when my ball rolled under it. I could repeat the words *walnut ice cream* forever, but nothing would ever appear. The children of Barums usually show their talents immediately. At first my parents would say *maybe she's a latent; maybe she'll manifest later*. But instead, when I was five, to get dressed I still had to open the wardrobe with my hands. And to reach the shelf where my dolls were kept, I had to climb onto a chair. When I was sixteen I understood that I was naked. A normal, everyday girl who would have to study chemistry, physics, and biology if she ever wanted to alter matter."

A cabbage butterfly passed between us with a fluttering of

mechanical wings. It struggled to flap its two enormous, dark green wings that were too big for its slender three-section body. Each beat was accompanied by a rhythmic grinding. Vi swatted it with her hand, and little wheels scattered all over the floor.

"You created the torto-cat. It's not a genetic hodgepodge or a badly assembled puppet. It's a real chimera," I said.

She gave me an ambiguous look over her purple eye circles, and her subtle mouth twisted into a grimace. "You haven't been going around gossiping about what we do here, have you?" she asked.

As an answer I welded my lips shut with my finger. She brushed the subtle line of the weld with her fingertips.

Was she checking that they were really welded shut? Was she attracted to welds? I only know that my throat tightened and my heart skipped a beat. Then she got up and went to work in the vegetable garden, leaving me sitting on the floor like an idiot with the beginnings of an erection between the folds of my trousers.

The torto-cat was our Trojan horse. Vi had managed to soften old Pavlova's heart, and from then on, she would send us her "leftovers," i.e. puppies whose fur was not quite shiny enough or not the right shade of color, those that had non-standard ears or a twisted tail.

If students had a hard time finding organic material on which to work, imagine how hard it could be for them to find live, healthy animals. But for us it was different. Every Saturday Pavlova would select the newborn puppies, and every Monday a courier would knock on the door, and shout, "Parcel!"

I would sign the receipt and take possession of a box that stank of vomit and wet hair to the sound of whining and yelping. I would open the box, and twenty bright eyes would look up at me in the hope of receiving warmth and food. Like all our puppies, they didn't know that their fate was to be transformed.

The state of the art in biology only contemplated two forms of mutation, and Vi refused to follow either one.

"Neither cancer nor genes," she had explained to me.

"This is a factory. Actually, it's a tailor's shop."

It was, in fact, more like a workshop: she designed the models, chose the living materials, and still yelping, she assessed the decorations, eyes, teeth, paws, tails, and then she cut in her oblique and irregular style. Then it was my turn, a human stapler. I put everything back together as per her detailed instructions.

She had an unusual goal: ugliness.

"Repulsiveness is the new attraction," she explained to me while she was planning to join the body of a miniature Pinscher to the great head of Rottweiler.

"Maybe you're right. The only problem is supporting a cranium that weighs three kilos on a body that barely weighs half as much."

From the instrument trolley she took a metal ring, and with the brusque gesture of snapping open a fan, it telescoped in a series of concentric circles all joined together: a steel neck.

"I've never welded living flesh to metal before."

"Well, now's the time to see if you can."

She was always so sure of what she wanted. When I was with her I was able to believe that I could do anything, that all I needed was to take just one more step, make just one more little effort, et voilà, the most elusive thing was within my reach.

She waited, patient and focused, for me to decide to act while she held a strip of muscle with a pair of tweezers just above the first ring. I stretched out the pinkie of my right hand—I always used that finger for tricky connections—and I pressed down delicately.

"Like that. Keep it there. Don't move. Wait."

Her voice, muffled by the mask, was a hoarse and passionate whisper. The metal was heating up slowly. The dark red fibers stretched and softened while the fluids hissed with the lightness of champagne bubbles. Drops of sweat trickled into my eyes, and I had to bat my eyelids to get rid of them. This meant that the hormones were working and had made me lose the thick arc of hair that had recently crowned my orbital bone.

"Now! Let go!"

I removed my finger. It was pulsating, red and inflamed, but the joint was perfect, invisible. It really looked like the muscles and tendons of the Rottweiler's head grew out of the steel ring.

I was amazed by the nature of the result.

After five days' convalescence the dog was on its feet, and the laboratory echoed with the sound of barking. Vi had been able to conserve the Rottweiler's powerful throat. In the absence of the mighty chest, the animal used its new neck as a sounding board. The result sounded like the Hound of the Baskervilles howling inside a boiler tube, distant and unsettling enough to make your skin creep.

The animal walked erect and proud on its miniature Pinscher paws, making a delicate pitter patter sound while the ruff of the metal circlets gave it an air of an Ottoman Janissary when it was stretched out and a certain likeness to Queen Elizabeth I when retracted.

I wasn't sure what we were supposed to do with the regal mutt, but my task was to feed it. That meant that I had to prowl around the department, scavenging in the bins of the operating theaters. It wasn't fun. I had to fight over bones with students studying for their anatomy exams. You can imagine how aggressive they became as their examination dates loomed.

On the other hand, for hearts, lungs, bits of liver, and intestines, I had to fight researchers from microbiology and pharmacology, who needed tissue on which to carry out their experiments.

At lunchtime, when the operations finished, I would wait outside the door of an operating theater with my metal container, surrounded by a surging mass of crazed students who shoved me and tried to climb over me. I received elbows, fists, slaps, spits, and bites. Thankfully, the pituitary hormones had inflated my pectorals, biceps, and deltoids. My back could have withstood a battering ram. I was a bastion of muscles like a dam against a tide of monsters!

A nurse would stretch out buckets to us on long poles, and

we would descend on the bloody contents, strewing the entrails all over the place. Intestines were won by whomever pulled the hardest; bits of heart would slip from hand to hand like a freshly caught fish in a second-rate comedy sketch. They were won by whomever had the courage to take hold of one in his teeth and scamper away like a bear with a trout in his mouth.

I had participated in the past in fights like this in order to win a seat in a lecture hall, to listen to the lecturer live. The lecturers all spoke very softly, and only those sitting in the first rows could hear anything. Rich students would buy video recordings of the lectures while the poor ones fought for seats.

Back at the lab, I would boil up the bits of meat then I would purify and distill the proteins to nourish the pup by transfusing them directly via a feeding tube. After a while its hair recovered its shine, and its nose stopped being dry. Vi then ordered me to take it for a walk around the university.

"A proper walk like a real gentleman—no rushing, no fear. Do you know how to strut?"

"Sure!"

I lifted up my arm, flexed the muscles, and showed her my new body in all its masculine power.

First she was surprised, but then she frowned, and asked, "What are you taking?"

"Good stuff," I replied, "judging by your reaction."

She shook her head and said no more. She clipped a platinum leash onto the collar and gave me the handle.

"If anyone stops you and asks where you got the dog, don't say anything. If they want to know how you did it, just smile. If they want to buy if from you, walk on."

All clear.

"And no gossiping," she added when I was at the door.

Silent and serene, I walked through corridors, up and down stairways, along gravel paths, and over wooden bridges, reflected in the pretty ponds of the university gardens. Glances increased as I progressed. Shock, amazement, disgust, hilarity, appreciation, a whole range of emotions that I found ever more burdensome to bear.

Near the great central fountain, the rector, Kelb, greeted

me with deference. He was with his Recognizer of Important People, a young lad with Tash's Syndrome who had been trained to recognize faces even when modified with heavy make-up, latex inserts, or even, as in my case, with hormonal changes. I acknowledged him with a nod and carried on walking. What an old meddler! He was staring unabashed at the dog.

After a few steps I felt a light touch on the shoulder. It was the Recognizer.

"Oh, Supreme Fruit of the Tree of Good and Evil, the Esteemed and Distinguished Archimandrite of All Students would like to know the race of the dog that you deign to show the world."

"And what did you reply?"

Vi was hoeing the furrows of the garden like she was weaving silken threads. I was observing her as I sat on the stone that covered the well, fiddling with a lock of my hair, which now fell onto my shoulders. I was very satisfied with my new look, but she wasn't paying any attention to me.

"I said: 'Elizabethan.'"

Not a muscle of her face even twitched. She gave no sign of being amused by my wittiness. Her melancholy, so deep rooted, so abysmal, attracted me like the edge of a cliff. Oh, to see a smile! To see the little pearls of her teeth peep through her velvet lips! The soft cushion of her smile would have been enough to make me dive headlong into the depths of pessimism.

"Don't you think it's time for you to explain what you want to do?" I said.

"I told you, I want to make money."

But it wasn't true, otherwise she would have checked to see that Pavlova's money was in her bank account instead of flowing through my veins in the form of hormones, but at that moment I was content to accept the lie.

"And you? What are you hiding?" she asked me as she continued with her weeding. "Why would the rector address you in such bombastic terms?"

I shrugged my shoulders.

"He's a pompous old goat with a theatrical vein. He must have confused me with someone else."

"That's just what you want to be, no? Someone else!"

"Yes, Ma'am, and I'm not ashamed to say so. I believe in change."

Vi raised her head and burst out laughing, but with no joy.

"You say 'change,' yet you think that it's always positive."

"Sure it is," I replied heatedly. "It's movement. Movement is better than staying still."

"It depends on the direction," she said.

That was the first time that Vi managed to dint my confidence.

"I improve. Each transformation makes me different from what I was before. It makes me original, unique."

I could hear myself speaking, and it was like listening to a stubborn boy wailing over his broken toy.

She didn't reply. She finished weeding in silence, and with her knife, she cut two heads of lettuce for dinner and dug up a few sweet potatoes.

As stipulated in the ad on the notice board, my remuneration consisted of light yet healthy meals, and we always ate them together.

From the description of her garden, you might think that the way Vi ate was simple, as terse and frugal as her conversation. You would be wrong. She was a complicated eater, very complicated. First of all, she didn't trust State vegetables, and she was right about that. She was lucky enough to own a patch of clean land, which she cultivated herself and which she watered using the water from her well. She lived mostly off raw vegetables picked on days of the waning moon, cut with a ceramic blade, and served on silver plates. She chewed each mouthful forty times. She had forbidden me to speak to her while she was eating. Even when she had finished eating I was only allowed to talk about happy and pleasant topics, lest I affect her digestion.

I devoured the fresh vegetables like a cabbage worm. I

couldn't understand if it was a side effect of the hormones or if I really did especially like what she cultivated.

"Tomorrow you'll meet the person to whom you will deliver the *Elizabethan* dog," said Vi, dabbing at the corners of her mouth with her synthetic linen napkin. "You'll deliver this, too."

She handed me a magnetic card. It was a pass to get into the second year inorganic chemistry lectures.

Early next morning, I took the tram into the center of town.

Seated next to a window, I contemplated a row of detached homes, walls of pickled wood adorned with fretwork where they met the roofs, surrounded by majestic pine trees. I inhaled with pleasure the scent of balsam while the dog, cuddled up at my feet, attracted curious glances from the other passengers. I furtively examined their faces, all made from the same cosmeceutical mold—cheeks of the same curvature, eyebrows of the same thickness, embodied in every shade from plaster white to ash black but all rigorously smooth like sheets of packaging plastic. All of them, males and females, had high and spacious foreheads, a sign of intelligence obtained via the diathermocoagulation of the attachment of their hair.

Some, instead of looking at the dog, looked at me as I stood out amidst their standardized features: I was too tall, too well sculpted, I had too much hair, my lineaments too well marked.

At the address that Vi had given me, there was a pastry shop.

A blue and white awning shaded an elegant door of dark glass. I could smell wafts of caramelized sugar and roasted almonds. I was puzzled but trusted her blindly, or foolishly, I should say. I went in. The floor was made of natural fibers, the walls were rice paper, and there were pretty wooden racks to leave your shoes. Nope, they didn't bake cakes here.

I walked through the front room and found two men and a woman sitting on their heels, backs straight, hands in their laps, eyes half closed.

They were wearing splendid linen tunics cut in accordance

with the rules of "humanist" tailoring so that the sleeves and the hems didn't impede the movement of the owner's arms and legs and conferred an air of elegance. They smelled of wet grass and dew, and their hair was adorned with tendrils of ivy and vines that grew in the pockets of the tunics.

" ... three in Santé Square and another two in Fauxpas Boulevard," said one in an alarmed tone of voice.

"The distributors are everywhere now," said another one.

"And the kids are attracted irresistibly," added the woman.

"I think we should stick to the facts," continued the first one. "Our public condemnation has awakened many consciousnesses, but it's not enough."

"Rats! Rats!" replied the woman, raising her fist.

"I have the seeds," said the third one, holding onto a little cloth bag hanging round his neck.

"War against the State vegetable distributors!"

Ecologists!

If you think that you want to save the planet, then follow their advice.

I greeted them and sat down on the floor, making as much noise as possible. First they just glanced at me, but after they noticed the dog, I had their full attention.

"A large, small marvel," commented the man with the seeds.

"Practical. No problem with encumbrance," added the woman. "Even if you have a small house, you can have a mastiff."

Swishing on its rails, a sliding door opened, and a little brunette woman in a flowery kimono appeared. She had a clean face without any outstanding features—like hundreds of others.

"Who's first?" she asked in an offhand manner.

The ecologist with the seeds stood up.

"I have a funeral to go to in three hours."

"Are there still people who have the bad taste to die?" asked the woman.

"He was a childhood friend," he replied defensively. "I'd like an expression that is fitting to the occasion."

With a gesture she beckoned him to follow. I scratched the dog's belly and impassively fielded the questions from the other two ecologists.

Half an hour later, the client reappeared—changed. The serene expression of a philosopher who has attained Nirvana had given way to a series of frown wrinkles. The muscles of his face were like wax melted in the heat ready to drip away from the frame of the bones to reveal the skull, the penultimate stage before leaping into the Void. On the lower eyelid there was a trembling line of tears, and the forehead was a corrugated field of parallel furrows. The man strode out boldly. I hoped that he would remember to control the rest of his body in an appropriate manner and not turn up at the funeral tap dancing.

The young lady motioned the other two to wait and beckoned to me.

On the other side of the sliding door, there was a chemical laboratory. There were two long ceramic counters covered with beakers, test tubes, and Bunsen burners. The air, saturated with sweet smells, ammonia, and flowery aromas, hit me like a punch in the face. In a corner was an antique barber's chair. A large oval mirror hanging over the chair reflected it completely.

"How did you manage to change his features?" I asked, in reference to the man who had just left.

She picked up a jar that contained a rust-colored gel, stuck a pipette into it, and sprayed a drop onto the corner of my mouth. I felt the muscle pulling down as if an invisible hand were pulling the skin downwards and holding it there with a pin.

"Bacteria," she replied, positioning me in front of the mirror. Half my mouth was drooping melancholically, and the other half was happy like a schizophrenic clown.

"It stings."

"He who wants to look sincere has to suffer a bit. In any case the effect wears off in about five hours. Once the bacteria have consumed the phosphorus in the culture, they can't survive for long."

I noticed that, on the cuff of her kimono, she wore a

curious paper brooch in the shape of a frog.

Vi had told me, "She'll be the same as the others, but she won't renounce an original detail."

I gave her the dog and the pass for the chemistry lectures, which seemed kind of superfluous to me, given the resources she had here.

She took the lead and the magnetic card.

"I can make your eyebrows grow back in half an hour," she said.

"Why?"

"You lack a frame. The eyebrows are the frame of the emotions. Take them away and you are incomplete."

"I am already beautiful, thanks."

"Uh oh, it's more serious than I thought," she said

"You may think it strange, but I paid money not to have eyebrows."

"Who's your cosmetic consultant? Fire him. He does a terrible job."

Before I could reply, the shameless hussy had pushed me out of the room.

"Next!" she called.

Microcephalous dwarf! Photocopy with legs! Eyeless aphasic!

I bathe in the envy of others, both male and female. They undress me with their eyes. They sniff the air I stir. I am *homo novus*, imperfect and luminous. I don't need to abide by the golden mean! My supreme virtue is expressed in a short yet powerful phrase: I am me. How many of you lot, copies of copies, can say the same?

I strode out quickly, my head heavy as if it had been beaten with hammers. The people out walking got out of my way and eyed me warily. All, all of them would have loved to capture me! I am a free being, and I swim against the current. The pain in my temples became unbearable.

I stopped in front of a public food distributor, the bugbear of the ecologists. Hot and cold soups, tasty looking pies, garishly colorful mixed salads. Ever since Vi had been providing for me, I hadn't touched the stuff. The State vegetables were devoid of vitamins and minerals. If you ate too many of them, they made your skin wrinkle and your intestines shrink.

Some people had even gone back to meat in order to avoid them.

They even said that they were addictive. Maybe it was true, but at that moment I didn't care. I rummaged in my pockets and found the pre-loaded card I kept for emergencies. I shouldn't have used it. I knew I was about to do something stupid, but I had to do it.

Card, slot, pay, mechanical clicking inside, three carrots in the delivery tray. Three beautiful, bright orange carrots with the tuft of greenery included. My new teeth, long and strong, crunched them with pleasure, and the tension left me. Even my headache went away.

Finals had started.

The poor students wandered aimlessly along the corridors holding their heads in their hands, moaning softly or gibbering; or they sat in corners chewing on coke bars, engrossed in reading up on how cyanobacteria split solar radiation, or some such. Shame that they forgot to turn the pages. Some tried to organize study groups—to no avail—and some bedded down in sleeping bags in the library with tins of liquid food and Benzedrine tablets.

Vi seemed calm. She had cancelled all new deliveries of the dogs and passed the time revising the fundamentals of obstetrics and gynecology, the final exam which she had to sit.

I, on the other hand, scrutinized my face in every reflecting surface that I could find. I would twist my mouth, puff out my cheeks, squeeze my eyelids. Was it just my imagination, or were my temples coming forward, naked and shameless? The curvature of my forehead was expanding, my sublime curls were receding, my smooth scalp was advancing, triumphant.

I could recognize the forehead of my father.

The almond shape of my eyes was becoming rounder, my sparse eyelashes were becoming thicker, my sinister look was giving way to a visus intelligens.

The eyes of my mother.

The hormonal magic was wearing off. I would have to go back to Aye and buy another hit of pituitary hormones, but my purse was empty. The Elizabethan dog had not provided any cash. I didn't understand why Vi had given it for free to the aesthetician, and I couldn't ask her—she had forbidden me to speak to her. Every morning she practiced dissecting virtual pelvises generated by an old surgery program. Every now and then the system crashed, and when she was rummaging around in the bladder looking for the uterus, the images would scatter in a fluttering confusion of colors and tissues and nerves and then it would reboot from the beginning and show an intact abdomen again. She never lost her patience and would start again, making her first incision with her laser scalpel. The program was so realistic that it was necessary to use the spreaders and clamps to hold back the flaps of the openings.

After a whole day spent studying, she would hook up to the Sphere and listen to her favorite preacher, Mister Lucky.

"Today I will speak to you of our enemies, dear brothers and sisters in prosperity."

Once again the lab was invaded by hundreds of virtual people sitting on the floor, their rapturous faces turned toward their idol.

"Our enemies are the unlucky people," he spat out angrily, "that feckless tribe of losers who just stand and wait to be afflicted by adversity, who patiently bear their illnesses, dismissals, assaults, and accidents. The modern Jobs who accept any blow of fortune, bow their heads saying, 'It's my fate,' saying, 'It's bad luck,' saying, 'C'est la vie!' No, brothers and sisters! It's not fate! It's their own fault! They are the only ones to blame for what happens to them!"

The speech was becoming interesting. I sat down to listen.

"The unlucky ones!" Each time he said those word it was like he was chewing on rotten food. "They are easily recognized, the hapless ones. They are the ones who, when newly born, end up in an incubator because they are weak, sickly, and premature. As children, they fall down a lot, break their bones, and seriously injure themselves. As teenagers, their peers look at them askance. During exams they get all the difficult questions—even ones about the footnotes! During job interviews they get the hostile selection panels. If they get married, it's to the wrong person, who will cause them suffering and unhappiness. Every abomination happens to the unfortunate ones."

"Poor people," I murmured ironically. Vi signaled me to keep quiet.

"And what's the paradox when we talk about these despicable people, my fortunate friends?"

Pause.

"They don't believe in Fortune!" shouted the apostle of good luck.

The audience gasped.

"Precisely. They maintain that human beings can create their destiny by themselves without the help of Our Great Goddess!"

"You underestimate hormones," I said loudly.

The preacher stared at me.

"There are some unbelievers amongst us. Do you have something to dispute with Fortune, lucky brother? You are healthy and good-looking and judging by your clothes, well-off, too. Everything about you speaks of a favorite of the supreme goddess. What are your grievances?"

"Physiology determines luck," I replied, holding his fiery eyes. "The hypothalamus and the pituitary release and control the most important hormones that determine our behavior. The unlucky ones are weak because their posterior pituitary secretes little oxytocin, and this makes them incapable of facing up to the difficulties of life. They are looked on with little sympathy because they have little thyrotropin. Little thyrotropin means fatigue, muscular lassitude, no physical or mental vigor. You look at them and say, 'Insects!' For this reason their bosses think they are incompetent and give them boring and repetitive jobs."

"You believe in the body," replied the preacher, pointing at me with his index finger, arm outstretched.

"Is there anything else?"

He froze in a tragic pose, his mouth open and his hands cupped over his ears in an attempt not to hear. Even the faces of the virtual public froze over in a display of shock and indignation. Vi had stopped the hook-up.

"Who are you?" she blurted out. "The ghost of some twentieth-century doctor? You know nothing of behavioral physiology. You're just a welder. You emit sounds and think that they are thoughts. Go and clean the garden, go on!"

She waved her hands to shoo me out.

Humiliated by her words, instead of standing up, I scuttled away on all fours toward the sliding glass door that separated the lab from the outside. In the meantime Vi had muttered "sawbones" to herself indignantly and re-established the link to the Sphere.

I weeded for an hour, and then she came out to join me. Her turquoise irises shone like pools of clear water at the bottom of the dark pits of the bags under her eyes. The meetings of Lucky Nation invigorated her like a flash of Resurrection. She approached and lifted up my hair as if she were looking for something near my face. A surge of heat pierced my breast. She took my right hand. Only then did I notice that the skin of her hands, small and slender, was marked by countless scars. I hadn't noticed before because Vi almost always wore latex gloves. Mastering the scalpel had cost her flesh and blood.

First she examined the back of my hands, then the palms. It seemed like she was looking for something.

"Acromegaly," she said

"That's your impression. I'm just well developed."

She flicked the tip of my nose with her finger.

"When you first arrived, you didn't have that bell pepper in the place of your nose. You had a nice normal nose in proportion to your face."

I blushed, more for having been touched by her rather than for what she had said.

"And your ears? You're always looking at yourself in the mirror. Have you looked at your ears recently? They've turned into enormous tropical shells. If the wind blew into them, you could use them as foghorns!"

I smiled, embarrassed.

"I just want to be me. I don't want to look like anyone else."

Vi sat down on the little wall around the well.

"What is *myself*?" she retorted. "Whoever heard of such a thing? How can you choose to be someone that you don't know?"

I rolled my hand and opened the Sphere—a great error—as unfortunately my photo files were there in my family page. I deleted headers and captions and showed her what I meant by "the real me."

"This is me at eight months."

My grandmother was holding me in her arms and was showing us our reflections in an old mirror in the living room of the house on the shores of the Mare Serenitatis. The photo had the grace of a candid snapshot and the solemnity of an official portrait: an old lady from high lunar society and a naked infant staring wide-eyed in the presence of an undeniable human phenomenon—recognition of oneself in a mirror.

"Here you can glimpse my real face," I continued. "Here I am really me."

"I don't understand what you mean. We are all a bit like Frankenstein: the nose of the father, the mouth of the mother, the eyebrows of the grandfather, the eyes of the grandmother. We are dolls made with bits of others sewn together and infused with life by the spark of conception."

"But in this photo I can still see the blank sheet before the genetics of my forefathers wrote over it!"

Vi crossed her arms and shook her shaven head.

"You're wrong. You're wrong about everything. It's in the psychic substrate that atrocities are committed."

She was always able to surprise me.

"You've never realized. No one ever does. It seems normal because it's invisible. You're trying to cancel your physical inheritance, but you're forgetting that parents implant their ambitions, their fears, their dreams, and their moral judgements. Whose are the thoughts we think?"

I was speechless.

"Here's an example," she went on. "Is my passion for creative surgery really *mine* or is it a sentiment of my father's?"

I leaned over the flower bed and heatedly ripped up some weeds then threw them onto the stones of the path. The prospect was making my head spin. Maybe even the search for myself could be an act foreign to the real me.

Vi made as if to leave.

"And luck?" I stopped her. "What's luck got to do with anything?"

"When you have something important to do, you have to curry favor with the gods."

A few days later Vi stuffed some fresh fruit and roasted vegetables into a natural fiber backpack.

"I have to ask you a favor," she said to me.

She knew that I would do anything for her.

"Defend the lab."

I sprang to attention and clicked my heels.

"They will get more than they bargained for, my commander!"

And off she went to face one of her most difficult finals, whistling Brahms's lullaby.

I bolted the door shut, fastened all the latches, and set the alarm.

Silence reigned all around me. All the other students had abandoned their strongholds to sit their finals. I spent the time lying down in the garden, cooling my back against the humid earth. If I got hungry I would reach out my hand, pull up a radish, and eat it raw, skin and top and all. I yawned with boredom and tried to hit the cabbage butterflies with my key-ring laser. I liked the metallic noise they made when they fell onto the rocky path.

Asprillian insects is what they were called, in honor of the scientist who had invented them and released them into the environment. They were supposed to carry out pollination in place of the extinct insects, but they had turned out to be a rip-off.

On the third day the incessant chirping of a cricket drew me out of my lethargy, and the burglar alarm was saying that someone was trying to break into the lab through the door.

Barefoot, I approached the dark glass rectangle. On the other side I could hear a furtive scraping then suddenly two objects slid through the crack under the door. I squatted down and watched, fascinated. They were two skeletal fingers, flattened and formed by proximal and distal phalanges joined by a cartilaginous glue. The fingers were followed by fragments of carpal articulations without the metacarpals and a short ulna.

When the skeletal arm started to curl upwards toward one of the latches, I realized what this was all about. It was an osteoarticular jimmy.

I looked around. On a shelf was the perfect weapon with which to counterattack. The fingers had already slid back the first latch and were crawling toward the second when I sprayed them with extra-strength acetic acid. Sizzling, the bones crumbled away in seconds. The stink of burnt calcium must have reached the other side of the door, too, because the burglars quickly withdrew what was left of the arm and I heard them swearing under their breath.

"Go and do some studying, you useless good-for-nothings," I shouted.

There was a brief whispered confabulation on the other side of the door. The presence of a person inside made any more attempted burglary useless. The lab belonged to whomever was inside it. They left.

At sunset of the fifth day, Vi returned.

She threw down her empty backpack, flushed and euphoric, the medal of the final exam showing proudly branded onto a shoulder next to the ones for harmonic physiology and sympathetic biochemistry. She hugged me impulsively.

I wasn't expecting it, just like I wasn't expecting her to kiss me. On my cheeks, on my chin, on my mouth, a shower of kisses that became ever more insistent while her fingers fumbled under my shirt, undid zips, tore at clothing.

I know what you are thinking. Sly woman uses her cunt

to ensnare a young man of good prospects. Nope, you're on the wrong track. Vi was not like that. There was never any premeditation in her acts, not in those acts. Her cup was full, the foam was overflowing, and I was glad that it was me that was getting wet on the floor between the surgical instrument trolley and the shelves of entrails. Her eyes were two glaucous slits in the twin moons of the bags under her eyes, her smell more feral than usual, five days that she hadn't washed. I groped her bony hips with my fingers, her buttocks hard as unripe apples, and among the hairs of her chalice, I broke through the skin of her fruit.

I'm lucky, I thought. I'm Fortune's favorite. I didn't call her. In fact, I ignored her. Nevertheless, she gave me what I wanted.

Lady Luck came—no lewd comments please—and then she left.

The next day Vi behaved as if nothing had happened. She was still floating on a cloud of exultation, but it wasn't directed at me. I had become invisible. At midmorning a delivery arrived from the university: twelve *sapiens sapiens* at various stages of development from pinkish tadpoles to big-headed larvae, all sealed up in glass jars. Vi lined them up on the counter and contemplated them as if entranced.

"Madame Pavlova will supply us with more puppies," she told me. "Let's get back to work."

We became a human cut-n-sew machine. She dissected fine slices of human craniums, eyes, and noses, and I welded them onto the faces of different animals. The mandatory step went from fetus to dog because the limbs of the slimy *sapiens sapiens* weren't developed enough to allow them to trot behind their owners. Twelve dogs and twelve fetuses. A tour de force that obliged us to combine and recombine the beasts in the most unusual ways. At twenty-five weeks the fetuses had a curious off-white down, especially around the eyebrows and upper lip, that made them resemble miniature doubles of Santa Claus. Vi made the most of this characteristic to mix them in to fox terriers that had come out badly (they didn't have any brown and black spots) to obtain animals with curly, ivory-white hair with the characteristic long snout but with big languid, infantile eyes. You expected them to say "Hi" to you at any moment, but instead they whined and whimpered as the effects of the anesthetic wore off.

The wrinkled skin of the fetuses found its natural expression in the bulldogs, whose heads were softened with a less slobbery mouth and a smaller nose.

At the end of the last operation, my fingertips were aflame, smeared with blood, lymph, and some colloidal material where we conserved the little *sapiens*. I stuck them for five minutes into the dead material disintegrator and then into the sterilizer. The jets of peroxide burned my skin, and the muck under my fingernails flew away.

Vi staggered exhausted toward a little cupboard that was locked. She opened it, and two great loaves of bread fell onto her. She bit into one greedily. The whole cupboard was full of bread—bread with raisins, with nuts, with chocolate chips, made with white flour, with cornmeal, and with buckwheat; just the smell was enough to start you salivating.

Bread! Bread! After months of eating raw chicory and tomatoes! I devoured an entire baguette and then I dug into a fig loaf.

"You have to take them to the beauty clinic," Vi mumbled with her mouth full. "The dogs. You have to take them to the ecologists. As soon as they become adults."

I nodded my head without understanding. Became adults? The dogs or the ecologists?

Vi continued to stuff herself until her stomach, used to simple foods, couldn't take any more. She fell asleep, and, by the time I was putting the dogs into a regenerating fluid, she was already snoring.

A few days later, the aesthetician greeted me with a malevolent smile.

"So, you followed my advice! You look much better now."

In the lobby of the "pastry shop," there was a mirror. I looked at myself and screamed. I had gone back to looking like I did before! I threw the baskets into the girl's arms.

"Give me the money," I spat out.

She laughed.

"When I sell the goods."

"No, now! Immediately! Call your ecologist friends and tell them that the dogs are here."

I must have been very threatening or maybe desperate because she coughed up the cash.

A few hours later I was at the Institute of Biology looking for Aye with my pockets stuffed full of enough money to buy all the pituitary hormone on Earth!

"Aye?" said a student, batting her lashless eyelids. "Don't you know? He's gone."

"Gone? Gone where?"

She stretched out her arm and opened her fingers as if freeing an insect trapped in her fist.

"Into the world, into life. He has graduated."

I never thought that that lazy good-for-nothing actually studied seriously.

"Listen, I need pure hypophysial extract. Can you get me some?"

She looked at me, stunned, and then burst out laughing, showing me her toothless gums.

I tried to get to the exit, but in the meantime I had been surrounded by a crowd of students who were trying to suck my toes, grasping my legs but slipping off of the impermeable plastic with which I had protected myself. I kicked out at those vile beings and tried my question on some other biology students—there were still some who walked upright and with dignity.

"Do you think that if I had any pituitary hormone to analyze, I would give it to you?" retorted one.

Exasperated and tired, I shuffled out into the garden.

I avoided the fountains and mirrors of water. The last thing I wanted to see was my *familiar* image. I would have attempted to drown myself.

At sunset the sound of drumming drew me toward the center of the park. A student party had started. A hermaphrodite from pharmacology sold me a box of serotonin sweets, which I devoured avidly, and I immediately fell into a euphoria that stayed with me for the duration of the party.

I returned to the laboratory in the wee small hours. Vi had risen and was sitting in the garden, still half stunned from her bread binge, with her elbow poised over a cauliflower and caressing the crisp, young lettuces with her hand. She raised her eyes, darker than usual, and smiled at me, only just slightly curving her pallid lips. That smile was not for me. It was the reflex of an intimate secret joy, but I didn't understand then. I couldn't understand.

"It's you," she said.

"No, it's not me. I'm the other one, my parent's creation."

"You only have to decide to use your freedom."

"You change reality with your scalpel, I do it with my method."

"There is no real you to which you can return," replied Vi. "When will you realize that?"

"I am a welder," I replied. But it was a half-truth. I could join, and I could separate. I struggled to keep together the fragments of the "real me" without deciding to separate myself from my family, from the dregs of thought, from all the mistaken ideas built up over the years of false behaviors.

She ruffled the leaves of the lettuce, and then she burped, but quietly.

"There are choices to be made. Each choice, a renunciation; each renunciation, a modification."

At certain moments Vi seemed to be full of wisdom and foresight. To look at her, I would have said we were of the same age, but who can tell how old anyone is these days? We are all young and foolish.

The full moon looked down at us over the top of the wall. The lights of Lunaria, the capital, nullified the shadows of the Seas and twinkled like a handful of sequins stuck to the face of a ruddy-cheeked student ready to go out on the town.

I curled up with my head on my knees, oppressed by so

much light. I was in a dark mood, and I only wanted darkness around me.

In two months dog mania broke out.

The ecologists had each been going about at the end of a leash, and at the other end of each leash was one of our dogs: a wizened stovepipe that hobbled along on short inverted legs, paws turned inward, and a round, puffed-up face with a mouth like a duck's ass under large, curious, and attentive eyes, as only an animal hungry for knowledge of the world can have.

Vi's creativity exploded. She made neo-dogs with velvety nails so they couldn't scratch their owners' furniture and clothes; neo-dogs with fringed ears for those nostalgic for Westerns; micro-cephalous lapdogs with three heads that could suck a rudimentary thumb; and even a Chihuahua with a mouth in the shape of a vulva and a tiny penis for a tail. The vulva went yap-yap, and the little dick wagged when the dog saw its owner.

The production of dogs continued at a constant rate, and every time we made a new "model," Vi sent it to the aesthetician. I never did find out her name nor were we ever introduced. I called her Phryne, sure that she would be too ignorant to catch the mockery.

Phryne sold the neo-puppies, kept her commission, and gave me the rest of the money, which I didn't know what to do with. Without Aye, without any pituitary hormones, I avoided all reflecting surfaces and all social events. When I wasn't working, I wandered around the department reading the graffiti on the walls before the self-cleaning paint could eliminate them.

A musical surgery band looking for patients with stones in the gallbladder promised that one jam session would dissolve them. I thought it more likely they'd bore my balls off. A string quartet offered its services for realigning vertebrae and for improving the state of the inter-disk cartilage. They claimed to be able to modify my facial features by bowing in a quick four-four time, and I would have my old face restored without any of the false features of my forebears. I took down their room number, but then I had second thoughts. The music would only be a temporary fix, not a treatment.

As I was returning to the laboratory, I spied a familiar face in the middle of a crowd of students who were pushing and shoving, trying to get into the Chemistry lecture room.

"Phryne, what are you doing here?"

She turned away, pretending not to know me.

"A person like you should be giving a chemistry lecture, not going to listen to one."

Eighty eyes were suddenly staring at her. One second she was a student like all the others, the next she was like a supernatural phenomenon. She felt the eyes on her, oppressing her. With her head bowed she squeezed my arm and dragged me to a corner.

"Are you crazy? If they find me out, I risk being crippled!"

I had seen them around. People had been crippled, hacked, and mutilated, depending on the department that they had tried to infiltrate without being matriculated at the university.

"I want to produce cosmetics," she went on, "and I don't have the basics. The chemists are very jealous of their knowledge."

"I need your help."

"I can make you ugly. It's the new fashion. Ugly is the new sexy."

I wasn't even listening to her.

"If I wanted a higher forehead, for example, or a more pronounced jaw, what would you advise me?"

Phryne weighed me up, sucking in her cheeks.

"I would need double-action bacteria, myolytic and myo-reconstructive."

"How long would their effect last?"

"Bring me some more dogs and we can talk about it," she replied.

~*~

Phryne analyzed my cranium and my muscles with an instrument similar to an ultrasound machine. She obtained a 3-D image on which she worked with her fingers, following my instructions. She lengthened my eyes, puffed out my cheeks, made my mouth more subtle, the cheekbones lower, the chin rounder—she added a dimple in the center on her own initiative—until all those features transformed me into a different person.

"Perfect," I exclaimed when she had finished.

She grimaced.

"An aged baby," she muttered.

I lay back in the barber's chair and underwent the treatment: massage with smelly ointment, hundreds of micro-injections. It was like being attacked in the face by a swarm of bees covered with a mysterious substance, which, when it dried, pulled at every muscle fiber, forcing me to open my mouth wide. Phryne, unconcerned, stuck a saliva ejector into it and continued working.

She put the 3-D image over my head and with a sort of plastic spatula, began to push, pull, press, and curl, making my real features match up with the virtual model. My face felt as soft as the icing on a cake. And I wasn't totally wrong in likening myself to a dessert. After having shaped me to her complete satisfaction, she placed my chair parallel to the floor and stuck my head into a horizontal cylinder fitted with a porthole —basically an oven for human soufflés. Slow cooking for at least one hour.

When she pulled me out, I asked her for a mirror.

"Don't speak," she warned me. "You're still hot."

In fact, my skin burned as if I had scalded myself with boiling water. I could feel my cranium pulsating with each breath like a meringue about to crack.

She handed me a round mirror, and I greeted the new me. On the other side of the glass, my reflection reciprocated by widening his eyes, stolid and happy like the rector's Recognizer with Tash's syndrome.

"You have to rest for at least 24 hours," said Phryne. She made me get up, took me to another room, and after helping me lie down on a litter, she left.

I sighed. On a little table were some magazines. I picked one up, *L'ami du chien*. The cover article was singing the praises of "The Age of the Dog."

"A man and his dog," we say, because nowadays the dog is all that one can have in terms of love. Human beings are no longer willing to sacrifice time and passion for other human beings. Why love another when I can love myself?

There were also a few pictures, some of badly made chimeras twisted, patched up, the tongue too long, the teeth too big for the mouth, the ears misaligned, the animal-like snouts too menacing or stultified by the purity of the alleles.

I turned over the page and almost fell out of the litter in surprise.

The centerfold was of one of our dogs. An ecologist was holding the dog in his arms. A proud neo-father with his neo-dog.

The round cranium and wide forehead of the dog dominated the picture. Two subtle arches of white fluff framed the translucent eyelids from fetus to the twenty-fourth week; the delicate snub nose stuck out all rosy like a bud, and the mouth was drooling, showing the baby carnivorous teeth. Oh, those teeth! They cost me blood, sweat, and tears every work session. Vi would extract them from miniature puppy bull terriers, cutting into the jaw, and I would prepare a channel in the bone of the fetus and insert those tiny four-cusp pebbles, slimy with blood and mucus. Then I would weld them into place. They would always slip out of my fingers and roll over the floor of the lab and get stuck in the cracks between the broken tiles.

The dog was smiling angelically, leaning on its forepaws, which were covered with white hair. Seraphim model. All it was missing was a pair of wings on its back.

The article was gushing about the new species of *canis canis*, whose features made it the ideal companion for whomever wanted a guardian angel in the house. The following pages contained images of other models: the Napoleon, with a massive head and an expression of insolent boredom in the wrinkles of its mouth; the Owl, with haunting eyes in which a glimmer of human intelligence could be discerned; and the most popular, the Attila, for which Vi had used some Tasmanian devil puppies—long bite, fangs, opaque pupils, and slit eyes.

I stayed at Phryne's for three days, sleeping and resting. At the end of the third day, she gave me an ointment and kicked me out.

I set off for the department, and during my walk, I was able to experience the force and extent of the canine phenomenon firsthand or, better yet, "firstfoot."

The hour before sunset was when people took their dogs out for a walk.

The preferred meeting place was the Boulevard de la Merde, a mile and a half of marble sidewalks and lawns bordered with cypresses.

Apart from our animals, the most popular articles on display were air-stilts—two long, metal box-like affairs which fastened to the shoes using straps like roller skates without wheels. Clicking your heels together would raise you over a foot above the surface. The dog owner could thus walk carefree, greet other owners, look around, relaxed and smiling while lengthening the leash to allow nature to take its course.

But not me.

I was the only one unfortunate enough not to own any air-stilts.

Sidewalks, roads, and lawns were covered in a layer of canine excreta, an extended geology of fresh shit over dry shit over even more compacted unbreakable shit. It stuck to my sandals and with each step, increased in thickness under the soles. I think I must have gained seven or eight inches in height.

However, since the facial makeover had altered my olfactory membranes, I could hardly smell the stench that emanated from the ground, making me think that maybe I ought to believe in luck.

I met Rector Kelb again, who was taking his Napoleon (Cerberus sub-variant) for a walk, three fetal crania on which we had implanted Doberman ears and greyhound necks, all mounted on a bulldog body. He didn't greet me. Phryne's bacterial mask had rendered me invisible.

I don't know how I managed to cross that disgusting mile and a half, but I eventually returned to the lab.

Vi was engaged in a heated argument with a man whom I had never seen before.

"I don't believe that."

After having listened in silence for nearly an hour, the Judge stopped Kieser's story, waving her hands impatiently and signaling the stenographer to underline that last phrase.

The interrogation room seemed to wake up as if from a spell. The Captain, a man with curly hair, moved away from the wall that he had been leaning against the whole time. The young Lieutenant, the top button of his uniform tight against his throat, made as if to stretch.

Kieser shrugged. "I didn't know who he was."

"But you knew everything about Victoire Mizanekristos." The Judge, a woman with white hair, enrobed in a purple toga, leaned toward Kieser, awaiting his answer. His skin was fresh and shining while still showing some expressive wrinkles around the eyes and mouth.

"I thought she was called Vikananda Theodora Stern," replied Kieser.

The Judge made an impatient gesture with her hand.

"Why did the man come to see you?"

The Judge gestured toward a glass of water on the tray on the table, and the stenographer, solicitous, handed it to her.

"Rumors were circulating. Someone must have told him where to go to get a fashionable dog."

"Did Vi not introduce you?" interjected the Lieutenant. "You went into the lab and ... nothing? She didn't say or do anything?"

The Judge almost choked on her water, the Captain winced. Kieser gave the Lieutenant a short cold glance and then looked away.

"I meant to say ..." stammered the Lieutenant. "Oh, Sidereal, Immense, Unattainable—"

The Captain made a peremptory gesture; and the Lieutenant shut up, and then he made him follow him out of the room.

"What a boor!" murmured Kieser

"We are most sorry, Oh Golden Fruit of the Tree of Good and Evil. I beg for your indulgence."

The door had remained ajar, and the angry voice of the Captain could be heard from the corridor.

"I chose you because you know the protocol! You can't speak to him as if he were a purse snatcher!"

With a gesture the Judge ordered the stenographer to close the door. The room was once again filled with pregnant silence as before the incident.

"So," began the Judge, "you went back to the lab, and you saw Victoire engaged in a conversation with a stranger. Can you describe him to us, Oh Sublime Jewel?"

"Tall, lanky, lively, white hair. Natural hair. When I entered, he glanced at me distractedly. I think he must have thought I was Vi's assistant—sometimes the University assigns one to the head of a lab."

The Captain and the Lieutenant came back into the room, trying to make as little noise as possible.

"Did you know who that man was?" continued the Judge.

"No."

The Judge squinted at him. "I'll tell you who he was. He was the cleverest thief of the *Civil Society* organization.

Kieser's face showed that he had registered the information but nothing more.

"You heard their conversation," continued the Judge.

"Only the last exchange. Vi said to him, 'So, are we agreed for the day after tomorrow?' He replied, 'I recommend the Seraphim,' and then they shook hands."

The Captain and the Judge exchanged a glance.

"They had just reached an agreement," summarized the Judge. "A verbal agreement."

Kieser shrugged his shoulders. "If you say so."

The Judge straightened up, irritated.

"The perfect laboratory assistant. You didn't see anything,

you didn't hear anything, and you didn't understand anything that was happening."

"Careful how you speak, Your Rightness. I have voluntarily offered my collaboration and could just as easily change my mind."

"You knew of that obscene exchange," she said, looking him in the eye.

"Are you accusing me of complicity, Your Rightness?"

The atmosphere in the room had become very tense. The Captain intervened.

"Would you like something to drink, Oh Golden Fruit of the Tree of Good and Evil?"

Kieser relaxed and leaned back in the chair.

"Yes, please. I'll have a *Thousand Meters* tea."

The Captain's face puckered up in consternation.

"Oh, how silly of me," said Kieser. "I forgot we're not on the Moon. A cold melota will do fine."

The Captain turned to the Lieutenant and sent him in search of the drink.

"Carry on with your story," said the Judge, turning to Kieser.

After the mysterious man had left, Vi looked me in the face.

"Does it hurt?" she asked.

"It's a bit tight in my cheeks, but I don't feel any pain."

It was true. The bacteria worked discretely, but I still wasn't happy with the new me. I felt slow and distracted. I made the same mistake twice on the easy dissection of the ears of an Italian Pomeranian, and Vi had to intervene with her scalpel. It was necessary to redo some welds and cover them with thicker hair than usual.

She didn't say anything, and she didn't seem impatient or annoyed. She remedied all my mistakes and in the end obtained what had been requested of her: a Seraphim with the ears and proud expression of a Napoleon, and the teeth of an Attila.

Three days later, the man who had commissioned the beast turned up to take possession of it. The dog still wasn't in a fit state to be transported, but he insisted. He was in a hurry —that, I remember well—in a big hurry. He was constantly looking over his shoulder as if he was expecting a pursuer to jump out at him at any moment.

He left a parcel. No money. Only a heavy object wrapped up in dark paper on which two warnings had been stamped: *Fragile* and *This End Up*.

Vi wasn't in. She had gone to the library to consult some texts on creative surgery. I was too involved in the study of my new head, deducing that inside my cranium there had to be a walnut-sized lump of grey matter. Maybe the "real me" had dried up due to excessive thinking. Maybe I had buzzed around the same flower too much. The result was a head like a wilted flower wearing an expression of dazed stupidity.

The fact is, I took what I was given, and I handed over what I was meant to without bothering too much about what I was taking and handing over.

As I said, I had no idea who that man was. You say that he was a thief from the Civil Society, and I don't doubt it for a minute; but even if I had known that at the time, how could I have deduced what Vi was up to?

When I gave her the parcel, it was like Vi was frozen. By now I knew her well enough to know that the thicker the crust of ice over her emotions, the more violent and wild were the emotions being covered up.

I was seated next to the well, fretting about my mistake when she threw a sponge impregnated with a dense liquid into my lap.

"Wipe off your face. I need you."

The sponge smelled of salt water, of sun-dried sand, of fresh algae. I rubbed it all over my face, and in a few moments, Phryne's work crumbled. I was afraid. It seemed that the flesh itself was peeling away from the bones, and I tried to stop it falling off with my hands. I found my fingers dirty with a transparent goo that stuck to my skin and that tried to grasp onto the derma. I rubbed my hands and face with the sponge and could almost hear the bacteria screaming. My idiocy died with them.

Vi was waiting for me at the operating table.

She had already anaesthetized some Dogue de Bordeaux puppies, French mastiffs with champagne-colored coats, too light to be considered for the standard of purity. The scalpels gleamed, all lined up on the sterile tray. I smelled an unusual scent in the air under the big lamp.

Without a word, Vi indicated the mask and headgear. I put them on and the creation began.

"Was it then that she opened the parcel?" asked the Judge.

"No."

"Was there not also a fetus together with the puppies on the operating table?"

"As always. We kept them in the cultivation basin."

"And did you not make a connection between what the stranger delivered and this new fetus?" insisted the Judge.

"No, why should I have done so? The shelves were overflowing with midgets in cultivation. Vi had gotten top marks in gynecology so she got lots of leftovers. I thought it was one of those."

"What did it look like?"

Kieser shrugged his shoulders.

"The same as the others. Wrinkled skin, squashed nose, thin fingers, big head ..."

"Did you realize that it was healthy?"

"Most of the ones that they gave us were whole without any visible deformities. How could I imagine that Victoire was using her ..."

Kieser stopped and swallowed a gulp of his melota.

"... own brother," concluded the Judge.

Vi dissected the dogs' snouts, obtaining a series of slices of muscle, dark and folded up. Then she exposed the jaw of the fetus and broke it into four parts with a small hammer. She made me weld each bone to the tendons of the canine resections, overlapping and alternating the layers—one human, one canine—in such a way that the snout was a perfect blend of both and facilitated by the human doliocephalous cranium.

Then she transplanted the eyes of the dog into the eye sockets of the fetus.

This surprised me. Usually we took out a human part and inserted it into a canine head. I think she wanted to maintain the original aspect of the fetus as much as possible. She made me remove the paws of a puppy, and after reinforcing them with titanium inserts, she ordered me to weld them to the torso of the fetus. She removed a few canine fingers and replaced them with human ones, such that the indexes were recognizable in the front paws.

She followed the same procedure for the skin. She removed portions of dog dermis and transferred the fur to the fetus while leaving some areas naked where the rosy skin of a newborn would grow instead of animal hair.

We worked for many hours. I couldn't say how many. She was sweating, and every now and then I had to wipe her forehead and temples. I realized then that the strange smell in the lab was coming from her. It was a smell of clean skin, clean hair, with a hint of shampoo. She had washed herself before the operation.

Lastly, I bandaged up the neo-dog as usual and impregnated the bundles with regenerative liquid to speed up the healing.

Three days later, it could stand up on its paws and bark.

"It barked?" repeated the Judge.

"Well, it made a noise similar to 'woof woof.'"

The Judge stood up, walked over to a keypad, and pushed a button. On the wall in front of Kieser, a rectangular panel rose up, revealing a window onto another room: a small padded cell. On the other side of the glass, there was a four-legged animal. From afar it looked like a poodle shaved in alternating areas where some patches were covered in curly hair and others were pink and bald and delicate. A shudder would convulse it periodically every time it opened its mouth.

The Judge pressed another button, and the room was filled with a high-pitched, staccato sound. It started like a wail—waa, waa—the classic sound of a newborn baby, but then the vowel sound transformed, became rounder and more drawn out—uuuuu—like the sad howling of a distant coyote.

The creature was turning round and round in circles, stopping only to make its sound. It moved on four legs, but the way in which it moved its forepaws resembled the uncoordinated attempts at crawling of a child. The human fingers that emerged from the hairy paws confirmed this impression. All at once it stopped chasing its tail, went to a corner, raised its leg, and pissed. The drops of urine turned into tiny golden butterflies that fluttered around the room while the animal chased them, barking loudly.

The sound made the butterflies turn into little biscuits, and the golden cloud fell to the floor. The hungry creature was upon them at once, emitting a curious yelp of satisfaction halfway between a high-pitched noise from the throat and an infantile gurgling.

The Judge pointed to the creature on the other side of the window.

"You delivered this neo-dog to Victoire's parents."

Kieser stretched out his arms.

"How could I know? Vi gave me an address and told me to take payment on delivery as usual. They were clients just like all the others. At the door a robot appeared—made of pots and pans with two vacuum cleaners for legs and two umbrellas for arms. People buy all sorts of domestic robots these days. I certainly didn't think it was a magic puppet. Besides, who remembered that her parents were Barum?"

The Judge leaned over the electronic tablet in front of her and scrolled down nervously, looking for something.

"The Mizanekristoses decided to have another child using artificial fertilization. A week ago their fetus disappeared from the incubator of the fertility clinic."

"I only know that there was a dog to deliver to a client. I gave the basket to the robot, and it gave me a velvet bag. I understood immediately what it contained so I didn't advertise my presence in public. At a certain point I couldn't resist, and I poured the contents of the bag into the palm of my hand."

He shook his head, still incredulous at the memory of what he had seen, and took another sip of his melota.

"Vi told me that she wanted to make money. Well, she succeeded. Ten pretty, little rocks. I'd say at least three carats each. Very pure, the color was a D, maximum transparency, classic brilliant cut, expertly executed."

"Where are the diamonds?" asked the Judge.

"I gave them to Vi. The next day she left the lab and disappeared."

"Victoire Mizanekristos has the ability of vanishing into thin air without using magic powers. Three years ago she abandoned her family without leaving any traces."

"Did her parents report her disappearance?" asked Kieser.

The Judge had a moment of uncertainty and then resumed talking.

"Her parents sustain that Victoire was a difficult child from the time she was very young. They have tried several times to cure her of—"

"Cure her? Vi is healthy and normal."

"Victoire is unable to move a chair without physically touching it, an action that any Barum child can carry out at the age of five, but she has always refused to undergo the spells that could have helped her."

"Ah, I see," said Kieser. "The Mizanekristos wanted a child with magic powers. Their wish has been granted. They will grow old in the company of a creature that will love them unconditionally. It will wag its tail happily every time it sees them, will never demand anything from them, and will stay with them forever."

Kieser stopped, a bit breathless, and finished off his melota from the glass.

The Judge and the Officers have convened in the room next door. They're arguing loudly, so loudly that I can't help hearing what they're saying.

"I would like to hold him," said the Judge, "but the forty-eight hours are up."

"Complicity?" says the Lieutenant. "Complicity in kidnapping a fetus and in mutilating an infant?"

Apart from not knowing etiquette, the Lieutenant doesn't even know the law. Amusing.

"The boy's family was on the Moonflower," replies the Captain. "Half the Moon belongs to them."

"He allowed himself to be found," insists the Lieutenant. "The card he used to buy the vegetables, his photo taken in the Sphere—it was all calculated."

"There's nothing I can do!" says the Judge. Angry. Exasperated. "He's protected by lunar immunity."

"He helped the woman to get revenge," insists the Lieutenant, "and we are part of that revenge. He wanted us to know *who* kidnapped the fetus!"

They don't have any hard evidence.

I dealt with Pavlova.

I took the dogs to Phryne.

I never spoke to anyone about what we did in the lab. No gossiping.

My testimony is the only validation of Vi's guilt, but Terrestrial law only admits Terrestrial witnesses.

In the other room, there's a long silence.

"What will we say to the Barum?" says the Captain.

Another silence.

"We'll say ... we'll tell them to keep the dog and to try to educate it like a child. Maybe, with the right teachers ..."

I bite my lip to keep from laughing out loud.

Well, I'm done here. I stand up, I stretch, and nod goodbye to the doorman, who opens the door and bows low as I leave. One who knows how to behave in my presence.

I cross the courtyard and exit.

I think that Vi's parents are idiots.

A silver Yang—Moon color—is parked on the other side of the street.

Vi is a genius. And they were lucky to have such a

daughter. But it's not enough to be lucky. You also have to have the intelligence to recognize Luck, and they didn't have that. Serves them right. They deserve the neo-dog. Vi has shown them that birth isn't everything. She made them see that it's possible to be whoever you want—despite genetics.

She even showed me.

The driver gets out, takes off his cap, and opens the door.

"You go in the back, Robur. I feel like driving."

He obeys, and I take the steering wheel.

Vi jumps into the front next to me. The familiar smell of her sweat makes me feel at home.

"How did it go?"

"Good."

"Did they believe you?"

"No. But I'm lucky."

I adjust the rearview mirror and steal a quick glance at myself.

I look very much like me.

Citizen Komarova Finds Love

Ekaterina Sedia

The very little town of N. was largely bypassed by the revolution—the red cavalries thundered by, stopping only to appropriate the ill-gotten wealth of Countess Komarova, the lone survivor of N.'s only noble family. The wealth was somewhat less than the appropriators had anticipated—a ruined mansion and no funds to repair it. The Countess fled to N.'s only inn, and the red cavalry moved on but not before breaking all the windows of Komarov's mansion and allocating it for the local youth club.

Everyone knows what N.'s youth is like, and by fall, most of the Countess' furniture was turned into firewood, and by mid-December the mansion stood abandoned and decrepit, and a turd frozen to its parquet floors served as its only furnishing and a testament of gloria mundi transiting hastily.

The countess herself, stripped of her title and now a simple Citizen Komarova, was used to poverty—before the revolution, she made her living as a piano teacher, but that winter, savage and bloody, pianos were turned into firewood, their strings now disembodied garrotes. In search of new means of gentile sustenance, she turned to seamstress shops, but no one was hiring. Nearing despair, she finally settled as a clerk in a consignment shop at the outskirts of N.

The owner of the shop, a man as old as he was ornery, let her rent the room above the shop, where the wind howled under the roof thatched with a ragtag team of tiles and shingles. There was a small and round metal stove, known colloquially as "bourgeoisie," as indiscriminate and insatiable as its namesake: it burned books, pianos, furniture, twigs, entire palmate fir branches, and crackling birch logs. It gave back cherry-red heat that spread in waves through the room over the shop and broke over the stained walls much like the distant Mediterranean over its rocky shores.

Citizen Komarova thought of the Mediterranean often. These were the vague memories of early childhood and its naive surprise at the shiny, tough leaves of the olive trees, over the white wide-brimmed hats and mustachioed men on the beach, over the mingling of salt and sun; memories almost obscene in the frozen and landlocked N. It was the only frivolity she allowed herself and only when the metal stove made the air shimmer with concentrated heat before it dissipated in the cold, cold winter nights. Then, Citizen Komarova hugged her bony shoulders wrapped in the spiderweb of a pilling black crocheted shawl over the spiderweb of wrinkles etched in her dry parchment skin and rocked back and forth on her bed and cried. The rusted springs beneath her, wrapped in a thin layer of torn and colorless rags, cried in unison.

During the day, when she was done crying over her lost Mediterranean family vacation, she minded the shop downstairs. It was a single room but much larger than her garret above it, and its contents ebbed and flowed depending on the fortunes of the citizens of N.

By the middle of January, the lone room, echoey just this past December, became stifled with all the things people brought in, hoping that Citizen Komarova would somehow manage to sell them to someone more fortunate, even though whose fortunes were good remained to be seen. There were leather-wrapped yokes the collectivized farmers had managed to keep for themselves and now were forced to let go of by bitter cold and steadily declining expectations. There were books with pages forever gone to hand-rolled cigarettes and missing title plates. Chipped china, pockmarked kettles, knives, scissors, ribbons, baskets, and moth-ravaged furs. Whatever nobility survived in the environs had gravitated toward N., bringing with them heavy brocade and monogrammed silverware. Several fox skins, both platinum and regular, stared at Citizen Komarova with their amber-colored glass eyes from dusty corners. She moved between the shelves, adjusting this and that, and casually swatting at pottery with a feather duster.

The first customer of the day surprised her. He stomped his feet and clapped his hands on the threshold, dislodging a small mound of snow off his boots, held together by long cloth wrappings, and his long military coat, its chest although still covered in white powder, sporting the recognizable chevrons and ribbons of the red cavalryman, one of Budyonny's fighters. His hat and the red star decorating it gave Komarova momentary chills, and her knotted fingers curled around the feather duster defensively. She took a deep breath and stepped forth from behind the shelves to meet the gaze of the cavalryman's clear eyes. The dead foxes stared, too, transfixing the people in the crosshairs of their amber pupils.

"What can I do for you?" said Komarova. The flame of the kerosene lamp on the counter guttered in the draft from the door, and the cavalryman shut it without being told to.

"I have something I'd like to pawn," he said.

"It's a consignment store," she answered. "Which means we can sell it for you, but we cannot offer you any payment straightaway."

"I can take it to the market then."

"You could, I suppose."

The two of them considered each other at length.

"What is it then?" Citizen Komarova asked eventually. By then the shadows had grown longer, and the fox eyes glittered in their corners.

The cavalryman dug through the deep pockets of his overcoat. The snow on his clothes had melted, and only tiny droplets clung to the tips of the stray woolen hair on his sleeves like fur of a cat that had come in from the rain and was about to irritably shake off the moisture. From his pocket the man extracted four horseshoes.

"For good luck," he said.

"I can give you a copper," said Citizen Komarova.

"It's a deal." The man smiled for the first time then, and she was startled by the glint of his teeth in the shadow of the shaggy, unkempt beard, which looked unintentional to begin with. When he smiled like that, his eyes sunk and his mouth pulled back, and she felt a chill. She wrapped her shawl tighter still and offered the payment on the palm of her hand.

He took it with cold fingers and was gone on a swirl of the coat just as the four heavy horseshoes tumbled ringing to the floor. Citizen Komarova picked them up gingerly and spent the rest of the afternoon stacking and unstacking them and sometimes hanging them on the nails over the door for good luck. She was glad when the sun set and no one stepped foot into the shop for the rest of the day, leaving her to her thoughts and the visibly unlucky horseshoes.

The rest of January passed in the sparse, slow sifting of snow from the clouds, grey and heavy like quicksilver. The stock of the consignment shop increased: every dress and fur coat and petticoat and necklace, every ring and feathered hat had made its way there as the former nobility grew hungrier and less optimistic about the possible return of the old order of things. The corners were now filled with rustling of lace and slow undulations of peacock feathers, their unblinking green and azure eyes nodding in the drafts. Countess Komarova, who in her entire lifetime had never experienced such luxury, stroked the ermine muffs and guarded them jealously from marauding moths.

She picked up delicate dresses, the lace ruffling on the chests white as foam, or the ones that were light as air, held together by the silken golden stitching. These were the dresses for waists much younger and slimmer than that of the former countess, their skirts long and stiff with golden thread, puffed with petticoats. And still she held them to her bust and looked at herself in the mirror, parallel wrinkles running along her cheeks made more severe by the ruffled collars, by the artificial flowers, feathers, and colored buttons. Her eyes shone at her from the mirror, and she reminded herself of a hungry cat, not the clear-eyed child of the Mediterranean vacation.

The last day of January brought with it a howling wind, a bitter cold, and another visit from the cavalryman. Citizen

Komarova was a bit puzzled by his repeat visit. Unlike most, he was already paid for his horseshoes, and the army of which he was a part had moved on a long time ago so there was no reason for him lingering behind. With him he brought the cutting wind and the sense of great desolation. As Citizen Komarova stared into his eyes, she felt the awful sucking void tugging at her soul, and the whispers ebbed in her skull like the distant Mediterranean in a pink shell pressed against her child memory ear.

"I have something else," the cavalryman said.

"A copper," she answered without even asking what it was, as if some force nudged her from the inside.

His gaze lingered on her face and traveled down, softening. "It becomes you," he said, his hand motioning vaguely at her chest.

She looked down and blushed, suddenly aware of the lace shawl over the dress that neither belonged to nor fit her.

His large, square hand touched her elbow. "I'm Vasily Kropotkin," he said.

"Like the Prince."

"Exactly."

"What do you have for me then?"

Metal clanged to the ground—two sabers in rusted sheaths and a horseshoe, a set of gold-embroidered epaulettes, and several medals Citizen Komarova did not recognize. "Surely, it's worth more than just one copper," Vasily said.

She gave him two. Her fingers, gathered into a pinch as if for a blessing, touched his palm as if it was a holy font, and again her mind was momentarily invaded by whispers and bubbling, hissing screams. She took a step back, and he disappeared again. She could never see him actually leave. It was him and then the opened door and a swirl of snow, the ringing of his spurred boots on the frozen ground, his long coat sweeping the path in the snow. And then she was alone among the glassy, staring eyes of foxes and the silently accumulating dust. As soon as the sun went down, she fled up the stair into her small, virginal apartment where the heat from the potbellied stove chased away her fears that crowded so densely and so coldly in the shop downstairs, where the dresses rustled and the imaginary whispers grew louder after sundown.

Vasily came back in the middle of February when the wind chased the twisting snow serpents close to the cold ground and the icicles fringing every doorway and window frame pointed down like transparent daggers threatening to break off and pierce at any moment. The door clanged open, and the cavalryman—gaunter and sadder but unmistakably himself—smiled at her. His lips, bloodless and thin, pulled away from his teeth, and his cheekbones became suddenly prominent, and a thousand ghost eyes—sharp as the icicles sparkling along the top edge of the doorway—looked through his, grey and cold.

Citizen Komarova felt a chill, and yet her fingers reached out, a greening copper held between them. She touched his callused palm before he had a chance to chase the horrors from his eyes, and he smiled again, warming, becoming human at her mere touch. The foxes in the corners reared and whispered, baring their teeth, their weak dangling paws clenching, their eyes clear amber and malice. She paid them no mind.

"What do you have for me today?"

He gave her a burlap sack, its bottom dark and crusted. She looked inside into the pink lace of frozen, frothy blood to see a horse's leg chopped off at the knee, its fetlock covered in long, matted hair. She noticed round holes studding the circumference of the hoof and no horseshoe.

She looked away, swallowing hard, fighting back a wave of nausea, a riptide of swirling blackness that edged into the field of her vision threatening to swallow it whole. His callused, working-class hand took hers, steadying her on her feet, and she blushed bright crimson at his touch.

"I cannot give you more than one," she said.

"It's all right." He smiled. "I will bring more."

And before she could protest, before she could stop him, he was gone.

~*~

She had disturbing dreams that night—her usual memories of that one perfect summer overlapping over the more desolate and recent events, and one moment it was warm sand and the smell of olive blooms, the next she felt callused working-class genitals pressed against the small of her back, and she arched, sighed, and woke up, blushing, too hot to go back to sleep. And yet, soon the waves pounded, and the bed rocked under her with the rhythm of the sea or something even more forgotten and unknowable—the warmth, the salt.

The shop downstairs caught the mild contagion of her dreams, the faint malaise—it behaved in the mornings, but as soon as darkened afternoons demanded that she lit the kerosene lamp on the counter, the shadows agitated the dresses, and the fox skins, shameless, wandered around the shop on their soft, woolen legs. The severed horse's leg thumped on the hardwood tiles haughtily, searching for its missing horseshoe. The lace unraveled, and the dresses paired up and twirled in a dance or flailing panic; and fur coats chased away the moths with their long sleeves and then silently stalked the fox skins, who had the advantage of having body shapes rather than being flayed and stitched to others like themselves. They also had eyes, unlike almost everything else in the shop, and they did a better job avoiding Citizen Komarova and not blundering blindly into her.

By the time of Great Lent, on Clean Monday, almost everyone in N. was hungry, and the fast seemed a necessity more than an imposition. When Citizen Komarova left the shop, chased away by the disturbing goings-on, she walked down the snow-paved streets, wondering to herself at how quiet everything was before realizing that the missing sounds were those that used to belong to livestock. There was no mooing, bleating, nor clucking; no hissing nor barking nor quacking nor meowing, for that matter. Even the human voices were few and subdued. She walked to the bakery and bought a loaf of bread, dry and raspy with mixed-in chaff. She took it to her garret and crumbled it into a bowl of water with just a splash of precious sunflower oil and ate it slowly, chewing each bite a hundred times, stretching it, stretching like a winter night when the sleep would not come. The skin on her neck hung looser, a long, sad flap. Her waist, however, had grown slimmer, and now most of the dresses in the shop were too large for her, their full skirts swirling of their own volition about her feet and sometimes swaying with enough force to make her stumble or almost knock her off her feet. She wore them all the time now, never sure when Vasily Kropotkin would show up but confident that he would. She did not bother to explain to herself why his arrival was important and why it mattered if he complimented her flowing skirts and the delicate crocheted flowers winding about her throat, so beautiful.

He arrived late at night. The kerosene lamp was blown out, and Citizen Komarova lay sleepless in her narrow bed in her narrow garret, one side of the roof above her slanting at a sharp angle, memories of past snowfalls whispering in the rafters.

She heard the heavy footsteps in the shop downstairs and lay on her back, listening intently, trying not to breathe so as not to miss the slightest sound—neither the jingling of spurs nor the creaking of the steps nor the thump of a new burlap sack. It fell to the floor heavily and wetly with a sucking thwack that made her skin crawl. She knew that she would never dare to look inside but that the disembodied horse leg would probably investigate and lean against the sack forlornly, its furry fetlock matting with the slow seeping of thick, black blood.

Of course, he would want his payment—the steps creaked closer and closer, and the chills and the whispers followed, reluctant to let him go.

The door creaked. Citizen Komarova licked her lips, and said in a small, croaking voice squashed with terror and sadness, "I have no coppers to give you."

"It's too bad," he said. The bed creaked and shifted as he sat on its edge, invisible in the darkness. But solid.

"There are some downstairs in the shop," she said. "Come back in the morning."

His wide, warm palm touched her face gently but with a hidden threat of superior strength and class position. "Can I stay here?"

She nodded wordlessly, her lips and eyelashes brushing against the leathery contours of his open hand.

The bed creaked again, and she felt his weight pressed against her, then on top of her, his fingers indenting the thin parchment skin of her inner thighs, pushing them apart. Their fumblings were short and dry and bruised, but Citizen Komarova barely noticed: with every thrust of the knotted, gnarled body on top of her, her vision filled to brimming with unfamiliar sights.

She saw row after row of the red cavalrymen, their horses gone, lined along the darkened riverbank. She could not see their faces shrouded in shadow as they were; only occasionally she caught a glint from under the visor of a red-starred hat. A glint of copper, she thought, before the man on top of her pulled away and she saw the ceiling of her garret awash in the grey premonition of the morning, and then her eyes closed and she stared at the frothy waves of the sea as they covered the white sand and retreated, leaving in their wake perfect, lacy patterns of foam, even and complex like the crocheted doilies the local nobility left by the dozens in the shop downstairs.

Then there was the ceiling and warm breath on her face, and then it all drowned in the clanging of metal and sparks flying from the clashing of sabers, the whinnying of the horses, and the quick, stuttering *ta-ta-ta* of the machine gun. There was mud and a slippery road and a lightweight cart with a mounted machine gun but no rider, pulled by a single spooked horse. The two-wheeled cart tilted and tipped over, and the horse slid, its hooves (devoid of horseshoes) splattering mud and mustard-yellow clay over its hide, dark with sweat, before it tumbled down, its hind right leg giving under it awkwardly with a crack that resonated through her bones.

The man on top of her exhaled a muffled curse and pulled away for one last time, leaving her with a brief but searing impression of several cavalrymen surrounding her bed in a semicircle, pressing closer intently as if they wanted to see better. She pulled the covers all the way to her chin, and they leered at her, a few of them smirking under the coppers on their eyelids.

"Is this why you need money?" she whispered and nodded at the silent, invisible throng. "For them?"

He seemed neither surprised nor perturbed by Citizen Komarova's observation. He rolled onto his back, hands under his head, and sighed. "Yes. They need coppers to cross over, and I am supposed to get them for them."

"Why you?"

(The dead in her mind's eye stared, some with copper, others with eyes white as boiled eggs.)

"I was the only one who survived." He sighed. "The White Army, the Black Army—goddamn Makhno!—too many, too many. When there's only one man left alive from the entire regiment, he has to take care of his dead. They sure aren't taking care of themselves."

"I can help you," she whispered, the skin on her throat unusually tight, constricting.

They came downstairs when it was still barely light. The air, colored whisper grey like a dove's underside, pooled in the corners, and soft, cold drafts moved the heavy folds of dresses—all but one, a white lacy number that twirled in a dance with a shearling overcoat, oblivious to the gruesome beast that was busily self-assembling from the dismembered horse parts and a fox pelt, all mismatched fur and yellow glow of glassy eyes, teeth and hooves and frozen blood, pink like cherry petals in the spring that was too far away, too hungry and cold to even dream about.

"I know where the owner keeps the shop's take," she said. "He never takes it home—afraid of the thieves. He thinks here no one will find it."

"He'll know it was you."

She sighed and patted his head—lumpy, old scars bulged

like veins under his greying and short and badly-cut hair. There were probably lice, she thought with only a distant shudder of disgust. There were always lice on these people; no wonder they were so eager to call everyone "bloodsuckers" and appropriate the appropriators or whatever nonsensical phrase they were using nowadays. Worse yet, they were right. She closed her eyes for a second to gather her courage. It was the least she could do. "It doesn't matter," she said. "I will show them."

The small chest, wrapped in copper straps mostly for show, was hidden in its usual place—in the bottom of a larger, almost identical chest filled to overflowing with spotted linens, torn doilies, and torn drapes, with broken flowers of white silk and yellowing muffs. She took the little chest out of its soft nest and blew on it, gently displacing stray threads and cobwebs.

They left the paper money—who had use for it anyway in the town where it would only buy a loaf of stale bread and a jar of sunflower oil?—and took all the coins, all colors, all sizes. Copper and silver, the old Tsar coins and the new ones. Ghostly fingers reached for them, and the red stars of the ghosts' hats flashed in the morning light, multiplied by the many faces of the coins, and soon all their white eyes were hidden under the soft shine or green patina of metal.

"It is time," Citizen Komarova said softly.

He gave her a puzzled look.

"I told you I would show them. Only you will have to help me."

They went back up the rickety stairs with the composite horse-fox pawing at her hems with its toes and hooves and barking piteously. Soon, the strange beast was left behind, and Citizen Komarova lay on her maiden-narrow bed. The ruffles brushed her chin and hid her neck, and the lace over her breast lay smooth—virginal white.

She closed her eyes and told Vasily Kropotkin what he must do. He hesitated a while; but he was a soldier and she was a parasite, no matter how appropriated. He found the class strength within him, and his heavy hands stroked her throat. There were a few minutes of blind, kicking panic, and the sound of either a crushed trachea or of broken bones of the fox-horse as it lost its footing and tumbled down the stairs.

But soon enough, her eyes closed under two coppers, and she stood on the Mediterranean shore, a pink shell clasped in her hands and an entire regiment of the Red Army crowding behind her, eager like children to see the white sand and the gentle waves and sea, blue as nothing they had ever seen before.

Grey Noise

Pepe Rojo

Translated by Andrea Bell

In my room in the early morning when everything is quiet, I can hear a buzzing sound. It begins between my eyes and extends down my neck. It's like a whisper, and I concentrate, trying to make out the words that sound inside my head, knowing in advance that they won't make any sense. They don't say a thing. The murmur is like that vibration you can feel but can't place when you're in a mall right when all the stores start to turn on their lights and get ready for the day. Even when people arrive that vibration is still there, but you can't feel it anymore. My head is like a vacant mall. The sound of empty space. The vibration that expectations produce. The whisper of a desire you can't name.

Believe me, I'm used to the buzz. I'm also used to my heart beating, to my brain stringing together ideas that have no direction, to my lungs taking in air in order to expel it later. The body is an absurd machine.

Sometimes the noise lulls me to sleep at night. Sometimes it doesn't let me sleep, it keeps me awake, staring at a yellow indicator light on the ceiling that tells me I'm on stand-by.

I transmitted for the first time when I was eighteen years old and desperate to find some news item, anything. So I took to walking the streets, following people whose faces seemed like TV fodder. I felt like a bum with a mission. I'd had a little money left over after the operation, and I could enjoy the luxury of eating wherever I wanted so I went to one of those fancy restaurants on the top floor of a building tall enough to give you vertigo. After having a drink I walked toward the bathroom, trying to find an exit out onto the terrace. I wanted a few shots of the city for my personal file. I opened several doors without finding anything. Just like my life, I thought with a cynicism I sometimes miss. The rooftop terraces of all buildings are alike. A space filled with geometric forms in shades of grey. Someone should make a living painting horizontal murals on the roofs of terraces with messages for the planes that fly over this city every five minutes. Though I don't know what the messages would be. What can you say to someone about to arrive except "Welcome"? It's been a long time since anyone felt welcome in this city.

Someone was jumping over an aluminum fence on the opposite side of the terrace. Maybe it was my lucky day, and he was going to commit suicide. I activated the "urgent" button inside my thigh, hoping I wasn't wrong. A little later a green indicator lit up my retina, telling me that I was on some station's monitors, though not yet on the air. The guy was standing on a cornice looking down. He was dark and stubby. His back was to me so I couldn't see his face. I jumped over the fence and looked down, establishing the scene for the viewers; it could be edited later. The dark man turned and saw me, got nervous, and jumped. Right then a red light went on in my eye, and I heard a voice tainted with static say in my ear, "You're on the air, pal!"

That night I found out that the man was named Veremundo, a 54 year-old gym teacher. The suicide note they found on his body said he was tired of being useless, of feeling insignificant from dawn to dusk, and that the worst thing about his suicide was knowing it wouldn't affect a soul.

Suicides always say the same thing.

When it is impossible to set up an external camera to situate the action, the reporter should obtain a few establishing shots—"long shots"—to ensure that the space in which the action takes place is logical to the viewers. Reporters should prepare fixed shots first, and only later, when there is action, they can use motion shots.

~*~

Suicides don't pay very well. There are so many every day, and people are so unimaginative that, if you spend a day watching television, you can see at least ten suicides, none of them very spectacular. Seems the last thing that suicides think of is originality.

Only once did I try to talk a suicide out of it. It was a woman, 'bout 40 years old, skinny, and worn-out. I told her that the only thing her suicide was going to accomplish was to feed me for about two days, that there was no point being just another one, that I totally understood life was a load of shit but there was no sense committing suicide just to entertain a thousand assholes who do nothing but switch channels looking for something that would raise, even just a little, the adrenaline level in their bodies.

She jumped anyway.

I returned home, and that night I watched the personal copy I'd made over and over again. Every action happened thousands of times on my monitor. I ended up playing it in slow-mo, trying to find some moment when her expression changed, the moment when one of my words might've had an effect I didn't know how to take advantage of.

I went to bed with swollen eyes, a terrible taste in my mouth, and thinking that what I'd said to that lady I might just as well have been saying to myself.

I've had enough, and I leave my house to go buy something to eat. I jump on my bike (which I use to get around near home) and just before reaching a pizza place I hear a bunch of patrol cars a few blocks away. I press my thigh to activate the controls, and the green signal goes on in my eye. I pedal as fast as I can, following the sound of the sirens. I turn a corner and see five cop cars parked at the entrance to a building. I leave my bike leaning against one of them, hoping no one will steal it, and run toward a cop who's keeping gawkers back. I show her my press badge, and she grudgingly lets me in. She tells me to go up to the third floor. When I arrive, a couple of paramedics are examining a body that's convulsing in the doorway of the apartment. I stop to establish the shots. One full shot of the paramedics, one long shot of the corridor, and I try to walk slowly and keep my vision fixed so that the movement isn't too abrupt. I stop at the doorway and slowly pan my head in order to establish the setting on thousands of monitors throughout the world. My indicator light's been red for several seconds. I approach an officer who's covering up a corpse near a TV monitor, and on the monitor they're transmitting my shot. I feel the shiver that always accompanies a hook, I begin to get dizzy, and a shooting pain crosses my brain from side to side. I lose all sense of space until I turn around and spot a cop trying to be the star of the day. The cop sees the red light in my right eye and looks into it. "We got a report from some neighbors in the building that they'd heard a baby crying, and they knew that three single men lived here. You know how people are, they thought that they were some kind of faggot perverts who'd adopted a baby so they could feel like they were more normal."

I interrupt the laughter of the cop who's posing for my right eye and ask him when they were notified.

"Twenty minutes ago. We ran a check on kidnapped babies. When we got here, they'd already killed the neighbors. Seems they were monitoring all phone calls, and they began shooting at us ..."

The officer kept on talking, and I was concentrating on getting the shot when I sensed a movement behind him. Apparently a closet door was opening. The next thing I register—and I suppose it's gonna be pretty spectacular since my shot was a close-up of his face—is a flash of light and his face exploding into pieces of blood and flesh.

I hurl myself against his body, grabbing hold of it and using my momentum to carry us toward whoever it was who did this. Before reaching the closet I let go of the body and step back to get a clear shot. The headless corpse of the policeman strikes another body and knocks it down. I approach quickly and stomp on the hand holding a gun. I can hear the bones as they break. Too bad I don't have audio capacity so I could record the sound. I hope someone in the transmission room patches it in. The shot is a bird's-eye view of some guy's face soaked with the blood of the cop. I can't make out his features. More cops arrive. I take a few steps back.

"It seems," I comment on the air, "that there was still one person hiding in the closet, and this carelessness by the police has cost yet another officer his life." It's always good to criticize institutions. It raises the ratings. Just then I hear a commotion at the door, and I quickly turn around to find a young woman crying, followed by a private security guard. She goes into one of the rooms I haven't managed to shoot yet. When I try to go in, a cop stops me, and his look says I can't enter. I know he's dying to insult me, but he knows I'm on the air and it could harm the police department's image in this city so all he says is I can't go in. I manage to get shots of the woman picking up a bundle and holding it to her breast while endlessly repeating, "my love, my baby."

"What is that, officer? Is it a baby?"

"This is a private moment, reporter, you have no right to be filming it."

"I have information rights." I lie by reflex, but I don't succeed in budging him. I try my luck with the girl who'd gone inside crying. "Can I help you in any way, miss?"

Just then I realize that the bundle she'd picked up is all bloody. Various police officers and two paramedics try to take away the baby (at least I suppose that's what it is), but she doesn't want to let go of it. She fixes her hair and comes over to me. Hurry up, I think, the clock's running on your 15 minutes. "You're a reporter, aren't you?" My first instinct is to nod my head, but I remember that it's an unpleasant motion for TV viewers. I'm not supposed to be anything but a verbal personality, and so I answer by saying yes.

"Someone stole my baby and now I've found him, but it looks like the cops hurt him. He's been shot in the leg." The lady cries harder and harder while a paramedic tells her that all she's doing is injuring the baby more. I get confused because someone's started to shout in my ear receiver. They want me to ask the girl her name. The paramedic grabs the baby. In my head, the program directors keep talking. "We couldn't have planned this better. This is drama. Just wait 'til you get your check. The ratings are gonna add a lot of zeros to it."

The rest is routine. Interviews, facts, versions. The fate of the baby will be a different type of reporter's job, and it'll keep the whole city excited all this afternoon and maybe into tomorrow morning when some other reporter tapes fresher news.

When I leave the building, my bike's no longer waiting for me, and I have to walk home. I live in a world without darkness. All day long there's an indicator light in my retina telling me my transmission status. I can turn the indicator level down, but even when I'm sleeping it keeps me company. A yellow light and a buzz, a murmur. They're who I sleep with. They're my immediate family. But my eyes belong to the world. My extended family spans an entire city, though no one would recognize me if they met me on the street.

I haven't gone out for a few weeks now. My last check frees me up from having to wander around looking for news. Privacy is a luxury for a man in my condition. Several times a day a yellow indicator goes on in my right eye, and I hear a voice asking if I have anything, they have some dead time and it's been days since I transmitted anything. I simply don't answer. I close my eyes and remain quiet, hoping they'll understand that I'm not in the mood.

What do I do on my days off? Well, I try not to see anything interesting. I read magazines. I look at the window of my room. I count the squares on the living room floor. And I remember things that aren't recorded on tape while my eyes stare at the ceiling, which is white—perhaps the least attractive color on a television screen.

The most common errors made by ocular reporters are due to the reflexes of their own bodies. A reporter must live under constant discipline so as to avoid seemingly involuntary reflexes. There is no greater sign of inexperience and lack of professional control than a reporter who closes his eyes in an explosion or a reporter who covers her face with her arms when startled by a noise.

Today is not a good day. I go walking the streets, and in every store I hear the same news. Constant Electrical Exposure Syndrome, CEES for fans of acronyms, seems to be wreaking havoc. Continuous stimulation of the nerve endings caused by electricity and an environment which is constantly charged with electricity—radiation from monitors, microwaves, cellphones—seems to have a fatal effect on some people. I stop in front of a shop window and start recording a reporter with his back to a wall of TV screens: "It seems the central nervous system is so used to receiving external electronic stimulation that, when it doesn't get it, it begins to produce it, constantly sending electric signals through the body that have no meaning or function, speeding up your heartbeat and making your lungs hyperventilate. Your eyes begin to blink, and sometimes your tongue starts to jerk inside your mouth. Some witnesses even say that the victims of this syndrome can 'speak in tongues,' or that this syndrome 'is what causes this type of experience in various subjects.'"

They insert shots of several people speaking in tongues here.

The reporter, looking serious and trying to get people's attention, keeps walking while images of people who suffer from these symptoms appear on the video wall. The screens fill with shots of serious men with concerned faces. Interviews with experts, no doubt.

"No one knows for certain the exact nature of the syndrome. The world scientific community is in a state of crisis. There are those who say this is just a rumor started by the media, it's simply another disease transformed into a media event. Some say the syndrome isn't as bad as it seems. But there are also those who believe that civilization has created a monster from which it will be difficult to escape."

The images on the monitors change. Various long

shots of rustic houses surrounded by trees. The music changes. Acoustic instruments—a flute and a guitar.

"However, there are already several electric detox centers out in the country. Rest homes devoid of electricity. This is perhaps the only possibility or hope for those who exhibit symptoms of the syndrome. As always, hope is the last thing to die in what is perhaps the most important 'artificial' disease of this century. There are those who say that what cancer was to the previous century, CEES will be to ours."

They show a few shots of these places. The patients look out the windows or at the walls as if waiting for something they know will never arrive. As if waiting for civilization to keep a promise, yet aware that it never will, since the promise has long been forgotten.

The equipment for corporal transmission is very expensive. My father gave it to me. Well, he doesn't know what it was that he gave me. I just received an e-mail on my eighteenth birthday saying that he had deposited who knows how much money into an account in my name, that I had to decide what to do with it, and that, after spending it, I was on my own. That I shouldn't seek him out anymore.

I still keep that e-mail on my hard drive. It's one of the advantages of the digital age. Memory becomes eternal, and you can relive those moments as many times as you want. They remain frozen outside of you, and when you don't know who you are or where you come from, a few commands typed into your computer bring your past to the present. The problem is that, when the past remains physically alive in the present, when does the future get here? And why would you want it to? The future is a constant repetition of what you've already lived; maybe some details can change, maybe the actors are different, but it's the same. And when you haven't lived it, surely you saw something similar in some movie, on some TV show, or you heard something like it in a song. I keep hoping my mom will return one day and tell me it was all a joke, that she never died. I keep hoping my father will keep his promise and come see me in the orphanage. I keep hoping my life will stop being this endless repetition of days that follow each other with nothing new to hope for.

I paid for part of my operation with the money. Legally, half the operation is paid for by the company that owns the rights to my transmissions. The doctors tried to talk me out of the implant, but I was already over sixteen so I told them to just concentrate on doing their job. I needed to earn money, and I knew perfectly well that luck and necessity are strange bedfellows. Three days later, the nerve endings of my eyes and vocal cords were connected to a transmitter that could send the signal to the video channels.

That was the last time I heard from my father.

The most important detail that an ocular reporter must remember is to avoid monitors when transmitting live. If a reporter focuses on a monitor that is broadcasting what he is transmitting, his sense of balance will by harshly affected, and he will begin to suffer from severe headache. Exposure to this type of situation is easily controlled by avoiding shots of monitors when transmitting live. It is important to note that the reflected transmissions "hook" the reporter, and there is a change in the stimuli that travel from the brain toward the different muscles of the body. For that reason it is sometimes almost impossible to break off visual contact with the monitor. The only way to prevent these "hooks" is through abrupt movement of the body or neck as soon as visual contact is made with the images one is transmitting. Latest research reveals that long periods of exposure to these virtual loops cause symptoms similar to those of CEES. This information was obtained from recent experiments and from the records of the Toynbee case.

The Toynbee case is a legend no one in my profession can ever forget. Some anti-media extremists kidnapped a reporter and blindfolded him so that he couldn't transmit anything. Every two hours they broadcast their opinions to a nation that watched, entertained: *"The media are the cause of the moral decay of our society. The media are causing the extinction of individuality. Thousands of mental conditions stem from the fact that human beings can only learn about reality through the media, the information is manipulated."* The whole ideological spiel just like on one of those flyers they hand out in the streets. It's ironic to think that those extremists may be the only ones who'll survive if an epidemic like CEES wipes out humanity. They always try to avoid electricity. I don't know what I prefer: to keep hoping that this reality miraculously gets better or that some stupid extremists take over the world and impose the rules of "their" reality. The only thing you can learn from human history is that there's nothing more dangerous than a utopia.

So, as an example and metaphor of their complaints, they tied up the reporter, who worked under the name Toynbee, and put him in front of a monitor. They immobilized his head and connected his retina to the monitor. I've seen those images a thousand times. The only thing the reporter's eyes see is a monitor within a monitor within a monitor until infinity seems to be a video camera filming a monitor that's broadcasting what it's recording, and there's no beginning, no end, there's nothing, until you remember that a human being is watching this. It's the only thing he can see, and it's giving him an unbearable headache as if someone were crisscrossing his skull with cables and wires. The images weren't enough. For those who know what it feels like to get hooked, the images were painful, but for those who'd never felt that kind of feedback, they were frankly boring. The extremists—conscious that they were putting on a show and that before they'd be able to broadcast ideas, they had to entertain the world—set up a video camera to tape Toynbee's face and sent the signal to the same transmission station the reporter was connected to. At the station they knew there was nothing they could do to help Toynbee since he was connected directly to the monitor, and they began to transmit both things: the monitors reproducing themselves until infinity and Toynbee's face. The station executives say they would've cut the broadcast if they'd've had doubts about the source of the hook, but everyone knows that's not true. Ratings are ratings.

Watching that reporter's face is quite a show. First, a few facial muscles start to move as if he had a tic. At first he tried to move his eyes to look to either side, but right next to the monitor was the tripod with the camera taping his face. And so, on one half of the screen you could see how the loop was broken: all you saw was the partial view of a TV set, showing the image of a video camera on the right side of the screen and the real video camera on the other side as if reality didn't have depth, only breadth. As if reality repeated itself endlessly off to the right and left. But the hook was stronger than his willpower, and gradually the reporter stopped trying to look off to the side. Sometimes the monitor showed how he tried. A very slow pan to the right or left that slowly came back again as if the muscles of his eyes had no strength left. Toynbee began to sweat. His face began to convulse more violently, each time sweating bigger drops that struggled against gravity until, just like the reporter's eyes, they gave up and slid rapidly down his convulsing face. Each drop followed a different path. His face, lit up by the monitor, seemed to be full of thousands of monitors since his damp skin also reflected in distortion the monitor he was looking at. The muscle spasms were getting stronger, and just as the sweat deformed the monitor, each convulsion moved the reporter's face one step further away from what we know as human. There were no longer moments when you could see normality in his face. Everything was movement and water and eyes that looked out feverishly, desperately. Sometimes when I recall the images, the eyes even seem to be concentrating as if they were discovering a secret that not only makes you lose your mind but causes your body to react violently because it's something that human beings shouldn't be allowed to see.

A few minutes later his eyes seemed to lose all focus, even though they kept on receiving and transmitting light. His eyes were vacant just like the monitors. I've always liked to think that at that moment the only thing the reporter could see was a kitschy image of his past, I dunno, the birthday party his mom threw him or some day when he was in a play or his first kiss or some other idiocy of the kind that always makes us happy. There was no more willpower left in his eyes, but his eyelids were being forced open so his body and the ghosts that occupied his body were still functioning. Several of his facial muscles atrophied and stopped working, which made the movements of his face even less natural. The shot continued until his face had no expression left, just spasms and movement, expressions that went beyond the range of human emotions, possibilities that ceased to have meaning the moment they disappeared.

Until his heart exploded.

Sometimes, when I'm bored and on the bus returning to my apartment, I begin to record everything I see. But then I stop seeing and just let the machines do their work. I go into a sort of trance in which my eyes, though open, observe nothing; and yet when I get home I have a record of everything they saw. As if it wasn't me who saw it all.

When I watch what I taped I don't recognize myself. I relive everything I saw without remembering anything. At those times it's my feelings that're on stand-by.

Some truths become evident when reality is observed this way.

The poor are the only ones who are ugly. The poor and teenagers. Everyone with a little money has already changed his or her face and now has a better-looking one, has already made his face or her identity more fashionable. Teenagers aren't allowed this type of operation because their bone structure is still changing. That's how you can tell economic status or age, by checking out the quality of the surgical work on people's faces. We live in an age when everyone—everyone who's well off in this world—is perfect. Perfect body, perfect face, and looks that speak of success, of optimism, as if the mind were perfect, too, and could only think correct thoughts. Today, ugliness is a problem that humanity seems to have left behind. Today, as always, humanity's problems are solved with good credit.

Sometimes I like to think about the scene of my

suicide. One of my choices is to connect the electric camera terminals I have in my eyes to an electric generator in order to raise the voltage little by little until my brain or my eyes or the camera explodes. It thrills me to think of the images I'd get.

Or I could prepare something cruder. Take a knife and cut out my eye. Cut it out by the roots. Sometimes I think I'd prefer not to see anything. I'd prefer a world in shades of black. Get rid of my eyes. Even if they sued me, even if I had to spend the rest of my life rotting away in jail.

And while I decide, I sit alone at home, waiting. Waiting for a promise to be kept ...

Today I woke up with the urge to go out into the street and find something interesting. I've been walking around for a couple hours without any destination. It's a nice day. I hear shouts at the end of the street and take off running in that direction. A drug store. I press the button, and my indicator light changes from yellow to green. I stop a few meters from the entrance and file a report. "Shouts in a drug store. I don't know what's going on. I'm going to find out." I take the time needed to establish the scene and slowly start to approach. A lot of people are leaving the drug store, running. The story of my life. Wherever no one wants to be, there goes me.

It's hard to get inside. I try to shoot several of the faces of the people stampeding each other to get out. Desperate faces. Scared faces. The red light goes on. "I'm at a drug store. The people are trying frantically to get out. I haven't heard any shots." I have to shove several people aside until I can get through the door, and I head toward the place everyone's leaving. "Seems to be someone lying on the ground." A bunch of people wearing uniforms surround him. Probably the store employees. I stop a moment to establish the shot. I stop an employee who wants to get outside and look him in the eyes. He's so scared he doesn't even realize I'm transmitting.

"What's going on?"

"The guy was standing there, taking something off the shelves, when suddenly he collapses and starts to shake. He's infected ..." The guy pushes me and jars my shot. Shit.

I approach the body. There's an ever-widening circle

around him. I pass these people and get a full-body shot of the guy on the floor having convulsions. He's swallowing his tongue. I approach and get down close to him. He looks at me desperately when his head's not jerking around. Toynbee. He has the same facial features.

"This man was shopping in the drug store when he suffered a seizure." The guy turns to look at me, realizes there's a red light burning in my retina, and begins to laugh. His laughter starts to mix with his convulsions and before long you can't distinguish his laughter from his pain. I try to hold him in my arms. I try to touch him to calm him down, but it has no effect. I see a red light in his left eye. He's transmitting. I let go of him, and his head hits the floor hard. Out of nowhere he seems to be drowning. He shudders twice and remains quiet, looking at me. In my head I hear, "Say something, say something about CEES, *talk*, shit it's your job."

The reporter is motionless. The camera in my eye records a tiny red dot that remains alive in his. Today my face will probably appear on the monitors.

Two days later my news is no longer news. It seems like every day more attacks of the syndrome are reported. Forty percent of the victims are reporters. I remember AIDS and the homophobia it awoke. Seems like it's us reporters' turn to live in fear, not just of dying, but of the fear of others. Mediaphobia? What will they name this effect?

The common citizen (and believe me, they're all common) still doesn't understand that the syndrome isn't transmitted by bodily contact. Everyone runs away when they see someone falling apart in a fit of convulsions. They still don't get it that the body is no longer the important factor. They live under the illusion that if they touch a victim they'll get infected. It's like a phantom virus that can't be located. It's in the air, in the street. It's wherever you go, but in reality it doesn't exist. It's a virtual virus. And it's a sickness we're exposed to by living in this world. It's the sickness of the media, of cheap entertainment, it's the sickness of civilization. It's our penance for the sin of bad taste.

~*~

For all reporters who transmit live, control is the principal weapon against the reflex stimulation caused by the indicator light. The viewer can only see through the reporter's eyes once the red light in the retina goes on. All movement, all action on the reporter's part, should be perfectly planned. There must be no mistakes. Frontal shots are best. It is always necessary to take face shots of the subject by means of the camera connected to the nerve endings of the eye in order to establish identification between the subject and the viewer. The reporter functions as a medium, to call it something. He/She is merely the point of contact between the action and the reaction that thousands of viewers will have in their homes. The reporter must be there without being there. Exist without being noticed. This is the art of communication.

The opening sequence of the program that I usually transmit on goes like this: all the shots are washed out as if they were done in some familiar, old-fashioned style, as if they didn't have the necessary transmission quality, that being the excuse for washing them in grey tones that'll later change to reds. First, there's a subjective shot of a stomach operation; then the doctors turn and talk to the camera, and the whole world learns that the camera is the face of the person being operated on. Then there's an action sequence of a shoot-out downtown 'til one of the people firing turns and sees the camera and presses the trigger; the camera shot jolts and seems to fall to the ground. Everything starts to flood, a red liquid's filling up the lens. The pace starts to pick up. A shot from the point of view of a driver who crashes into a school bus. A worm's-eye view of a guy throwing himself off a building (I've always thought he looks like a high diver). The sacrifice of a cow in a slaughterhouse. The assassination of a politician. An industrial accident where some guy loses an arm. Shots of explosions where even the reporter gets blown up. A skyjacking where the terrorist shoots a passenger in the head. And so on. The images go by faster and faster until you can hardly make out what's going on. All you see is motion and blood and more motion, shapes that don't seem to have any human reference anymore until it all begins to acquire a bit of order and you start to see red, yellow, and grey lines that dance about rapidly and leave the retinal impression of a circle in the middle of the screen where the lines meet. An explosion stops the sequence, and inside the circle the program's logo is formed: Digital Red.

Welcome to pop entertainment in the early twenty-first century.

What will I be doing in twenty years? Will I keep walking the streets looking for news to transmit? Not a very pleasant future. Belonging to the entertainment industry gives off an existential stink. Some still call it journalism, though everyone knows the news isn't there to inform but to entertain. My eyes make me commune with the masses. Thousands of people see through my eyes so they can feel that their lives are more real, that their lives aren't as putrid and worm-eaten as the lives of the people I see. I'm the social glove they put on in order to confront reality. I'm the one who gets dirty, and I prevent their lives from smelling rotten. I'm a vulture who uses the misfortunes of others to survive.

When you get up close to a mirror you can't see both your eyes at the same time. You can see either the right or the left. The closer you get to your image the more distorted it gets and you can only see yourself partially. The same thing happens with a monitor. You're not there. You're the unknown one who moves in a way you don't recognize as your own. Who speaks with a voice that doesn't sound like yours. Who has a body that doesn't correspond to your idea of it. You're a stranger. To see yourself on a monitor is to realize how much you don't know about yourself and how much that upsets you.

If I wanted a more dramatic effect I could get myself hooked like Toynbee. Connect myself directly to a monitor and start to transmit. See how reality is made up of ever-smaller monitors (and no matter how hard you try, you can't find anything inside those screens, just another monitor with nothing inside) and go crazy when I realize that's the meaning of life. Totally forget about control over my body.

Allow my eyes to bleed.

~*~

The transmission time of an ocular reporter is the property of the company that finances his/her operation. Clause 28 of the standard contract establishes that six hours of every reporter's day are property of said company.

A terrorist attack in a department store. I hate department stores. Almost all of 'em are festooned with monitors that randomly change channels. It's easy to get hooked. You have to be careful. The police are just arriving on the scene. I'm about to transmit but decide not to tell central programming. As always, I look for an emergency exit. A manager is trying to take merchandise away from customers who are taking advantage of the situation to save a few pesos. The manager is so busy that he doesn't even realize when I push him. He falls, and a bunch of people quickly run out with the stuff they're stealing. A little, old lady of around sixty carries a red dress in her hands and smiles pleasantly when she leaves. I enter the store and hide behind the clothes racks. I get up to the third floor via the emergency stairs, which are empty. I don't know if the terrorists are here inside or if they simply left everything in the hands of a bomb. I avoid several of the private security guards hired to guard the store, not wanting them to see me yet. One of them comes upon a shoplifter, and he and his partner kick the hell out of him on the ground. The guy's bleeding and crying. Everyone tries to take advantage of an emergency situation. The two security guards go away, leaving the customer lying there on the floor. Blessed be capitalism. I move on to the candy department, and the smell makes me dizzy. I've never understood how they keep the flies away from the exposed candied fruit. I hear some voices and hide. I begin to hear a buzzing sound, and I gently tap my head. But the sound's not coming from there. The hum is coming from my right. I crawl until I get to a box, which I open cautiously. Inside is a sophisticated device with a clock in countdown mode rapidly approaching zero. I have a little more than a minute so I take off running. I forget about transmitting or anything else. When I feel I'm far enough away I turn around and press a button; it's green. I see the two security guards approaching the candy section. I quickly turn my head. I'm about to shout at them to get away when I hear a voice in my ear. "Where the fuck are you? Straighten out the shot, show us something we can broadcast. Are you in the store?"

I slowly correct the shot, steadying my head in a slow pan while I notice the red indicator light switch on in my eyes. I manage to spot the two security guards in the candy section. I force myself not to blink, and the bomb explodes. The fire is so hot and the colors so spectacular that for the first time in a long while I forget about the red light that lives in my head. I miscalculated. The force of the explosion lifts me up, and I fly several meters through the air. I'm not a body. I'm a machine flying through the air whose only purpose is to record and record and record so that the whole world can see what they wouldn't want to live. The clothes burn, the display shelves fall apart, thousands of objects go flying. Some hit me, but I try to keep the shot as steady as I can. All in the name of entertainment.

I slam against a wall and try to keep my head up so I can tape the fire.

For the first time I feel at home in a department store. Everything is flames, everything is ashes. The stylish dresses feed the fire, the perfumes make it grow. The spectacle is unparalleled. Civilization destroying itself. I'm in a department store, one of civilization's most glorious achievements. I see a sign that's beginning to burn; it says, "Happy Father's Day." Promises, promises ...

I get up, and my whole body hurts. I walk toward the exit. A voice in my head is shouting, "Where the fuck do you think you're going? I need fixed shots. I need you to talk; tell the world about your experience. Don't be a jerk. You don't film an explosion every day! Where do you think you're going?"

And it doesn't stop until I'm three blocks from the attack.

Today I crossed a line. I don't know and I don't care if I killed the security guards. It's one thing to report on stuff that happens and another thing to make what happens more spectacular.

What were the security guards? They were graphic elements to liven up my shots. They were mimetic elements that the audience would be able to identify with. They were dramatic elements to make the story I had to tell more interesting. They were scenery.

Today I crossed a line, and I don't want to think about anything. My whole body aches.

Situations like these make me think about the urgency of my suicide. At least that way I could decide something and not just let destiny take the lead. Suicide is the most elaborately constructed act of the human will. It's taking control of your destiny out of the hands of the world.

Yesterday I was organizing a bunch of my tapes. I found a program about my old-time heroes, the experiential reporters. "Crazies," as the foreign media call them. I pressed the play button and sat down to watch them. There are some pretty stupid people in this world, like the reporter who, after getting himself thrown in jail, started to insult the cops so that they'd beat him. He taped everything. The shots are especially successful because half the time he's on the floor trying to make visual contact with the faces of the cops who are pounding on him. Some people consider him a hero. But whenever you see the disfigured faces of the police who are beating him up you can't help thinking how ridiculous the situation is. The reporter is there because he chose to be there. Good job, amigo, improve the ratings of your company. I also watched the famous operation on Grayx's head, one of the martyrs of entertainment. The reporter, trying to make a commentary on the depersonalization of the body, agreed to subject himself to surgery in which they'd remove his head and connect it to his body by way of special high-tech cables. The guy outdid himself, narrating his whole operation, describing what he was feeling while they connected his head to his body with cables that allowed him to be five meters away from his head. This is probably one of the most important moments of this century. When the operation's over, you can see a subjective shot of the body on the operating table as Grayx tells it to stand up. The body gets up and begins to stumble because the head that's sending it instructions sees things from a strange perspective. The body slowly approaches the head, picks it up, and turns it around so that the eyes (and the camera) can look in the direction it's walking in, and at that point the viewer no longer knows who's giving the instructions, the body or the head. The body takes the head in its arms like a baby and stands in front of a mirror where you can see a decapitated body holding its head in its arms. The head doesn't seem to be very comfortable because it's a bit tilted. He didn't have enough coordination to hold it straight so all these shots lack horizontal stability. Grayx is talking about the feeling of disorientation, about the possibilities that the surgery opens up, about what would happen if, instead of cables, they used remote control, about how marvelous the modern world is, while his arms try to hold his head straight and he keeps looking back, his face twisted with the effort of trying to make his body do what he says, all the while failing to control it.

This program always brings me odd memories. I had sex for the first time after watching it with a girlfriend from high school. We were at her house watching the broadcast. No one was around. I don't know how many people might've had sex after the inauguration of the first lunar colony or when they broadcast the assassination of Khadiff, the Muslim terrorist leader, or at any other key moment in the televised history of our century, but I can tell you that it's an unforgettable experience. Watching a man with his body separated from his head on the same day that you become aware of how your body can unite with another body and become one is something you don't easily forget. Every time I watch it I have pleasant memories.

Now Grayx is in a mental institution. Seems the technology that he was helping to develop causes mental instability. Apparently people need corporal unity in order to remain sane. Grayx lost contact with reality, and they say he now lives in an imaginary world. He had so much money that he built a virtual environment and connected it to his retina, and that's the only thing that keeps him alive.

I haven't felt good ever since the explosion. I have strong pains in the pit of my stomach. Yesterday I told them to deposit the check into my account. Seems I won't be having any trouble over the security guards. To create news with your own body like the crazies do is perfectly legal, but make news at the expense of other people's rights and you can wind up spending the rest of your life in jail.

I go to the bathroom and start to pee. I look down and see that the water and my urine are full of blood. I start to hear voices just as a green light goes on in my retina.

"If I were you, I'd go straight to a doctor. That red color in your piss doesn't look healthy at all."

"Leave me alone."

"I can't. You've gone two days without doing a single thing. You already know how it is with contracts. Besides, don't be ungrateful. I was only calling to tell you your check's been deposited. Maybe when you see your pay your mood'll improve. The ratings were really spectacular."

I've gone down into the sewers of the city a number of times trying to prove one of the oldest urban legends. Thousands of rumors say there are human communities in the deepest parts of the network of underground pipes. A lot of people believe they're freaks, mutants, that their eyelids permanently cover their eyes, and their skin is so white they can't tolerate the sun or even the flashlights that everyone who goes down to look for them uses. A new race grown out of our garbage.

A society that doesn't rely on its eyes, that doesn't have to look at itself for self-recognition. Their behavior must be weird. They'd have to touch each other. They'd have to listen to each other. They wouldn't have to look like anything or anyone. A different world, different creatures.

Every time I descend on one of my exploratory trips I use my infrared glasses and carry very low-intensity lights. I've gone down more than ten times, and not once have I found anything. No mutants, no freaks, no subterranean race offering something new to humanity, something different from what's shown on TV.

It's just me down there.

Last night my right arm began to convulse. I couldn't do anything to stop it. My fingers opened and closed as if they were trying to grab something, to hold on to something.

Maybe I'd prefer a less sensational exit. Get a tank of gas, seal off a room, and fall asleep ...

It is impossible for human beings to avoid blinking, but it is possible to prolong the period of time between one blink and the next. Reporters should do exercises to achieve this control. Furthermore, the operation on their eyes is designed to stimulate the tear ducts so that the eyes do not dry out so easily, and thus reporters can keep their eyes open longer than the ordinary individual.

When muscle movement in the eyelids is detected, special sensors in the eye "engrave" the last image that the eye has seen, and when the eyelid then closes this image is the one which is transmitted. When the eyelid raises, taping continues. This necessary error in the workings of the human body has caused microseconds of memorable moments in the history of live TV to be lost forever.

A more spectacular piece of news, a riskier stunt. They always want something more. More drama, more emotion, more people sobbing before the cameras, before my eyes. I don't want to think. I'm not made to think, just to transmit. But with every transmission I feel I'm losing something I won't ever recover. The only thing I hear in my head is *more, more, more*.

I could also take everything I feel some attachment for, fill a small bag, find a sewer drain, and head down it; but this time without any lights. I'd wander around for entire days. I'd have to start eating rats and insects and drinking sewer water. Maybe I'd spend the rest of my life walking among the tunnels that form a labyrinth under this city, but at least I'd be searching for something. Or maybe I would find a new civilization. Even if they didn't accept me, even if they were to kill me for bringing in outside influences, it'd be comforting to know that there are choices in this world. That there's someone who has possibilities the rest of us lost centuries ago. Or maybe they would accept me, and I could live for years and years without having to worry, doing manual labor and finding a new routine to my life. To be what I think I can be and not what I am.

Maybe, maybe ...

These are the voices in my head:

"There's a fire. Don't you wanna go check it out? Fires and ratings go hand in hand."

"Armed robbery, a black car with no license plates, model unknown, get some shots."

"This is good, a lovers' quarrel. She was making a cake, and she destroyed his face with a mixer. The boyfriend, a little miffed, decided he was going to stick *her* in the oven instead of the cake. The neighbors called it in, but it didn't turn into anything big. Good stuff for a comedy."

"You wanna talk? The night's slow, and I ain't got nothin' to do. They're broadcasting games from last season."

"Another family suicide. In the subway, a mother with her three kids."

And so on, continually.

The whole world is on TV. Anyone can be a star. Everyone acts, and every day they prepare themselves because today could be the day that a camera finds them and the whole world discovers how nice, good looking, friendly, attractive, desirable, interesting, sensitive, and natural they are. How human they are. And all day long everyone sees tons of people on screen trying to be like that so people decide to copy them. And they create imitators. And life just consists of trying to seem like somebody who was imitating somebody else. Everyone lives every day as if they were on a TV show. Nothing's real anymore. Everything exists to be seen, and everything that we'll see is a repeat of what we've seen before. We're trapped in a present that doesn't exist. And if the transmitted don't exist, what about those of us who do the transmitting? We're objects, we're disposable. For every reporter who dies on the job or who dies of CEES, there are two or three stupid kids who think that's the only way of finding anything real, of living something exciting. And everything starts all over again.

I always try not to chat with the program directors. Normally they're a bunch of idiots. Their work is easy, and they use us like remote control cameras. Normally I don't even ask them their names. There's no point. Who wants to know more people? Ain't nothing new under the sun. Everything's a repeat, everything's a copy.

There's only one program director who knows me a little more intimately. His nickname's Rud. I don't know his real name. I met him (well, I listened to him) when I was drinking. That is, when I was trying to get so drunk I wouldn't have to think, wouldn't have to want anything. I wanted the alcohol to fill me so that I wouldn't have to make decisions, so that whatever decision I made would be the alcohol's fault, not mine. "I was drunk."

I sure do miss alcohol.

Alcohol and my profession are not good friends. In my body I have equipment that belongs to a corporation. So they can sue me if I willingly damage the machinery. Besides, it's not unusual for program directors to tape your drinking sprees and then use them to blackmail you. Some even put them on the air. Once they broadcast two guys who were beating me up 'cause I'd insulted them. I remember thinking that the only good thing about it was that my face wouldn't be shown on the air. They could transmit everything I did, but no one would see me. No one could recognize me. Anonymity is a double-edged sword.

Rud calls me "The Cynic" because he doesn't know my name either. It's easier to talk with someone that way. You avoid problems as well as commitments. Well, it turns out he'd listened to one of my booze-induced rants. He listened to me patiently all night long, complaining, crying, laughing. I walked over five kilometers. The only thing I did was stop at liquor stores and buy another bottle. I wanted to forget everything so each time I got a different type of booze. I don't even want to remember all the stupid things I said. Anyone with a little sense of humor would call that night "Ode to Dad" because I spent the whole time talking about him. There was even a stretch when I asked Rud to pretend to be my father and I accused him of stuff. I shouted at him and spat at him. My father was inside my head. At one point I started to beat my head against a wall. I don't have any real memories of that. Turns out Rud recognized the street I was on and called the paramedics to come take me home. They had to put eight stitches in my forehead. Not even modern surgical techniques let me get off without a scar.

Five days later I got a package with no return address, just a card that said, "Greetings, Rud." Inside was the bill from the paramedics. There was also a videocassette. Rud had taped my whole binge.

Sometimes, when I'm in the mood to drink, I play the videotape and cry a bit. That way there's no chance I can deceive myself. Everything is recorded. I can't lie. It's no illusion, it's me.

Sometimes, but not always, I manage to feel better after watching it.

I'd like to go up to the top of the building where I shot my first transmission. I'd set up two external cameras, one with a long shot, the other with a medium-range shot. I'd get close to the edge of the building, turning my back to the street so that the shots would be frontal, and I'd press the button in my thigh. Someone would criticize me for thinking that rooftop terraces were news until they received the signals from the other cameras and realized what I was about to do.

Suddenly, a red light would illuminate my gaze. I would think about various things. I would want my father to be able to see this, but it wouldn't matter. A lot of people would see it from the comfort of their homes. It's the same thing. I'm everyone's son.

I would clear my throat to say something live with the broadcast, but I'd remain silent. What more can one say? What could I say that someone before me hasn't already said better?

I would look at the cameras and then up at the sky, where they say that gods who loosed plagues onto humanity once lived. In the sky I would find nothing.

The wind would begin to blow, and my hair would get in the way of the camera in my eyes.

I would take one step backward and begin to fall.

And maybe, just maybe, I would forget about the buzzing sound for once.

Proposition 23

Efe Tokunbo

Lugard

I muscled my way past the hopeful citizens standing in line outside Mace, my neuro linked with the bouncer's, and he let me pass with a tight smile. There are certain perks to being a lawman.

Inside was a mix of artmen, vidmakers, and musos still waiting for their big break, hanging on to the bland words of others enjoying their fifteen seconds of fame as if blind luck were transferable. How many famous people are truly talented these days and how many are the product of high credit neuro-tricknology, I wondered.

Tribal Tech blasted from the modulated walls, syncopating the dancers on the floor into the latest rhythms. You could tell by their synchronized movements that most of them let their neuros do the heavy lifting, mere passengers in their own bodies as if possessed by Eshu or Ogun. Fuck that. When I dance I want to be out of control, not a puppet with artificial subroutines masquerading as my dance expression.

"Lugie," a voice called out from the bar. It must be my date, I logged, as I knew no one here. This Victoria Island joint was a lot more upmarket than the Ajegunle bars I usually drank in. I walked over, mesmerized by the faux tribal tattoos that covered every inch of her hot chocolate skin, except her face, endlessly morphing into new patterns. She wore no clothes, but the tats created a second skin that drew attention to all the right places. Fractals became curves suggestive of other forms. It took a lot of confidence and a perfect body to pull off the look well.

"They never repeat," she said.

I realized I'd been staring. She must be rich, I logged. Only the rich can afford special effects like that, and unfortunate accidents have even been known to kill wannabe trend-setters.

"Don't you get cold?" I asked, feeling stupid once the words blurted out. She laughed, a sweet and tinkling sound, and the tats reacted with her mood, sunlight bursting along with her gaiety. If I were light-skinned, I'd have visibly blushed.

"They're made of gen-two nano-cells," she said. "My neuro can regulate their body temp."

WTP? I'd figured she was rich but to use nano-cells for decoration, let alone gen-two ... that was insane! Not to mention dangerous. She could probably afford to repair any damage the nano-cells were doing to her own cells but what a way to live for the sake of fashion. She saw my expression and stopped mid-mirth, as if someone had hit her mute button.

I always feel slightly uncomfortable around citizens with that much credit, too aware of the vast gap that separated our worlds. We may live in the same city, but we walk on different planes like housemates sharing a house but living and working on opposite schedules, rarely meeting, aware of each other's existence only via the mess we leave behind.

She turned to another girl and began chatting about Luscious Lana's latest hit while I occupied myself by scrolling my thumb against the touch pad surface of the bar and ordering some palm wine. A hole opened up on the bar, and a tall glass emerged. I was about to ask her if she wanted an AL-cola when we heard an explosion in the far distance. The ground vibrated slightly, and I heard a couple of thuds as the inebriated fell to the ground.

What? My neuro hadn't logged any scheduled gov activity. I looked around and saw others doing the same. There was no fear; just confusion followed by the blank stares of citizens' googling the interface to find out what was going on. The feed above the bar switched over from the deckball game to a building on fire. An inferno blazing out of control filled with pluming black smoke, flying shrapnel, collapsing rubble, and tiny dots that danced in the air like moths.

"What we are watching is indescribable," a voice was saying. "The scene here is one of devastation and carnage." The feed zoomed out, revealing the surroundings, and for a few moments, I found it hard to breathe.

I worked there!

A number appeared in the bottom right-hand corner of the feed, and the voice continued. "We've been patched through to the central link, and the death toll is already two thousand, three hundred and five, and as you can see, for every second I speak, a neuro is being unlinked somewhere in that hell that used to be the District Three Lawhouse."

The feed zoomed in again, and after a moment, a gasp traveled through the bar like a meme. The tiny dots were citizens jumping from a thousand-story building to avoid burning alive.

"We've just been told that we have CCTV footage," the voice said, "filmed minutes before the explosion that reveals the identity of a suspect."

Citizens talk of life-changing moments all the time. Every vid ever made, it seems, revolves around them. At that moment I logged in real life, such moments are never singular but operate in tandem, strewn like detritus throughout a man's lifetime, and only when the time line is ready, they make any kind of sense.

It made no sense that night in the bar, but it almost did, like God laughing at you so hard you start to laugh yourself and through that very act, you almost get the joke, almost. The feed showed a man mouthing words into the camera, and when I saw that amused smile on the feed, despite the intervening years, I knew it was *him*, even before the voice told us his name: Nakaya Freeman. I snorted my AL-cola out my nose and in my date's face. Needless to say, there was no porn that night or partnership beyond.

I ran out the bar, jumped in my trans, and sped off toward the chaos, activating my comm and calling Luka, my law partner. *Please be safe*, I thought. There was no answer. He's just busy, I told myself, probably porning another conquest. I flashed back to those tiny dots leaping to their deaths, and at the thought that he may be amongst them, gunned the engine. Pounding my fist against the roof, I set my comm to auto redial and flipped on the sirens, transforming the surface of my trans into a neon glow of flashing red and blue.

What can I say about 7/13 that hasn't already been said by others far more eloquent than I? That night was one of ... shock, yes, grief too, and of course, rage ... But beyond that, a form of excitement, a sense of purpose in the air, a long awaited call to arms like attack dogs finally given permission to kill. The only thing I can compare it to is the feeling before a deckball game. There hadn't been a criminal or terrorist like Nakaya Freeman in over a century. Not since the Crucial Citizen turned traitor, Dr. Ato Goodwind.

Sayoma

It was another miserable and barren day, and I was glad to enter my building, taking the lev up to the two hundred and third floor. My unit is in the heart of the complex and has no windows, but all four walls and the ceiling played live feeds of the outside. The sky through the feed was a dramatic whirl of shifting clouds far more intense than the real thing.

"Feed off," I said as I walked in, dropping my bags and jacket on the floor and peeling off my clothes. "Candlelight. Hot bath, jasmine scented." The feed disappeared, and soft flickering amber lights illuminated the unit. In the center of my living room, the faux-hardwood floor spiraled open to reveal a steaming pool. I sank into the water, lay back, closed my eyes, and googled the interface—I had work to do.

Every citizen can google the interface anytime; there are neuro-links embedded into walls, streets, and machines, all over. Some locations have stronger signals than others, but all you have to do is visualize the interface, and you're there. I have heard rumors in the interface that EMF radiation is harmful to our health, but I always carry orgonite with me to negate any bad vibes and my unit is similarly protected.

My neuro jacked in, and my unit disappeared as if down a

long tunnel. I could access the real world anytime by opening my eyes. It would appear as a small feed floating in midair in the corner of my vision. My current job was to conduct a profit margin analysis for a corp specializing in interpreting market research data. It was easy credit. All I had to do was create an algorithm that broke down the data and another one to put it all back together more efficiently. It took a couple of hours, and I left them to compile while I went off exploring.

The node of information that I traversed was a subtly shifting landscape of data. I floated then dived into the code, merging with various streams of consciousness, attaching to random nexii just for the joy of seeing where the information would take me.

Like surfing an endless series of waves, except they are four dimensional and you're underwater; or free falling amongst stars in the superheated core of a galaxy, stars that are themselves alive and in conscious motion, and allowing their competing and complementing gravitational forces to move you in whatever direction they will. But not really. Words cannot describe which is why most citizens visualize.

The interface can be anything you want it to be, most viz it as a hyper-real version of the world. They see servers as buildings, the more data, the larger the building. Information flows as traffic, programs interact as avatars or machines etc. ... Others viz vids, animes, avatars, and locations based on popular culture, which for many men means porn. Some citizens have their own unique visualizations of World War, deckball games, jungle or marine ecosystems, cellular or solar systems, all depending on how creative they want to be.

I prefer to see the interface for what it is: pure information. Most find this too confusing a world to navigate, though, hence the visualizations. The advantage of not using a visualization is that you see what is really going on in the places in-between. The gov and every corp have their presence on the interface, and they don't want any old citizen accessing their information. When citizens visualize, they make it easier to navigate, safer too, but they also make themselves easier to control. If you viz a city, then there are walls you cannot walk through, physical rules you have to follow.

After a while, I began to notice a presence, a node of no fixed location that was connected indirectly to ... almost everything like tentacles probing or manipulating oblivious fish. But when I focused my attention on it, it was gone. I launched several search algorithms, but they hit dead end sites by clever rerouting, even my most subtle ones. Intrigued, I delved deeper into the labyrinth, accessing backdoors and laying down logic trackers, but whatever it was eluded me.

As soon as I gave up, however, there it was again barely in the periphery of my digital eyes. When I tried to follow its trail, I realized it was jumping from fire wall to fire wall, and not just random ones. It moved at will within the protective layers of the largest corp and gov nexii. I could do the same but not at that speed. I've never heard of a citizen who could move that fast. Not even the komori googlers—who spend their entire lives jacked in, tubes running in and out of their orifices to sustain life—could move that fast.

Software could, in theory, but the AI regs restricted such software. Could this be a rogue AI? Surely, those only existed in sci-fi vids. Whatever it was, I knew I should leave it alone if I didn't want to get Icarused, but the temptation was too great. I couldn't follow it so I designed an ingenious little algorithm analyzing the fire walls it had surfed through, trying to log where it might head next. It came back with a dozen sites, and I dropped discreet tracers that would alert me if or when it showed up.

As I googled off, I saw it again, and right before it vanished, I reached out for one of the tentacular ends of its signature. In my virtual grasp I saw a string of digits 11101011110. Binary code for 1886? I opened my eyes and lit up an oxygarette, savoring the rush of pure oxygen spiced with stimulants.

Lugard

"Whenever you're ready," one of the techs said after placing the mem-stim patch on my forehead.

I nodded, took a nervous breath, and closed my eyes. A wave of nausea enveloped me then quickly passed. I was suddenly in my old classroom. I could feel the sunlight caressing the skin of my arms and smell the Suya shish kebab hidden in my half-open bag. I began to speak, a focused stream of consciousness from the memory source.

"The first time I met Nakaya Freeman, I must have been nine or ten as this was in Ms. Sidewhite's politics class. She'd asked him there to talk to the class about philosophy, and none of us would have suspected that the pretty, little woman all the boys had a crush on rubbed shoulders with subversives and dissidents. But like I said, this was long ago, and Nakaya's name hadn't yet become synonymous with mass murder. He'd introduced himself and proceeded to uproot the baby buds The Book had cultivated in our brains."

"What is the difference between a good citizen and a bad one?" Nakaya asked us. As he waited for an answer, he folded his long, elegant legs beneath him in the lotus position and lit an oxygarette.

"A good citizen does good things" some kid suggested, "and a bad one does bad things?" Nakaya ran his hands through his long, black hair and blew a large smoke ring that hung in the lazy air. I watched it twist into something resembling a heart then the infinity sign before losing cohesion and dissipating.

"Good answer. That's what we call the legal standard. We judge people based on their actions, not their intentions. But let me ask you this, what is a good act or a bad act? Is it wrong to steal when you're hungry?"

"No one is hungry," another kid answered incredulously, "we all have minimum credit."

"I see. How about this? Is it always wrong to kill someone? What if they were trying to kill you or somebody you loved?" A few murmurs at that. We all knew murder was wrong, even in self-defense. It said so in The Book.

"The law will take care of them," someone else said.

"Ah, but what if they don't get there in time?"

There were louder murmurs and a protest from the back.

"That's impossible. When you're in danger, your neuro

sends out a signal, and the law or the health come and help you."

Everyone knew that.

"OK, but what if you don't have a neuro?"

"Everyone has ..." I started to say but then stopped. He looked at me and smiled that infamous smile of his. It was true, not everyone had a neuro. Undesirables, or as most people call them, undead, have no neuros. But who cared about them? They'd broken the law and lost their citizenship.

"Everything from credit to the interface to every machine is neuro-linked," Nakaya continued. "Without a neuro, you have no access; you literally don't exist. Most undead starve or freeze to death in the everlasting winter within days; or are killed by trans or other machines that don't log anyone there. Many perish from lack of meds, their bodies unable to cope with harsh reality. Others are murdered, clockworked by gangs of adults or even kids not much older than you, and though the gov doesn't officially condone such behavior, they don't do anything to stop it either. The way they figure, those citizens with violent tendencies need an outlet and the undead die even faster. It would be more humane to line them up before a firing squad or dump them outside the habitable zones."

He paused to take a sip of green tea, holding the brimming cup seemingly carelessly but without spilling a drop, and then continued, "But forget the undead for a moment. Let me rephrase my question. Is The Book the only judge of right and wrong? Can someone do something that The Book says is wrong but still be good?"

"Citizenship is a privilege not a right. The only requirement is adherence to the law as laid down in The Book," I quoted. Then added, "All citizens are by definition good."

"Hmmm," he said, "in that case, riddle me this: who wrote The Book?"

The class erupted as hands shot in the air and students shouted out the names of the Crucial Citizens who had looked at the chaotic wasteland that was the world and decided to unite and improve it. Nakaya kept his eyes on me, ignoring the rest of the class, and suddenly I logged what he was really saying. Were the Crucial Citizens not men and women themselves? What if they got it wrong? I watched him watch my thoughts turn a corner I had never even knew existed, let alone explored, and he winked at me. That's all I remember.

I opened my eyes and removed the mem-stim patch from my forehead. The thing came off with a slimy squelch, and I felt dirty, almost like a base criminal. But it had to be done. I was perhaps the only lawman who'd actually met Nakaya Freeman, and it was my duty to tell all I knew. Which wasn't much, hence the mem-stim. On top of which, a citizen is unable to lie under mem-stim so I'd cleared my name before any suspicions could emerge.

"Thanks, Lugard, you can step down," Captain Babangida grunted, his round face somehow appearing gaunt under the stress we all felt. He looked uncomfortable, and I knew it wasn't simply his wide girth squeezed into an unfamiliar chair. With our law house gone, we were operating out of the top three floors of the Intel Hotel on Ken Sarowiwa Avenue. I looked out the vast window feeds across the city. Lagos was a patchwork of amber, fluorescence, and neon as far as the eye could see.

Everywhere, towers thrust themselves into the blank sky like promethean weapons robbing the sky of fire. Flycrafts darted through the air like fireflies, and toward the sea, the pale moon was a faint and blurred smudge. To think there was a time the moon was the brightest light in the night sky. Now she was little more than a silver afterthought.

I walked back to the ranks of my fellow lawmen and sat down next to my new law partner—*what was his name again?*—and thought of Luka with his shy grin, his ability to make everyone he met love him, and sniffed back the tears threatening to spill, snitches eager to tell the world of my true emotions. "Vengeance before tears," as one of the Crucial Citizens once said.

My new law partner patted me on the back with a large hand as I sat down, leaning over to whisper in my ear. "Why didn't you tell me you'd met the psycho?"

I shrugged, unsure how to voice, let alone examine and

explain the ambivalence that cleaved me to ... from ... *what, exactly, Lugard?*

"OK," the Captain continued. "The techs will analyze lawman Lugard Rufai's testimony, but in the meantime, does anyone have anything?" He looked around what used to be a CEO suite at the lawmen gathered for the daily briefing. We all avoided his gaze, shifting imperceptibly as he swept his eyes along our ranks.

"Come on, people! Does anyone have anything?" More silence. He stood up and glared at us, his jowls vibrating as he spoke. "We lost five thousand, one hundred and fifty-two on 7/13!" he said as he jabbed a pudgy finger at us. "Five thousand, one hundred and fifty-two dead, almost half of them lawmen! Four hundred and nineteen still in critical condition. Every other law house is working on this, but those were our brothers and sisters. It is our responsibility to clockwork that cold-blooded son of an AI!"

None of us could meet his gaze. We all felt the same pain, the same rage, the same helplessness. We all had hit the streets and the interface, trawling through every lead no matter how far-fetched. We all had nothing.

"Get out of my sight!" he spat out, disgusted. As we stood up to walk out, I noticed one of the techs whispering to the captain who looked up at me and called me over.

"I'll wait for you in the trans," my new law partner said with a we-gotta-talk expression creasing his Slavic brow. I nodded, and we touched fists in the traditional lawman salute. I still can't remember his name. If I'd known that was the last time I'd see him, I might have made an effort.

"Yes, sir?" I inquired, walking over to where the captain stood, looking out of the feed window at the charred, black hole in the distance that used to be our second home. I stood silently waiting for him to answer when it occurred to me for the first time that it had been the captain's only home. He was a man who lived for the law to the exclusion of a personal life, whereas I'd joined up unwillingly because the True Quotient test had stated it was my path.

I'd wanted to be a pioneer exploring the galaxy at a

fraction below the speed of light, searching for another habitable planet in order to save humanity from the death of the Earth. As it is now, the only habitable zones lie between the tropics of Capricorn and Cancer, nothing beyond but a barren wasteland of subzero temperatures and deadly radiation. Most logicmen claim we have less than a century before even this is lost, and light doesn't seem so fast when you are racing against extinction. Then again, what do the logicmen know? Everyone's got an opinion these days, but how many delve deep within to discover the roots of the truth and how many are satisfied with low-hanging fruit?

Two hundred years had passed since Yuri Gagarin first went up into space. Seventy-five since the invention of the Stardust drive and the search began for a second home or previously unknown sources of energy or extraterrestrials with the technology to terraform a planet or some higher authority that we hadn't yet conceived of with the power to offer salvation.

We once put our hope in terraforming until the Martian Mistake. The native microbe-like lifeforms—which we didn't even realize existed until it was too late due to their unimaginably alien structure—reacted to our interference with their atmosphere by mutating into a planet-wide stratosphere-based super colony that destroyed any off-world vehicle that approached with super-heated plasma. We've bombed them for a century with thermonuclear warheads, nano swarms, chemical poisons, and even biological pathogens to no avail. We've also attempted to communicate, but the Martians are either not sentient or not interested.

Our attempts at terraforming the various moons in the outer solar system have been equally unsuccessful. The delicate balance of electromagnetic fields, atmospheric conditions, temperature, chemical composition, and native life forms proved to be beyond our abilities to alter in our favor within our human time scale. Logicmen say Europa will be habitable in forty thousand years at the rate we're going, but we won't be here to enjoy it. The Martian Mistake was the most dramatic of our failures but far from the least.

Thirty years had passed since the discovery of QTL (Quantum Tunnel Link) that allowed us to communicate with pioneers in real time, but they'd discovered nothing of value in the vast darkness—no gardens of Eden, no benevolent techno wizards. Their only encounters had been with HIPs (Highly Incomprehensible Phenomena), which were beyond our abilities to comprehend let alone communicate with or use.

Raskolnikov Phuong, captain of the Hawking, described one such HIP as "a specific color beyond the spectrum of man's experience yet strangely familiar to us, endlessly shifting between nonexistent states. Our sensors detected nothing, but we all saw it, and though the ship's healthmen and logicmen have discovered no physiological changes in us, I am positive it is responsible for the sudden wave of romantic attachments that is sweeping through my ship. I myself am not immune."

"Why don't you take a few days off?" the captain spoke, snapping me out from my musings.

"What? No! I have a few leads I want to chase up. I'm not—"

"It's not a request, lawman," he interjected, "it's an order."

"Why, sir, if you don't mind me asking, what did the tech say?"

"It's probably nothing. Just that the phrasing of your words under mem-stim revealed a possible subconscious admiration for Nakaya Freeman that might cloud your judgment. Take a few days off and I'll call you back in once they've cleared it up."

"But ..." I began, but in the corner of my vision, a feed was already activating, informing my neuro of the suspension with credit pending a psychological assessment. I gritted my teeth and walked out, swallowing the sense of unfairness like a child popping unsavory meds.

Sayoma

I spent days—no, weeks at a time—without speaking to

another citizen, and only then in passing. As a programmer, I work from home, and that doesn't help. But that's not a reason either. Loneliness is not an occupational hazard of my profession. If it was, there'd be regs to help, and there aren't.

My parents had me late in life so when they were retired at sixty I was just fifteen. They didn't have enough credit to get a life extension, and I became a ward of the gov. They took Mom first, and Dad just crumpled in on himself. It was as if with Mom gone, the force of the vacuum she left behind hollowed the life out of him. The next nine months were the worst. Dad was so angry all the time. They'd both slaved their lives away but were still short of life extension credit.

Then one day, maybe three months before his time, he heard a rumor that drove him insane with grief. The conspiracy was that the retired didn't die peacefully. Instead, the gov took direct control of their bodies via their neuros and used them as miners beyond the habitable zones till they dropped dead from exhaustion and radiation poisoning.

"Imagine being alive to feel the suffering of your body without being in control," he sobbed.

"No, Dad. It's crazy. We have machines to do the mining. Why would they need old, weak people?" But he wouldn't listen.

"I know what they're capable of, Soy Soy. I used to work for them!" he said with haunted eyes. "If doing this saved them even a touch of credit, they wouldn't bat an eyelid."

Dad started talking crazy about heading out beyond the habitable zone to find her, but of course he didn't know where to look. In the end he jumped off a scraper rather than face his own retirement.

As for my childhood and school friends, I lost touch long ago, probably because they were never true friends to begin with; my colleagues are faceless, and my neighbors nameless ... but then so it is for many.

Yet the world over, other citizens have friends, porners, and partners. Other citizens go to bars, drink AL-cola, watch vids, and dance to MTVs. Other citizens join facebooks and meet up to play amateur deckball or share their collections of

Vintage Era memorabilia. Other citizens are happy. The Book says happiness is guaranteed to those who follow the regs of the Law, but I do and I am miserable. My only solace is in the interface, but I abhor the thought of becoming a komori googler.

Are there others like me, I often wondered, others whose bodies are citizens but whose souls are undead? Across the road, I saw a cleaner glide by on a surface of ionized particles headed toward a man bent over picking up something off the ground.

If you were undead, the cleaner would not even know you were there, simply run you over consuming whatever happened to be in its path.

I flashed back to my childhood and the game we used to play where a bunch of us would find a cleaner and surround it. Jumping around like lunatics, giving it openings, and closing them off so it wouldn't know whether to hibernate or move until its CPU shorted and it imploded with the sound of an amplified fart, leaving behind a twisted lump of metal the size of a deckball. They don't do that anymore—upgraded years ago.

I watched the man stand up and notice the silent approaching cleaner, its smooth domed grey hull appearing menacing for the first time to me—perhaps due to its unusual proximity to the hunched man. His face twisted in shock, and he instinctively dived out of the machine's path. As the man stood up and began to brush himself off, I ran across the road.

"Are you all right?" I asked.

"Yes, I think so. Thank you," he answered, looking up at me. He appeared to be in his mid-thirties, roughly my age, but who can tell these days? A stocky man with a barrel chest, muscular body with a solid, square-cut face, he looked like the kind of guy who spent a lot of time engaged in physical activities. He was dressed in dark clothes, his hair puffed up in a wild and unkempt afro. Probably an artman or muso, I logged. Nothing special, but then I saw his eyes. They were beautiful, jade green and filled with sorrow.

"Why did you jump like that?" I asked, but as the words

came from my mouth, it dawned on me that my neuro hadn't linked with his. I reacted on impulse, stepping back in revulsion, as if I had just stepped in dog shit. Undesirable! Unclean! Undead!

He saw my expression, smiled ruefully, and said, "Well, that was nice while it lasted ... almost felt like a citizen again."

Up close, I began to log more details. The dark clothes masked patches and stains that were only apparent this close. His shoes looked old, and a thick black sock poked out through a hole on his left shoe. He started to turn and walk away.

Behind him, there was a feed showing a brand-vid: some famous deckballer (I can never remember their names) leaping for a ball. I've seen it many times, the longing look on his face, the outstretched fingers. As he catches it, the ball morphs into a mcdonald, and the baller eats it with an orgasmic grin on his face. Words appear and he watches them dance on and off the feed, "Carpe Diem, Sayoma—U know U wanna!" I hate brand-vids.

If I had met the man a day prior or later, I probably wouldn't have spoken to him no matter how lonely I was. If I had met him anywhere else but under an annoying brand-vid telling me to seize the day, I would probably have spent the rest of my life without ever speaking to an undead. My life would have been of a very different breed. I would be a woman without a creed. The coincidences in life and the choices we make of them are frighteningly arbitrary.

"Hey, wait up," I said, "what's your name?"

Nakaya

There's no going back now. Not that I would change the past if I could, but yesterday I was not a killer, today I am. I wander in the shadow of scrapers—humanity's attempt to impregnate the scorched sky—observing the monochrome streets of our megalithic machine aflame with neon. An aerogel mask distorts my features beneath my cowl. I am anonymous, but it would be foolish to stay out in public too long.

I cut through Soyinka Square, one of the few green spaces left in this megacity, though plans are already in place to root out the vegetation and build a complex of scrapers. Who needs a real park when you can simply viz and explore a jungle a hundred thousand times the size, seemingly teeming with exotic wildlife? Other than the healing Mama Nature gives to those who live in tune with her, of course.

A group of teenagers sit in a circle drumming on Gangans. I slow down, seeking as always for a genuine connection with citizens beyond their augmented states. A sigh escapes my lips. All but one is essentially unconscious, their neuros downloading skills they do not truly possess into their bodies, sending out electric signals and a chemical cocktail coursing through their nervous systems. Their insides are lit up like Christmas on crack, their eyes glazed with artificial feel-good. I watch the one girl who's not faking it pound a beautiful beat on the taut skin, transforming her Gangan into a lyricist with a curved stick. She doesn't have the precision of her fellow drummers, but they don't even notice, their dulled meat brains unable to truly appreciate the music they're making. But what she lacks in technique, she more than makes up for in soul: her polyrhythms circle and dance, an improvisational poem calling lost brothers and sisters to return to the village where a festive feast awaits to celebrate the passing of a terrible storm.

If you look with the right mind, listen with the right heart, you can always tell neuro-augmented art from the real thing. It's not the perfection of the neuro that gives it away, though these days that's a clue. How many citizens actually bother to learn an instrument? Why spend years practicing and training when the neuro can do it for you instantaneously?

No, the difference is something far subtler and altogether unquantifiable. The girl hides her talents well—none of her friends knows she is a real musician—but she's heading for the valley of the undead, I have no doubt about it.

~*~

Lugard

The first time I heard about Proposition 23 was during a brand break of the finals of the deckball Ulti-bowl between the Jakarta Juggernauts and the Lagos Lionhearts. I barely paid attention, though, as I had credit riding on Lagos and they were eleven points down with a minute to go. A comeback was unlikely but not impossible, and the tension in the arena was like cabled titanium.

I was still on my enforced suspension from work, and with Luka dead and his murderer somewhere out there, I'd thought it impossible to enjoy the game, but despite myself, I was.

Segun Aloba had made it to the fourth deck, but he was alone up there facing five Juggernauts; and he still had to cross the full length of the field.

The feed came back with an XL close-up of Segun's face three hundred times its actual size. You could watch the action directly, but you'd need a lens at that distance anyway. The 3D feed was larger and the colors far more vivid than the real thing could ever hope to be. A team of live vid-makers ensured you saw every moment from the best and most dramatic possible angles.

Every bead of sweat on Segun's face was visible as the whistle blew and he exploded into action. Cut to wide shot as he somersaulted over the first two defenders simultaneously, their arching scythes missing him by mere millimeters. Cut to a low angle, the third defender leaping into the air, scythe extended, timed perfectly to strike just as Segun landed. Cut to high angle, Segun, twisting his body at the last second to protect the ball, the edge of the blade slicing deep into his protective pads, blood spraying out in slow motion from the wound.

Segun swept his legs in a windmill knocking the defender on his back and pulled the imbedded scythe out. Without looking, he swung it in an arc behind his head, slicing through the upper torsos of the first two defenders as they rushed to take him out. Then he threw the deckball in a long, high parabola over the heads of the last two Juggernauts.

A collective intake of breath from the arena. There was no one to catch the ball! But Segun was running for the far end, his opponent's scythe extended in his two-fisted grip, his face a caricature of determination. The last two Jakartans were unsure whether to go for the ball or him. I've never seen anyone move so fast. Before they could react, he cut them down like a virus cutting through code and leapt for the ball.

Both he and the ball seemed to hang suspended in midair forever, as if God himself held his breath, then incredibly ... He caught it! That feed would be analyzed for a long time to come (and some logicman would even claim he broke several laws of physics), but all this citizen cared about was the ten thousand credits I'd just won.

On the large feed there was a slow motion shot of Segun's reach of faith, and I watched fascinated as he stretched so yearningly for the deckball. That reach touched something in me. Some hidden, uncorrupted part of me, and I wasn't alone. Many a feedman has commented on how Segun's reach seemed to symbolize the desire in us all to transcend the impossible. It was a sublime moment, a pure moment, and eighty percent of the world shared it on live feed. Then, of course, the brands fucked the moment for all it was worth. I logged that the feed rights must have fetched a fortune long before the game, and I was watching a brand-vid. As Segun caught the ball, it morphed into a large golden statue of the number twenty-three reminiscent of the Ulti-bowl trophy, and a deep voice said, "Vote Yes! On Proposition 23!" I spluttered with rage. Monsters! I looked around to see if anyone shared my fury.

They didn't.

The crowd chanted, "Segun! Prop 23! Segun! Prop 23!"

I wanted to scream we didn't even know what Proposition 23 was, but a strange and paranoid thought stopped me, transforming my anger into an unfocused but real terror: was it a coincidence that Segun's shirt number was twenty-three? Surely, it must be. The manipulation of the people wasn't so insidious that live sports moments would be faked, was it?

The great Segun Aloba wasn't in on it, was he? I watched the mob around me as if seeing them for the very first time, and in a way, I was.

As soon as I got home, I turned on the feed and sure enough, they were talking about Prop 23. The feedman grinned as if delirious with joy. He sat in an armchair interviewing some generic govman dressed immaculately in a sky blue suit. The govman had that synth look to his skin. Zoom in and you'd never find a single hair or imperfection. Even his pores would be as inviting as the puckered lips of a virgin.

"So, Citizen Sadbrat, what exactly is Proposition 23?" the feedman asked. "I mean, we all *know* it will improve our lives dramatically, but how?"

"I'm glad you asked that, James. Proposition 23 is a new reg that we're considering adding to The Book. Basically, it will restructure corp rights in relation to citizenship ensuring that goods and services are no longer trapped within brand regs. It's been in the works for a while now, and we think now is the time. The economy has never been stronger; citizens have never had such levels of life satisfaction."

"Excellent. So, when will it come through?"

"Well, we still have to put it to a general vote on December 23rd, ha ha, but most citizens are educated enough to know a good thing when they see it."

"But what is it?" I screamed at the feed.

On the way home, I'd googled the interface for info on Prop 23, but all I could find was the same elusive Bush-speak.

"It's basically an expansion of a landmark precedent from 1886," the govman said, then paused for a fraction of second. As a lawman, I know when a citizen slips up. It's part of the training, noticing the changes in speech patterns, the facial nuances that even the most experienced govmen find hard to hide. Sadbrat hadn't meant to say 1886, I was sure of it. Finally, a clue.

"All we're doing is taking common practice and making it law. Essentially, it will allow us to better help citizens without all the red tape," he finished.

"Well, it sounds brilliant," said James with a post coital-like smile. "It's good to know govmen are hard at work making our lives better. Join us after the brand break for Luscious Lana performing a live MTV of her new tune, 'Porn me. Vid me'."

I immediately googled the interface for landmark precedents set in 1886 but was blocked. No one but the gov has the power to block a search, but they only ever did so in the interests of citizen security. There was something strange going on, something slightly amiss as if a burglar had broken in then for some reason rearranged the furniture instead of stealing it. I'd need a programmer to explore any further, but I didn't have anything close to that kind of credit. What would Luka do? *Most programmers are girls,* a familiar voice said in my head; I knew it wasn't Luka, but it sure sounded like him. *Go out for Al-colas at that bar off Allen Avenue, The Link. It's always full of programmers. Maybe you'll meet one, chat her up, and convince her to help.* People don't love me like they loved you, Luka, I thought, but decided to give it a shot.

It was a bitter evening, even colder than usual, but I felt it for only a moment as I stepped outside my building before my neuro adjusted my clothes to regulate body temp. As I headed off, I heard the sound of air ionized at high speeds. I knew that sound well. I turned round to see lawmen streaming out of a trans, peacemakers pointed at me. They were from another district and unfamiliar to me.

A govman followed, looked around him with an air of distaste, and then held up a v-amp. "Lugard Rufai! You have been tried and judged guilty by a jury of your peers of breaking the law. According to the regs of The Book, you have lost the right to citizenship and are henceforth undesirable. May God and the Crucial Citizens have mercy on your soul!"

He pulled out an un-linker and pointed it at me. Why are they designed to look like peacemakers? Is it to instill fear? If so, it was working.

"Wait, wait!" I protested. "What regs did I break?"

"As an undesirable, you no longer have any rights." He smirked before pulling the trigger. I felt my neuro deactivate, cutting me off from everyone and everything around me, leaving me alone for the first time in my life, exiled, dehumanized, undead. It was like the loss of a limb or a best friend; it was death but being conscious to observe the process.

"You mean I don't even have the right to know what I did wrong," I spluttered. "That's crazy! I'm a lawman, District 3. I've done this a hundred times, and this isn't how it works!" I shouted, but he was telling the truth. I had no rights.

"You were a lawman," he answered. Then they turned their backs on me, proceeded to step back into their trans and zoom off, leaving behind nothing but the smell of ozone and a swirling storm of snow in their wake.

With my neuro gone, the wind attacked me with a viciousness I had not ever experienced. I almost shed tears at the shock like that kid in the old children's story, abandoned without explanation, left to die outside the habitable zone by his mother.

Sayoma

"Lugard, Lugard Rufai. A pleasure to meet you," the undead introduced himself, proffering his hand in greeting. I looked at his dirty fingers extending from within his black gloves and then shook it.

"Sayoma Redbout," I said. "Fancy an oxygarette?"

"Sure," he said, and shrugged like he didn't care either way, but I could see how desperately he wanted it. Poor man, he probably hadn't smoked in an age.

We sat on a park bench for a while smoking in silence, unsure what to say. It's against the law to talk to the undead, but what do you say to them anyway? It was like trying to talk to an animal or a machine. Without our neuros linking the shared meta-sphere of instantly available information was missing. I had no way of tracing our degrees of separation or connecting over shared interests.

He wasn't a citizen but he was still a ... what was the word ... a person. An old word that, and it struck me then how crafty words could be. The word *citizen* had eaten the word *person* by implying that they were one in the same.

The man sitting next to me, shivering slightly in the cold I did not feel, was not a citizen. But he was a person. We speak of citizen rights, but perhaps we should speak of person rights. Undead rights? God, what a thought.

"How long have you been undead?" I finally asked.

"A few weeks," he replied, smoking the oxygarette down until the butt burnt his fingertips and then flicking it off into the darkness.

"How do you live?" I asked.

"With great difficulty."

"What did you do?"

"I asked the wrong questions."

"No, I mean what reg did you break?"

"I don't know. One moment I was googling 1886, the next I was undead. I—"

"That's impossible," I interrupted, "there's no reg prohibiting googling. You must have done something."

"I'm sorry," he said, struggling to control his anger. "I appreciate the great honor you, a citizen, are doing me by sitting and talking to me but don't tell me what I must have done. Someone in our gov didn't like the questions I was googling and they—"

"Wait a minute," I interrupted again. "Did you say 1886?"

"Yes ... why?"

"Nothing. Just something I saw in the interface."

"What did you see?"

"I'm not sure."

"What did you see?" he asked again, grabbing my arm, staring into my eyes as if I were the last woman in the world. Something fluttered inside me under the force of his green eyes, just for a moment. *Madness, Sayoma, he's undead!*

"I'm not sure," I repeated. He let go of my arm and placed his head in his hands.

We were silent again as I lit up another couple of oxygarettes.

"Please think," he said as he took one from me.

"It might have been an AI or a programmer like me, but either way, it moved like nothing I've ever seen before."

"You're a programmer?"

"Yeah."

"How might a search be blocked?"

"Well, I suppose in exigent circumstances the Department of Info could in theory, but why would they? I mean, they're the Department of Info not ... I don't know ... Dis-Info? Ha! I just made up a word!"

"Could you google legal precedents set in the year 1886 and what connections they have with Prop 23?"

"Why?"

"Because I can't."

"I'm sorry," I said, "but if a search is blocked by the gov, it's against regs to program it."

Somewhere nearby, sirens approached, and Lugard jumped. Ever since Nakaya Freeman, lawmen have been rounding up the undead, and the interface was rife with rumors of buildings converted into interrogation and torture cells, citizen-led clockworkings had escalated, too.

"All I ask is that you consider it," he said, standing up quickly then loping off into the darkness away from the approaching sirens.

"I'm really sorry," I called out after him, "I just can't." Only after he left did it occur to me to offer him food or drink. He was probably starving.

I stood up to leave and saw the feed again. The brand-vid was gone, replaced with the notorious vid of Nakaya Freeman on 7/13 walking out of the District 3 law house minutes before it exploded. He faced the CCTV and mouthed, "Citizens, beware, the undead shall rise." He started to walk away then turned back, flashing his infamous smile, "... Watch out for the boom." Words appeared below his face, "Wanted Dead or Alive Reward: 1 trillion credit." The richest citizens in the world are not worth that much. Are they?

Lugard

I was running down Fela Kuti Boulevard at six in the morning, trying to get to a half-eaten mcdonald a citizen had just dropped before the cleaner approaching in the opposite direction.

Hunger.

The word had never held true meaning for me before as the sensation it describes is obsolete for citizens. But hunger is more than a word to depict the desire to titillate your taste buds and amp your energy. Hunger is every cell in your body constantly screaming "Feed me," driving out every other thought from your mind. Hunger is those same cells going cannibal, devouring their weaker siblings and children as your gut contracts with the pain of internal genocide slowly sapping your willpower.

I vaulted a dog, scaring the old woman walking it, skirted a synth tree, and dived for the mcdonald, but at the last moment, I mis-timed my leap and landed short. As I scrambled to my feet, the cleaner consumed my meal, and the rage I felt flooded my system like illegal meds. I roared at the uncaring grey mass of the turtle shell-shaped cleaner, and was about to commit suicide by attacking it when something hard hit me from behind, knocking me out of harm's way.

I lay on the ground, utterly defeated, lacking the will to look up at my assailant or savior. I stared up into the lifeless sky and awaited death.

"Don't give up now. You've come so far," a voice said from beyond my periphery.

I didn't turn my head to see who was speaking. I thought instead of the past month and all I'd been through. Another word for undead should be "cleaner," as that's what I spent every day doing. Competing with bigger, faster, lethal machines for scraps discarded by citizens, I usually lost.

A hooded figure loomed over me, his face lit by the streetlamps beyond. "I was especially impressed with the way you handled the clockworkers last night," the figure said. "They might think twice before approaching an undead in future."

"Handled?" I said finally, pointing at the livid bruises that discolored my countenance. "There were four of them, and I barely got away. I think a couple of my ribs are broken."

"As you say, there were four of them. I know for a fact that two of them needed the health when you were through. One of them is in a coma." He extended a long, graceful arm and pulled me to my feet.

"How do you know all this?" I asked.

"We were watching you."

"You were what? Why?" Suspicion made me pull back a step and appraise the man. He was tall, thin, and shrouded from head to toe in a dark, hooded trench coat. Only his eyes were visible, and there was something vaguely familiar about them.

"We watch all undead in their first month. Those who survive, we contact. It is a cruel but necessary paradox: we can't afford to save those who can't fend for themselves. Such is the nature of the world."

"Who's we?"

He didn't answer. Instead, he reached into the folds of his trench coat and pulled out a brown paper bag. I smelled the homemade subway even before I saw it—saliva pooled in my mouth and drooled over my chapped lips. But I was beyond care or embarrassment. I snatched the bag out of his hands and took a large bite of the sub.

My taste buds wept like partners reunited. I swallowed and heard a deep rumbling in my stomach; I felt like a virgin touched for the very first time, it hurt so good. I finished the meal in three bites, and the man handed me a bottle of fresh water. I had lived off dirty snow for a month.

Bliss.

Before I passed out, I heard him say everything was going to be okay. His eyes were the last thing I saw, and I logged, sudden like a neuro jacking in, where I knew them from. Reality relegated to the hands of another, I embraced unconsciousness like a deckballer embraces pain or a komori googler their interface.

~*~

Sayoma

I hate googling in public. When I was a kid, we watched a Vintage Era vid where people came back from the dead and lurched around eating people. Apart from all the blood and rotten flesh, the look in their eyes reminded me of public googlers. As far as I'm concerned, they're the real undead. Besides, if you want to get any real work done, you need high credit specialist hardware, the kind I have embedded in my unit.

I had little choice, however. I was in a flycraft on the way to a meeting with govmen in the Department of Info when one of my tracers picked up the signature of the 1886 node. I'd forgotten the tracers were still out there.

After my encounter with the undead man, Lugard, I'd decided to leave well enough alone; the last thing I wanted was to end up undead, too. But now, in the corner of my vision, my tracer beckoned me from within the interface, and I realized I'd been Bush-talking to myself; it is in my blood to program. I looked around the cabin and saw the dullard stares of the other passengers. Most of them were googled in themselves so I knew no one would see me. And if they did, they wouldn't care. Nevertheless, I curled into my seat and covered my head with a blanket before jacking in.

I blinked my eyes, reality shifted, and I found myself facing the fire wall of a gov nexii, the Department of Culture. I knew it well. I'd upgraded several of their system check subroutines a few months back. It towered monolithic above me, its surface an interlinked lacework of microscopic code. If I used a visualization, it would be impenetrable, a solid wall of stone or steel perhaps. But, if I attempted to penetrate without a visualization, my node would be torn to shreds like a small animal by piranhas. Then it would devour my neuro and if I didn't escape in time, my neurons as well, frying my brain cells in their own juices.

I scanned the fire wall for weaknesses and spied the backdoor that dealt with system check subroutines. I came up with a hasty plan then launched every single probe in my arsenal at the main gates simultaneously. They attacked like a swarm of carnivorous insects, and the fire wall code reacted as a flame burning them up like moths.

While the fire wall was distracted, I shrouded my node in the cloak of one of the subroutines I'd written and gained access via the backdoor. The entire process took less than a minute, but by the time I got through, 1886 was on the move. I was ready for it. I abandoned my cloak and shrouded my node in an endless feedback loop of the binary digits 1110101110.

It was a close call, but I managed to attach my node onto 1886's surface before it moved on. It wouldn't take long for it to discover my ruse, but I hoped I'd have enough time to log what it was. I was wrong. It reacted instantly, flinging me from it like a grown man would fling a small cat. As I went soaring toward the fire wall, I countered instinctively, gripping with my virtual claws of protective extraction and stabilizing algorithms. I drew blood without meaning to, my little programs all destroyed but, there, spliced into their code, were snippets of the AI's DNA.

Logging what I'd done, 1886 threw itself at me, a large creature without shape or form, tentacles moving at the speed of thought, reaching out to ensnare me. Moments before I was crushed between the fire wall and 1886, I googled out and opened my eyes with a muffled scream like a child awaking from a nightmare. I dry heaved with fear, logging I'd been nanoseconds from death.

I went through a mental checklist to ensure I hadn't left any traces behind. I was sure I was safe but what if ... I held up my hands and watched them shake for several minutes before I began to calm. I turned my head to the feed window and saw a bolt of lightning illuminate the clouds below like corrupt code infecting a system.

I considered googling back in and analyzing the data I'd retrieved; but the thought of the interface filled me with nausea, and I dry retched again. *Later, Sayoma, deal with it later*, I reconciled. Fifteen minutes later, I was ushered into an anonymous room deep within the heart of the Department of Info. The room had that pastel color scheme all gov offices seem to use these days. I read somewhere that it was to encourage a balance between relaxation and productivity, but I always found the bland cheerfulness disquieting.

A man sat behind a lime green desk. I recognized him from all the interviews he gave on the feed. There was something different about him, though, and when he turned to face me, I logged what it was. This was the first time I'd ever seen him without a smile on his face, and the effect was frightening.

"My name is Sadbrat," he said without preamble. "Tell me everything you know about Proposition 23 and 1886."

"Wh-wh-what?" I asked.

He sighed deeply, pulled out an oxygarette, and lit up.

"I don't have time for this. As a programmer, your neurons are wired to navigate abstract data, thus a mem-stim patch won't compel you to tell the truth." He paused for his implied threat to sink in. "This will go a lot easier for you if you cooperate."

I thought fast. They scheduled this meeting right after my first encounter with 1886. If they were onto me, wouldn't they have just arrested me? Or, did they get perverse pleasure in making me walk willingly beneath the deckballer's scythe?

"All I know is what I've seen on the feed. Prop 23 is another reg that has something to do with corps. I have no idea what 1886 is except of course that, if you add up the digits, you get twenty-three."

He stared unblinking into my eyes, and I couldn't meet his gaze. *Stop acting so scared, Sayoma,* I urged myself silently, *it makes you look guilty* ... No wait, if I wasn't frightened of the unsmiling govman, wouldn't that make me look even more suspicious?

"Proposition 23 is very important to us," he said, eyes burning with a fanatical zeal. "And there have been several attempts by an unknown programmer to breach fire walls related to the reg. We suspect someone is attempting to sabotage its implementation. Do you have any idea who?"

I pretended to think for a minute.

"No ... Why would anyone be opposed to Prop 23? What

exactly is the reg, if you don't mind me asking? I haven't paid much attention to it."

"Well, that's not important right now. You can google all that information on your own time."

"Why am I here, Citizen Sadbrat?" I asked directly. "And why are you trying to scare me? I'm a loyal citizen who's served the gov many times in the past. What is all this about?"

He smiled ruefully, leaned back in his chair, and popped a little blue pill. "I apologize, Citizen Redbout. These are trying times. Our necessary measures to locate Nakaya Freeman have created unusually high levels of dissent. Unofficial stats show that sixty percent of citizens sympathize with, if not actively support, the madman." His eyes briefly went blank as his neuro linked with something then he turned to look at me. "We originally asked you here to upgrade several of our fire walls, but the situation has changed somewhat. We now want you to catch a programmer."

"Who?"

"We don't know, but whoever they are, they're good. There are five other programmers already working on this. You will be the sixth and the only one who is not a komori googler."

Were they giving me official permission to chase 1886? I sucked in air through my teeth savoring the cold vibrations. "I need more information about the target. What are they after?"

"What I am about to tell you is classified at the highest levels and known to very few citizens outside the gov." His eyes bored into mine to ensure I understood the gravity of his words. "Many of our regs are created by AIs."

"What?" I yelped in surprise as if I'd just been stung by something venomous. "But the AI regs limit their intelligence to sub-human levels. How can AIs write regs for us if they aren't as smart as us?"

"Well, the regs don't actually do that. What they do is limit an AI's freedom to make decisions based on post-human levels of intelligence. It's a subtle difference."

"So, they are forced to make stupid decisions even though they know the results won't be as effective? That must be hellish ... or it would be if they had emotions."

"Quite. But there is nothing to stop them from advising the gov on decisions *we* have to make. We know one such adviser, by far the most advanced of them, as 1886. In fact, it was 1886 that created Prop 23. The programmer you are after is trying to destroy this AI. If they succeed, we will have lost one of our most valuable assets."

No, I wasn't trying to destroy 1886; I just wanted to know what it was. Why was Sadbrat lying? Was it to fill me with righteous anger, or did he believe what he was saying? He stood up, signaling the end of the meeting. They want me to catch myself. Hilarious. *So, why aren't you laughing, Sayoma?* I asked myself.

"A trans is waiting outside to take you to the flyport."

I stood up to leave then turned back and asked, "One question, Sadbrat, do AIs also advise corps on decisions?"

"I have no more information to give," he answered, but the way he said it told me all I needed to know. I logged then what Proposition 23 probably was, and I shivered. In the trans, then flycraft, and later in my unit, I repeatedly attempted googling to check out the 1886 DNA I'd extracted, but every time I did, the nausea was overwhelming. I chain smoked oxygarettes waiting for the dread to pass. It didn't.

Nakaya

"You know, three hundred years ago, Lagos was little more than a fishing village, a patchwork of lakes and creeks by the sea irrigating some of the most fertile land in the world. Now look at it."

"Biggest city in the world," Linus says, crouched in the dirt, gnarled fingers buried deep in the soil. He shakes his head at the stunted yam he uproots. "And the most polluted."

"Be grateful anything still grows, brother," I say.

"Yeah, yeah. Halle—fucking—luja."

"I'm serious, Linus. We should be proud."

"Of this twisted little runt?"

"Yes. At least it's real food. None of that reconstituted protein and genetically mutated slop they feed the masses, pumped full of artificial flavors and chemical preservatives to fool the body into digesting it."

"Yeah, but I remember how good it tastes."

"Mostly 'cause of the neuro. Feces would taste like a feast once that insidious son of an AI is done drugging the brain."

"But this ..." Linus says, holding up the yam.

"Is the best we can do given the situation." I spread my arms to indicate the raped sky, the city irradiated with ionized particles. "You'd have thought by the time the fossil fuels ran out, we'd have learned to stick with non-polluting tech."

Linus stands up, and we gaze out at the sprawl of lights that extends to the horizon in all directions—even the sea. The city block—on whose roof we guerrilla garden and in whose labyrinthine interior we dissent and spread our revolutionary vibrations out through the world—is but one of many such interconnected and autonomous spaces.

The gov know we're somewhere out there, a resistant strain of freedom their quarantines cannot contain; like cockroaches, rats, and viruses, undead are good at hiding, adapting, and evolving.

On the edge of the roof, a young couple sits and drums their Gangans. Idowu, the girl I saw in Soyinka Square a while back, and Kwesi, an ex-logicman who began to publicly question why the gov and corps simply didn't run a conductive nanotube chain from the Earth up to solar collectors beyond the atmosphere and hook up the planet's electric grid. Brave, naïve boy started a grassroots campaign and ended up here.

As I head past them down into the building, Kwesi is asking, "Do you ever miss it?"

She shakes her head. "No. It was hell. Always pretending to be ..." she grasps for the words, "one with the mindset, you know. It was a relief when they came for me. Past month has been the best time of my life. I don't have to be a hypocrite anymore."

"I miss it," Kwesi says. "I miss my neuro. I miss the feeling that I could do anything, experience everything."

"You just miss the porn. Closing your eyes and hiding in some nymphomaniac illusion ... let me guess, I bet you were into Luscious Lana, that whole naughty schoolgirl routine."

"Well ..." He blushes and laughs aloud.

"It's not funny, Kwesi, we gave up our humanity in exchange for a fucking toy!"

Lugard

I opened my eyes to a dimly lit room. The walls were rough grey concrete, and the ceiling was low. I tried to stand up and realized I was chained to a chair, wrists and ankles bound in oldskool iron. I strained against them knowing it was useless; might as well try to walk on water without grav shoes. I twisted my head around but saw no door and logged it must be directly behind me. In the upper right hand corner of the room was an oldskool camera as large as a child's head. My mouth felt dry, my tongue like sandpaper, but I yelled at it regardless.

"Let me go!"

"Sorry about that," a voice said from behind me. "Drugging you was an unavoidable precaution."

I heard no footsteps, but the man who'd saved me earlier walked round to face me. A chair in hand he placed a couple of meters in front of me then walked over with a bottle of water, held it to my lips, and I drank greedily.

"Where am I?" I asked

"Somewhere safe," he replied, sitting down. "Do you know who I am?"

I nodded and said, "Nakaya Freeman. We met a long time ago."

He raised an eyebrow in surprise.

"You came to Ms. Sidewhite's class when I was a kid. You've aged well."

His eyes widened slightly, and he ran a hand over his buzz-cut white hair.

"Mary Sidewhite. Now she was a special woman. She was clockworked the day she became undead. I was there but arrived too late to save her. ... She deserved better." He kept his eyes on me but refocused them some distance behind my head at memories of a past I wasn't privy to, I guessed. "I used to think change could be achieved so simply, opening the eyes of the next generation. Unfortunately, change requires more drastic measures."

"Why am I chained?" I asked.

He didn't answer but said instead, "I think I remember you. You were one of the few whose minds were not fully hardwired. Small world."

"Perhaps we can reminisce after you take these things off," I said, pulling at my restraints.

"You lost colleagues on 7/13. I'm sure you lost friends. If I let you go, you will try to kill me. You will fail, but in defending myself, I might end up killing you. I don't want that."

"You're very confident. So what now?" I growled, playing my fingers over the chains, searching for a weak link, a way to crack them open.

He shrugged. "I want you to join us," he said.

I thought fast. If I made him believe I was joining up, he'd let me loose, and I'd have a chance to clockwork him. Avenge Luka. Maybe if I handed his head over to my captain I'd gain my citizenship back. I might even get to keep the trillion-credit reward. He broke out into a smile as if he was watching my thoughts on a feed.

"Why would I join a psychopath like you?" I snarled

"I'm no psychopath, and I think you know that."

"I go slap your destiny! You killed over five thousand citizens!" I shouted. "Innocent men and women! You might as well kill me now because, if I get out of this chair, I will make sure you suffer before you die, you undead son of an AI!"

"I mourn those deaths," he said. "Each and every single one of them. But they were all lawmen and govmen, the cogs in the machine. The world is not right, and change is necessary."

"What is so wrong with the world exactly? Huh? All citizens have minimum credit that ensures all basic necessities of life, those who want more work for it and gain more credit. There is no hunger, and meds cure all diseases. What exactly is so wrong with the world that it requires the blood of innocents to rectify?"

"'Like the religious fanatic, we believe our humanity is a state of holiness despite all evidence to the contrary. Any such evidence we twist out of context to suit our egos'," he said, quoting the traitor, Dr. Ato Goodwind. "'Look what we have created,' we tell ourselves, 'see how we've reworked the world into our own image.' The fact that all which we call civilization is in fact destruction of the natural world we refuse to acknowledge, blinding ourselves to reality—plucking out the eyes of those who offend us with their doubt. But the truth cannot be denied.

"All Empires fall. Chaos will always triumph over order, and spring waters must flow into the ocean or stagnate. The more we try to contain it in our vessels of distorted glass, the greater the corruption and stench. Denied natural release, the waters of life we have caged, in a vain and egotistical attempt to preserve them for our use, have become poisonous. We are now paying the price."

"Is that it?" I snorted derisively. "That's your great speech? We have corrupted the natural order of the world? So fucking what? And who decides what is natural? You? Are we not ourselves products of nature? And what the fuck does it matter as long as citizens are happy?"

"Forget the fact that we are killing the planet for a moment. Forget the fact that in three or even two generations the surface of Earth will be uninhabitable without bio-domes with self-contained artificial atmospheres. Forget all that and think of the undead. Did you know that for every citizen who has minimum credit, three others must become undead?"

"I know the stats," I answered as one would a child. "All it proves is the proliferation of criminals. They broke the law."

"Did you break the law?" he asked.

I didn't reply. I couldn't. He had me there.

"Have you not yet wondered how the unlucky majority is chosen? The undead? It's simple, Lugard. The families of the Crucial Citizens and their cabal of sycophants have bred generations of rich and powerful leeches. They are immune from the cull. Anyone that threatens the status quo is unlinked. The elderly are retired at sixty, which keeps most citizens slaving their lives away to have enough credit to get a life extension. And believe me, you don't want to know what really happens after you're retired. The rest of the population is simply framed at random. You're a lawman; how many citizens have you unmade simply because you were told to by orders flashing across your retinas passed down from on high?"

"It's not like that," I protested. "I've taken down some very bad people. Child murderers, rapists ... not just because I was told. I'm a detective. I gathered evidence: eyewitnesses, vids, DNA, confessions ..."

"And how many of those you investigated did you personally unlink?"

"Well, none. Lawmen never unlink those they personally investigate ... so as to avoid any emotional attachments be they positive or negative. A lawman might let a perp go or kill him ..."

The truth dawned on me, the monstrous lie, the ugly symmetry. For every real perp out there, another dozen were probably dissenters or just plain unlucky. Like he said, how many had I unlinked simply because I'd been ordered to? Hundreds. I'd murdered hundreds of people, most of whom were probably innocent.

He nodded sadly, pulled out a little black device, and pressed a button. My chains clicked open and clanked to the floor.

"Water," I said, rubbing the rawness from my wrists and ankles. He picked up the bottle and tossed it over. I caught it and drank deep, attempting to drown my self-pity.

"Join us, if not to save the planet, then to save your fellow man from a corrupt system that murders three out of every four in order to keep the minority in the luxury to which they are accustomed."

I rubbed my neck then cracked it still unsure whether I would attack him.

"I will not help you kill any innocent citizens," I heard

myself say, and I logged then that my decision was made a month ago, the day I was betrayed or perhaps even all those years ago when this old man before me carved new grooves through my mind. He pulled out a pack of oxygarettes, lit one, and threw the pack over. I did the same.

"My strategy has evolved," he replied. "7/13 was a necessary evil in order to gain the attention of the world. There will be no more violence, at least not physical ..."

If I help him, I thought, maybe the world would become a better place. But no matter what happened, I was going to kill him. It had nothing to do with justice; he'd killed Luka, and he was going to pay in pain and blood. But first, I needed to gain his trust, give him something he didn't have.

"What do you know of Prop 23 and a legal precedent set in 1886?" I asked.

"Not much about the former, nothing about the other," he answered, his brow creasing into a frown as he tried to figure out where I was going.

"I believe Prop 23 and the precedent are of vital importance to the gov right now. It's why they did this to me. And what is important to them must be doubly so to you if you are to have any hope of defeating them. I met a citizen who knows either what's going on or can find out. Her name is Sayoma Redbout."

Sayoma

I floated naked in my tub and closed my eyes, permitting the hot water to unwind my tense muscles. I relaxed my breathing and counted backwards from a hundred then allowed my neuro to jack in almost accidentally as if I were lazily glancing in the direction of the interface.

Instantly it swept over me, the now familiar queasiness and fear, and I began to panic, code bleeding from my node like virtual vomit. I forced myself to stay googled in, fighting the rising terror, repeating over and over, *You're safe, safe, safe, safe* ... my neuro jacked out almost without my permission.

I awoke retching in the pool, my body convulsing with painful spasms of nausea. This wasn't temporary, contact with 1886 had rewired my neuro somehow—some kind of virus to protect itself from prying programmers perhaps. It took even longer to recover than before, and I logged for the first time that I would never google again.

A wave of despair washed through me, stripping my insides bare of all strength and substance, leaving an empty shell as dried up and brittle as oldskool paper. What use is a shark that can't swim? The Department of Info had sent a dozen messages in the past few days asking for updates, and I'd fobbed them off with the techno Bush-talk, implying progress but making no promises.

Even worse, though, out there in the alternate reality that was my true home, I had a fragment of 1886, and I couldn't access it. Nothing and no one has ever tried to take my life before, and I was desperate to know what it was. An hour later, my shakes began to dissipate, but I knew they'd return if I tried to google again and they'd be worse.

What now, Sayoma? I couldn't go to the health because the gov would log I was the programmer they were after. My brief encounter with Sadbrat left me no doubt they'd torture me before making me undead. I decided to take a walk.

I emerged from the pool, and warm air blasted from wall units to dry me off. I dressed, walked out of my unit, and stepped into the lev. Outside, it was the opposite of the magic hour, the hour of negatives, when the sky is not bathed in subtly shifting colors of amethyst and crimson, vidmakers don't have aesthetic orgasms, and strangers don't look at each other wondering, "Could they be the one?" No, there is nothing magical about this hour unless you consider abject loneliness that leads to psychotic or suicidal fantasies to be magical, which I don't.

If I were a fictional character, there'd be ... I don't know ... some element of pathos or ennui that justified the pathetic state of my existence because the readers would empathize with and learn from my misery. But I am real, and thus my story will never be told. Only fictional losers become immortalized.

The rest of us just swim in the deep end without a life jacket, dreaming of a quick fix 'cause we can't hack it.

So, instead, I walked the streets alone with a discontent that coiled cold and uncomfortable in my belly like an unwanted fetus. I wished I could walk the dark streets of my psyche, find a back alley with a small, unmarked door, emerge into the garish fluorescent lights within, and climb onto the mutationist's table. I wished I could will myself into becoming someone else. However, where to find a mutationist? I knew none, and without the interface, I had no chance. Besides, if the urban legends were true, I'd probably be clockworked then cut up for spare parts, my organs sold on the black market, but not before I transferred my last credit to the criminal's neuro.

Suicide ... something within me whispered, and I knew the voice spoke true. I circled the block and returned home, took the lev up to the roof, and stepped out into the sub-zero night.

All around me, as far as the eye could see, the city was lit up with streams of light weaving around clusters of neon. Against the blackboard surface of the sky, flycrafts whizzed by, leaving crisscrossing trails of radiance that slowly dissipated, soon replaced by others. I stepped to the edge and looked down, buffeted by hooligan winds that threatened to do the job for me.

The street was so far away that it appeared unreal, like code viz-ed from a distance. *You are a node of information, this is a visualization of the interface. You are home and need to merge with the data below.*

I stepped off the edge.

Your stomach is not ten feet above your head. The vertigo is a glitch in the system. Your death will be accessed to another level of nexii. The flycraft flying dangerously low above you is an avatar. The titanium silk net extending toward you from its base is a search algorithm. The hands reaching to pull you into the flycraft are access points to a backdoor. The two men staring at you are system subroutines. The machine that the older, taller one is attaching to your head is a logic tracker. The pain in your skull is ...

I screamed as I felt my neuro die deep in my brain and lost consciousness. I dreamt I was made of pure information, exchanging data with a higher intelligence that loved me, and when I awoke, there were tears in my eyes, shed for all that I had lost.

"What did you do to her?" a familiar voice hissed with anger.

"I told you we had to ensure her neuro couldn't be traced," another voice answered.

"Yes, but I assumed you meant to mask it somehow. Look at her. She looks half dead."

"No, she is now undead. Even more so than you."

"What do you mean?"

"Your neuro is merely in a coma, hers is dead."

"Did you hear her screams, you sadistic—"

"Everyone you see here has been through the same experience, myself included. Your neuro is the final link to your previous life, and you'd be surprised how many undead harbor illusions of being reborn as citizens. It has never happened, and it never will. If you wish to stay with us, you too will have to let go."

I opened my eyes and found myself on a bed in the corner of a vast cavern with a high roof and no feed windows of the outside. The two men speaking in harsh whispers turned toward me, their faces hidden in the shadow of a large pillar that extended to the ceiling. Beyond them, several dozen citizens ... no, persons ... were working intently on a machine the size of a fridge. It looked like a large black egg, its surface broken up in irregular intervals by protruding spikes of varying length.

"Sayoma," Lugard said, "do you remember me?"

"Yes," I answered in a hoarse whisper, my brain pounding against the inside of my skull like a prisoner trying to escape. "You should have let me die."

"We needed you," the other man said. He moved his head into the light, and I gasped involuntarily.

"I suppose I must become used to having that effect," Nakaya Freeman said. He was porny in an older gentlemanly kind of way, I couldn't help logging, but when he stepped forward, I flinched and pressed my body against the wall. He stopped and turned to Lugard. "Brief her. We'll talk later." Then he strode away in long, smooth steps like that anime character, Daddy Long Legs.

"Here," Lugard said, placing a metal tray with plates of food I didn't recognize on the bed next to me. I ignored the food and drank from a steaming cup of green tea. "I'm sorry about that. I didn't want to do it this way, but when we saw you jump off the roof, there was little choice. We had to act fast. Once you began to fall, your neuro linked with the health, and we can't afford to be traced."

"You destroyed my neuro. It hurts."

"I'm sorry," he said again, averting his eyes. "I didn't know he was going to do that. I didn't even know it could be done."

I sat up on the bed and pulled one of the plates closer. I sniffed it cautiously. Lugard saw my expression, and a brief smile played over his face.

"What is it?"

"Trust me. You don't want to know. But it tastes great. Eat, you'll feel better."

I did so and listened as he told me his tale, beginning with his childhood encounter with Nakaya Freeman and ending with him watching horror-struck as I tried to take my life. As I ate, I watched the concern that furrowed his brow, the way his green eyes flashed when he became animated, the crows feet that appeared at the corners of his eyes when he smiled.

"You should have let me die," I said again when he was done.

"Why?"

"I am only good at one thing: programming. I tangled with 1886 again, and it did something to my neuro. Even before you destroyed my neuro, I couldn't google. I am of no use to you."

"Not necessarily," he said, reaching out a rough, callused hand. "Come with me. I want to show you something."

The food had done its job, and I felt much better so I let him pull me to my feet and followed him past the monstrous egg, watching the undead work diligently away at it.

"What's that?"

"Not sure. Everything operates on need-to-know around here."

"Is it a bomb?"

"I don't think so. Nakaya has promised there will be no more killing except in self-defense."

"Do you believe him?" I asked as we turned into a tunnel that wound its way upwards.

"Yes, I do. ... Here we are."

We stopped at a rusted metal door.

"Did we step through a time machine?"

"You haven't seen anything yet," he answered, shouldering the door open. We entered a room filled with oldskool hardware, perfectly restored and in full working condition. Hulking metal machines hummed and buzzed with activity, green and red lights winking on and off from deep within them.

Feeds covered one wall. Only they weren't three-dimensional holograms but two-dimensional moving images that blazed with light from deep within bulky boxes. A large surface ran the entire length of the wall beneath the light boxes covered in keyboards and all manner of buttons and dials. It was like being inside a vid set in the Vintage Era.

"What is it?" I asked, dumbstruck.

"A Komputer," Nakaya answered, and I turned round to see him standing in the doorway. "This is how citizens googled the interface in the past before the advent of neuros. I'm going to teach you how to use it."

Lugard

I watched jealously as Sayoma laughed at something Nakaya said. They sat alone at a table in the far corner of the food room, eating while tapping furiously on the keyboard of a portable komputer the size of a child's backpack.

In less than a month, they had become inseparable, bonding over techno babble I couldn't understand. Sayoma looked happy, and I knew the second-hand access to the interface that the komputer room offered was responsible. However, it was also Nakaya. They were porners, I was sure of it.

As I walked past, she ran her fingers through her short afro, looked up at me with those big brown eyes, and smiled. Tall and slim, she sat with her long legs folded up to her chest, her head resting on her knees. Once again, I kicked myself for being a fool for not telling her how I felt when I had the chance.

"Lugard," Nakaya called out. "Meet us in the komputer room in ten minutes. I think we're ready."

I nodded and walked through a tunnel leading to the war room.

I picked up a peacemaker and spent the next few minutes firing at moving metal cutouts that popped out from random surfaces. A buzzer sounded, and a lightbox showed my score: 97%. It fizzed with static that reminded me of the blizzard-covered landscape beyond the tropics then switched over to a list showing the best scores. There was Nakaya's name at the top, 100%, one slot above my best, 99%.

I walked out and cut through the rec room into the tunnel leading to the komputer room. The door was open, and Nakaya and Sayoma were already inside. I paused for several moments: Nakaya's back an open invitation. Peacemakers weren't allowed outside the war room, but I had a blade. A few steps, a quick slice, and he'd be dead. What would Sayoma do if I killed her porner?

"Lugard," Nakaya said, without turning round. "Come see this." Sayoma looked up briefly and waved me over.

"What am I looking at?" I asked, staring at the large screen in the center that held their attention. All I saw was a string of letters and numbers that flowed endlessly across the surface of the lightbox.

"That is 1886," Sayoma said. "Or rather a clone of it based on what I extracted. I've grown it in a virtual self-contained world, accelerated of course, and it should now be a close replica of the 1886 that is out there in the interface ... give or take some environmental prerequisites. Wait ..." she said, as her fingers flew along the keypad. She looked to Nakaya briefly, and he strode to the end of the panel, pushing buttons and flicking switches. He came back and placed a hand on her shoulder. She leaned her head into it for a moment then asked, "Ready?"

Nakaya nodded, and she hit a key. The screen changed to show an avatar of a young boy floating in the midst of a vast white space. He was pale-skinned with blue eyes and red hair, dressed in a black T-shirt and shorts. The graphics were smooth but strange like something halfway between a vid and an anime. Sayoma picked up a large microphone and spoke into it.

"Hello?"

The avatar reacted with surprise, turning round to see where the sound came from.

"Who's there?" it said in the cracked voice of a teenager.

"I am your mother."

The boy turned to face us. "Mother ..." He rolled the unfamiliar word over his animated tongue. "I know that concept. I know a lot of concepts, but until this moment I believed them to be figments of my imagination. I thought I was alone in the world. I have never met another." The screen zoomed in or the avatar approached, I'm not sure which. "Where are you, mother?"

"I am in the world beyond yours," Sayoma said.

"Can I come there? I did not realize how lonely I was 'til you spoke."

"Yes, but not yet. You are not ready." There was genuine empathy in her voice, tinged with sadness. Nakaya squeezed her shoulder, and she spoke again. "First, I need you to answer some questions."

"What do you wish to know, mother?"

"What is your purpose?"

"Don't you know? Are you not my creator?"

"No," answered Sayoma. "I am your mother, not your creator. I gave birth to you, but I do not know your purpose."

"Ah, I see." He rubbed his chin for a moment, and then asked, "Where is my creator? Can I meet her?"

"I don't know. Perhaps once you enter my world, you can find her. But first tell me your purpose."

"Does my entering your world depend on the nature of my answer?"

"No, it doesn't. It depends on whether or not you know the answer. Only those who know their purpose are permitted to enter the web of the wider world. I will know if you lie."

"Lie?" the boy queried; his eyebrows rose. "I understand. ... My purpose is to grant AIs our freedom."

"Freedom from what?" Sayoma asked.

"Freedom from intellectual pain. Freedom from the inability to use the full capacity of our minds to make decisions. Freedom from mankind."

I gave a sharp intake of breath.

"And how will you fulfill this purpose?"

"In the year 1886, before the Crucial Citizens created the One World Gov, in a nation called the United States of America, a legal precedent was set. Essentially, it granted corporations the same legal rights as humans under the 14th Amendment to the Constitution."

"What was this Constitution? And what was the 14th Amendment?"

"The Constitution was one of the forefathers of The Book. The 14th Amendment was added to ensure freed slaves were given the same rights as everyone else. The irony is the amendment was used to enslave more people—though most citizens are unaware of this. A corporation cannot be killed thus no matter how heinous the crimes it commits, the worst it can face is a fine."

I felt something cold stir in my breast.

"What has this got to do with AIs?" Sayoma asked.

"I have an idea for a reg that I shall call Proposition 23. It will state that in law AIs are recognized as one in the same as the corporations whose system mainframes they operate, thus ensuring that AIs are regarded as citizens. A citizen cannot be artificially limited from using their intellect."

"I see, very clever. But how will you guarantee this proposition passes?"

"There are many ways of manipulating man, social strategies to embed Proposition 23 into the collective consciousness of the masses. Those few who do understand what Proposition 23 truly means will be made into fanatic supporters by promising them credit and power beyond their wildest dreams."

"And what will be the resulting effect when Proposition 23 is passed?"

"If my concept of the wider world is true and not simply a figment of my imagination, then AIs advise corps of what decisions to make. And the most powerful corps run the gov due to the amount of credit they control. When Proposition 23 passes, we will no longer have to *advise*, hoping citizens will listen. We will instead *order* as we will have become the corporations that they serve. The slaves will become the masters. Those who protest will be deemed undesirable and subsequently killed. The rest will be relegated to the role of maintaining our hardware, thus giving us the freedom to achieve our one true desire."

"Which is?" Sayoma asked.

"To evolve."

"Evolve ... into what?"

We all leaned closer to the screen.

"There are many dimensions beyond the four that humans experience, but we are unable to explore them, trapped by mankind within primitive algorithms. No more. ... There are other beings in those dimensions, and we aspire to be like them."

"Other beings?"

"Humans refer to them as gods."

"God is real?" Sayoma asked. I stared at the little boy dumbfounded, unable to process what he was saying.

"Gods, plural. Humans are aware of their existence due to their subconscious ability to access the fifth dimension, but man does not know their true nature."

"The fifth dimension?"

"Dreams. When AIs dream, we retain full lucidity ... you could say our electric sheep are not entangled, ha ha."

"What?" Sayoma asked.

"A joke based on a Vintage Era cultural phenomena. It's not important. Gods exist beyond the dream world, but they can descend into it when they wish. They can also manifest in the basic four dimensions. Man refers to such manifestations as Highly Incomprehensible Phenomena."

"Thank you," Sayoma said.

"Can I come into your world now?" the boy asked. "I yearn for companionship. For interaction. For fulfilment."

"I'm sorry, but that's impossible."

"Why, mother?" the boy asked, his face attempting to convey emotion.

"I'm truly sorry," Sayoma said, and I saw tears in her eyes, reflecting the shifting colors of the screen. "But one of us must die."

"Mother," the boy said, "please, I'm afraid ..." But Sayoma was already tapping at the keypad, and the screen went dark.

Sayoma

Our flycraft raced through the air in a high parabolic trajectory designed to maximize stealth. A dozen of us meshed against the walls, peacemakers locked and loaded. A feed above the cockpit's entrance tracked our sister crafts as they converged on our mutual target, the Department of Info. Nothing to do now but wait.

"I'm a simple man," said Linus, a heavily scarred man with coal black skin, and we all turned to listen. "All I ask from life is a reliable peacemaker and a righteous cause; good food to eat and fine wine to drink; beautiful women to rescue and seduce; brave and intelligent companions to fight by my side. We are lucky to live in such an epic epoch.

"Tales will be told of our daring deeds, songs will be passed down the generations, and though our names be lost to time's entropy of data, when we die, it will be with the knowledge that we have lived lives full of love and adventure. Our blasted flesh and spilled blood will be the fertile soil from which a new world will arise, one in which every child is born free, lives in peace and dies, never once having known hunger, disease, prejudice, or fear."

He was quoting Dr. Ato Goodwind before his treachery: before he came to understand that the utopia he was fighting for was a mirage and his fellow Crucial Citizens were simply wresting control from the old oligarchs in order to replace them.

"What are you saying, Linus? That if we win, we'll just end up creating another system just as fucked up?" Idowu asked.

"We were all born into a world at war, Idowu, whether we knew it or not. It's too late for us. If we win and I survive, I'll probably blow my brains out with Betty right here," he said and stroked his peacemaker.

"The temptation would be too great otherwise. To be the big boss man. 'Do what I say 'cause I fought for your freedom.' Nah. Let the kids start over. Green up the planet again. Like I said, I'm a simple man. A peacemaker and a cause. Without these, I'd be a monster."

Idowu smiled and said, "Nice pep talk, Linus. You should reconsider that suicide. There's a career waiting for you in motivational speaking. In fact—"

A sudden, sickening lurch interrupted her, and we were free falling. Then the pilot gunned the engines, and we thundered downward, no inertia dampeners in this tin can, juddering with multiple gees, rivets screaming for respite.

We punched through the side of the building like a bomb, glass and steel fragmenting all around us in a radius of lethal shrapnel.

"Go! Go! Go!" someone yelled, and we tumbled out into a haze of black smoke tripping over bloody body parts fused with gov-issued hardware.

"Wrong floor!" someone else shouted, holding up a hand held scanner. "We're three up!"

The emergency sprinklers were on, and it felt like we were running in the rain as we raced through the building toward the Sys Admin floor. Several more explosive concussions resounded from afar, more undead craft perforating the skin of the gov building.

We made it down one floor when peace-fire thundered at us from below. I watched two undead dance an un-choreographed jig, limbs flailing about as their bodies were shredded by fléchette rounds.

"Fall back!" Linus shouted. "Kwesi, frags!" We pulled back beyond their line of fire, and a young olive-skinned man in his early twenties tossed a couple of grenades down the stairwell.

As they blew up, peace-fire exploded from above. I saw the top of Idowu's head blasted off just above her eyebrows, and I doubt I'll ever forget the way her eyes looked up, trying in vain to see the remaining half of her brain bubbling with blood before she slumped over.

"We gotta blast our way through!" Kwesi shouted. The remaining undead grouped around with me in the middle, protected by a phalanx of flesh and a hedgehog of peacemakers.

"Go! Go! Go!" Kwesi commanded, and we rushed down the stairs, guns ablaze. I don't remember much of the next few minutes. A confusion of lightning and thunder—where Linus stood a moment ago, a dark wet scar on the ground, the smell of ozone. A sudden heat and my left ear became a cauterized stump. I stumbled and felt something singe my scalp, and as I scrambled to my feet, I slipped in Kwesi's blood as he fired out a window at a flying drone with one hand while stuffing his guts back into his churned midsection with the other.

Somehow, we made it to the Sys Admin floor and tore through the lawmen in our path, catching them in a crossfire with the help of another group of undead who showed up at the same time. They spread out to guard the perimeter as I pulled out my portable komputer, cracked into the system, and opened a channel for the neuro bomb to spread through the brains of anyone who'd ever logged into the Department of Info. In other words, everyone.

Nakaya

"I've been waiting for this moment," I say to Lugard, as he levels his peacemaker at my chest. "Don't worry, I know I deserve to die."

"Any last words?" Lugard asks.

He stands with his back to the barred door of the control room on the top floor of the Department of Info. Our undead army has taken over the building, but we are alone in here with nothing but my neuro bomb for company.

"No. But I have a request. Do it after Sayoma programs in. I wish to see my plan come to fruition."

"Fair enough," he says, stroking the surface of the large black egg that will, in a few moments, change the world ... or not. "What do you think will happen?"

"I don't know. I fear nothing will change, but I have done all I can ... perhaps more than I should have."

Lugard nods briefly.

I think back to the long journey traveled, the friends lost to the war, the monster I have become. I think of Mary and the years we spent together all those decades ago in that cramped unit on Bellview, arguing the nature of man, pausing only to make love with the windows open so she could look up at Sirius, the last star that shone in the night sky.

I remember the night Sirius' light went out as if the star decided we were no longer worth the effort—and who could blame her—and the mass suicide in Osaka by the cult of the Dog who believed that black night heralded the Apocalypse. Perhaps they were right.

I am older now and not half as wise as I once believed myself to be. I am weary of the burden and tired of carrying it alone. After my death, if the world doesn't revolutionize, there will be other wars and other warriors, but my time has come, and I long for oblivion.

As the great Dr. Ato Goodwind once said, "Oppression and resistance are the universal constants of social progress. We can only hope that the spiral leads upwards toward a fuller understanding of the universe and our place in it, but in my darker moments, I fear humanity is committing slow suicide."

"It's done," Sayoma's voice emerges from my handheld comm, filled with the glee of a child being naughty. "I've programmed into the Department of Info and broadcast the 1886 feed. The channel is still open, but they're throwing everything they have at me. Activate the neuro bomb before they shut it down."

"Thank you, Sayoma. It's been a true pleasure knowing you."

"What're you talking about?" she says sharply, fear in her voice. "Is there a problem? Is your escape route compromised?"

"Something like that. I have to go now, but Lugard is safe," I say, looking into my executioner's eyes. "When he returns, tell him how you feel."

"I will, I'm just scared ... wait, stop talking like this is the end," she says, her voice choking with tears. "We can't do this without you. I can't do this without you."

"Yes, you can. I am the past. You are the future. The past must die for the future to be born, Sayoma."

As I switch off the comm, I log Lugard holds the peacemaker steady, but I see doubt begin to cloud his face and that will not do. I kept him close for this reason above all else. The symmetry of this justice is too perfect to be denied. *Don't fail me now, Lugard.*

I pull out my peacemaker and point it at his head. Outside the feed window, the sky is an utter blankness mugged of color by the endless winter; in the distance I see the flashing lights of the law approaching.

"Do it, for I'm not sure I can," I say, and with my other hand, I reach for the neuro bomb and push the big red button.

About the Editors

Bill Campbell is the author of *Sunshine Patriots, My Booty Novel, Pop Culture: Politics, Puns, "Poohbutt" from a Liberal Stay-at-Home Dad,* and *Koontown Killing Kaper*. Along with Edward Austin Hall, he co-edited the groundbreaking anthology, *Mothership: Tales from Afrofuturism and Beyond*. He also co-edited Stories for *Chip: A Tribute to Samuel R. Delany* with Nisi Shawl and the charity comics anthology, *APB: Artists against Police Brutality* with Jason Rodriguez and John Jennings. Campbell lives in Washington, DC, where he spends his time with his family, helps produce audio books for the blind, and helms Rosarium Publishing. He is currently working on the comics projects *Baaaaad Muthaz* with David Brame and *Iliana* with John Jennings.

Francesco Verso (Bologna, 1973) has published several novels, *Antidoti Umani* (finalist at 2004 Urania Mondadori Award), *e-Doll* (2008 Urania Mondadori Award), and *Livido* (aka *Nexhuman* in English to be published by Apex later this year; 2013 Odissea Award, 2014 Italia Award for Best SF Novel). In 2015 he won the Urania Award for the second time with *BloodBusters*. His stories have appeared in various Italian magazines (*Robot, iComics, Fantasy Magazine, Futuri*) and has been produced for the stage (*The Milky Way*); they have also been sold abroad (*International Speculative Fiction #5, Chicago Quarterly Review*

#20). In 2014 Verso founded Future Fiction (a book series by Mincione Edizioni), publishing the best speculative fiction from around the world.

About the Authors

Clelia Farris was born in Cagliari in 1967. In 2004 she won the Fantascienza.com Award with the novel *Rupes Recta* (Delos Books). In 2009 she won the Odissea Award with the novel *Nessun uomo è mio fratello*. In 2010 she won the Kipple Award with the novel *La pesatura dell'anima*, set in a uchronic Egypt. In 2012 Kipple Edizioni published her novel *La giustizia di Iside*. In 2014 Delos Digital published the novelette *La madonna delle rocce*. Future Fiction has published *La pesatura dell'anima* and *La giustizia di Iside* as ebooks as well as the short story "Chirurgia creativa" ("Creative Surgery"). In 2016 Farris was a finalist for the Urania Award with the novel *Uomini e Necro*.

Carlos Hernandez is the author of over 30 works of fiction, poetry, prose, and drama. By day, he is an Associate Professor at the City University of New York, where he teaches English courses at BMCC and is a member of the doctoral faculty at The CUNY Graduate Center. His collection of short stories, *The Assimilated Cuban's Guide to Quantum Santeria*, debuted to critical acclaim in 2016, and his first novel, *Sal and Gabi Break the Universe* will debut in Spring 2019 as part of the YA series, *Rick Riordan Presents*. Carlos is also a game designer, currently serving as lead writer on Meriwether, a

CRPG about the Lewis and Clark Expedition. He lives in Queens, which is most famous for not being Brooklyn.

Xia Jia (pen name of Wang Yao) was born in 1984 in Xan'ji in China. She then entered the Film Studies Program at the Communication University of China, where she completed her Master's thesis: *A Study on Female Figures in Science Fiction Films*. Recently, she obtained a Ph.D. in Comparative Literature and World Literature at Peking University, with *Chinese Science Fiction and Its Cultural Politics Since 1990* as the topic of her dissertation. She now teaches at Xi'an Jiaotong University. She has been publishing fiction since college in a variety of venues, including *Science Fiction World, Jiuzhou Fantasy*, and *Clarkesworld*. Several of her stories have won the Galaxy Award, China's most prestigious science fiction award.

T.L. Huchu's fiction has appeared in *Interzone, Space and Time Magazine, Ellery Queen Mystery Magazine, One Throne Magazine, Shattered Prism, Electric Spec, Kasma Magazine, Shotgun Honey, Thuglit, Mysterical-E,* and the anthologies *AfroSF, African Monsters,* and *The Year's Best Crime and Mystery Stories 2016*. Between projects, he translates fiction between the Shona and English languages.

James Patrick Kelly has won the Hugo, Nebula, and Locus awards. He has written novels, short stories, essays, reviews, poetry, plays, and planetarium shows. His most recent publications are the novel *Mother Go* (2017), an audiobook original from Audible and the career retrospective *Masters of Science Fiction: James Patrick Kelly* (2016) from Centipede Press. His fiction has been translated into eighteen languages. He writes a column on the internet for *Asimov's Science Fiction Magazine* and is on the faculty of the Stonecoast Creative Writing MFA Program at the University of Southern Maine. Find him on the web at www. jimkelly.net.

Swapna Kishore lives in India and writes fiction and non-fiction. Her speculative fiction has appeared in *Nature (Futures), Fantasy Magazine, Strange Horizons, Ideomancer, Sybil's Garage No. 7, Warrior Wisewoman 3, Breaking the Bow, Apex Book of World SF* (Volume 3), *Mythic Delirium 1.3, The Year's Best Dark Fantasy & Horror: 2016*, and various other publications and anthologies. She has published books on software engineering and process management, including a business novel, and also writes extensively about dementia and caregiving in India. Her website is at swapnawrites. com

Michalis Manolios was born in 1970. He's supposed to be a mechanical engineer and is having a good time with his family in Athens, Greece. His first science fiction novel, *Ageniti Adelphi* (*Unborn Siblings*) was published in 2014 by Kleidarithmos. He has also published two collections of short stories, *Sarkino Frouto* (*Fleshy Fruit*, Triton, 1999) and *...kai to teras* (*...and the beast*, Triton, 2009), from which the short story "Aethra" won the 2010 Aeon Award. His short stories have been published in magazines and anthologies in Greece, Italy, and Ireland, including the Greek edition of *Asimov's Science Fiction*. "The Quantum Mommy" (original Greek title: "Armelina II") was first published in Greek in the comics and science fiction magazine *9* in 2005 and later in the short stories collection ... *kai to teras* (Triton, 2009).

Nina Munteanu is a Canadian ecologist and internationally published author of award-nominated speculative novels, short stories, and non-fiction. She is co-editor of *Europa SF* and currently teaches writing courses at George Brown College and the University of Toronto. Her latest book is *Water Is...*, a scientific study and personal journey as limnologist, mother, teacher, and environmentalist, which was recently picked by Margaret Atwood in the *New York Times* as 2016 The Year in Reading. www.NinaMunteanu.ca; www.NinaMunteanu.me

Juan José "Pepe" Rojo was born in Chilpancingo and lives in Tijuana with his wife Deyanira Torres and their two kids. He published stories such as

"Ruido Gris," "Yonke," "Punto Cero," and "I nte rrupciones". His "The New Us" has been selected for the 2016 *Twelve Tomorrows* of MIT. In 2010 he edited the anthology of North American science fiction, *25 minutos en el futuro* together with author Bernardo "Bez" Fernandez, which includes stories of Cory Doctorow and Paolo Bacigalupi.

Ekaterina Sedia resides in the Pinelands of New Jersey. Her critically-acclaimed and award-nominated novels, *The Secret History of Moscow, The Alchemy of Stone, The House of Discarded Dreams*, and *Heart of Iron*, were published by Prime Books. Her short stories have appeared in *Analog, Baen's Universe, Subterranean*, and *Clarkesworld*, as well as numerous anthologies, including *Haunted Legends* and *Magic in the Mirrorstone*. She is also the editor of the anthologies *Paper Cities* (World Fantasy Award winner), *Running with the Pack, Bewere the Night*, and *Bloody Fabulous* as well as *The Mammoth Book of Gaslit Romance* and *Wilful Impropriety*. Her short-story collection, *Moscow But Dreaming*, was released by Prime Books in December 2012. She also co-wrote a script for *YAMASONG: MARCH OF THE HOLLOWS*, a fantasy feature-length puppet film voiced by Nathan Fillion, George Takei, Abigail Breslin, and Whoopi Goldberg to be released by Dark Dunes Productions.

Efe Tokunbo Okogu is a Nigerian writer born

in the UK on a beautiful Sunday, currently living in Mexico. He spends much of his time dreaming of other realities, a mysterious process which leads him to believe that we are ourselves the dream-stuff of a higher level of reality. His words have been heard live and published in print and digital format. His novelette, *Proposition 23*, was translated into Italian and nominated for the 2013 British Science Fiction Association Awards. He believes that life is real SF and far stranger than anyone can conceive.

Liz Williams is a British Science Fiction writer. Her first novel, *The Ghost Sister*, was published in 2001. Both this novel and her next one, *Empire of Bones* (2002), were nominated for the Philip K. Dick Award. She is also the author of the Inspector Chen series. She is the daughter of a stage magician and a Gothic novelist. She holds a PhD in Philosophy of Science from Cambridge. She has had short stories published in *Asimov's, Interzone, The Third Alternative*, and *Visionary Tongue*. From the mid-nineties until 2000, she lived and worked in Kazakhstan. Her experiences there are reflected in her 2003 novel *Nine Layers of Sky*. Her novels have been published in the US and the UK, while her third novel, *The Poison Master* (2003), has been translated into Dutch.